"Vanessa!" Jeff's shout almost covered the chimes. A split second later, Vanessa heard Nathan's low scold, "You're not a Scud missile, Son. Use your indoor voice and your manners."

" 'Kay, Dad. Where is she?"

"I'm down here," Vanessa called. She lifted a hand and waved over the counter.

"Hey, Van," Nathan said, "about ready to go?"

Embarrassed to the core of her being, she looked up at Nathan and shook her head.

"No?"

"I'm um. . .stuck."

CATHY MARIE HAKE is a Southern California native who loves her work as a nurse and Lamaze teacher. She and her husband have a daughter, a son, and two dogs, so life is never dull or quiet. Cathy considers herself a sentimental pack rat, collecting antiques and Hummel figurines. She otherwise keeps busy with reading, writing, baking, and being a prayer warrior. "I am easily distracted during prayer, so I devote certain tasks and chores to specific requests or persons so I can keep faithful in my prayer life."

Books by Cathy Marie Hake

HEARTSONG PRESENTS
HP370—Twin Victories
HP481—Unexpected Delivery
HP512—Precious Burdens

Love Is Patient

Cathy Marie Hake

Heartsong Presents

To those who love and sacrifice and to those who patiently walk alongside and wait. God bless you.

I'd like to thank Rick Wilcox of Guide Puppies for the Blind. He was a wonderful resource. All of the right information about the dogs is his; any mistakes are mine.

A note from the Author:
I love to hear from my readers! You may correspond with me by writing:

> **Cathy Marie Hake**
> **Author Relations**
> **PO Box 719**
> **Uhrichsville, OH 44683**

ISBN 1-58660-806-1

LOVE IS PATIENT

Scripture quotations marked nasb are taken from the New American Standard Bible, © 1960, 1962, 1963, 1968, 1971, 1972, 1973, 1975, 1977 by The Lockman Foundation. Used by permission.

PRINTED IN THE U.S.A.

one

Granite Cliffs, California

Big, brown, puppy-dog eyes—Vanessa Zobel had always been a sucker for them. It was why she'd opened Whiskers, Wings, and Wags. Right now, she had not one, but two sets of large, soulful brown eyes trained on her. "May I help you?"

"Nobody can help me," the little brown-eyed boy across the counter said in a despondent tone.

Vanessa looked to the adult for an explanation. The tall, sable-haired man stared back at her for a moment, then glanced down at his shuffling son.

"We need to return this." The man set a quart-sized Zip-Tite plastic bag on the counter. It tilted toward the edge, so he caught and scooted the bag closer to the register. Blissfully untroubled by the changing current, the goldfish inside continued to swim tiny laps.

The little boy stuck out a grubby finger and rubbed the edge of the clear plastic bag. "I done wrong."

His confession didn't reveal much information, but he'd admitted responsibility for whatever the problem was. Vanessa hummed. "Is that so?"

"I really, really wanted Goldie. I knew he'd stay little and he'd be quiet."

The man rested his calloused hand on the boy's shoulder. "Jeff—"

"I know, Dad. I done wrong." The little boy hung his head.

5

Kids sometimes shoplifted. Vanessa had experience dealing with customers in that realm, but she knew Jeff couldn't have stolen the fish. She looked at the father in puzzlement.

"I understand you give coupons to the school for free goldfish. Jeff forged my signature on the parental permission line."

"Ohh." The picture became clear. She looked from the child to the fish and back again at Jeff. His lower lip protruded in a quivering, almost-ready-to-cry pout. "Oh, my."

"Dad says I gotta—" His little chin rose as he sucked in a gulp of air. "Gotta give Goldie back to you."

Vanessa shot the broad-shouldered father a quick glance. The left side of his mouth kicked up into a rakish smile, and his eyes stayed steady as could be. He stood behind his son and kept a hand on his shoulder.

To Vanessa, it looked like a show of support during a difficult time. Still, the father's other palm flattened and scooted the baggy farther away. Taking her cue from him, she walked around the counter and knelt in front of the little guy. Since she didn't know if he would be afraid of her dog, she rested a hand on Amber's golden coat in a silent show of reassurance. "Jeff, I think you're a mighty lucky young man."

"You mean I getta keep Goldie?" Hope flared in his big eyes.

"No, I'm afraid not." Vanessa took his little hand in hers as she shook her head. "I think you're blessed to have a daddy who loves you so much, he wants to teach you to be an honorable man."

"Is honor'ble like being honest?"

"That's part of it. It means being honest and fair and that folks know they can trust you to do the right thing."

Jeff twisted the toe of his well-worn sneaker on the

linoleum floor. The sound of the rubber squeaking mixed with tweets, yips, and a parrot squawk. He jammed his hands into his pockets and muttered, "My dad's honor'ble."

"I try to be, Son. It's not always easy."

Tears filled Jeff's eyes. "I wanna keep Goldie. Goldie likes me. What if he isn't happy here?"

"I'm sure the lady has lots of goldfish to keep Goldie company."

"Yes, I do. Goldie will need to get used to the water, though."

Though lines of bafflement creased his brow, a devastatingly handsome smile tilted the father's mouth. "Goldie's already a very good swimmer."

"I'll need to let him get used to the water temperature. It might be a bit of a shock to him otherwise, so we'll just slip him—bag and all—into the tank until the temperature equalizes. Then we'll let Goldie out so he can make friends with all of the other fish."

"We will? Do I get to help?"

Oops. Me and my big mouth. She wrinkled her nose and looked up at the father again. "It'll take about fifteen minutes."

Jeff tugged on his father's paint-splattered sweatshirt. "Dad, you said we were going to bring Goldie back if it took all day!"

Vanessa tried to smother her smile. She doubted the father meant he was willing to stick around for a fish reacclimation.

The father chuckled and rumpled Jeff's hair. "We can spare fifteen minutes."

Vanessa took the bag from the counter. "The fish tanks are right back here."

"Can I carry Goldie?" A quick look back into the dad's eyes let Vanessa know it was okay. "Sure." She handed the squishy package down to Jeff's little hands, then shoved up the right sleeve of his lightweight sweatshirt. "We'll even have you put his bag into the tank."

Jeff carried his tiny contraband through the store. Vanessa thought they made quite a procession—the boy and his fish, his father, then she and Amber bringing up the rear. Amber quietly sat at heel while the father clasped his big hands around his son's waist and lifted him. Jeff solemnly lowered the bag into the goldfish tank. Big tears filled his eyes.

"I know it's hard for you, Son, but this is the way it has to be." The father set him back down.

"I knew it was bad to tell a lie. Writing a lie is wrong too, huh?"

"Yes, it is."

Several of the fish in the tank darted by the plastic bag. A few nudged it. "It looks to me like Goldie's got a lot of fish who want to be his friend," Vanessa said. "You can watch them for awhile if you'd like. I need to do a little work around here, but I'll come back to help you let Goldie out of the bag."

Vanessa walked past several more tanks teeming with fish, around the corner display of hamsters, gerbils, and mice, then shoved a protruding bag of dog food into place on a shelf before she reached the back room.

"All done," Valene declared as she pulled a load of towels from the clothes dryer.

Vanessa smiled at her identical twin. "Hang on a second." She unfastened Val's clip, quickly finger combed the shoulder-length, honey blond tresses back into order, and popped them back into a tidy ponytail that matched her own.

Val's blue eyes twinkled. "If you tell me I look pretty, I'm going to accuse you of being vain."

"Your soul is beautiful," Vanessa shot back. "I didn't say a word about the package God put it in."

"Oh, so He gave Mom and Dad a two-for-the-price-of-one deal on us?"

"Spoken like a business major." Vanessa laughed at their silly banter as she plucked a green jacket from amidst the towels and fastened it over Amber's back. "Speaking of deals, what would you think of us putting together a puppy package?"

"Not a bad idea—especially since you filled every last cage and pen last night."

"What do I say?" Vanessa spread her hands wide. "I love dogs. I need to get back out there." She smoothed the golden retriever's jacket, gave the animal an affectionate stroke, and started to push a cart out the door. "Let's go." She murmured the command, and Amber sedately walked alongside her.

"Watcha doin'?" Jeff asked from over by the hamsters.

"I'm going to give all of the animals some fresh drinking water."

"Can I help?"

"You need to ask your daddy."

Jeff's father turned around from admiring a parrot. "I'll let him help. . . ." Glints of gold sparkled in his brown eyes. "If I can too."

Jeff scampered over. "Your dog's wearing clothes now!"

"Yes, she is. She's a special dog. Her name is Amber."

Jeff pursed his lips and squinted at the writing on the green jacket. He pointed at it. "That doesn't say Amber."

His father squatted down beside him. "Why don't you read it, Sport?"

"J-joo-eye-dee." His little features twisted. "Jooeydie? What is that?"

"Sound it out again. Use the other sound for G, and keep the first vowel silent."

Jeff's face puckered. "Teacher says, 'When two vowels go walking, the first one does the talking.'"

"That's usually true, but this word is a rule breaker."

"G-eye-dy. Guide!" Jeff beamed as he ran his forefinger along the white lettering. "Guide pup-py in train-ing!"

"What a smart boy!" Vanessa smiled at how the father beamed from her praise every bit as much as the son.

"Jeff's six. I'm Nathan Adams." Laugh lines around his mouth deepened. "I'm sure he'll be glad to tell you how old I am, what we ate for lunch, and that I occasionally drive too fast."

"Vanessa Zobel," she provided with a quick laugh. "Twenty-four, a taco, and no speeding tickets. . .yet."

"Did Amber eat a taco too?"

"No." She played with Amber's soft ears. "Amber isn't supposed to be a pet. She's going to be a working dog. We want to teach her to do her jobs without getting treats. It makes her happy for me to pat her and tell her she's a good girl."

Nathan hooked his thumbs in the front pockets of his tattered jeans. "So you'll train her and give her away?"

The gentle quality of his voice made Vanessa's heart melt. Most people focused on what a wonderful thing it was for the blind to receive such a dog. She did too—or she wouldn't be training the dogs. Still, few ever understood the ache involved in relinquishing a puppy.

"This is my fourth guide puppy." She petted Amber and added, "She's a good dog. I'll miss her, but I know she'll be a wonderful companion helper for someone who needs her."

"Does she sleep here at night with all of the other animals?" Jeff continued to trace the letters on the jacket.

"No, Amber goes everywhere with me. It's my job to make sure she learns how to behave nicely wherever we are. In a few months, she'll go to San Francisco to a special doggy school where they'll teach her how to help a blind person."

"Someone's going to be lucky," Nathan said slowly as he

looked into her eyes. "It looks like you've trained Amber magnificently."

"Does she wear that thing on her face 'cuz she's a working dog?"

"Yes." Vanessa glanced down at the green halterlike device. "It's a training tool called a gentle leader. That part around her muzzle is loose, so she can still open her mouth."

"Can she still eat?"

"Yes, she could, but I've trained her only to eat at special times from a bowl. She won't eat food she finds on the ground or that people offer her. See how the other part of it goes under her chin here and makes a collar? If I give the leash just a tiny pull, it steers her."

Nathan gave her an astonished look. "Power steering for puppies. Wow."

"How come all of the other dogs and cats are noisy, but Amber is quiet?"

"They're just babies. They need someone to love and train them." The door chimed. Vanessa craned her neck and spied one of her regular customers trundling into the shop. "Excuse me. I need to help Mrs. Rosetti."

She sold the usual pound of lamb-and-rice biscuits her regular bought each week, then came back to the father and son. "Would you like to help me give the animals fresh water to drink?"

In no time at all Nathan, Jeff, and Vanessa had refilled all the water bottles and dishes for the reptiles, rodents, birds, and kittens. Jeff's enthusiasm for the task far outstripped his ability, and his shirt showed it. Still, his father ignored the wet clothing and patiently helped his son. At each cage, habitat, or pen, Jeff decided he'd love to have that particular pet the most.

"Looks like you have a bona fide animal lover on your hands," she said to Nathan.

"He's decided anything worth having is worth collecting. We already have a rock collection, at least two hundred baseball cards, three oatmeal canisters of seashells, and enough Matchbox cars to jam our own freeway. If I let him have one pet, I'm sure our whole house would turn into one big menagerie."

As Vanessa raised a brow, she asked the teasing question, "And the problem with that would be. . . ?"

"I'm not about to debate that issue with you." Nathan shook his head and gave her a rueful grin. "Your bias is clear."

"True. I think pets are great." Vanessa parked the cart in the corner and spread her hands wide. "I can't think of anything better than being around animals!"

"Why are you stopping?" Nathan asked her.

"We can go release Goldie now."

Jeff stood on tiptoe and peeped over the edge of a pen holding a pair of cocker spaniels. "I wanna see the puppies. They're so little!"

"I tell you what: We'll use up the rest of the water in the pitcher. Then, we can let the goldfish free. Afterward, I'll take care of the rest of the dogs."

Nathan snagged one of a pair of cocker spaniels that bounded out of their pen when Vanessa opened the sliding door. She hastily grabbed the other and laughed as it licked her cheek. "You're gonna run me ragged, aren't you, Frack?"

"Frack?" Father and son asked in unison.

"Frack." She held up her wiggling puppy. "You snagged Frick—for which I'm eternally grateful."

"I wanna hold a puppy too."

"I don't mind your holding a puppy, but perhaps we could find one that's a little less active." Vanessa playfully tousled Frack's ears, then set him back in his pen.

The shop's bell chimed again, announcing another customer.

"If you don't mind, I can help Jeff release the goldfish while you take care of those folks," Nathan offered.

"Fine. Thanks."

Lord, she prayed as she walked off, *see that guy? Gorgeous brown eyes, fabulous sense of honor and ethics, even a dollop of humor. You can find me one of those whenever You're ready.*

Two little girls stood with their mother at the door. "We've come to look at kittens."

"I hope all of the good ones aren't taken!" one girl said.

"I hope not too." Vanessa smiled at them, *but I'm not talking about kittens.*

two

Nathan watched the perky woman and her retriever head for the front of the shop. Her blond ponytail bounced as she walked. It had been a long time since he reacted to such a natural beauty. The moment they made eye contact, his brain went into a free fall, and he'd probably made a total fool of himself gawking at her. She hadn't laughed at how he fumbled and almost dropped that dumb goldfish—a fact for which he was grateful.

Most of all, he appreciated how she'd taken her cues from him and supported how he wanted to discipline Jeff. She hadn't made a big, hairy deal out of the matter, but the way she stood firm about putting Goldie back in the tank reinforced his parental decision. Still, the compassionate way she allowed Jeff to make sure Goldie had new friends would undoubtedly keep him from doing a total meltdown when they left.

"Dad, do you think Goldie will be okay?"

"The lady here is nice, Sport. I think she'll do a great job keeping Goldie happy."

"Prob'ly." Jeff sighed. "I guess we can let him out of his bag now."

Jeff took his sweet time telling Goldie a half dozen "important" things. He then spoke to the rest of the tank's occupants, earnestly telling them all about their wonderful companion as if he'd owned the silly creature for months instead of overnight. Lower lips quivering, Jeff finally freed the fish.

Nathan watched tears fill his son's eyes. He quietly took the soggy bag from Jeff's hands and wished again he hadn't needed to do this. As kids went, Jeff was a great, but Nathan wanted him to grow up to have integrity. Rewarding his dishonesty by letting him keep the fish would be a mistake.

"I can't tell which one is Goldie." Jeff trembled. "Can you?"

Oh, it would be so easy to lie.

"No, Son, but I figure that's a good thing. It means Goldie fits right in and everybody is already playing with him."

"How are you doing, Big Guy?" Vanessa asked softly as she rounded the corner. Nathan watched as she knelt, opened her arms, and Jeff ran to her. She hugged him. "It's not easy to say good-bye, is it?"

Jeff shook his head and burrowed closer to her.

"I'll bet you'd rather grow up to be a good man like your daddy than to keep one little old goldfish."

"Yeah," he agreed, his voice muted against her shoulder. "I done wrong, but Dad said this would make it right."

"The next time you have to choose how to act, I'll bet you do a better job," Nathan said as he slipped his hands around Jeff's waist and lifted him high.

"We can't go yet, Dad. She promised I could hold a puppy."

"I need to get more water. Why don't you two go look at the dogs and decide which one Jeff wants to hold?"

Whiskers, Wings, and Wags certainly boasted a bumper crop of animals. Nathan and Jeff sauntered along the puppy wall. Every breed from Afghans to wiener dogs snuffled, yipped, and wagged from the bright clean pens and cages. A pair of puffball-sized huskies tussled over a toy, and a little shar-pei that looked like a rumpled tan sock napped in a corner.

"Does she got any spotty dogs like on the movie?"

"Does she have any spotty Dalmatians?" He tried to correct Jeff's grammar when they were alone. If other folks were around, Nathan preferred to ignore the usual childish mistakes. Evie had loved fine literature, and she would have wanted their son to be well spoken.

"Yeah, Dad. Dalmatians. I forgot that name."

Nathan scanned the pens. "Hmm. No, I don't see any."

"I don't carry them," Vanessa said as she approached. Amber walked at her side, yet a frisky black Lab strained every last inch of the leash Vanessa held in her other hand. "Dalmatians are charming to look at, but they tend to be very high-strung so the pound ends up with lots of them. I'd rather let somebody rescue one than support someone to breed more litters."

Nathan listened to every word she said, but he was even more aware of Jeff's reaction. His son reached up, clutched his hand with a near-death grip and quivered with sheer excitement.

"Is that one for me?"

"Sure," Vanessa said. "Maybe we could let you go into a meeting enclosure so he'll stay corralled."

Jeff rocketed into the three-foot tall enclosure, and the Lab galloped right after him. Vanessa laughingly controlled him until Nathan closed the gate. It wobbled, and he inspected it. "You've got a loose screw."

"Plenty of folks have told me I have a screw loose. No one ever told me I have a loose screw."

Jeff still clutched the leash for dear life. "My dad's in the 'struction business. He knows all 'bout screws an' lumber and stuff."

"You've got a handy dad."

"Uh-huh. Honor'ble too. I wanna grow up to be like him someday."

"Good for you. Those are fine qualities."

The minute Vanessa unhooked the leash, the Lab and Jeff tumbled into a tangle of legs and noise.

"Looks like they're getting along okay," she said after a minute. "I'll let them goof off while I give the rest of these babies a drink."

"Let me help," Nathan offered.

She held up her hand. "I'd rather you stay with Jeff. The puppy is already settling down, but I don't like to leave kids alone with unfamiliar dogs."

"Makes sense. Tell you what. Find a Phillips screwdriver, and I'll fix the hinge for you." Nathan grinned at how the Lab licked the hip of Jeff's jeans. "Do you have food in your pocket?"

"Beef jerky," Jeff confessed. "I wanted a snack while you got your hair cut. He's really smart to find it so fast, isn't he, Dad?"

"Yes, he is."

"Can he have some jerky?"

"No," Vanessa called over. "I have a jar of puppy biscuits on the ledge there. You may give him one of those."

The minute the puppy heard the rattle from the jar, he skidded over and sat on Nathan's foot. *Cute little thing. Hardly longer than my shoe.* "Hungry, Boy?"

A yip served as an answer.

Vanessa went up front to help a few more customers. When she came back, she leaned over the wall and chuckled. Nathan didn't feel self-conscious in the least to have Jeff and the puppy both in his lap. As a matter of fact, he was enjoying every minute of it. He'd be hard pressed to say which one of them wiggled more.

"I try to give each of the puppies a temporary name. The owners are free to change it, but it lets me love them a bit more while they're here. Do you guys have any suggestions for him?"

"Blackie?"

Nathan ruffled Jeff's hair. "That's not a bad suggestion, Sport, but lots of dogs get named that. Why not think of things that are black?"

"Wheels. Tires. Licorice."

"Licorice!" Vanessa clapped. "I like that!"

"Lick for a nickname," Nathan added as the puppy laved his son's face.

Truthfully, Jeff and Lick were getting along famously, which surprised Nathan. Jeff had never shown much interest in animals, but he seemed to be enjoying this little jaunt to the pet store. *I didn't even realize he wanted that dumb fish, either. Maybe I should take him to the zoo. . . .*

"I'll make a little name tag for Lick's pen. He just came in last night."

"You've got a bumper crop of puppies." Nathan tilted his head toward the far wall.

"Spring." She smiled. "The early litters are here, and I just took in several new puppies last night. I'd rather sell puppies and kittens for Easter than bunnies."

"I like dogs better than bunnies," Jeff declared. He stroked Licorice and giggled as the puppy licked him avidly in response.

Nathan focused more attention on Vanessa than his son since Jeff seemed content to play with the puppy. "What's wrong with rabbits?"

"Nothing." She shrugged. "Some folks do beautifully with them, but others don't realize the cute little bunny won't stay tiny and that he likes to eat plants."

"Dad, look. He's so neat!"

Nathan glanced down. "Yeah, he is." He looked back at Vanessa. "Sounds like you're more interested in making good matches than in making a buck."

She flushed with obvious pleasure. "I try."

"Can I give him another biscuit?"

"Sure," Nathan answered absently. The jar rattled. "I'll bet the dog treat manufacturers make a bundle off of you, Vanessa."

A wisp of hair came loose from her ponytail as she shook her head. She tucked the sunny strand back into the clip. "I like to use affection instead of treats."

"Dad, he's got lots and lots of little teeth."

"Yeah, he does." He couldn't recall the last time he'd been around anyone so cheerful. "Working here really suits you."

"It's a blessing to have a job I love."

"You found a screwdriver?"

"Yes—if you really don't mind. . . "

"Not at all."

Nathan shifted into a more comfortable position and continued to carry on some small talk with Vanessa as he fixed the hinge. Jeff broke in with little observations and nonsense, but since he and Licorice kept each other entertained, Nathan continued to focus on Vanessa. Jeff got more insistent, and Nathan put both hands on his son's shoulders to transmit that he needed to settle down and hush a bit.

"I'm gonna get it, aren't I?"

At the same time Jeff spoke, Vanessa asked, "Are you guys about done in there?"

"Yes."

"Wow, Dad. Thanks!"

"Huh?" Nathan gave his son a quick look. His little face radiated with joy.

"I'll take really good care of him. I promise!"

"What?" Nathan cast a baffled glance at Vanessa. She gave him a troubled look.

"He asked if he could have the puppy," she whispered, "and you said yes."

three

Oh, great. The one time I don't give my kid undivided attention, I tell him he can have a dog? I didn't mean that he would get the dog; I meant if he kept interrupting he was going to be in trouble! Nathan took a deep breath and turned back to crush Jeff's hopes.

"Jeff," Vanessa said as she entered the pen. She knelt and made direct eye contact with him. "This is all my fault. Your daddy was answering my question. He wasn't telling you that you could have the puppy."

Jeff wrapped his arms around the puppy's neck, hugged it close, and shook his head. His voice went adamant. "My dad is honor'ble. He said I could have my dog."

"Your daddy is an honorable man, but this was just a misunderstanding. A mistake," Vanessa tried again.

Nathan took a deep breath. "It's a fine puppy."

"See? My dad doesn't lie!"

Vanessa let out a soundless sigh.

"Why don't you let us talk about this for a few minutes?" Nathan asked her.

She stood, clasped her hands at her waist, and tilted her head toward the puppy. "The three of you, or the two of you?"

"Three," Jeff answered promptly. From the way he held onto the little Lab, she suspected a six-point earthquake wouldn't shake them apart.

Vanessa didn't say another word. After she let herself out of the enclosure, Nathan noticed she walked away without that cute bounce she'd had earlier.

Several minutes later, she returned. She seemed subdued.

Instead of wearing that dazzling smile, she avoided making eye contact.

"Hey," he called softly. "We're going to take him. A boy needs a dog."

"Labs make good pets," she said as her face brightened a bit, but it still missed that sparkle he'd noticed earlier. "They do well with children."

"I guess I'd better buy some kibble." Nathan let himself out of the enclosure. "Jeff, you and Lick play for a few more minutes."

"Okay, Dad."

Ten minutes later, Nathan dumped the contents of a red plastic shopping basket onto the counter and shook his head. Two chew toys, a bottle of puppy shampoo, a leash, collar, food and water bowls, all accused him of being a pushover. The large sheepskin bed and the forty-pound bag of puppy kibble leaning against the counter proved he'd done a royal job of painting himself into a very expensive commitment.

Me and my big mouth. I try to teach my son to show integrity and end up buying half of a pet store!

Vanessa caught a jingly ball that started to roll off the counter. From the minute she'd whispered that he'd accidentally agreed to get the dog, she'd changed. She couldn't seem to meet his eyes.

From their conversation, Nathan knew making a good match was important to her. He strove to find a way to reassure her. "Do you have a good vet you recommend?"

"We have a terrific vet who comes here one Saturday a month to give vaccinations, Dr. Bainbridge. If you buy the puppy shot package, it saves you all of the office visit charges."

"Good idea."

She leaned down and pulled out a few leaflets from beneath the counter. As she tucked them into a bag, she said,

"I'm giving you the information on that package, as well as one of the vet's business cards."

"Thanks. I appreciate it."

She continued to avoid looking at him. "I'm also giving you a pet ID tag order form. Fill it out, and we'll order the tags. They're complimentary."

He reached over and captured her hand as she reached for one of the toys. "You don't need to throw in anything. Seriously, this was my choice."

"Hey, Dad!"

"Just a minute, Sport."

Vanessa flashed him a strained smile and pulled away from his touch. "We've been putting together a new puppy package. The first bag of food, a toy, and the tags are included at no charge."

The nape of his neck started to prickle. Nathan wheeled around and stared at Vanessa as she quietly walked up to him and asked, "Are you sure you want to do this? I'll come up with some way to explain it to Jeff."

"There are two of you. Twins." He cast a quick look over his shoulder, then concentrated back on Vanessa. Even though her eyes radiated concern, that little spark was still there—both in her eyes and somewhere deep inside of him. He'd missed that with the other gal.

"We're identical. I'm sorry if you were confused. I didn't realize Valene had come out and started helping you."

He glanced down at Amber. "I should have guessed something was wrong. I didn't see your companion."

"Daa-aad. Look out. There are two—" Jeff galloped around the corner and skidded to a stop. Licorice didn't halt. He charged ahead.

"Whoa!" Vanessa dove for the little puppy.

Nathan got to him first. Licorice sniffed his neck and let

out a happy sounding yap. Vanessa knelt right next to them. Nathan dipped his chin to keep the puppy from licking the ticklish spot beneath his left ear. "I don't want to hear another word about not taking this little fellow home. It's obvious he's chosen us."

&

"Vanessa!" Nathan called as he hastened toward the young woman locking the pet shop door.

She cast a quick glance over her shoulder and grinned. "Hi. How are things going?"

"Not good. We need to talk." Nathan raked his fingers through his hair in a single, impatient swipe. "I'm going insane."

"And you think I have the directions to get there?" She finished locking the shop. "Why does everyone think I'm the crazy sister? No, wait. Don't answer that."

He eyed her white-and-orange baseball uniform with dismay. "Cleats?"

"They're a lot more comfortable than heels. My church team is playing across the street tonight."

A sick feeling churned in his stomach. "And you play."

Her smile gleamed. "Believe me, if I didn't, nobody would ever wrangle me into wearing this uniform. I look more like the Great Pumpkin than the shortstop."

He tilted his head to the side. "Shortstop, huh. No kidding? I would have pegged a bouncy gal like you to be the team mascot."

"That was back in high school. Valene was the class valedictorian; I was the class clown and mascot. I shouldn't complain about this uniform. Nothing could ever be as uncomfortable as the shark suit I wore."

"You wore an outfit made of sharkskin?"

"Worse," she moaned. "I wore a great big, gray-and-white plush—"

"Plush? A shark?"

"Oh, yes. Fins and all. You're looking at one of Granite Cliffs's great whites—retired, of course."

"Since you've retired, you'll have enough time to help me." Nathan felt a small spurt of satisfaction that he'd segued this smoothly. "We're um. . .having some trouble."

"We are?" She pointed across the street to the ball diamond in a silent invitation to walk along with her.

Nathan automatically stood to her left so he'd be on the outside. "Yeah, well—"

She didn't follow along. "I'm sorry, Nathan, but Amber walks at heel. You need to be on my right."

"Oh. Okay." He shifted.

"Let's go," she said, and they fell into step.

"See? That's what I need. Jeff and Lick are romping everywhere and tearing up the house and yard. I need obedience and control tips. Amber heard you and fell right into step with us."

"One down, one to go." She winked and added, "I think you do fine with Jeff. The puppy might take a bit of time."

"If you saw my place, you wouldn't say so. My son's decided wherever he goes, Lick should be there with him. Last night, he waited until my back was turned and decided Lick belonged in the tub with him."

"Oh, no!"

Nathan rubbed his forehead at the memory of the wet puppy, the soggy bathroom, and the water trail down the hallway. That was just a part of the trials he faced with this new acquisition. "Yes. The dog won't eat his kibble. Instead, he's chewed the leg of a dining chair and gnawed on a pillow from the sofa."

They stopped at the corner and prepared to cross the busy intersection. Amber halted and sat without any cue at all. A cat streaked by, but the dog didn't react.

"I can't believe that. I've chased after our puppy twice because he can't leave cats alone. You've got to help me."

"I guess I sort of got you into this." Vanessa started to cross the street.

"Are you going to get me out of it?" He matched her stride and added on in desperation, "I'm more than willing to pay the going rate."

"Licorice is too young yet for training, but we can reserve a spot for him in one of the classes I'll have in a little over a month."

"My sanity could be measured in milliseconds, not months."

"Uh-oh. That sounds serious."

He rubbed his aching temple with his fingertips. "The only pets I ever had were cats. Cats take care of themselves."

"Ah, yes. Cats train their owners; dogs are trained by their owners."

"You nailed it on the head. So tell me: What's available right now to get us through the nightmare stage?"

"You mean something like private puppy lessons?"

He shot her a grateful smile. "I thought you'd never offer!"

Her eyes widened and a hectic flush filled her cheeks. "I didn't!" He continued to stare at her, and she scrunched her nose. "Let me guess. You bought the Lab because you misspoke and honored your word, so you're standing there thinking I ought to do the same thing."

"I'm flexible with hours."

Vanessa leaned her back into the fence. One of her knees crooked outward and her heel fit into the chain link. "We have to have an understanding. I'm not good at minding what I say. Valene—she's one of those 'think first, then talk' kind of people. Me? I'm impulsive. She got the brain, and I got the mouth." She laughed self-consciously. "If I'm willing to work with you, you have to promise not to use my words against me. I'll be sunk if you do!"

"Fair enough. When can we start?"

She shrugged. "Tomorrow at seven?"

"A.M.?"

Vanessa groaned. "Oh, don't tell me you're one of those morning people!"

"No." He watched someone dump several bats and balls out of a canvas sack. "I'd be a night owl if Jeff weren't such an early riser. He got that from my wife."

"If she's a stay-home mom, I could work with her from ten to eleven."

Pain speared through him. "Evie died five years ago."

"I'm so sorry, Nathan."

He nodded his head in acknowledgment of her sympathy.

"Nate? Nate Adams!" Kip Gaterie jogged over and shook his hand. "Did Van talk you into joining the team? We could use a slugger like you!"

"Do you play?" Vanessa gave him an assessing and hopeful look.

"Hang on a second here. I'm trying to get you to train a dog so I won't have to chase after him. Running after a ball isn't any more appealing."

"Pity." Kit looked at him steadily. "You can always change your mind. We'd be glad to have you, and we've got a bunch of rug rats about Jeff's age who could keep him company on the playground."

"Thanks, but I'll have to pass."

"That's a shame." Kip scuffed his foot in the red dirt. "Van, the park messed up on our reservation and only slotted us for an hour and a half. We're playing sudden death tonight, so we need to get out there."

"Okay."

As she turned to go, Nathan grabbed her arm. "Hey, if

you're only going to play for a little while, I can go home and get Jeff and Lick. Could you work with us after the game?"

"You're really desperate, aren't you?"

"In a word, yes!"

She glanced at her bright yellow Tweety Bird watch. "Be here at seven-thirty. I can't work miracles, but I'll try to give you a few starting tips."

"I gave up hoping for miracles years ago." He fished in his pocket for his keys, embarrassed by his sharp tone. "Have a good game. We'll be back later."

four

Vanessa wondered at the depth of the bitterness in Nathan's words, but it was neither the time nor the place to ask him what had caused that shift in him. Instead, she shoved on her mitt and jogged out onto the ball diamond.

After a cursory warm-up, the game began. Valene arrived and sat in the bleachers. She liked individual sports like tennis and badminton, but when it came to team sports, she preferred to be a spectator. By contrast, Vanessa loved all sports. She'd begged and wheedled to have her twin join several teams with her, but their youth pastor once gave a lesson on accepting loved ones instead of trying to change them. His words hit home—Vanessa had spent the whole ride to Seaside Chapel trying to cajole Val into trying out for the junior high volleyball team. She spent the drive home apologizing. Now it all seemed to work out beautifully. Val always brought the team banner and would watch Amber while Van dashed around the bases.

Kip sat down on the bench next to Van in the dugout. He nudged her shoulder playfully. "What's with you and Nathan Adams?"

Vanessa gave him a startled look. "Nothing. I just sold him a puppy, and it needs a bit of training. Why?"

He shrugged. "He's a good guy."

She gave him a piercing look. His tone a message she couldn't quite interpret. "But?"

"Nate took his wife's death hard. They used to attend Mercy Springs with me. He stopped attending, and I kinda hoped maybe he was starting back into fellowship."

"I don't know a thing about where he stands with the Lord. The only thing I know is, I'm in the doghouse 'cuz he bought a rambunctious puppy from me." She squinted as a ball sailed through the air. Hopping to her feet, she screamed, "Run! Run, Todd!"

The team cheered as Todd sped across home plate. Kip headed out of the dugout and hefted a bat. He looked back at Vanessa and wagged the end of the bat in her direction. "You never know what God will use to bring a sheep back into the fold. Keep your heart and eyes open."

❧

"There she is!" Jeff galloped toward the chain-link fence. Lick romped alongside him.

Nathan didn't need his son to point out where Vanessa was. He heard her first. She ran full tilt for third base, screaming like a heat-seeking missile the whole way. Her golden ponytail streamed behind her, and the left half of what had once been white-and-orange-striped baseball leggings now sported a calf-to-waist dusting of red that tattled on what must've been a world-class slide. She took a cue from the third-base coach and stopped. Energy high, she bobbed up and down on the base.

Nathan grinned as he continued to watch her. She cheered from third base, "You can do it, Della! Slug it!"

"I don't have your muscles, Girlfriend!"

Cupping her hands around her mouth, Vanessa yelled back, "Then use your brains. Anyone has more of those than I do!"

Everyone on the diamond chuckled, but Nathan watched as the outfielders drew closer to the infield. The ball whizzed over the plate.

"Strike one!" The second pitch went wide. The third zoomed over the plate again. Della stood there the whole time and didn't swing at all.

"Della," Vanessa hollered, "I said to use your brains, not your looks."

Della lifted the bat off her shoulder and took an awkward stance. "I'm not getting filthy dirty like you do."

"Don't worry about that. I already collected all of the loose dirt. You ought to be fine."

"Do you girls mind if we play ball?" the opposing pitcher asked in a humored tone.

"If you insist." Della nodded. "I'm as ready as I'm gonna get."

Nathan's jaw dropped as he heard the bat crack and the ball sailed far out into center field. Vanessa and the runner on second base both ran home. Vanessa skipped back and forth along the foul line. "You did it, Della! You did it!"

"Pretty clever strategy," Nathan said through the fence to Kip. "Lulled the other team into complacency."

Kip shook his head. "Nope. We can't believe it, either. Della's never even connected. Van took her to the batting cages this week."

"What in the world is Della doing on a team if she can't hit?"

"It's not about winning—it's about having a good time." Kip stared at him. "Though I wasn't kidding that we could sure use you on our team."

Vanessa bounced over. "Jeff! Lick! Hiya, guys!"

Licorice jumped up onto the fence with a happy yip.

"Off." Vanessa's voice took on a firm quality. She added, "Give the command and jerk back on the leash."

"Off!" Nathan pulled the leash from Jeff and tugged it. To his surprise, Licorice got all four paws on the grass and gave him a baffled look.

"Good dog, good dog," Vanessa crooned. She glanced at her watch. "You're a little early. Val and Amber are over on the bleachers. You can join them, or I can meet you by the playground as soon as the game is done."

"No playground," Jeff said morosely. "Dad said I can't 'cuz I already took my bath."

"Maybe next time," Vanessa said.

Nathan watched his son brighten up again. Vanessa had a knack for saying the right thing. Licorice started to drag on the leash. "I guess we're off to the stands."

He greeted Valene and took a seat next to her. He leaned forward and read the scoreboard. "The Altar Egos?"

"Vanessa named the team when it got started. She came up with over a dozen possible names, but that one won the vote."

"Is she always this irrepressible?"

Valene choked back a laugh. "I don't think I've ever heard anyone label her that way, but you're right."

The teams swapped positions. Vanessa played shortstop.

"Altar egos. . . ," Nathan repeated as he spotted the big plastic banner someone had tied to the chain-link dugout. The bold black words on the orange-and-white-striped background intrigued Nathan: 'But may it never be that I would boast, except in the cross of our Lord Jesus Christ.' Galatians 6:14.

Kip said it was a game for fun—not for competition—but the banner's declaration backed up what might easily have been a politically correct comment.

Nathan watched as the Altar Ego's players teased each other as much as they congratulated the other team on good plays. Vanessa called, "Nice try!" to one of her teammates when he dropped a pop fly. He picked up the ball, fired it at her, and she snagged it in her glove. "Ned and his nuclear arm!"

She intrigued Nathan. If anyone had room to boast, surely it was Vanessa. A powerhouse hit and a talent for snagging line drives made her impressive to watch. Then again, so did her svelte figure. She'd been almost comical—a one woman cheering squad for her friends. When the clock ran out and her team lost by one run, her grin didn't fade a speck.

As she came over to the bleachers, Jeff hopped up. "Guess what?" He didn't even pause to allow her to guess. "I got new spelling words on Monday, and you'll never in a million years guess what one of the words was. Guide—just like on Amber's jacket."

"Betcha you ace that test," Vanessa said. "Val, we're going to work a little with Licorice to see if we can find a few ways to calm him a bit. You can stay if you'd like, or you can take my car home. Amber and I could use the walk."

"I'd rather go work on my résumé. I saw a few positions in the career section that looked promising." Val squinted at the distance. "I have enough light to walk home. You keep the car."

"Not a chance," Nathan interrupted. "Jeff and I will give Vanessa a ride. We're messing up your schedule. It's the least we can do."

"Really, I can walk," Valene insisted. "I walk or jog four miles every day."

Nathan saw the worried look she shot Vanessa.

"We won't stay very long, Valene. Jeff has school tomorrow, and I need to have him in bed by eight-thirty. After chasing him and Lick around this evening, I'll probably crash all of five minutes later."

"See? Pumpkin time isn't midnight; it's eight." Vanessa handed the keys to her sister. "Now promise me you'll juice up your résumé. It was too modest and bland."

"I'll see what I can do."

"What kind of job are you looking for?"

Valene shrugged. "I have my business degree. I kind of thought maybe a hospital business office."

"The minute you interview, you'll have every single hospital in Southern California after you," Vanessa declared. She stooped and said to Jeff, "My sister is a total brain. She's terrific at spelling words and math."

"Did you ever switch places for tests?" Jeff asked in a stage whisper.

Nathan wondered the same thing, but he wasn't sure he wanted to hear the answer—and he certainly didn't want Jeff to.

Vanessa wrinkled her nose. "It wouldn't have been right for us to swap places at school. We each got the grades we deserved. We did trade places at summer camp once so I could play baseball more and Valene got to swim."

"Van slid into second base and ruined my new jeans that day," Valene recalled.

"You look alike, but you're really different," Jeff decided.

Vanessa winked at Nathan. "That's one smart kid you have there. If your dog is half as clever, training him will be a piece of cake."

They spent about half an hour working with Licorice. Jeff started out like gangbusters, wanting to do everything. Licorice decided to yank free and make a mad dash across the park.

"Oh, no," Nathan groaned. He started to run after the puppy. It was the last thing he wanted to do.

"Nathan, clap and shout his name, but run the opposite way. He'll come chase you."

Less than a minute later, Licorice wiggled in Nathan's arms. "I can't believe it. That's all it takes? I've practically run a marathon twice today, catching this hairy little beast!"

Jeff plopped down on the grass and started to laugh. "Daddy needs to be trained more than the dog!"

Vanessa bit her lip and turned away, but from the way her shoulders shook, he knew she was thoroughly entertained. He bumped her hip with his and said in mock outrage, "Now look what you've done!"

"Saved you shoe leather?" she shot back.

"Who are you kidding?" He held up Licorice. "Knowing my luck, this little energetic four-legged headache is going to end up chewing on my shoes, anyway."

"Dad?"

Something in Jeff's tone made Nathan freeze. "What?"

Jeff ducked his head and lifted both shoulders. He said to his lap in a small voice, "He already did."

Nathan groaned. He turned back to Vanessa. "Shoes, a pillow, and a chair leg. Tell me the list of casualties ends there."

"You're in it for the long haul. It's not a three-strikes-and-he's-out proposition."

"You're the puppy pro." He couldn't help responding to her gentle humor and common sense. "Now what do I do?"

"Give him the chew toys. I don't have anything scheduled tomorrow evening. Bring him by the shop after closing, and we'll come up with some strategies."

"Okay. You're on. I can hold out that long."

❧

The door to Whiskers, Wings, and Wags flew open. "Vanessa!" Jeff's shout almost covered the chimes. A split second later, Vanessa heard Nathan's low scold, "You're not a Scud missile, Son. Use your indoor voice and your manners."

" 'Kay, Dad. Where is she?"

"I'm down here," Vanessa called. She lifted a hand and waved over the counter.

"Hey, Van," Nathan said, "about ready to go?"

Embarrassed to the core of her being, she looked up at Nathan and shook her head.

"No?"

"I'm um. . .stuck."

five

"Stuck?" Nathan repeated, leaning farther over the counter to get a better look.

"Stuck? Vanessa's stuck?" Jeff repeated. He raced around the counter.

"Oh, brother." Vanessa rested her head against Amber's side. "Ever hear the old saying, 'Be careful what you pray for?'"

"What did you pray for, and why are you stuck?" Nathan moved Jeff off to the side and hunkered down.

"I dropped a receipt. It slipped down here behind the drawers. When I reached up to get it, my ring caught, and my hand is jammed."

Nathan thoughtfully pinched his lower lip between his forefinger and thumb. He raised his brows at Jeff. "Son, it looks like we have a genuine damsel in distress here."

"Are we gonna rescue her?"

"Sometimes, Sport, a man's gotta do what a man's gotta do."

"Wait!"

"Did we scare you free, like Dad scares the hiccups outta me?"

"Don't I just wish." She looked up at Nathan. "Would you please flip over the Closed sign and lock the door?"

"Jeff, you heard her. You can do those things, can't you?"

"'Course I can!" His tennis shoes squeaked on the linoleum as he ran back around the counter. The dead bolt made a solid clunk, and cardboard scraped across the glass as the sign flipped over.

Nathan didn't wait for his son to finish those simple tasks.

He slithered onto the floor next to her and slid his hand up close to hers. With each inhalation he took, his chest pressed against her back. Every breath he let out ruffled her hair and made her shiver. He frowned and wrapped his other arm around her. "You're cold. How long have you been trapped down here?"

"Half of forever," she evaded.

"Oh. So she can't tell time, either," Jeff said from behind them.

"Son, we need to squirt some soap up onto Vanessa's hand. Go into the back room and see what you can find."

"Dog shampoo," she suggested. "It's the yellowish orange stuff by the big tub."

Nathan's fingers nudged the side of her hand. "Too bad we can't open the drawer, but it would knock you senseless."

"Thank you."

"Huh?" He twisted his head a bit and gave her a puzzled look.

"After finding me like this, I figured you were going to think I didn't have any sense at all."

"Just because Valene was valedictorian doesn't mean you're not bright. How about if you stop comparing yourself and always thinking you come out on the short end of the deal?"

If he'd barked the words at her or teased, it would have been easier. Since his voice went so soft and earnest, she gulped.

He tugged a bit on her wrist and muttered, "You're really jammed in there."

The whole situation struck her as so ludicrous, she started to giggle. "You know me—I took that old cliché to heart. 'Anything worth doing is worth doing right.'"

Nathan's arm tightened around her. "So you're saying this was worth doing?"

How am I supposed to answer that?

The patter of Jeff's shoes saved her from having to formulate an answer. "Here's the shampoo!" He climbed over their legs and sat next to Amber. While Nathan withdrew his hand and gooped it up with the unscented liquid, Jeff scratched his knee. "What did you pray for, Van?"

She jerked on her hand once again to no avail and confessed, "Patience."

"Here goes nothing." Nathan curled back around her and slid his hand up by her wrist. "My fingers are fatter than yours. If I shove my hand any higher, we'll both get stuck. Can you wiggle your hand to the side a little?"

"Which side?"

"That way." He nudged her a bit. "Good. I'll see if I can rub some of this slimy stuff on the metal bar here and on the edge of your hand. Afterward, if you jostle your hand over here, maybe we can work just enough of the soap under the ring to make your finger slip free."

"I don't even know if it'll come off." She fidgeted, hoping to spread the shampoo around. "Grandma gave one to each of us on our thirteenth birthday."

"You've never taken it off?"

"Nope."

"Wow," Jeff said. He gave her an incredulous look. "Dad said all rings have to come off sooner or later. He keeps his in his sock drawer."

Nathan went completely still. Vanessa closed her eyes for a moment, sensing the pain that rolled off him. He'd said very little about his wife, but what he had said made it clear he'd loved her dearly. It must have been heart wrenching to finally remove his wedding band.

He drew in a deep, steadying breath. In a tight voice, he ordered, "Now try to work your hand free."

A few, very long minutes later, she felt a little give. "Almost—it slipped a little bit."

"Good." Nathan clenched her elbow. "On the count of three. One, two, three!"

He yanked, she pulled, and her hand came free.

"Oh, thank you, thank you, thank you."

"So you got what you prayed for," Jeff said as he hugged Amber.

Nathan opened the drawer, pried the ring free, and shoved it back at Vanessa. He stared at his son and rasped, "Prayers are like dreams and wishes. Not all of them come true. Don't ever forget that."

&

At least once a week, Nathan arranged for Vanessa to work with him, Jeff, and Licorice. Every weekend, he brought Jeff to Whiskers, Wings, and Wags to buy a bag of kibble.

"I can order this in larger bags. It comes in twenty and forty pounds," Vanessa offered.

"Not a chance." Nathan plunked a ten-dollar bill onto the counter. "Don't even start down that path. You could charm a snake into buying a pedicure, but I'm impervious to this particular sales pitch."

"A pedicured snake?"

He ignored her entertained echo. "Our place is small. I don't want to have to go out to the garage or backyard to grab a scoop of chow for the little beast."

"Isn't that funny? For some odd reason, I figured a man in the construction business would have a big old house."

"Old, yes; big, no. Evie and I bought an 1865 saltbox back in Massachusetts on our honeymoon." For the first time, the memory flitted though his mind without tearing a jagged hole in his heart.

"A saltbox? How charming!"

"You wouldn't have said that if you'd have seen it. The poor thing was slated for destruction. Evie went wild over it and said all the rickety old house needed was elbow grease and love, so we had the place all numbered, dismantled, and shipped out here. I put it back together on a big lot." Under his breath, he recalled, "We always figured we could add on."

"Dad's building me a fort. A giant one with a swing set underneath."

"Neato! Are you helping?"

Nathan grinned. "He's sanding the shutters and is going to paint them."

"If you need an extra pair of hands, I'm willing to help." She lifted her arms and fluttered her fingers in the air. "A pair of nice guys rescued me, so I can offer to be useful."

"Dad's putting a zebra in the backyard. He said he'd need lotsa help with that."

"A zebra?" Vanessa gawked at him. "You really weren't kidding when you said if you got one animal, you'd end up with a menagerie!"

Nathan chuckled. "Jeff's got the wrong idea. It's a gazebo, not a zebra."

"No zebra?" His son gave him a dismayed look.

"No zebra. No cats, rats, birds, or lizards, either." He glanced about the pet shop and hoped he hadn't missed out on anything readily visible, because sure as the sun rose, if he missed something, Jeff would take that as a promise that he could have one. In the off chance he had overlooked a creature, Nathan shook his finger at his son—as much to keep his attention focused on him as anything else. "Don't press your luck. We have an agreement, and you're behind on your end of the deal."

Jeff blurted out a laugh and slapped his hand over his mouth.

"Just what is so funny?" Vanessa folded her arms on the counter and leaned forward.

"Dad made a joke about our agreement about Lick." Jeff whispered very blatant clues at a decibel only a first grader would consider secretive. "Behind. End."

Vanessa made a goofy face. "Well, Buster, you'd better clean up your act. I'm not coming over to help on a fort or a gazebo if I have to tiptoe through the tulips."

"We don't got no flowers."

"Have," Nathan corrected. "We don't *have* any flowers." *Evie loved flowers, and I still can't stand to tend them.* He shoved away the thought and cleared his throat. "I don't have time to mess with detailed gardening. If something needs more than routine watering and an occasional trimming, you can bet it's not in my yard."

"Juggling a thriving business, a kid, and an energetic puppy would be enough for anyone." Vanessa's lips pursed, and the impish gleam in her eyes warned Nathan he'd better prepare himself for whatever she'd say next.

"The best thing for you would be some free time. You know: recreation."

"Is that so?" he asked sardonically.

"Absolutely. Something fun. Let you get out a bit. Be with good people. Enjoy fresh air."

"Are you—" Jeff bobbed and weaved from one side of his father's long, lean legs to the other "—sending Dad to summer camp?"

"Nope." Nathan ruffled his son's hair. "I think Van's trying to rope me into playing baseball."

"Where's her rope?"

"With the zebra?" Vanessa ventured in a playful tone.

"Sport, I need a minute with Vanessa. Why don't you go see if you can spot Goldie in the fish tank?" He waited until

Jeff was out of earshot, then braced both hands on the counter. It took everything in him to keep from thundering, but he refused to lose control. "Forget it. Just forget this plan of yours to lure me back into church. I know the whole deal—sucker someone into an activity they like, then chip away the defenses until they start attending services. Well, it's not going to work, Vanessa. Not on me."

"Okay. I promise I won't ever invite you to worship. It doesn't mean you can't just have a good time with great people."

"You just don't get it, so I'm going to be blunt. My wife died. She was a devout believer. We prayed for a miracle, but she died an inch at a time of kidney failure. A good Christian man would have accepted it, but I didn't. I still haven't. Call me jaded or bitter or a backslider—I know all of the churchy terms for it. There's one thing I refuse to be, and that's a hypocrite. I'm not about to wear a mask and pretend everything is hunky-dory."

"Who said you have to?"

He slammed his fist on the counter. "I went to church the Sunday after the funeral. I needed God. I needed comfort. Instead, I ended up having to put up with half of the congregation weeping all over me. How was I supposed to console them when all I could do was look at my son and know God took away his mother?"

"I'm sorry you hurt." She slid her hand over his fist.

"What? No shock that I'd dare to be mad at God?"

Vanessa simply squeezed his clenched fist. "There's nothing wrong with being angry. God is bigger than your rage, and He's patient."

Her response caught him off guard. Embarrassed by his outburst, Nathan mumbled, "I'm not about to darken the door of a church."

"There aren't any stained-glass windows or sermons on a ball diamond." She waggled her brows. "And I'll help with your gazebo."

"You drive a hard bargain. Do you drive nails half as well?"

"Just you wait and see."

six

Vanessa sat on the edge of the deck they'd just made for the gazebo and winced as Nathan yanked a splinter from his hand. "Want some help with that?"

"Naw. It's no big deal. I get 'em all the time."

"When you said you were building a gazebo, I didn't imagine anything quite this grand."

The leather of his tool belt made a slight stretching sound, and some of the tools clinked together as he laid back and supported himself on his elbows. He gave her a taunting grin. "In over your head?"

"I'm holding my own." She gave him a saucy smile. "Except for when it comes to tools. Your cordless power stuff is really nifty."

"Occupational benefit."

"Oh, come on. Who are you kidding? Even if you weren't in the construction business, you'd still have the biggest and best power tools made because they're big boys' toys."

"I collect toys; you collect things with fur, fins, or feathers. From where I sit, it seems like you shouldn't be throwing rocks since you're living in a glass house."

"From where you sit?" Her ponytail swished impudently as she gawked around at the gazebo. "I might have glass walls to my so-called house, but this little house of yours has none at all!"

"Just you wait and see." He stood and pulled her to her feet. "This baby's going to be done in no time at all."

She picked up a drill, slipped her forefinger through the trigger loop, and made it whine. "Thanks to these toys."

"And thanks to you. It's a lot easier getting things done with an extra pair of hands."

"I'm having fun." She turned to go back to work. "We ought to be able to get the main beams up and the benches made today."

"I'm amazed. I thought Amber would go nuts over the whine of the drill. She just curls up out of the way, and the noise doesn't even faze her."

"It's all part of training her to ignore things. I've taken her to construction sites, parades, and high school basketball and football games. She's learned that noise, vibration, and movement aren't as important as being a good girl." Vanessa stroked Amber approvingly. "It's all a part of learning good puppy manners, and you are a perfect lady, aren't you?"

"Incredible. Why doesn't she stretch out?"

"That's part of her training too. We teach the dogs to 'be small.' She's going to have to fit under seats on a bus, ride in a plane and train, and be in auditoriums. If she stretches out, someone will step on her, or she'll become an obstacle."

"How'd you learn all of this?"

"There's a manual, and I go to puppy-raiser meetings twice a month."

"Meetings? What do you do?"

"One meeting is usually a combination business and obediencetraining meeting. The second one is normally an outing. We take the puppies somewhere so they can be exposed to a challenging environment or situation and learn how to respond appropriately. It's a great group of people and dogs."

She reached over for another length of wood he'd already cut to size. "If you have any wood left over, you could make a doghouse for Lick."

"Why bother? He's sleeping in Jeff's room."

"I know we're in California, but it does rain every once in awhile."

Nathan waved his hand to indicate the gazebo. "And this isn't enough shelter?"

"That all depends."

"On what?"

She gave him a look of owl-eyed innocence. "If you like eau de wet puppy."

"Okay. I'm convinced. A doghouse is my next project."

"Then we'd better get back to work and finish this up."

A few hours later, they took another breather.

"This yard is huge." Vanessa scanned. "I'll bet you have a cool lawn mower."

"It all depends on what you think is cool. I hired the kid next door to mow and edge. He wanted to earn money for football."

"He's probably rich enough to own the team by now. What is this—an acre?"

"Three-quarters of an acre. I tried to keep the gazebo to scale. It would have looked pretty ridiculous to have one of those little scaled-down jobs back here."

"Yeah, well, Jeff's fort is so big, I'm expecting the U.S. Navy to billet a few officers in it."

Nathan bent his head over his palm and plucked out another splinter as he mumbled, "Jeff wanted the extra level and the rope netting. It wasn't that much more work."

"Did you really camp out up there last Friday?"

"Yup. Lanterns, sleeping bags, and mosquitoes." He turned toward the house and yelled, "Jeff, where's that lemonade?"

The door opened. Jeff stuck his head out and shouted, "I can't reach the glasses."

"Aren't there clean ones in the dishwasher?"

"Huh-unh. We forgot to run it. I can tell 'cuz there's still pasgetti on the plates."

"I'll go help him." Vanessa sprang to her feet. Amber accompanied her across the lawn and into the house. The minute she got inside, Vanessa sucked in a deep breath. She'd never seen Nathan's house.

Clearly, a busy man, a little boy, and an undisciplined puppy lived here. School papers cluttered the refrigerator door and the coffee table. Both the telephone and the stove bore spaghetti sauce splatters, and a small bulletin board listed two baby-sitters, several fast-food places, and a few scrawled memos. Two pair of muddy shoes—one small, the other huge—sat on the hearth, and a track of muddy paw prints zigzagged down the hall.

"The glasses are up there." Jeff pointed to a cupboard on the right side of the sink.

Vanessa opened it and spied a set of earthenware dishes adorned with pinkish flowers around the edges. It seemed so absurdly feminine in a father-and-son home, but that fact tugged at her heart. Clearly, Nathan still held his wife's memory dear, and he clung to the little things that still kept her alive in his heart. She must've been someone very special.

Bypassing the glass tumblers in favor of three mismatched plastic cups, Vanessa said, "These look like good ones to take to the backyard."

"I'll pour the lemonade."

"Okay." She fought the urge to take over. Nathan encouraged Jeff to be independent, and it wouldn't hurt anything if they had to wipe up a spill. She took the time to scan the house a bit more.

A woman's touch was still very evident. Wallpaper of dainty sprays of antique roses covered the far side of the kitchen, echoed by linoleum flooring that held a pattern of tiles with little rose-colored flowers. A five-foot-long pine board hung from the ceiling. Several decorator-quality baskets dangled from pegs on it.

"Forgive the mess," a deep voice said from behind her.

Vanessa jumped at that sound. "It's a wonderful place."

"Consuelo will be back on Monday. She's spending a week visiting her sister. She manages to keep Jeff out of trouble when he gets home from school and keeps the place from being a total pit. Three days on our own, and we've just about demolished the downstairs. Jeff and I were going to pick up a bit before you got here, but—"

"We got busy watching cartoons," Jeff interrupted.

Vanessa watched red creep up Nathan's neck. "Don't be embarrassed. I did the same thing. I was supposed to be sorting through the pots and pans, but I ate my cereal in front of the TV and got stuck on good old *Rocky and Bullwinkle* reruns."

Nathan swiped two of the glasses from the counter and handed her one. "*Rocky and Bullwinkle*, huh?"

"My favorite."

"So even as a kid, you had a thing for animals."

"Guilty as charged." She took a sip. "Great lemonade, Jeff."

"Thanks. Can the dogs drink some too?"

"No," Nathan and Vanessa said in unison.

"Why not?"

Nathan looked at Vanessa. "You're the expert."

"People food isn't always healthy for dogs. Every once in awhile, if your dad lets you, you can give Lick some of your leftovers."

"Oh, great," Jeff sighed. "Dad always finishes everything. We don't got no leftovers."

"We don't *have* any leftovers," Nathan corrected.

"That's what I said. Poor Licorice is gonna starve!"

Vanessa walked out of the kitchen and into the backyard before she burst into laughter.

A short while later, Nathan pounded one last nail into a board and asked, "Why are you sorting pots and pans?"

"Valene bought a condo. We're trying to decide who owns what."

"You mean the Dynamic Duo is splitting up?"

"Hard to imagine, isn't it? Actually, I think it's a great move—pardon the pun. Val landed a job in the business office at the hospital. The condo is close, so she won't have to worry about a long commute."

"It's not all that far—about twenty minutes or so?"

"Close enough to still meet and go to church and do things together."

"Outgoing as you are, you'll stay busy." He stuffed the hammer into his tool belt without even looking. "Aren't you worried Val will feel a bit lost?"

"I think it'll be a good change for her—she'll need a little nudging, but she'll make friends. If anything, I'm going to be lost without her. She's so organized and capable."

"Capable? Look at you, Van. You own and run a store. You have an active social life. You're great at sports, volunteer in the community, and are better with a hammer and saw than half of the men I hire. Don't sell yourself short."

She looked into his coffee brown eyes and saw the sincerity there. His praise meant more to her than it probably ought to. Uncomfortable with the sudden closeness she felt, she wiped her palms on the sides of her jeans. "If I do something stupid like forgetting to pay the electricity bill so I lose my power, I'm going to sneak over and sleep in Jeff's fort."

Concern creased Nathan's forehead. "You're used to splitting rent. Are you going to be in trouble?"

"No, Val wouldn't ever leave me in the lurch. The shop's doing well. I can afford to live alone. Amber's good company, too, aren't you, Girl?"

Amber wagged her tail.

Nathan looked across the yard at Jeff and Lick as they tumbled in the grass. "Any chance you'll train him to sit quietly?"

"Are you asking about Jeff or Licorice?"

"Hey. For that, I'm not going to volunteer to help Val move."

seven

"Just how much stuff have the two of you squirreled away in this place?" Nathan took in the pile of boxes and blinked in disbelief.

"This place has a lot of storage space," Valene murmured as she glanced about the apartment.

"She's only taking her stuff." Vanessa capped the black marker with a flourish after she finished writing "Kitchen— dishes. Breakable!" on a box.

"Not really. Vanessa's giving me a bunch of things that probably are rightfully hers."

"It's really an excuse for me to go buy new dishes. I want to get something different."

The shuffle of booted feet at the doorway made them all turn. "Kip! You came." Vanessa waved him in. "I nearly fought Val to the death so I could keep the coffeemaker. There's a fresh pot in the kitchen, if either of you men need to get juiced up with caffeine before we start."

"What? No doughnuts?" Kip crossed the room and slapped Nathan on the shoulder in greeting. "These two women are going to work us half to death, then let starvation complete the job."

"I suppose this is my cue to say something like, 'I made Grandma's cinnamon coffee cake,' but I probably ought to confess that Valene is taking the couch."

Nathan stared at the big, pale blue, fluffy-cushioned couch and rubbed his forehead. "How about if I go for the coffee, cake, and no couch?"

Kip flopped down on the couch. "You've obviously never tasted Vanessa's cooking! Me? I'll take the coffee and move the couch. I've tasted something she made once. Believe me, once was more than enough. It wasn't fit for human consumption."

"Hey!" Vanessa tossed the marker at him and headed into the kitchen. "Just because you don't know dog food when you see it. . ."

"Dog food?" Nathan looked from Kip to Valene for an explanation.

A shy smile lit Valene's face. "Van made special biscuits for Mrs. Culpepper's poodle. She's got heart problems and needs low sodium treats."

"It was Valentine's Day," Kip groused. "How was I supposed to know they weren't heart-shaped cookies? She had them on a plate!"

Van came back into the room. She balanced four mismatched holiday paper plates that held plastic forks and big, fragrant chunks of pastry.

Nathan happily swiped one, handed it to Valene, and took one for himself as Kip scrambled off the couch and dove for another. "Wow. I thought you were kidding when you said something about your granny's recipe."

"It's not cinnamon; it's her lemon cream cheese loaf," Vanessa said.

Nathan took a bite. It melted in his mouth. He quickly licked a pastry crumb off his lip. "For this, I'll even help move the couch."

"Careful." Kip gave a wary look around the boxes. "They're bribing us. There's got to be a catch somewhere." His eyes narrowed. "Val, is your new condo an upstairs one?"

"Not a chance. By the time I get home from a four-mile run, I don't want to have to jog up the stairs."

Kip chuckled. "And I thought you were going to tell us Vanessa is afraid of heights."

Nathan gulped down the last bite of pastry and shook his head. "Vanessa is fearless."

She bumped into a stack of boxes and quoted, "I can do all things through Him who strengthens me."

"Then why did you want us to come help you move all of this junk?"

The move only took the morning hours. Valene had everything organized and ready to go, and the men managed to wedge everything into the truck she'd rented. After a single trip, they'd hauled everything out and taken it into Val's new place. The twins' parents were out of town, but they called from their hotel and arranged for a local deli to furnish lunch. A four-foot submarine sandwich with all of the trimmings was delivered just as Nathan wheeled in a dolly with the last stack of boxes on it.

As they ate, Kip tossed a can of soda to Nathan and said, "We still have a spot for you on the team."

"I'm not going to church."

Vanessa startled at the vehemence of his tone.

Kip shrugged. "I didn't invite you to church. Course you're welcome if you wanna come, but I'm talking about home plate, not the offering plate."

Aware he'd startled Vanessa and Valene, Nathan felt a niggling of guilt. He pushed it aside. There was nothing wrong with a man standing firm on an issue. Then again, there was nothing wrong with a guy playing ball, either. "Okay, here's the deal: I'll play. But don't expect me to warm a pew."

"We're in business."

"Business!" Vanessa glanced at her watch. "I have to mind the shop for a couple of hours. Jamie could only stay 'til two today. I'll be back at about six to help you unpack the boxes, Val." She hugged her sister, dashed for the door, and sang over her shoulder, "Thanks for lugging all of my sissy's stuff, guys!"

❧

Vanessa sailed back through her sister's door at a few minutes after six.

"Next time I get a great idea and decide to move," Valene sighed as she plopped down on the couch, "shoot me."

Vanessa stepped around a stack of towels, clung to a large roasting pan with oven mitts, and looked around the living room. "You've unpacked almost half of the boxes! We'll finish up later. For now. . ."

Valene gave her a weary smile. "Supper. Whatever it is, I'll eat it."

"Here you are." Vanessa set the roasting pan on the bare coffee table.

"Put the mitts under that! I don't want the wood ruined!"

Vanessa ignored her twin and lifted the lid with a flourish. "Ta da!"

"What in the world?" Val leaned forward and stared at the pan. Nestled inside was a cell phone with a colorful rectangle of paper taped to the bottom. She lifted the phone, and Vanessa started to laugh as Valene tore off the coupon and read aloud, "Free pizza?"

"But of course. Home delivery. And observe, Mam'selle. . ." She pulled out a red-and-white-checkered plastic tablecloth, spread it on the coffee table, and topped it with matching paper plates and napkins she'd stuffed into the roasting pan. "You go ahead and call. I already arranged for them to bring a large pizza with the works, soda, and salad."

"What? No dessert?"

Vanessa gave her a wounded look. "Have you ever known me to skimp on the essentials?" She pulled a small gold box of chocolate truffles from the roasting pan and set it in the center of the table with all due consideration.

"Perfect. How about if we eat those while we wait for the pizza?"

"Be still, my beating heart!" Vanessa patted her chest theatrically. "Is that my always-sensible twin sister suggesting something that decadent?"

"I am being sensible. If I turn my back, you'll eat the hazelnut." She leaned forward, lifted the foil box's lid, and plucked out her favorite. After she called for the pizza, she crossed one leg beneath her on the sofa and made direct eye contact. "I want to talk to you for a minute about being sensible."

"Uh-oh. You just pasted on your serious look."

"I am serious. Van, Nathan is a troubled man. He's really resistant to anything having to do with God."

"I know." She stared at her sister and sighed. "What kind of Christian would I be to reject him instead of coming alongside him? He's mad at God. Really mad. I've been there too. Remember when Grandma died? I hurt so badly, I didn't pray all summer."

"Yeah, but from what Kip said, Nathan's been bitter for years now."

"Nathan hasn't made any secret of it. God is patient, Val. I figure we can either push Nathan away, or we can draw him back to the Lord. It's not something that will be fixed overnight. Baby steps—it's a matter of baby steps. You heard him—he'll join the team."

"Don't fall for him, Van. It'll break your heart."

eight

Nathan peeked in on Jeff. His son was sprawled across the bed sideways, the pillow lay on the floor, and the puppy was curled up at the head of the bed where the pillow belonged. Letting out a sigh, Nathan crossed the hardwood floor. His footsteps made a solid sound, but he doubted a full-volume Sousa march would rouse Jeff. Licorice's head lifted, and his tail made a rapid *whump, whump, whump* against the oak headboard.

"You don't belong up here." Nathan planned to scoop the puppy off the bed, place him on the floor, and have him trot out to the back door for one last pit stop. Once he reached for the dog, his plans altered.

Licorice's tongue darted out and lapped at Nathan's wrist. The speed of his tail wagging a drumbeat against the headboard doubled. Nathan picked him up, cradled him in his arms, and left the room. As he walked down the hall and reached the squeaky third step on the stairs, the puppy squirmed and snuffled until his little wet nose nudged at the base of Nathan's throat.

Nathan stopped on the stairs and looked down. "I'm Granite Cliffs's biggest pushover, you know. You're the living proof of that. If you weren't so cute, it would be downright embarrassing that I put up with you."

The small metal tags on Lick's collar jingled.

"Yeah. I know." Nathan carried him down the rest of the stairs, through the living room, and out the kitchen door.

He put down the pooch and sat out in the gazebo. It was too early to turn in, and he had too many thoughts running though his mind to bother trying to follow a plot of any television show.

He took up a piece of sandpaper and started to rub out a small ding on the right edge of the western bench in the gazebo. After a few passes, his action halted. He didn't want to make that nick disappear.

Vanessa had been hammering trellis on the side of the gazebo, and her hammer slipped. She'd been upset about the blemish in the bench, but it was such a minor imperfection, Nathan knew he could sand it smooth. For now, he'd still leave that nick there—it was like a reminder of the golden afternoon when they'd constructed this.

Vanessa. He'd felt a spurt of emotion when Kip showed up at her apartment this morning to help with the move. Were they dating? The thought turned his stomach. He had no right to be jealous or possessive. None whatsoever. He and Vanessa were. . .*what are we?*

He couldn't exactly answer that nagging question. When Kip said he hadn't had any of Vanessa's cooking other than the dog biscuits, that had made Nathan breathe a little easier. As they'd all worked together to carry things out to the moving truck and haul them into Valene's new place, Nathan noticed Kip kept mixing up the sisters.

They both wore blue jeans and old, faded red Whiskers, Wings, and Wags T-shirts. Other than that, Kip must have been hit in the head with one too many wild pitches if he thought Van and Val were interchangeable. Val was a pretty young woman; Van was ravishingly beautiful. She just plain sparkled. Her moves carried an exuberance and grace that captivated Nathan.

They didn't even smell alike. Val wore something from one

of those fancy bottles she'd carried into her new place in a basket; Vanessa would have given Carmen Miranda stiff competition in the fruit bowl category. Her hair smelled of strawberry shampoo, she chewed watermelon bubble gum, and when she sat beside him in the truck, she'd slicked peach gloss on her lips.

If all else failed, Kip could have just glanced down and seen that Amber shadowed Vanessa everywhere she went. *Well, maybe that isn't entirely true,* Nathan admitted to himself. *Amber stays with Valene when Vanessa is on the ball diamond.*

Licorice woofed softly. He'd grown appreciably in the past month. He'd barely been able to make it up a step that first day. Now, he undulated like a playful dolphin as he bounded up the four risers into the gazebo. Nathan groaned.

"Lick, is that mud on your nose and paws?"

Licorice skidded to a halt, leaving telltale streaks in his wake.

"What did you dig up this time?"

The puppy sank down, buried his muzzle in his paws, and made a pitiful, guilty whimper.

"Looks like I'm going to have to consult with Vanessa about what to do with a naughty little digger." Nathan leaned down and petted Lick's sleek black coat. In truth, he wasn't overly upset. It provided another good excuse to be with Vanessa again.

᠄

"Do you have time for a puppy consultation?"

Vanessa clamped the receiver between her ear and her shoulder as she considered Nathan's question. She had her hands full, but she didn't want to miss what he had to say. "Uh-oh. What's Lick up to now?"

"Outsmarting me."

She didn't try to muffle her laughter. "Again?"

Silence on his end of the line might have meant he was offended, but when he spoke, his voice sounded more like he was chuckling than chiding. "You could be a little more sympathetic."

"Actually, I'm thinking how fortunate you are. Obviously Lick is a highly intelligent dog, so once he's trained, he's going to be a dream boat."

"Right about now, I'd settle for a leaky canoe."

"Well, he's a puppy, so I can guarantee he's still leaky."

"You did warn me that you'd been class clown," Nathan muttered wryly.

"Let me put Nero down so I can hold the phone." She set aside the receiver, placed the black Lab puppy she'd just groomed into an enclosure, and came back. "Thanks for waiting."

"Let me get this straight," Nathan said with a tinge of amusement. "You're fiddling with Nero while my Rome is burning."

"That's about the size of it. He and Lick are from the same litter. The family who took him didn't check with their landlord, and they've been told they'll be evicted if they keep him."

"And I thought I had problems."

"It's really no problem at all. Valene is a little lonely. She's used to me and a dog, so I've decided to give Nero to her."

"She doesn't have a yard."

"No, she doesn't. For just about anyone else, I'd encourage them to have a smaller dog if it's going to be a house pet. Val loves to walk and jog. If anything, Nero will get plenty of exercise and provide an extra measure of safety for Val. Anyway, enough about Nero and Val. What do you need?"

"Help. I'm desperate. I tell you what: Jeff and I will bring Lick to baseball practice tonight. We'll snag some Picnicin'

Chicken on the way. If we get to your shop right as it closes, we can eat in the park, and you can give me some pointers on what to do with the puppy."

"Sounds great. Feed Lick before you come—otherwise, he's going to want people food."

"Okay. Gotcha. Good tactic. See you later."

❧

Van and Amber were standing outside the pet shop when Nathan drove up. He drew alongside the curb and parked.

"There they are!" Jeff scrambled out of his seat belt and twisted to unlatch Lick from his puppy seat belt. The windows were rolled down, and he shouted, "We brought chicken and hot cherry flipovers for dessert!"

"Turnovers, Sport." Nathan identified with Jeff's eager scramble to get out of the car. Clearly, if he and Vanessa did decide to pursue a relationship, he wouldn't have to worry whether Jeff liked her. Nathan got out of the car, grabbed the rustling plastic bag holding their supper, and snatched his mitt from the dashboard.

"All set?" Vanessa stooped and paid generous attention to Lick.

"You betcha." Jeff gawked around. "Dad said you gots another dog just like mine. Where is he?"

"I do have another puppy that's Licorice's brother. I left him in the shop, and I want to keep him a big surprise. I'm giving him to Valene after the game tonight. Can you keep it a secret?"

"Yep!" Jeff hopped in place.

Nathan tilted his head and slanted his eyes toward the clouds as he shrugged, hoping Vanessa would understand his meaning. Six-year-old boys weren't exactly reliable when it came to keeping confidences.

Vanessa's eyes twinkled with understanding. She rose and lifted an electric blue athletic bag.

"I'll take that." Nathan reached for it.

"Then put your glove inside. No use carrying a bunch of loose gear." She unzipped it and opened the flaps.

Nathan made a show of leaning forward and peering inside the bag. "You don't have a python in there that'll eat my all-time favorite mitt, do you?"

She let out a theatrical sigh. "I knew I forgot something!"

"Good thing. You'd be in big trouble if anything happened to my glove. I worked at a Christmas-tree lot my sophomore year of high school so I could earn enough money for it."

"Ah, yes." She gave him a pert smile. "The old sweeter-'cuz-I-earned-it item. Val and I shared our biggie, but I suppose that wouldn't come as any surprise."

"As different as you are from one another, it is. So tell me—what did the two of you want so badly?"

"A sound system for our bedroom. When we moved to our apartment, it was the only thing in the living room."

He dropped his mitt inside. As she zipped up the bag, he mused, "It didn't occur to me until now, but you don't have any snakes in the shop."

"Snakes are icky," Jeff declared.

"Val and my mom agree with you. The day I signed the papers for this shop, they made a point of telling me not to count on their help if I kept a single snake on the premises."

As he lifted the bag of gear, Nathan asked, "It's not much of a sacrifice, is it? You already offer a wide array of animals."

"I couldn't possibly handle snakes. They don't have wings or whiskers, and they don't wag. Are we ready to go?"

"Ready!" Jeff and Nathan declared in unison.

Jeff trotted ahead with Lick sort of trying to stay at heel. The two of them tangled about every third step, but that rated as a definite improvement.

Nathan stood to Van's right so Amber could walk at heel.

With the supper bag in one hand and the athletic bag over the opposite shoulder, he didn't have a free hand. For a fleeting moment, he considered switching the picnic to his right hand so his left hand would be free to hold hers, but he dismissed that concept as soon as it flashed though his mind. He wasn't ready to jump into anything deep yet, and she seemed comfortable with matters as they stood. Most of him accepted that fact, but he still felt a twinge. He hadn't realized how lonely he'd become until he'd met Vanessa.

Laughter bubbled out of her as she watched Jeff and Lick. That sound acted like a breeze, shoving away his gloomy clouds of thoughts. Nathan started to do something he hadn't done in years.

nine

As they strolled down the street, Nathan started to whistle. It felt right, just puckering up and letting loose a stream of notes. It wasn't until they were waiting at the light that he realized what tune he'd chosen.

Vanessa said the title just as his own awareness dawned. " 'How Much Is That Doggy in the Window?' "

He gave her a sheepish look. "I guess I'd better be careful not to give away the secret, either."

Jeff took his hand before they crossed the street. "I 'membered to look both ways."

"Good going."

"Dad, did you tell on Lick?"

He squeezed Jeff's hand. "Vanessa needs to know what Licorice is doing so she can help us make him a better puppy. She's not going to stop liking him just because he did something bad."

"Like the way you still love me, even when I done wrong?"

"Do wrong. And yes, just like I will always love you, no matter what you do. Still, that's not an excuse for you to do bad things. When you love someone, you try your hardest to do things that please them."

"Then everybody is happy. Right, Dad?"

"Right."

They reached the other side of the street, and Jeff shook free from his grasp. "We'll run over to the big tree. Can we sit under the tree for our picnic?"

Nathan shot Vanessa a quick look. "Wouldn't you rather sit

at one of the picnic tables?"

"How about if we sit at a table under a tree? I don't mind sitting on the ground, but Lick is going to help himself to the food if it's down at his level. It's not fair to tempt him. He's too young to know better."

After they were seated and had started eating, Vanessa peeked under the table and asked Licorice, "So are they going to tell me what you did this time?"

"He dug a hole—a great big hole." Jeff drew a sizable circle in the air with his drumstick.

"Hmm."

"I read a few suggestions on-line," Nathan confessed. "I tried two of them. Both were abysmal failures."

"What did you do?"

"I blew up a balloon, put it in the hole, and covered it with dirt. Supposedly the loud pop was supposed to be a deterrent. The only thing it did was send him running to another spot, where he promptly started digging a new hole."

"Persistent little monster, isn't he?"

Nathan thought her voice held a blend of sympathy for him and a tad of amusement. He broke eye contact and scooped in a few hefty bites of coleslaw.

"So what else have you tried?"

"A squirt gun!" Jeff guffawed.

Nathan gave Vanessa his if-you-can't-beat-'em-join-'em grin. "We discovered Lick loves water. Silly animal came charging toward me and tried to drink from the Super Squirtmaster."

"So I gotta Squirtmaster to play with now." Jeff's delight couldn't be more clear.

"So much for my foray into effective canine discipline."

"Labs are water dogs." Vanessa took a quick sip of soda and set the can back onto the sun-bleached wooden tabletop. "The nice thing is, he'll love going to the beach with you."

"If he digs there," Nathan grumbled, "maybe he'll fall all of the way through to China."

"Dad! You wouldn't let that happen, would you?"

"No, he was just teasing, Jeff. There are some things you can do to stop the digging. If you play with him more and tire him out, he won't have the energy to dig. There are a few products out on the market that keep a dog from digging, and you can spray them on the ground in a few key places where the digging will destroy special plants."

"Okay. I know the shop is already closed, but can I go ahead and pick up some of that tonight?"

"Sure." She slanted him a questioning look. "Have you been gardening?"

"Yeah. How'd you guess?"

"He planted flowers." Jeff's little body swayed back and forth in cadence with how he swung his legs. "But Lick dug most all of 'em up."

Vanessa's brows arched in surprise. "I thought you said you weren't much on flowers."

"A certain person who helped me build the gazebo pointed out the backyard would look a lot better if I planted some."

Her brows wiggled as she did a truly pathetic Groucho Marx imitation. "I'll bet that person was right."

"Who knows? The little black beast made mulch of them."

Vanessa rested her forearms on the picnic table and leaned forward. Her voice softened. "Nathan, Lick saw you digging in the dirt. He thought it was okay. Until he gets older, you'd do well not to set an example you don't want him to follow."

"Oh, brother! Do I feel stupid!"

"Now I'll make you feel downright smart: Go get some chicken wire. Put about an inch of dirt over it, and just comb flower seeds into the soil. He won't be able to dig, and you'll only spend a fraction of what you would for pony packs of flowers."

"For that, you deserve a cherry turnover."

❧

That Friday, after the game, Vanessa gathered her gear and collected Amber from Val. "Wanna go out for some ice cream?"

"Double fudge?"

"Double dips," Vanessa promised.

Deep laughter from behind them made her turn around. Nathan rested his hands on his hips. "Double scoops of double fudge for twins. Don't tell me you don't see the humor in that."

"Dad, can we get ice cream too?"

Vanessa saw the question in Nathan's eyes. "Sure, you guys can come along. We'll sit outside the shop so Nero and Lick can come along."

Jeff knelt between the two Lab puppies. Both turned as if on cue and licked him. "What about Amber? Won't she come?"

"Amber is allowed to go into most places like church and restaurants and stores because she's a service animal."

"Sis?"

Vanessa turned to Val. "Huh?"

"I hope you don't mind, but I changed his name. Nero was a madman, and I wanted something a little more. . .noble."

"I don't care one bit. What did you decide on?"

"Hero."

"Oh, that was clever. I'll bet he's responding to it right away."

Valene beamed. "He is. He's so bright. I want him to start in with the next session of puppy obedience. When does it start?"

"Next Saturday."

Nathan knelt and scratched both Lick and Hero behind the ears. "Did you boys hear that? You're going to be classmates."

"Can they have ice cream too, to cel'brate? You taked me out for ice cream when I started school."

"I don't know." Nathan looked up at her. "You didn't let us feed the dogs at our picnic."

"Amber eats twice a day. I give her treats, but not while I'm eating or socializing, because I don't want her to turn into a beggar."

Val hitched the strap of her purse higher on her shoulder. "We probably ought to use the same system we did back when you had Thane."

Vanessa nodded and explained to Nathan and Jeff, "I had my first guide puppy in my senior year of high school. We still had our family dog, a poodle named Fluffy. Fluffy wanted treats like she used to get—she was pretty spoiled. We taught the dogs that Fluffy got a treat when Thane got to go on an outing."

"Then I guess going on the trip is enough. Lick won't get a lick of ice cream."

Jeff giggled. "That was funny, Dad."

"Ice cream?" Kip sauntered up. "Are you going out for ice cream? I'm inviting myself along."

As they sat on the little wrought-iron patio set outside of the ice cream parlor, she watched Nathan wipe a dab of Very Berry from Jeff's face. He looked up at Vanessa just as she realized a little chocolate had dripped on her chin. He beat Kip to the stack of napkins in the center of the table and handed one to her. "So you got your first dog in high school. Why?"

"I love animals, and it seemed like a neat thing to do. Since we'd be in college in a year, it wasn't right for me to get a dog of my own and leave it behind with my folks."

"That makes sense, but then I'm running into a logic problem. You told me this is your fourth guide puppy, so you had to have a dog or two while you were in college."

"I listed puppy training on my college application under community service. The college admissions officer noticed it and mentioned that he'd give me clearance to have a puppy in classes as long as we didn't have any major accidents or disruptions."

"Did you?"

"Mom does a lot of volunteer work, and Dad was able to take the dogs to work with him at the phone company some days. Between Val and me juggling class schedules and our folks filling in, we breezed through college with the pups. Our first dog, Thane, was the biggest challenge. He was a riot."

Val choked back a giggle. "He about caused a riot on more than one occasion. The poor thing pitched a full-scale fit the first time he spied you in your shark suit. She came into the auditorium for a school assembly, and I think Thane thought the shark had eaten her."

"If Val hadn't let go of the leash, it wouldn't have been such a disaster. It took all but one member of the football team to catch Thane." Vanessa ignored her sister's don't-you-dare look and added, "The quarterback was a little preoccupied, flirting with my sister."

"Which is why she'd let go of the leash?" Nathan ventured as he gave Val a knowing grin. "Can't fault a man for having good taste."

"Sure can't," Kip agreed in a hearty tone.

"Thanks, guys—but you'll notice, my sister had the full attention of the rest of the team."

"Yeah," Vanessa snorted. "And who wouldn't, dressed up like a huge stuffed shark with a growling puppy clamped onto the fin?"

"What did you do?" Jeff wondered as several rivulets of ice cream ran down the cone, onto his hand.

"Yeah, Van," Kip nudged her arm. "What did you do?"

"A very funny dance," Val answered. "You started this, Van, so I'm telling the rest of the story. The dog wouldn't let go of the shark, and the shark kept running in a circle and wouldn't let go of the dog. There's a great picture of it in our yearbook as one of the football players took a dive toward them. The caption is BAIT AND TACKLE. "

"Oh, well," Vanessa laughed. "What do I say? She's brainy, and I'm zany. I think I keep her guardian angel and mine busy enough for both of us."

"My mom is with the angels." Jeff's comment immediately changed the focus of the conversation.

"Then she's in a very happy place."

Vanessa heard her sister's sweet words as she watched Nathan wrap his arm around Jeff's shoulders. "That's right, Son." His action bespoke support and love, yet he didn't let anyone give him that same comfort.

If he were a puppy or a kitten, she would have known a score of ways to coax him to draw close and let her give comfort. Originally he'd seemed bitter; now he had become matter-of-fact, like someone who woodenly recited a rote prayer but the meaning behind the words didn't register. Nathan built walls and constructed defenses she couldn't begin to get beyond. Until he was ready, no one would be able to reach him. All she could do was pray the Lord would work in his heart. . .and trust that when the time was right, God would have someone there to show His comfort and consolation to Nathan.

ten

Nathan sat in the shady courtyard with five other puppy owners. Had anyone asked, he would have said Vanessa looked like a luscious slice of lemon meringue pie, dressed in her crisp yellow walking shorts and a gauzy white blouse. He watched Vanessa demonstrate the simple commands she'd be working on with the "puppy kindergarten" members. Amber obediently followed each order.

"Just how long before Marzipan does all of those tricks?" one woman asked.

The burly man next to Nathan tried to untangle his beagle's leash from around his own legs and muttered, "Right about now, I'd settle for this mutt learning to sit. I'm going to fall and break my neck if Soupy keeps running circles around me."

After the session was over, folks wandered into Whiskers, Wings, and Wags to make some purchases. Jamie, the clerk who had been minding the store, slipped out for her lunch break. Nathan saw several other customers browsing too.

"What if I hang out with Hero and Licorice for awhile in one of the enclosures so Val can help you out?"

One desperate glance at the line at the register, and Van gave him a grateful smile. "Bless you!"

Nathan watched the puppies frolic and listened to Vanessa's cheerful voice as she helped her customers. Her zest for life appealed to him. She was every bit as sunny and bouncy as her hair.

For the past five years, he'd had a deep shadow of grief over his life. Evie begged him not to run from life, to feel free to fall in love again. "God has someone special in store for you and Jeff. I have an assurance about that."

He'd shaken his head. He didn't want any other woman. Since Evie died, not a day went by that he hadn't looked around the home they'd lovingly restored and missed her. . . until he met Vanessa. Oh, there had been plenty of beautiful women who made it abundantly clear they'd be happy to be the new Mrs. Adams. Not one of them deserved a second look or thought.

How could it be? In one slim month, Vanessa crashed right through all of his defenses. One month? One day. That very first day he'd been here, he'd changed. Nathan could hardly imagine it, but now he was sitting on the floor, two little black Labs playing with his shoelaces, and feeling perfectly content to hear Vanessa talk to old Mrs. Rosetti about the lamb-and-rice dog biscuits.

A father couldn't exactly dive into dating and courtship. Nathan resolved to take things slowly. He had Jeff to think of. Then again, he needed to kick things up a few notches. The thought that Vanessa and Kip might be an item had had him in knots. Now that he knew this wasn't the case, he wanted to be smart enough to start reeling her in. He wasn't about to sit back and let another man steal his sunshine.

"Who are your pals?"

Nathan didn't have to look up to identify the speaker. "Val, if you can't recognize your own four-legged kid, your sister's going to disown you."

She laughed. "It wouldn't be the first time she's been tempted."

He clipped a leash back onto Hero's collar, lifted him over the hip-high wall, and placed him in Val's arms. "Jeff's hoping you'll bring Hero to the park next Thursday for our baseball practice. He thinks the brothers need to play together."

"Smart kid you have there." Vanessa refilled the treat jar by the enclosure. "Puppies need to socialize so they learn to get along well."

Val agreed to the plan and left, but Nathan found he wasn't eager to go. He sauntered to the front of the shop and watched as Vanessa deftly straightened up a display of squeaky toys. He liked that about her—she managed to keep things tidy without making a big fuss or to-do about it.

"Do you think I'll ever manage to train Lick to be as obedient as Amber is?"

"I think you have an excellent start." She gave him a hundred-watt smile. "You have to remember I've worked with Amber for ten months. She was only eight weeks old when I got her, so we've had plenty of time to develop rapport. Several months from now, you and Lick will be a great team."

"Yeah, but probably not like you and Amber. You're with her twenty-four/seven."

"That bonding and intense teamwork do pay off. I won't pretend otherwise, but the world is full of well-behaved dogs that haven't been with their owners any more than you're with Lick."

"I hope you're right. I watched Val, and she seems to have Hero well in control—much better than I do Lick, and I've had him longer."

Vanessa's eyes twinkled. "She was moaning about how much better you are with Lick."

"No kidding?"

"It's the absolute truth. Everyone wants a cute little fluff ball, but they forget that the little guys have to learn the rules of the home, just like a child would. The first month with a puppy is always challenging. As of this week, you've passed that mark. You've had him for five weeks. Things ought to start improving a lot."

Her words carried the assurance he sought, but he wanted to keep visiting. Nathan shifted his weight and wondered, "Are you as hungry as I am?"

"I'm starving. Why?"

"Two reasons. First, because I thought we could go snag a burger. The second is, I think it's going to be a persistent issue after these Saturday classes."

"Why would that be?"

"Because every last dog in the class is named after food!"

Vanessa tickled a kitten through a cage and mused aloud, "Oh? I didn't even notice. There was Marzipan. And Pepper."

"I've got Licorice, and that guy next to me had Soupy. The English pug is Cheerio."

"But Val's dog is Hero. It doesn't—"

"Hero sandwich," Nathan reminded her.

Vanessa's laughter pealed through the air. "Know what? I limit the class to six. I had another request that I slotted for the next series: 'Brownie.'"

"So what do you say? Jamie ought to be coming back from her lunch break soon. She can hold down the fort while we fill up after our brainwashing ordeal."

"What about Lick?"

Oops. Blew it on that account. Nathan tapped the toe of his athletic shoe on the linoleum floor, then grinned. "How about if he takes a nap in the grooming room?"

"Poor baby. Is he plumb tuckered out after his first day of puppy kindergarten?"

"Yes, but his daddy is trying to get on the teacher's good side by offering to take her out for lunch."

"I always thought you were supposed to take the teacher an apple."

"Oh, that's for teachers who have children for their pupils. Dogs are a different story entirely."

"Do tell." She shot him an entertained look.

"Kids take apples to the teacher; puppy owners take the teacher to apple pie."

"I thought I liked my job. I was wrong—I love it!"

Ah, Vanessa, he thought, *if only a slice of apple pie could change how I felt about my life and job. There was a time when I had that same enthusiasm you have, but it's been gone for years now.*

❧

Vanessa fumbled for the telephone. It shrilled again, and she groaned as her fingers curled around the receiver and lifted it. "Hullo?"

"Vanessa?"

"Nathan?" She squinted at the neon orange numbers on her alarm clock—4:17? *This has to be a nightmare. It's not really happening.*

"Listen, I'm sorry to bother you—"

She shook herself. "Is it Jeff? Is something wrong?" In an instant, she was blazingly awake.

"No, but yes. Here's the deal: I just got an emergency call. The night watchman from the apartment complex I've started over on Beach and Tenth says it looks like the second story is buckling."

"Oh, no!"

"Jeff's class is going—"

"Whale watching today," she remembered aloud. Jeff had chattered about the trip every chance he got. He'd been looking forward to it for three weeks. "As I recall, you were supposed to go along."

"I'd ask Consuelo to go, but she gets seasick. I know Mondays are your day off, and I hate to ask. . ."

"Oh, I love whale watching! I'd be happy to go."

"Even with a class of six year olds?"

"The more, the merrier. I need to take Amber out on a boat, anyway."

"You're a lifesaver. I'll bundle up Jeff and be there in about twenty minutes."

"Don't bother. I'll come there."

Vanessa hung up the phone, hopped off the mattress, and flung the covers up in a hasty pretense of making the bed. Knowing the sea breeze would be stiff, she wore a T-shirt beneath a fleecy sweatshirt. Jeans, thick socks, and a battered pair of tennis shoes finished the outfit, then she dashed into the bathroom to grab her toothbrush.

Vanessa stopped dead in her tracks and burst out laughing. She'd fallen asleep, reading in bed, so she hadn't taken off what little makeup she normally wore. Mascara formed smoky rings around her eyes, a crease from her pillowcase looked like an earthquake fault line down her left cheek, and static electricity made every last strand of hair stick straight out in a bizarre impression of an atomic dandelion.

"Maybe I am having a nightmare, after all." She quickly scrubbed away the raccoon rings with a damp washcloth and brushed her teeth. Practically snatching herself bald due to the hairbrush getting caught in numerous tangles, Vanessa grumbled, "I'm going to have to talk to that man. He'll just have to understand he needs to arrange to have emergencies at a decent hour."

Amber woofed from beside her.

"Hey, don't stand up for the man. We girls are supposed to stick together." Vanessa grabbed a handful of essentials, zipped back into her bedroom, and recalled lending Val the big leather purse. Without it, she knew she had to make do.

Fifteen minutes later, she stood on the doorstep to Nathan's old saltbox in the predawn chill. She shivered and tapped quietly on the door. It opened almost instantly.

"Van, I can't thank you enough. I—what in the world?" He stared at the bulging pillowcase in her hands and gave her a baffled look.

Vanessa cruised past him and refused to look him in the eye. "I'm not trick-or-treating. If you dare say anything, you're dead meat. I told you I'm not a morning person."

"I didn't say a word."

She tried to act calm, cool, and collected as she pulled her windbreaker from the pillowcase. She should have put it on for the drive over, but she hadn't been functioning well enough to reason out that minor detail. Next, she withdrew Amber's leash and bright green jacket. A digital camera, a hairbrush, a tube of lip balm, a scrunchy for her hair, a visor, and a pair of sunglasses tumbled onto the coffee table as she upended the pillowcase.

Pretending to ignore Nathan's chuckle, she tossed the pillow onto the end of the couch, punched it a few times, toed out of her shoes, and flopped down. As she closed her eyes, she yawned.

Amber's paws pattered on the hardwood floor as she turned around in her customary triple circles before she plopped down directly next to the sofa. In contrast, Nathan's work boots sounded like a whole platoon of infantrymen as he approached. He detoured somewhere—but she refused to peek. All she wanted were twenty more winks. . .no, make that forty. A door latch popped open, then shut, and the infantry marched closer. "Here," Nathan growled softly. He covered Vanessa with a big, heavy blanket.

She didn't know where he'd gotten it from, and she didn't really care. As she snuggled a bit deeper into the cushions and blanket, she mumbled, "Better dig up an alarm clock for me."

"You won't need one. Jeff gets up at six-thirty on the dot."

"I'm not going to open my eyes, because if you're smiling at that revolting news, I'll have to crawl off the couch and leave."

"Thanks again, Van."

"G'night. G'bye."

The lock on the door clicked, and she dropped into a deep sleep filled with wild, disjointed dreams centering on talking puppies.

"I can't find my dad. Can you help me?"

"He's in the yard," she told the terrier.

"Thanks." The little pup trotted away. A door banged, and cold air washed over her as the little dog hollered, "Dad. Daaad! Where are you?"

Vanessa bolted from the couch. "Jeff!"

eleven

Vanessa stumbled over Amber and skidded through the kitchen. The clock on the stove read 6:33. She sped through the doorway in her stocking feet and ran out onto the wet lawn. "Jeff!"

Where was he? She nearly got whiplash, scanning the property. Red-and-blue plaid pajamas made him easy to spot once she turned toward the far end of the backyard. Both of his feet—bare feet—were on the rope ladder to his fort.

"I can't find Dad. I thought I'd climb up here. I can see better if—"

"Honey, your dad's not out here. He had a problem at work."

"But you told me he was in the yard." Jeff hung there and gave her a bewildered look.

"I must've been talking in my sleep. Come on back in the house."

Jeff jumped onto the grass and headed back toward the door. He turned and watched Amber and Lick both take care of business and pointed at them with shameless glee. "See what good puppies we have?"

"Terrific ones." She took a step. "Eww yuck! Your lawn is soaking wet!"

"Unh-huh. Dad made the timer on the sprinklers to go on early so the grass is dry for me to play on all day." Jeff trotted past her, into the house, with both dogs in his wake.

She squished after him. Once inside, she peeled off her socks and scowled at them. "What time does school start?"

"Eight."

"Great. I can toss these in the dryer." She mentally clicked off the minutes before they'd have to leave and felt a burst of relief that there was plenty of time for her to regain dry socks. At least there was one good thing about Jeff being an early riser—it gave a bit of space for solving odd predicaments that came up.

"Dad's gotta get home 'fore then, though. We're going on a field trip, and we've gotta be at the school early."

"Just how early?" She decided to break the news about being the substitute chaperon after she finished mopping up all of the wet foot and paw tracks on the linoleum.

"I dunno. It's on the paper." He banged his palm on the refrigerator door. The sheet of directions beneath his hand had a sketch of a whale in the upper right-hand corner.

"Thank You, Lord!" Vanessa snatched the page away from a pizza delivery magnet. She looked down at Jeff. "Know how I told you your dad had a great big problem at work? Well, since he figured he wouldn't get back in time, Amber and I are going to go with you instead."

"A dog can go to school?" Jeff's eyes got wider. "A dog wants to watch whales?"

"Isn't that cool?"

"Wow! Can I take Licorice too?"

"No, Sport. Amber's allowed to come along because when she grows up, she'll be a working dog. Give me a second here so I can get the scoop on what we're doing today."

" 'Kay."

Vanessa read the paper. The teacher had chosen a picture that depicted the kind of whale they'd most likely see—a point in her favor, and one she promptly lost when Vanessa spotted the second-to-the-last line, "Be sure to be here early! We're leaving at seven-thirty!"

Vanessa flipped the paper onto the kitchen counter and

glanced at the clock again. "We're on a tight schedule, Sport. We have to be at school in less than an hour. You'd better hurry up and get dressed."

Jeff rocketed up the stairs and reappeared five minutes later in an orange tank top and blue-and-purple-striped shorts. "I'm ready!"

"Only if you want to turn into a snowman. You'll freeze your toes off in that outfit. C'mon. Let's go find you something a bit warmer." Vanessa took his hand and climbed the stairs. She felt a little funny, wandering around the private part of Nathan's house.

What had to be the master bedroom was directly across from the landing. Early morning sunlight slanted through a beautiful, oval stained-glass window and splashed puddles of amber, rose, and blue over the rumpled, eggshell-colored sheets of a sleigh bed. In his rush, Nathan had dropped several coins that lay in a haphazard path from the antique oak dresser to the door.

It took but a second to take in that view, and Vanessa wanted to hurry on past it. Three doors gaped ahead. "Where's your bedroom?"

"Over here." Jeff tugged her past a bathroom where the towels hung askew, into what still looked like a nursery. The wallpaper featured pastel zoo animals, yellow gingham curtains dressed the window, and a baby blue, three-drawer dresser stood against the far wall. All three drawers were ajar.

"Boy, you really were in a hurry," Vanessa said as she took in the garments spilling from each drawer. "How about if you find a pair of jeans, and I'll come up with a shirt?"

" 'Kay."

Vanessa straightened out the drawers as swiftly as she could while trying to be unobtrusive. She pretended to consider different shirts before settling on an undershirt and a bright yellow sweatshirt that would make him easy to spot in a crowd. She made his bed and set the clothes on it with a pat. "You change while I see about some breakfast."

"It's Monday," he said as though that fact had special significance.

"What does that have to do with breakfast?"

"Waffles and orange juice! We always have them on Monday." He even nodded as if to assert it was the routine every decent home ought to follow.

Once Vanessa reached the kitchen, she glanced at all of the cupboards and cabinets. Where does Nathan keep the waffle iron? She could wait a few minutes 'til Jeff came down to answer that question. In the meantime, since there wasn't a carton of orange juice in the refrigerator, she opened the freezer. There, in the door, just next to the can of orange juice, sat a box of toaster waffles.

"Quick and easy." She grabbed both items and spun around toward the counter. It struck her as odd that Nathan bought juice that had to be prepared and waffles that were premade, but then again, he probably grabbed them during a dash through the frozen-food section.

Jeff plunked down the stairs, and they sat at the table and ate while the puppies chomped on kibble. Jeff banged the heels of his tennis shoes on the rungs of his chair. "What did you make for lunch?"

Lunch! Oh, great. How could I forget about that? She gave him an I've-got-this-covered look. "We're a team. We're making lunch together."

He dawdled over a second waffle as she wiped down the toaster and put it away. Mouth full, he pointed at a cabinet. "We gots granola bars and fruit rollies up there."

It didn't take long to slap together a decent lunch. They brushed their teeth, and then Vanessa groaned, "I forgot to put my socks in the dryer!"

"You can wear some of mine."

"Thanks, but my feet are a bit bigger than yours."

He opened the dryer and fished out a crew sock with two black stripes at the top and another with no color striping but gray patches at the toe and heel. "Here. You can wear Dad's. We aren't gonna be late, are we? Teacher said if we're late, the bus will leave without us."

Vanessa yanked on the mismatched socks, ignored the fact that the heels poked out at ankle level, and shoved her feet into her tennis shoes. "You put Lick in the backyard. I'll grab my stuff, and we'll be outta here."

"Are you sure Dad won't come with us? The three of us always have fun together."

"Yeah, we do manage to have fun together, but if your dad woke me up early for anything other than an emergency, I'd dump him right off the boat."

She gathered all of the gear, snapped the leash and jacket on Amber, and they raced out the door. Jeff's school was a brisk half-mile walk, and they chattered the whole way there. The minute they reached the edge of the school grounds, Vanessa spied a tall, dark, handsome man leaning against a cinder-block wall. "Nathan!"

૨&

Nathan strove to look casual, but it wasn't easy. Luckily, Jeff gave him a moment of diversion.

"Dad! You're here! You'd better be careful. 'Nessa said she'd dump you over the side of the boat if you showed up."

Vanessa's pink cheeks tattled that she hadn't counted on that little quip getting repeated. Nathan chuckled at her. "Gotta watch what you say around Jeff. He's got a knack for remembering the smallest things and repeating them at the most inopportune moment."

"So I noticed." She shrugged. "I deserved that. I ought to think before I speak, but that's a real weak point for me. I take it the apartment emergency isn't a massive crisis after all?"

"Yes and no. The watchman thought the second floor was buckling. It isn't. We designed it so the upstairs of the deluxe apartments will have either sunken baths or a raised platform for the bed and a lower conversation or play area."

"I see."

Nathan thought of how tired she'd been when she'd dragged herself to his front door earlier that morning. He quickly added, "But while I was there, I looked at the ceiling beams for the main entrance and noticed they're already warped a little. They'll continue to twist until they torque the supports and weaken the vaulted ceilings. I had to track down the manufacturer back East and read him the riot act. He's sending replacements on the train today. It's going to set us behind schedule a full three days. If I hadn't caught that, it would have been a real embarrassment."

"Doing quality work matters to you."

"Yes, it does." He raised his brows. "Am I forgiven, or are you planning to go through with that plot to dump me overboard and feed me to the whales?"

"There's nothing to forgive. Jeff and I had a fun morning. He's a great helper."

"Yeah, I fed the puppies and got Van some of your socks." Jeff giggled. "Hers got wet."

Nathan gave Vanessa a stricken look. "Lick didn't. . .um—"

"No! Oh, no, he didn't. I tromped out in the backyard on your just-watered lawn."

"Ah. Gotcha. One of the hazards of having a puppy."

"Nope. She didn't come out to get the puppies; she came out to get me!"

"Sport, what were you doing out in the backyard?"

"Vanessa said you were out there." Jeff tugged on Nathan's belt and stood up on tiptoe. In a stage whisper, he added, "Dad, she talks in her sleep!"

With a mock look of exasperation, Vanessa propped her hands on her hips and tapped her toe on the sidewalk. "And you, Jeffrey Adams, talk waaay too much while you're awake!"

"Yep!" Jeff giggled at her theatrics. With a gleeful look, he added, "Dad, guess what? Your socks are too big on her. Waaay too big."

"No kidding. Your dad's feet are huge." She pinched her jeans just above the knees and hiked them up several inches. "Have you ever seen anything so ridiculous?"

Nathan tilted back his head and roared.

"Listen, Mister, it's not that funny!"

"Oh, yes, it is." He couldn't stop chuckling. "Let me guess. Jeff got those out of the dryer."

"How did you know?" Vanessa and Jeff both asked him.

Nathan copied Vanessa's action. He hiked up his own jeans and displayed a plain sock and a striped one. "I was in such a hurry to get out of the house this morning, I grabbed whatever was handy. I'm wearing the matching set!"

The look on Vanessa's face was priceless. She blinked, her face split into a huge grin, and giggles spilled out of her. When she finally calmed down, she announced, "It looks like you have everything well in hand. They don't need me as an extra chaperon, so I'm taking your funny socks and going home."

Nathan dared to reach over and grab her hand. "Actually, we do need you. When I got here, Miss Sanderly was having a conniption fit. It seems one of the mothers who offered to accompany us woke up with a toothache."

"You'll come, Vanessa, won't you? Pleeeze?" Jeff jigged at her side.

"Of course she is. She wouldn't miss this trip for anything."

Nathan didn't want to give her an opportunity to back out. He knew he ought to feel guilty about roping her into this; the truth of it was, he didn't feel anything other than pure anticipation.

twelve

"Val, you wouldn't have believed it," Vanessa told her sister as they met at church for the midweek service. "One of the other kids on the field trip didn't have a jacket. Nathan grabbed one out of the jump seat of his truck and gave it to the little boy."

"That's good. Remember the time we went whale watching and nearly froze?"

"Yes, but I thought we were done, and it turned out that was just the beginning."

"Oh?"

"They could live out of that truck for a week. No exaggeration—they have so much stuff all organized in the cab, NASA ought to ask for packing tips. Nathan started rummaging for food so he'd have a lunch to take."

"Well, we have energy bars and water in our cars."

Vanessa shook her head. "But we don't have cheese-and-crackers snack packs. A juice box."

"Sis, Jeff's a little kid. Nathan's got to keep munchies for him."

"If it stopped there, I wouldn't think a thing of it. Then he started pulling stuff out in earnest. Beef jerky. Dried apricots. A little can of peanuts. Granola bars. Those individual cups of applesauce and plastic spoons!"

Valene's eyes grew huge. "The man even had spoons?"

Muting her voice since they were entering the sanctuary, Vanessa said, "Yes. Spoons. And paper towels. Nathan packed a better lunch than I did!"

To her credit, Val muffled her laughter. As they slid into the pew, she wondered aloud, "Had he just gone grocery shopping or something?"

"No." Vanessa plunked her purse down and muttered, "He keeps earthquake supplies in his truck and car." She gave her sister a daffy look. "To top it all off, we cruised all day and didn't see a single whale."

"That's too bad."

"Jeff was so disappointed."

The music started, so their conversation ended abruptly. Vanessa stared at the back of the pew in front of her and let out a silent sigh. She'd struggled to get Jeff ready, lunches made, and the two of them to school on time; Nathan did it every single school day, and he managed it quite well. He operated on a smooth, near-perfect level, and she could be the poster girl for Insecurities Anonymous—well, she would be if they had anything more than a friendship. *But we don't. We're just pals.* That realization flooded her with an odd sense of relief. *Yeah. It's good Nathan is so good at handling things on his own. Sure it is. It works out well for him and Jeff.*

She continued to think of them until Kip slid into the pew and somehow managed to bump Val over so he sat between them. Once the service got underway, Pastor MacIntosh made announcements. After he mentioned one particular upcoming activity, Vanessa and Valene both leaned forward to make eye contact and exchanged a meaningful look.

&

"He'd have such a good time."

Nathan stared out of the dugout, not wanting to look at Vanessa's pleading face. Kip sent a ball sailing into center field and made it to second base while folks cheered. Nathan hoped Van would get involved in the game and drop the subject.

"I'm working, but you can go with him, Nathan. If you're already busy, plenty of the parents are going, and they'd keep close watch on Jeff."

He didn't respond.

The shortstop caught a fly, and Kip got tagged out on third. Nathan bolted off the bench, eager to get out on the field, away from the conversation.

Vanessa halted him. "I'm sorry, Nathan. I didn't mean to pressure you. I promised I wouldn't invite you to church—I didn't stop to think you'd consider a primary department outing would fall under that heading. I knew Jeff would enjoy going to the tide pools, and well—" She let out a gusty sigh. "I understand. It's with the church's primary department. I can see now it was a mistake for me to say anything."

Tears glossed her eyes. Nathan drew in a quick breath. Part of him caved in; the other part rebelled. She wasn't just a do-gooder, trying to involve his son in church—she really cared about Jeff. *But I'm not getting sucked into all of this church stuff.*

"I really blew it, didn't I?"

"Vanessa, let's just drop it for now and play ball."

"All right." She paused and added, "I'll drop it." As he began to walk off, he heard her mutter, "For now."

In the last inning, Nathan channeled all of his churning emotions into his swing. His grand slam bought the Altar Egos's triumph. As he ran the bases and touched home plate, the team and crowd went wild. Only he knew deep inside, the last thing he felt was victorious.

❧

Saturday, after the puppy kindergarten class, Nathan curled his hand around Vanessa's arm. Shock jolted through her at the intensity of his gaze.

"Can you give me a minute?"

"Um, yeah. Sure. What is it, Nathan?"

"Saturday mornings aren't working out well for me." He let go of her. "The next few weeks will be impossible. Can you work with Jeff and me on training Lick on a catch-as-catch-can basis?"

A sick feeling churned in her stomach. She'd pressured him about the tide-pool trip for Jeff, and this seemed like a polite version of "So long, see ya later."

Lord, I'm so sorry. I need to learn to be patient. I acted in haste, and I've pushed him away from You.

Nathan tugged on Lick's leash to pull him back from sniffing at a patch of grass. Nathan kept his gaze trained downward. "Jeff really wants to go to the tide pools next Saturday. I can't be in two places at once."

"He'll love it! Be sure to take your camera and get pictures!"

Nathan looked up, and the sparkle in his eye warmed her heart. He wasn't trying to bail out or to mollify her—she could see that he really wanted to go.

"It's been so long since I dug out the camera. Evie always took snapshots. I just haven't had the heart. When you took your camera whale watching, I got an attack of the guilts."

When he mentioned his wife, the sparkle in his eyes dimmed, and it made Vanessa want to comfort him. She sensed he'd not welcome anything overt, so instead, she went for simple reassurance. "Not that I got any great photos, anyway. We didn't see a single whale."

Nathan shrugged. "Since he didn't get to see any whales, I thought you were right—he ought to get a chance to see sea creatures somehow."

Vanessa nodded. If she said something right now, she'd probably make an utter fool of herself, either hugging him or blubbering for joy.

"It's not just next Saturday. If it were a matter of missing a single class, we'd probably be able to catch on and catch up. It's more complicated than that. The following Saturday, I'll be out of town, and the week after, I have an appointment with a client. Lick's just too knot-headed for me to believe we can miss three sessions in a row and train him to be obedient."

"I'm sure we can work out a few private training sessions."

"Great. If we can get him to behave, I'll be a happy camper. I don't expect him to ever be a model citizen like Amber."

"When we're through with him, he will be. It just takes patience. With patience, you can do just about anything."

๛

Late that evening, Vanessa pulled a diskette out of her computer. *Lord, I just wanna say something here. I know I told Nathan all it took was patience to get things done. I did qualify it with a 'just about.' Well, I've been trying to make the accounts balance, and they won't. I can't. This doesn't just take patience—it's going to take a miracle!*

She grimaced at the memory of her sage words, then turned that grimace toward the shoebox full of receipts. Practice—she practiced plenty of things, but patience wasn't one of them. That commodity just hit an all-time low.

In sheer desperation, she filled a bag with gourmet doggy treats and hit the road. She tromped into Val's condo and cried, "I'm throwing myself on your mercy. I even brought bribes for Hero."

"It's the end of the month." Val arched a brow. "Let me guess: You can't get the books to balance."

"Bingo."

"Hero will be happy to have the treats. I, on the other hand, refuse to be bribed."

"Val, come on. I'm dying here."

"So am I. Here's the deal: You give Hero the rest of his

puppy shots. I can't stand to do it myself, and Dr. Bainbridge's office is only open during the hours I work."

"I'm more than willing to do that. You've got a deal." Vanessa poured herself a cup of tea. "Then again, I would have been willing to do it for you anyway."

Val laughed. "I know. Just like I would have straightened out your record keeping for you anyway."

While Val clicked around on the computer and resolved all the quirks and misfiled information on Vanessa's ledger, Van dug through the cabinets and found a vase.

"What're you up to now?"

"Don't pay any attention to me. Just crunch the numbers." Vanessa pulled a variety of silk flowers from her athletic bag and put together an arrangement for Val's living room.

"All done," Val said.

"Me too. Take a look."

Val walked into the living room, and her face lit up. "That's perfect! I don't know how you do that kind of stuff. Arts and crafts are my waterloo."

"Yeah, well, you got the smarts; I got the crafts. Believe me, if I had to pick, I would have taken the brains."

"You do have brains," Val protested. She then grimaced. "But I'm worried you're not using them. We need to have a talk."

"Now what did I do?" Van turned sideways on the couch and watched as her twin searched for the right words. *Uh-oh. Whatever this is, it's a biggie. . . .*

Val paced across the floor and turned back. "I think you need to draw a definite line with Nathan."

"Draw a line?"

"He's not a believer. Well, he is, but he's not living his faith. He's bitter toward the Lord, and that's not the kind of man you ought to be dating."

Vanessa snorted. "Dating? You've gotta be kidding me. We have his son and two dogs everywhere we go. It's nothing romantic at all."

"Just because it starts off innocently doesn't mean it'll stay that way." Valene sat down and curled her hand around Vanessa's wrist. "You'd be wise to spend less time with him and more time with a man who is practicing a strong daily walk with Christ."

"We're not dating, Val, and Nathan will eventually restore his relationship with the Lord. Christ didn't turn his back on those who strayed. He said as a shepherd He'd search for every lost lamb. If all I ever do is hang out with Christians who have no doubts or questions, who's going to reach out to those who are out of relationship or hurting? That wouldn't be living my faith."

"You have a point, but I'm trying to make you see the difference between being casual friends and losing your heart. Nathan is handsome, well-to-do, and kind."

"I have several guy friends who are handsome or well-off, and they're all good-hearted. They're just friends."

"But how many of them would have called you at four in the morning to pinch-hit for their kid's field trip. Why did Nathan call you?"

"Let's see. For starters, my other friends don't have kids. As for Nathan, it was a Monday. Most people work on Mondays, but it's my day off. Nathan knows I love the ocean. Jeff and I are buddies. Besides—it's good for Amber to go on all different modes of transportation, and she hadn't been on a boat yet."

Val gave her an I'm-not-buying-your-story look.

"Get this: One of the kids came up to us and asked Jeff, 'Is she your dad's girlfriend?' and I said, 'Nope. Amber is my dog, not his.' See? I made it clear I'm not romantically entangled."

Val laid her head on the back of the couch and groaned. "Why did I have to be right? I just told you, you have brains, but you're not using them. This is going to be a disaster."

"Let's see." Vanessa ticked off points on her hand. "Jeff learned a lesson about integrity. I sold a dog. I'm even earning money on training." She wiggled those three fingers in the air. "If that isn't enough, look at the more important issues: Nathan is now playing ball with the church team, and he's renewed his friendship with Kip. Jeff is going to the tide pools with the primary department—and Nathan is taking him!"

All five fingers stuck up in the air. She then tightened them together to form a scoop, turned her hand palm up, and lifted it toward heaven. "It's really not in my hands at all, Val. It's in God's."

thirteen

Once or twice a week, Nathan managed to find a time slot that Vanessa had free. They met at the park across from her shop and worked with Lick's training. Sometimes Jeff stayed at home with Consuelo. Other times he was at a birthday party or at a friend's house. About half the time, he came along and enjoyed learning too.

Nathan liked how Van paid attention to Jeff and never acted like he was a tagalong. The two of them often traded silly jokes and romped, yet she still earned and held his respect.

If they did puppy training in his backyard, she made a habit of bringing a snack of some variety and insisting that they all wedge into the fort to share it. Having deduced that he was all thumbs in the kitchen, she frequently managed to bring something she'd baked—cream puffs, cookies shaped like dog biscuits, apple tarts, or cupcakes with cherries made of gumdrops decorating the top.

Two adults, one wiggly boy, and two puppies in the fort's tight space always turned out to be the highlight of the day—and not because of the food. Nathan could sit close to Vanessa, relish her sunny laugh, try to determine what odd combination of fragrances she'd put together, and swipe a nibble from her fingertips.

Whenever he and Vanessa met without Jeff, Nathan tried to find ways to prolong their time together. They'd eaten at several fast-food places that featured outdoor picnic tables so the dogs wouldn't have to be left in the car—something neither he nor Vanessa would consider. It didn't exactly qualify as the most romantic way to edge into a relationship, but he didn't care. Just being with Vanessa made his day.

One hitch bothered him. When they ate, she prayed. He knew the Lord was an integral part of her life. She'd mention things about a program at church or occasionally quote something he knew came from Psalms or Proverbs. If anything, he sensed she made a concerted effort not to swamp him with religious stuff.

He appreciated her restraint. It made him uncomfortable when folks got all churchy around him. Nathan knew it was guilt. He flatly refused to explore that emotion. God took Evie away. How could God ask for a man's soul when He robbed him of his heart?

Over time, he'd begun to feel less awkward when Vanessa would say a simple, quick grace. He'd turned down a few invitations to church by a couple of the guys on the team until Vanessa had grabbed the bull by the horns. After practice one evening, she'd faced the whole team and announced, "Nathan knows he has a standing invitation to church. I promised him I wouldn't wheedle or plot so he'd get roped into attending. When he's ready, he'll come. Until then, let's leave it be." Integrity. She had it in spades.

What kind of man was he, to want to court a woman who walked so closely with the Lord? He knew all about being in step with the Lord. He'd been that way once upon a time, and he'd willingly worn the mantle of the spiritual head of his home with an awareness of its responsibilities and blessings. His marriage with Evie blossomed under God's grace and leading—until Evie died, when simple faith suddenly wasn't enough. Vanessa deserved a man of faith. *But I can't let her go. What kind of man does that make me?*

❧

"Dad, that was so much fun! Can we go again? Please?"

Nathan looked down at Jeff's sun-kissed cheeks and silently agreed. They'd had a terrific day down at the tide pools. The group got there just as the tide went out, and the pocked rock formations held countless wonders. Children darted from one pool to the next, shrieking with joy. They'd squat next to a little hollowed-out retreat and point at darting, tiny fish or touch limpets. *Yeah, I could go for a day like that again. It was relaxing, fun. . . .*

"Please, Dad. I wanna go back there."

"I had a great time too. Maybe we could do it again. What would you think about taking Vanessa and Amber with us?"

"That'd be super-duper! Let's go tomorrow."

"Sorry, Sport." He lifted the blankets, and Jeff tumbled into bed. Covering his son, Nathan said, "Tomorrow's Sunday. Van works in the afternoon after she goes to church. The animals have to be fed and watered."

"But we could go in the morning!"

Nathan shook his head. "Van goes to church."

"Dad? Why don't we go to church? I gots lots of friends who go to Van's church. We're all good buddies."

"Church isn't just supposed to be about who you go to see."

"Then what is it about? I know!" Jeff popped up and gave Nathan an earnest look. "It's 'bout God and Jesus and stuff—like in the songs the kids were singing today, huh?"

"Yeah." Nathan tucked him back in, ruffled his hair, and kissed his forehead. "Enough talk. Go to sleep." Before Jeff could pursue the conversation, he left the room.

❧

"I'm going for the fives." Dad set aside two of the dice and dropped the other three back in the cup. They made a hollow, rattling sound before he dumped them out again. They tumbled across the flower-patterned vinyl tablecloth and came to rest a few inches past a small crease that acted as a speed bump.

Vanessa leaned back in the molded plastic patio chair and relished the night breeze off the sea. It rustled through the mulberry tree in the corner of the backyard. She laughed. "Remember that year Val and I did the silk project?"

"Fourth grade," her mother recalled. "Those silkworms you raised were disgusting."

"Now I thought they were interesting, Mom." Dad set aside another five and plunked the last two dice into his cup. "The teacher said our Van was the only kid she ever had who actually kept them alive and spinning."

"Because we had the mulberry leaves. It wasn't hard at all—I just picked a few leaves and dumped them in each morning. We got a good grade on the project because of Val. She wrote a great paper to go along with it."

"And your illustrations were amazing," Mom added.

Dad sent the dice across the table and bellowed gleefully, "Yahtzee!"

"Can you believe that? The last roll of the game, and Dad gets a Yahtzee!"

As they put away the game, Mom asked, "What made you think of the silkworms?"

"The mulberry tree."

Dad took another sip of his tea. "It's a good source of shade, but the berries sure make a mess. Every year, I say something about taking it out and putting in something that won't be such a hassle, but Mom won't let me."

"Why not?"

"She's sentimental. You used to hold your animal hospitals under it."

Vanessa grinned at the memory. "It's amazing you didn't

go broke, buying me gauze and tape for all of those bandages I made."

"What's amazing is, all of those animals just sat there and let you mummy wrap them!" Mom laughed. "Dad's just as sentimental as I am. He sticks nails into the ground by the hydrangea so the flower petals will turn pretty colors. Remember how you and Val used to play "Wedding" and use those poufy flower balls as your bridal bouquets?"

"And the yellow chenille pipe cleaner rings!" Vanessa looked over at the hydrangea, then back at her parents. "We had a storybook childhood."

Dad cleared his throat. "Speaking of weddings. . ."

"Is someone getting married?"

"We're talking about you, Sweetheart." Mom scooted her chair closer. "You're spending an awful lot of time with that Adams man."

"Did Val put you up to this?"

"Nope." Dad leaned on the table and shook his head. "Honey, we reared you to do the right thing, to live by the Bible. You know you're not to set your heart on a man who isn't walking with the Lord. My understanding is Nathan Adams lost his wife, and he's bitter toward God."

"He is."

"Then why are you dating him?" Mom frowned.

Vanessa sighed. "Once and for all, we are not dating. I get paid each time we meet, and you certainly didn't rear me to be that kind of woman!"

Her mom's eyes widened, and she chided, "Vanessa!"

"Okay, Mom. Sorry. I got a bit carried away, but all of this concern feels like such an overreaction." When her parents didn't respond, she hastened on. "I'm giving him puppy obedience lessons. Most of the time, we have Amber, his black Lab, and his son with us. We've never eaten out unless you count an ice cream cone or fast food. He's a friend."

"Friends can become more than friends"—Mom looked her in the eye—"especially when the woman is as compassionate and sympathetic as you are. Your whole childhood, you gravitated toward people and animals who needed special attention. You've grown into an empathetic woman who cares freely and deeply. I'm worried that you're getting absorbed into Nathan Adams's world. He's a wounded man, and you can't fix him."

Vanessa rubbed her face with both hands and looked away for a moment, then looked back at her mother. Quietly, she admitted, "I know I can't. I'm just trying to come alongside him as a Christian sister."

Mom dipped her head ever so slightly and looked at Vanessa with her I-mean-business glare. "Sister? Friend? Those are nice labels, but my radar is sending off boyfriend alarms."

"Mom, I'm not dating him. I'm so busy with the shop and the private lessons and the baseball team and the puppy training club, there isn't time. My life is full, and my heart isn't empty. I figure God will put the right man in my life when He wills it."

"Nathan is on that team, isn't he?" Dad asked pointedly.

"Yes, he is." Vanessa grinned. "And he just took his son to the tide pools with the primary department today. I have faith that the Good Shepherd will bring back His straying lamb. It's a matter of letting God be God."

"Don't get involved romantically with a man and expect him to change." Dad stood. "It's wrong, Honey."

"I agree, Dad. I need to get going. I'll see you at church tomorrow."

❧

Nathan lay in bed and stared at the stained-glass window. A streetlight shone through it just enough to make the pattern apparent. Evie had surprised him with the window the year she was carrying Jeff. It was a Christmas present, and she'd managed to save up the money for it by squirreling away her change. He'd been so surprised. *Little things add up. Just think—we're going to have the best little thing of all.* She'd wear that dreamy look and rub her tummy.

Then, too, once he set the window into their bedroom wall, she'd lie next to him and imagine all the different things the window could mean. *Three flowers. . .you, me, and the baby. Or is it the Trinity? Father, Son, and Holy Spirit. . .the ribbon holding them is love. I'm sure of that. Nothing is stronger than love.*

Now, he lay there, and her words echoed in his mind. So did Jeff's. *Dad? Why don't we go to church?*

He rolled over and smacked his pillow.

God, You know why I don't go to church. I refuse to be a hypocrite. I'm not going to go and pretend I understand. I don't. I don't have the kind of faith that makes everything okay and lets me dump everything into Your hands. I'm mad. No, I'm livid. Bad enough, You took my wife, but how could You rob Jeff of his mother? I wouldn't want someone who held a grudge against me in my home. Why should I go to Yours?

Sleep wouldn't come. Hearing a light, puppy whimper, Nathan shoved aside his blankets and got up. He took Lick out to the backyard and grumbled, "Okay. Do your business."

How many times had he heard Vanessa give Amber that same command? He'd chuckled the first time he overheard it. That was back when he didn't know the special commands she used in training. Now it all made sense and came as second nature.

Lick complied, then ran to the other side of the yard. "Come." Nathan waited, but the puppy ignored him.

He squatted down and reached out. "Come, Lick."

The puppy continued to wander on his own path.

"Lick, come on, Boy."

Lick perked up his head, his tail wagged, and he bounded across the yard, straight to Nathan.

Nathan felt a spurt of irritation, then squelched it. He couldn't punish this silly little, wiggly ball of fluff. Lick had obeyed the call and come. If he got punished, he'd be less likely to come again in the future. Instead, Nathan cradled the puppy in his arms and took him inside. As he stuck Lick back in his bed in the corner of Jeff's room, Jeff stirred.

"Dad?"

"What?"

"You never answered my question. Can we go to church?"

Nathan stayed motionless and stared across the dim room at his innocent little boy. *I don't have to make a big deal of this. We'll go just once. That'll satisfy him.* Even that agreement felt like a huge concession.

"I wanna go."

Each word strained his vocal cords as Nathan said, "We'll go tomorrow."

fourteen

His shoes pinched. His dress socks had a hole in one toe, courtesy of Licorice. One of the buttons on his suit dangled by a thread, and he'd forgotten he'd tossed his favorite tie in the drawer the last time he wore it, so he had to settle for another one that had a small mustard stain. For being a successful businessman, he looked like a bum.

Man looks at the outward appearance, but the Lord looks at the heart. The verse ran through his mind, and as Nathan pulled into a parking space, he muttered, "I'm striking out on both accounts."

Giggling, Jeff bounced along the sidewalk as they headed toward the sanctuary. "Hey—there's Andy! He's in my class at school."

It didn't take much time to settle Jeff into a Sunday-school class, then Nathan stared at the sanctuary. Each step took resolve. *I could just leave and come back to pick up Jeff, but I said we'd go to church. If I don't stay, I would be lying.*

He hadn't attended Seaside Chapel before and was surprised to discover how that very fact actually made it easier to go inside the sanctuary. Instead of having to endure the inevitable flood of memories from Mercy Springs, there was simple curiosity on his part. A greeter shook his hand, and an usher handed him the bulletin—familiar rituals that should have given comfort, but just left him feeling hollow. He could endure one day of this.

He saw Valene sitting near the aisle. Amber was lying curled up, "being small," just to the side of the pew. A couple sat beside Val—her parents, he presumed. Nathan slipped into the pew directly behind her, set down the bulletin, and leaned forward. Tapping her on the shoulder, he murmured, "Don't look now—the roof might cave in. I came to church."

"You'd better look," she whispered back. "I'm Val."

"I know." He flashed a quick smile at her. "Van couldn't sit as still as you do or stay quiet. She'd be chattering up a storm with half the congregation and make a last-minute mad dash for a seat." He glanced around, hoping to see Vanessa. With Amber right here, she had to be close—a fact that made him feel a little less anxious. Until now, he hadn't realized how much he was counting on her being there to be his lifeline. "Where is your sister?"

"Van's singing in the choir today. Amber's supposed to stay here, but I'm keeping an eye on her."

"She looks a lot more comfortable than I feel." He couldn't believe he'd blurted that out.

She gave him a timid smile. "I'm glad you came. Have you met our parents, Ellen and Bill?"

"No." He stood and shook Ellen's and Bill's hands. "You have wonderful daughters."

"Thank you. We hear you have a terrific little boy," Ellen said.

"And a powerhouse swing," Bill added. "The team's finally winning a few games this year."

"Why don't you come and sit with us?" Ellen invited.

Just then, another family entered from the side and filed right in next to the Zobels. Nathan grinned. "Thanks, but I'm fine." He took a seat and pretended to study the bulletin.

Nathan figured it served him right that he assumed Vanessa would be waiting to sit next to him. She probably served on a few committees and substitute taught a Sunday-school class too. He'd never met anyone with her vitality. If something needed doing, she'd be in the middle of it.

Valene and her parents were gracious, but it just wasn't the same. He knew Van and Val were identical, but the odd thing was, he really never gave Val a second thought. Vanessa kindled something inside of him, and beside her, all other women paled to insignificance.

Shy Valene sat in front of him and dipped her head as she meditated before the service began. He'd noticed Vanessa tended to turn her face toward heaven when she prayed. She acted just as open with the Father as she did with people.

How can she trust the Lord and rely on Him so completely? Innocence? Is it just that she hasn't been burned by life yet? God let loose a nuclear bomb in my life. Nothing's left of my soul but a charred shell. I believe in Him, but how can I ever trust Him again?

He didn't have much time for reflection. The worship leader got up to the microphone and welcomed everyone. He directed them to all stand and greet someone. A couple of the guys from the baseball team came over and shook his hand.

Part of Nathan liked already knowing some of the folks— it made it seem a little less foreign. On the other hand, he felt trapped. Just because he came this once, he didn't want them to all start bugging him to show up again.

While his attention was diverted, the choir filed in. Nathan looked up and spotted Vanessa at once. She perked up and smiled at him. *Best welcome I got. . .* Close on the warmth of that feeling, his common sense kicked in. *But this is just a onetime deal.*

The pianist played a couple chords, and the choir started in. Soon, the music director had the whole congregation singing.

Funny thing, hymns. They're classics. Never paid attention, but they can be welcoming and comforting—probably the familiarity of

them. Odd, after five years, I remember almost all of the words. Two
of the worship songs were new—he didn't know the tunes, but
that forced him to attend to the lyrics more closely. All in all,
the music time didn't feel too awkward.

Nathan followed the music minister's directions to stand
and sit when everyone else did. He took his seat again as an
elderly couple tottered from the front row of the choir to the
microphone and started to sing, "It Is Well with My Soul."
Clearly, their hearts were in the right place, but their vocal
cords weren't. Nathan never pretended to have a whole lot of
talent in the music department, but even he knew they were
each singing in completely different keys. To make matters
worse, one of them wore a hearing aid that managed to buzz
off and on. The microphone picked up the high-pitched tone
and turned it into a shrill siren.

Amber stood up, right there in the center of the main aisle
and started to "sing" along in howl.

"Hush!" Valene tried to silence Amber, but Amber wagged
her head from side to side almost as if she were saying no. She
tilted her head back and continued to howl.

Nathan glanced up at the choir and saw Vanessa's incredulous expression. Valene glowed bright red in embarrassment
as she continued to whisper very softly, "Hush, Amber.
That's enough."

Having spent a lot of time with them, Nathan remembered the command Vanessa used on the rare occasions when
Amber needed correction. He leaned forward and used her
tactic. In a firm voice, pitched low enough to mean business,
yet not so loud as to travel through the entire sanctuary, he
said, "That's enough."

Immediately, Amber went quiet.

"Down," Nathan commanded.

Amber backed up a few steps, lay down, and rested her

chin on the edge of his pew. Nathan glanced up at the choir, and Vanessa mouthed, "Thank you."

Fortunately the man in charge of the sound system managed to adjust the microphone so the duet finished without any further technical or canine embellishment. Nathan knew he'd never forget that hymn.

After the benediction, Bill Zobel turned around. "I have a hankering for Chinese. Why don't you collect your son and meet us all at the Paper Lantern?"

"Only if he'll promise to order something with some zing," Vanessa declared as she walked up. "My parents and Val all have sissy mouths. I'm tired of sharing bland stuff."

"The hotter, the better." Nathan grinned. "But Jeff is going to be a traitor. He always wants something sweet like orange chicken."

"My favorite!" Ellen smiled.

"See?" Vanessa groaned.

"I'll order hot-and-spicy Hunan beef if you get firecracker shrimp or kung pao chicken." He got a kick out of seeing how Vanessa perked up. The woman was so bright, she could masquerade as a thousand-watt lightbulb.

Val wrinkled her nose. "I'll order beds for both of you at Community General after you burn holes in your stomachs with that stuff."

Nathan shrugged. "If my cooking hasn't sent me to the hospital, nothing will."

❧

"Dad, what is the duck peeking at?"

"Peking used to be a place in China, but they changed what it's called to Beijing," Van explained as Nathan gave his son a baffled look. "The people at that table across from us want to try a dish that is named after the city."

"Oh. So those people wanna eat funny stuff." Jeff leaned

closer to Vanessa. "Did you hear them? They're getting mushy pork."

"Mu shu pork sounds good to me." Vanessa's dad closed the menu. He grinned at Jeff. "It's sort of like skinny pancakes they fill with pork. They're good. I'll get that, and we can try it together."

"My dog eats pancakes. My dog and Valene's dog are brothers. I wish I had a brother."

The muscle in Nathan's cheek twitched. His eyes narrowed for a split second. He took a long, deep breath, and his features smoothed. Poking his forefinger into Jeff's ribs, he rumbled, "Oh, no. You're enough for me. Between you and Lick, I've got my hands full."

Jeff giggled and squirmed. "Lick got one of Dad's socks today. He ran all over the house with it in his mouth."

Nathan looked into Vanessa's eyes. She felt her pulse speed up a bit. "See what kind of trainer you are? You swiped my socks, so now the dog's doing it too."

"His socks?" her mother echoed. "You swiped his socks?"

Shaking his head, Jeff blabbed, "She wore Dad's socks. Dad and Van both had one with stripes and one that didn't have stripes. They matched each other."

Mom about spilled the tea she was pouring into Dad's cup as she croaked, "How did you end up wearing his socks?"

"Vanessa talks in her sleep." Jeff wiggled with delight. "She told me—"

Uh-oh. This is unbelievable. Damage-control time here. "Nathan had an emergency. At work. I went over—to his house, not to his work. He called me." She knew she was babbling, but she couldn't help herself. "Early in the morning—"

"Vanessa bailed me out of a tight spot. About a week ago, I had to dash off to a construction site, so she baby-sat Jeff for me." Nathan finished the explanation smoothly. It didn't escape her notice that he made it abundantly clear he hadn't stayed in the house with her there.

Whew.

"You ready to order?" The waitress held her pen poised over an abused pad of paper.

"Mom?" Dad prompted.

"I heard Jeff likes orange chicken, so I'd better order something different so we'll have an assortment. I'll go for some sweet-and-sour ribs."

"I'd like the mushroom chicken, please." Val snapped the menu shut.

"Mu shu pork," Dad added.

Jeff got up on his knees and leaned across the table. "Are those our pancakes?"

"You better believe it!"

"Goody!"

Jeff managed to give them all a rundown of his Sunday school lesson. The whole time he spoke, Nathan kept his arm around his son's shoulders, but with his free hand, he pensively turned his teacup in slow, exacting clockwise clicks.

What is he thinking?

When the food came, Jeff changed topics. "Looky, Dad! Looky! That thing in the middle of the table is a merry-go-round!"

"It's called a lazy Susan. We'll all put our food on there and spin it around so anyone who wants to can have a taste. Pretty nifty, huh, Sport?"

"Can you put one in our table? It's cool!" He turned to Vanessa. "My dad can do anything. He can make anything!"

She thought of the beautiful, old oak pedestal table she'd seen at Nathan's house. "Your table is round like this one, but I think it would look kind of strange with a lazy Susan. It's just right the way it is."

"On rainy days, Consuelo puts a big blanket over it and lets me pretend it's a tent."

"Jeff, you need to quiet down," Nathan said matter-of-factly. "It's time to use your mouth to eat, not to talk."

As she dished rice onto her plate, Val piped up. "Yeah, well, Amber wasn't very quiet today, either. I wanted to crawl under the pew when she started in!"

Van muffled a laugh. "Nathan took care of it. And get this, Nathan: Eulla Mae and Harold came up to me in the narthex and thought it was hilarious that Amber wanted to make it a trio with them. They weren't upset in the least."

"Eulla Mae is gifted with grace," Mom said.

Nathan snorted. "I'm certainly not."

His words stunned Vanessa for a moment until she followed his rueful gaze. He'd managed to drop a shrimp, and it had slithered away from the serving spoon, leaving a thin, messy, pinkish streak across the table.

"You can't escape me!" Vanessa nabbed it with her fork. "Ta da! Gotcha, you little rascal."

"Catching a shrimp isn't a big deal. I wish you woulda gotten a whale." Jeff's lower lip poked out in a classic pout. "I didn't get to see no whale on our trip."

"No, we didn't get to see any whales, but we did see lots of cool sea creatures yesterday at the tide pools," Nathan reminded him. "You saw anemones and urchins and hermit crabs. . . ."

"Van? Dad said we can go back to the tide pools again. Wanna come with us?"

"I'd love to!"

After the meal was over, Nathan swiped the check and paid the bill. They all walked out to the parking lot, and after he left, Dad and Mom bracketed Vanessa.

"Honey, he's a good man," Mom said.

"But he's not walking with the Lord," Dad said. "He's

fallen away. I hate to see you get more deeply involved. It's a big mistake."

"Involved? It's friendship. And for the record, I have a deal with Nathan. He knows he has a standing invitation to come to church, but I don't bug him. Today was the first time in five years he's attended church, and I'm thankful for that answer to prayer."

"We're glad he came. We hope he continues, but Van, don't start wading into 'missionary dating.' You know it's wrong."

"Yeah. I understand. Just notice that it was Jeff who asked me to go to the tide pools—not Nathan."

Inside, she felt a niggling about that fact. She really wished Nathan had asked. . . Then again, she was glad he hadn't—not because of her family's misgivings, but because she didn't want to have to start examining her feelings about him too closely. Deep down, she knew full well if he was an on-fire believer—*No. I'm not going there. This is about God and His relationship with Nathan. I'm not in the picture. I'm not. Well, okay, so I am—but just a little bit.*

fifteen

"You want me to what?" Vanessa stopped dead in her tracks on the aisle between the birdseed and kitty litter. Her hand wrapped around the cordless phone receiver more tightly. Amber stood patiently at her side, oblivious to the ridiculous suggestion Nathan had just made.

"Jeff mentioned it the other day at lunch—the tide pools. Why are you sounding so surprised?"

"I'm not exactly surprised you asked, but—"

"You're off on Monday, and I'm at a point in my projects that I can take a day off too. Jeff's school booked a student-free day for the teachers, so he won't miss any class."

"So far, I'm fine with that—"

"You also said Amber is allowed there," he tempted without taking a breath, "so that's not a hitch."

Vanessa marveled at his delivery. He'd reasoned out all of the contingencies and her possible objections and delivered his sales pitch as smoothly as he banged a nail into place with a hammer. She grimaced. He'd failed to take one major point into account.

"C'mon, Van. Whadda ya say?"

Vanessa stuffed an outdated tablet of rebate coupons in the trash can under the counter. "You were doing fine until you started discussing high and low tides."

"You have to get there right as the tide is going out so you can see the best assortment of all of the sea life. Those first hours are awesome!"

"I have to be awake so I can see." She wiped off the counter and headed toward the kittens' cage. She'd sold all but two of

110

them, and they looked like they could both use some attention. "I couldn't pry my eyes open at 6:43 if you dropped a
python on me."

Nathan chuckled.

"I don't really even think," she mused as she dangled a
feather teaser toy at one of the fluff balls, "the world is alive
yet at that hour."

"It is. I assure you, it is."

"I'll take your word for it." She laughed at his impatient
snort as well as at the kittens' antics. "I'm not about to actually discover that for myself."

"You already have. When you bailed me out that night, Jeff
had you up by six-thirty."

"Boy, oh, boy. I do a guy a favor, and he tosses it right back
in my face."

"It's a good cause. Think about how disappointed Jeff was
when we didn't spot any whales when we went whale watching. A trip to the tide pools will help make up for it."

"Nathan, you already took him."

"But you weren't there."

"Yeah, well, it's a safe bet that I'm going to be a no-show for
anything that requires me to crawl out of bed before sunrise. My
alarm clock and I have an ironclad agreement: It doesn't wake
me up before 7:23, and I keep it plugged in."

"7:23?"

"And not a second sooner. I have a routine all worked out
so I can stay in bed until the very last minute." She tossed a
jingly bell in for the kittens and fastened the cage's catch. "I
told you I'm a night owl."

"You're not exaggerating at all?"

"Okay, I confess—Val dragged me out of bed and poured
coffee into me so I'd make seven-thirty classes in high school
and college."

"So you can get up and function."

"Not really. She and I are polar opposites—she's a lark, and I'm an owl. It's probably one of the reasons she got As and I didn't in all of those crack-of-dawn classes. I was just sleep-walking with a commuter mug in my hand."

"Ah ha!" His baritone laughter rippled over the phone line. "I've discovered your weakness. Jeff and I will bring a giant mug of coffee for you."

"Not good enough."

"No? Jeff will be so disappointed, Van. He really wanted you and Amber to go with us."

"Life is made up of all sorts of little disappointments." If anything, Nathan sounded rather downhearted himself. She couldn't tamp down her smile, even though he couldn't see her. "Chocolate has caffeine, you know."

"You'd eat chocolate at six in the morning?"

"As far as I'm concerned, if I'm breathing, it's a good time to eat chocolate. I'm a firm believer in eating my vegetables, and cocoa is a bean."

Nathan spluttered for a moment, then recovered wryly, "I suppose that is an example of the kind of stuff you, ah, 'learned' in one of those early morning science classes."

"The benefits of a good education." She laughed. "I probably ought to set a good example for Jeff, though. I'll settle for hot cocoa."

"Great! We'll pick you up at six on Monday."

"Six-fifteen." After she hung up, Vanessa put the phone back on the base and folded her arms akimbo. "That man missed his calling in life. He should have gone into retail sales where he'd get a hefty commission. He'd be rolling in the dough in less than a month."

Amber looked up at her as if she understood and agreed with every last word.

"Come on, Girl. We have work to do." Amber stood and followed along as Vanessa went along the aisle with all of her fish tanks. She sprinkled food along the surface of the water and watched as the fish tumbled about in the water like colorful sprinkles in a kaleidoscope.

When she and Val had worked here when they were in college, she'd hated cleaning out the fish tanks. It was a slimy, messy, smelly job. Her boss really liked fish, though. Pete would stand and admire the nearly translucent fins, the way the colors went iridescent, and the grace with which the fish cruised through the tanks. He'd actually had a second aisle of exotics. She'd gotten accustomed to caring for them.

All along, she'd thought to go into veterinary medicine—well, until she'd gotten into anatomy and physiology. She'd sat in the corner of the lab and tried to force herself to participate, but she couldn't dissect the cat. It looked just like Elvira, the sleek black cat she and Val had for several years. As a compromise, she'd done her "dissection" on a computer instead. When she went to turn in all of the necessary pages, Dr. Bainbridge was visiting her professor.

Her professor made a disparaging comment, but Dr. Bainbridge came to her defense. He'd been the family vet for Elvira; the poodle, Fluff; and later her first guide puppy, Thane. He'd gently suggested she was excellent at caring for healthy animals—perhaps she ought to think about running a pet store or kennel instead of going into veterinary medicine. He'd even put in a good word with Pete at the pet store, who promptly hired both Van and Val.

Val had enjoyed running the register, pricing things, and keeping the books. Van, on the other hand, had gone wild over the animals. She'd groomed them, played with them, kept the pens and cages spotless, and found tremendous satisfaction in helping customers find the perfect pet.

Pete had often remarked his business took off once the twins worked there. He chalked it up to their beauty. Van teased it was because Val finally straightened out his books so he could keep track of his funds. Val declared it was due to Vanessa's knack for selling not only the pet, but all of the necessary start-up gear. Whatever the truth, the job had paid for the rest of their schooling, and Pete had happily set their work schedules around the hours they needed off for classes.

Pete had waited until Van was almost ready to graduate before he told her he was thinking of selling his pet shop. Just the year before, Grandma had passed on and left a sizable legacy to her and Val. Val used her share to buy the condo. Van prayed and felt the Lord was opening doors. . . .

But not fish tanks.

She'd bought the store, renamed it, and promptly sold off half of the stock of fish. Now, she had five shiny tanks full of freshwater fish. Adding more puppies, dog chow, and gear made the store far more profitable—and she didn't have to clean as many tanks.

Nonetheless, the goldfish tank qualified as essential equipment. She often donated coupons to schools and the church to give to children for a free goldfish. Frequently those children came back to get another fish, or their parents bought inexpensive little aquarium accessories. When that family felt ready to get a different pet, they frequently came back to Whiskers, Wings, and Wags because they were familiar with it. Vanessa smiled to herself. Nathan and Jeff were the record holders for the shortest turnaround time.

Van polished a few fingerprints off the front of the last glass-fronted tank and watched the fish dart around. No doubt Jeff would want to know why she didn't stock sea urchins, sea stars, and hermit crabs. Under her breath, she murmured, "Nathan, your kid is as cute as you are."

❧

Sunday morning, Nathan set out cereal and grabbed a banana for Jeff. It was the last one—good thing too. It had reached the eat-now-or-toss-it stage. They needed to do some grocery shopping. Nathan would rather haggle with a city inspector over a building variance than walk the aisles of the grocery store. Jeff always wanted to buy all the junk food he'd seen advertised. Invariably, Nathan would skip a row or two just to get out of the place faster, only to stand at the register and remember something he needed and hadn't seen.

There were times when he thought about asking Consuelo if she'd take on the grocery shopping and cook suppers, but that went against one of the lessons he wanted to teach Jeff. A man could get some help with a few things—even delegate—but overall it was important to be capable of coping with issues. Someday his son would have to face life on his own. Nathan knew he needed to equip Jeff with skills like shopping and, well, basic stuff like opening cans and nuking frozen junk in a microwave.

He took a swig from his mug and made a wry face. The aroma barely qualified as coffee, and the taste didn't. He'd used the last few spoons of grounds out of the bottom of the can to make this pot. He scribbled "coffee" on the shopping list and underlined it.

"Sport, turn off those cartoons and come eat. We've got stuff to do today."

"We do?" Jeff had been lying on the floor next to Lick, watching TV. He stood and pushed the off button.

"Yeah. I'm gonna hop in the shower. I already poured milk on your cereal, so it'll get mushy if you don't eat it right away."

Nathan walked up the stairs and climbed into the shower. As he scrubbed, he made a mental list of other things he should have put on the grocery list and forgotten. He'd yanked up his jeans when Jeff traipsed in, covered from neck to toes with mud. "What happened to you?"

"Lick wanted out. You told me to be sure to let him out right away any time he wanted to go so he wouldn't have any accidents."

"I fenced off the dirt in the backyard, though." As he spoke, Nathan stripped Jeff out of his clothes and shoved him into the shower.

Jeff's scrawny little chest puffed out with pride. "Lick wanted to go out the front door."

"You didn't—"

"He was really good, Dad. He did his business, and when he started to run away, I called 'Come!' to him, just like Van told me to. He turned around and came right away."

"Let me guess: The living room is as muddy as you are."

"Nope." His grin took on a decidedly cocky flair. "I helped Lick wipe off his paws on the doormat."

"Judging from your clothes, he thought you were the doormat. Clean all of that off."

As his son showered, Nathan finished dressing and tossed the muddy clothes into his hamper. Consuelo did laundry—a chore for which he happily paid her extra. She'd definitely earn her money with that load. Nathan knew she wouldn't bat an eye at it. The clothes he wore to construction sites often came back equally gritty.

Thank God for Consuelo.

He stopped dead in his tracks. He couldn't remember the last time he'd actually been thankful to the Lord. In this case, he had to confess, it was a heartfelt emotion. Without her, he wouldn't have made it through the last five years.

"Dad?"

"What, Sport?"

"It's Sunday, right?"

"Yep." He globbed a dab of toothpaste on his brush, started to work on his molars, and froze. He caught sight of Jeff in the bathroom mirror. His son had pulled back the shower curtain and looked at him with hope shining in his big brown eyes.

"Can I go to Sunday school?"

Slowly Nathan pulled the toothbrush from his mouth. He spat in the sink, then turned around. "You already went to Sunday school last week."

"Unh-huh. It was fun."

"Why do the same thing again?" He hoped he sounded casual. This wasn't in his plan. He'd thought it would be a one-shot deal, then Jeff would latch onto some other activity. Normally, he grew distracted or bored and moved on to a new thing.

"We're going to the tide pools again. You told me we'd see different creatures. The Sunday school teacher told me they hear a new story every week, so it'll be different there too."

Miscalculated on that score, Adams. Now what're you gonna do?

"Listen, Sport—I thought maybe we'd go out for—"

"Lunch with Vanessa and her family again? Yippee!" Jeff disappeared behind the shower curtain.

Nathan turned back to the sink and ordered, "Wash behind your ears." He looked at his reflection. A thin line of toothpaste outlined the center of his lower lip. Deep, harsh grooves bracketed his mouth. *What have I gotten myself into?*

sixteen

Nathan sat in the sanctuary and thumbed the edge of the bulletin. Jeff was so excited about going to Sunday school, he'd gotten ready in record time, and they'd arrived a bit early. Nathan sat in the same pew he'd occupied last week. He hoped Van wouldn't be in the choir today. She could sit next to him and make it so he didn't feel quite so lonely or out of place.

Last week, the organ music made the hair on the back of his neck prickle. Today, the softly played hymn flowed over his nerves. It fit his mood like his favorite hammer just kind of fit in his hand when he was working on a project around the house.

The bulletin featured the morning's hymns and Scripture, then had another segment, "Looking Forward." It listed all the upcoming activities and events. He smiled as he noticed the last ball game of the season was listed. A plea for tools and willing hands for building a church in Mexico piqued his interest a little. *What am I thinking? I didn't even want to go to church. Why would I get involved in a project like that?* He swiftly turned the bulletin over.

LOOKING AROUND mentioned a birth, a wedding, and the names of those who were or had been in the hospital. Fair enough. It was nice to see this place really functioned like a cohesive church family—really caring for its own.

There was one last little section LOOKING BACK. It simply asked, "How was your walk this week?"

Nathan drew in a sharp breath. He set aside the bulletin and wished he hadn't read those words. *How was my walk? My walk? God, I'm the walking wounded.* He bowed his head in weariness. *This week.* The last two words of the question echoed in his mind. This week? This week had gone better than. . .well, than since he'd torn out of church five years ago. The realization stopped him cold. It really had been a better week. Less empty. Not the same struggle. But why? What had made the difference?

"Nice to see you here, Adams."

Nathan looked to the side and stood at once. He shook hands with Bill Zobel and glanced down at Amber. "What happened? You're missing all but one of your gals."

"Ellen volunteers in the nursery once a month. Val is working this weekend. Someone at work is sick, so she's been putting in a lot of extra days and overtime."

"That's a bummer." He tried to sound casual and fought the urge to look around. "What about Vanessa?"

"She'll be here in a minute. She made cupcakes for a bake sale, and I'd rather baby-sit Amber than carry a tray of food. I'd either accidentally dump it on someone or eat half of them before I reached the kitchen."

"You have more self-control than I do, because I've tasted her cupcakes. I'd have eaten all of them." The small talk wasn't exactly difficult, but Nathan knew he didn't measure up to Bill's dreams for his daughter's future husband. Granted, Bill behaved more than just cordially. Vanessa must have inherited her friendly, outgoing nature from him. Even so, there was a world of difference between accepting someone as a friend and welcoming him as the man who was dating your daughter.

Nathan wanted to sit at the edge of the pew so he could simply scoot over to allow Van to take that place and be close to Amber. With Bill standing there, he'd have to scoot in farther and have Bill sit between them. *It's probably exactly what he wants.*

"Your boy liked Chinese last Sunday. How do the two of you do with Italian?"

"I love it; Jeff wears it." Nathan grinned. "You saw him with the chow mein noodles last week. He's worse with spaghetti."

Bill chuckled. "How 'bout we all go out to Ruffino's for lunch?"

"Sounds good."

"I pick up the tab this time."

"Hi, guys!" Vanessa slipped up and gave her dad a hug.

It was a sweet sight. Vanessa was an affectionate woman, and her warmth never seemed out of place or forced. The way she acted around her family made Nathan think of how long it had been since he'd been on the receiving end of any such fondness. Sure, Jeff and he hugged and wrestled around—but the sentimentality a woman put into a hug—that was different. How would it feel to wrap his arms around Vanessa and have her put her arms back around him? To hold and be held—even for a fleeting moment? Five long years of not wanting any such contact ended abruptly, and the realization shook him. *Being in church really has me off balance.*

"Did I hear you say something about Ruffino's? I can already taste the veal scaloppini."

"Songs and sermon before the scaloppini." Bill pushed her closer to Nathan and glanced at his watch. "I forgot to sign up for the men's pancake prayer breakfast. I'm going to duck back and do that before the service starts. I'd be happy to have you as my guest, Nathan. It's Wednesday. What do you say?"

Nathan thought for a moment, then pulled a small palm computer from his pocket to check on a date. "I have a site inspection Wednesday morning." He felt an unexpected twinge of regret and paused for a second before proposing, "Maybe another time?"

"I'll hold you to that."

&

Vanessa hummed all afternoon at the pet shop. *He came to church today! Two weeks in a row, he's come and heard the Word. Lord, please do a mighty work in Nathan's heart. There used to be a bitterness about him, but now there's just a sadness. Leech away the grief and pour Your love out on him.*

The bell at the door chimed. Patsy Dinnit zipped into the shop with her pedigreed Border collie on a hot pink, rhinestone-studded leash. "Van! Jazzy's going to have a litter. Do you want to take the puppies on commission again?"

"Amber, stay." Vanessa left her and went around to the other side of the counter. Amber normally did well around other dogs, but Jazzy tended to act high-strung when she carried a litter.

Stooping to give Jazzy a couple of strokes, Van asked, "Did you use the same sire? The last litter was gorgeous."

"Sure did! Sire's owner would get pick of the litter, but you can have all of the rest. I'll do an even split on the proceeds with you again."

"Let me grab my calendar and see what I have booked. When is she due?"

"In about four weeks."

Vanessa went back to the register. "Good girl." She patted Amber and reached for her calendar. "That would make it about the twenty-eighth, give or take a few days." She then flipped two pages. "If I take them when they're about eight weeks, that'll be in August. I have dachshunds and Labs coming in about the same time. That'll be a nice variety."

A secretive smile lit Patsy's face. She looked this way

and that, then whispered, "Jazzy's not the only one who's expecting."

"Patsy! Really? How wonderful!"

"You have no idea what a miracle it is. Hugo and I have been trying to have a baby for almost four years. I'm so excited, I can hardly stand it. I haven't said a word to anyone until today. We went and had an ultrasound Friday. Wanna see the picture?"

"I'd love to! When are you due?"

"January second. Hugo is already talking to the baby. Last night, he tapped my belly and told the kid to come early so we'd have a tax deduction!"

"Oh, no!" Vanessa giggled. "It's a good thing Hugo and Val didn't fall in love and get married. They're both so into business and accounting, they'd breed a whole tribe of bean counters."

Patsy gave an exaggerated wince. "They'd name them Lima and Chili."

"Those beans have some class. I was thinking more along the line of Jelly—can't you see it now?" Vanessa spread her hands in the air like she was holding up a banner. "Jelly Dinnit."

Patsy gave her a mock look of hurt and rubbed her still-flat tummy. "How could you say such a thing? I planned for something more affectionate. . .Sugar. Sugar Dinnit."

"I just finished lunch, but this is making me hungry!"

"I saw you go into Ruffino's with that gorgeous hunk. Who is he? He was at church last week too. You work fast, Girl!"

"He's just a friend. We met my family there. I sold him a dog, and he's taking obedience training."

"He is, or the dog?" Patsy gave her an impish wink.

Vanessa waggled her forefinger at Patsy. "Your husband is going to have his hands full if this baby is half as spunky as you are."

"You're calling me spunky? Ha! Now you—your kids are

going to be balls of fire."

"Predictions like that are enough to make me stay a spinster."

"Not a chance. That guy—you and he are going to be an item. I can feel it in my bones. Mark my words: In a few months, you're going to be gliding down the aisle."

"Me? Glide? Only if I were on a skateboard. You're mixing me up with Val. She'll glide, for sure. If you see me going down the aisle, it'll be in a bridesmaid's gown."

"Nope. You're not going to dissuade me. It's my vision, and the groom was that fine-looking man you sat next to in church."

"You know. . ." Vanessa tapped her cheek and looked at the ceiling, as if lost in important thoughts. "I seem to recall prophets who are wrong are put to death. You're so wrong about any entanglement there, it's downright dangerous."

Patsy giggled and dug through her purse for the picture of the ultrasound. "Look at this. This is a miracle."

Vanessa turned it around and looked at the wedge-shaped picture. "Amazing. Just amazing. Look! I can make out his profile! Is it a him or a her?"

"We told them not to tell us. It's so delicious, just knowing we're having a baby. I like leaving that secret in God's hands until He puts this baby in ours."

"Oh, yes. Like Psalm 139 talks about Him creating us in our mother's womb. I'm so thrilled for you. What a blessing."

Patsy agreed and carefully tucked away the ultrasound picture. She smiled. "That is my blessing and good news. I'm standing by what I said earlier, though. Go ahead and call it dangerous thinking, but I'm sure you and that guy are going to be an item."

Patsy left, and Vanessa looked down at Amber. "Dangerous. Even thinking Nathan could ever change and find me attractive is so far from possible, I'd be a fool to waste my time considering it." She turned and saw her reflection in the shop-window. *Am I looking at a fool?*

⋟

The alarm clock went off, and Nathan groaned. He'd been lying awake for the last twenty minutes, hoping the rain would stop. Instead, it kept falling. If anything at all, it seemed to be intensifying. There was no way they could go to the tide pools in this kind of weather. Reluctantly, he picked up the phone and dialed.

" 'Lo?"

"Hey, Sleepyhead, it's raining."

"You woke me up to give a weather report?"

"We won't be able to go to the tide pools." He sat up and stacked several coins on his bedside table. Jeff would come in and swipe them. He loved to plink the dimes, nickels, and pennies into the enormous, multicolored plastic dinosaur-egg bank in the corner of his bedroom.

"Nathan Adams," Vanessa moaned over the phone, "you are rotten to the core. Cruel. Mean. There probably isn't a person on the face of the earth more vile than you." Her bed squeaked, and her blankets made a loud ruffling noise, tattling that she'd rolled over.

He smiled at how zany, impulsive Van could be so pre-dictable about this one particular aspect of life. She'd been more than honest when she confessed she wasn't a morning person. "Need another minute to wake up?"

"Wake up? Why?" She yawned. "I'm going right back to sleep as soon as I tell you how barbaric you are to dare calling me at this ridiculous hour."

"Come on, Van. You can't be mad."

She yawned again—a long, luxurious, stretched sound that let him know she could easily shut her eyes and coast right back off.

"You were going to wake up now, anyway," he wheedled shamelessly.

"Not really. I had it all planned out. I'd get dressed, sleep in your car, and sleepwalk on the beach. Amber would rescue me if I accidentally walked into the surf."

"Don't forget that plan. We'll put it into play some other day." Nathan swept the quarters into the jar beside his bed for the once-a-month pilgrimage he and Jeff took to an arcade. The arcade! His heart galloped in anticipation. He'd come up with a great substitute for them. "I have an alternative plan for the day."

"It better start with, 'Van, sleep in 'til noon.' "

"Eight."

"Eleven." Her voice still sounded husky with sleep.

"Nine, and you still get hot chocolate."

Vanessa muttered something unintelligible and hung up the phone.

"Dad?" Jeff stood in the doorway, curling his toes on the cold, hardwood floor. "You promised we'd go to the tide pools again to see the sea creatures today."

Nathan opened his arms, and Jeff scampered across the room and launched into a hug. Nathan held his son, rubbed his bristly cheek in Jeff's sleep-mussed hair, and growled like a bear.

Jeff giggled and wrapped his arms as far around Nathan's chest as they'd reach. He paused a second, then asked in a sad tone, "Papa Bear, what're we gonna do? Vanessa and Amber wanted to go to the beach with us."

"I know you're disappointed, but I have a plan. . . ."

seventeen

"It's rain-ing, it's pour-ing, the old man is snor-ing."

Vanessa stared at Nathan and Jeff as they stood on her doorstep. She yanked them through her door. "Are the two of you crazy? Standing in the rain, singing. . ."

She paused, then huffed, "Without me? Seriously. I'm hurt."

Nathan closed his huge black-and-gray-striped golf umbrella with a loud snap. Jeff continued to sing as water dripped off his bright yellow slicker. He fiddled with one of the fasteners. " 'Nessa, d'you know that song?"

"Yep. Val and I used to sing it when we were little. I forgot all about it." She looked at Nathan and frowned. A water-splattered plastic grocery bag hung from the crook of his elbow. "What is that?"

"Your hot chocolate, Madame." He opened the bag and pulled out a carton of chocolate milk with a flourish.

"Nathan, I hate to break it to you, but that isn't hot."

He gave her a supercilious look. "Not yet, it isn't. My faithful sidekick, Master Jeffrey, will assist me in the delicate operation of preparing it for you." He helped Jeff peel out of his slicker and cleared his throat. "Come along, young man. We have serious work to do."

"Oh, boy. This I've gotta see." Vanessa tagged along behind them as they headed into her kitchen.

"Pop fly!" Nathan picked up his son and sat him on the kitchen counter.

"Pop fly?" Vanessa echoed. "How'd you come up with that saying?"

"It's from baseball, Silly," Jeff said.

"And I'm his pop, and I made him fly." Nathan opened a cupboard, shook his head, and shut it.

Vanessa didn't say a word. She backed against the counter on the far side of the kitchen so she'd be out of the way and still have a bird's-eye view of the goings-on. Nathan opened the next cupboard and shot her a quick look over his shoulder. "Wow, this is impressive. Even if we hadn't tasted some of your goodies already, all of this junk in here tells me you make more than just cupcakes on a pretty regular basis."

She shrugged. "I like to bake."

"I like to eat!" Jeff gave her a greedy smile.

Nathan's smile matched it perfectly. "Me, too! Especially your stuff. We're willing to sacrifice our taste buds and stomachs to the cause anytime."

"I'll keep that in mind."

The third cupboard held the coffee mugs Nathan wanted. He pulled out the first one with a wave worthy of a game-show host. "Ta da!"

"You didn't have to search. I could have just told you where they were."

"Oh, but this is an adventure, and Master Jeffrey and I are sleuths."

"I hate to break the news, but sleuths are for mysteries, not adventures."

Vanessa watched Nathan get out more mugs and unbutton the sleeves of his tan-and-green plaid flannel shirt. He methodically rolled up those sleeves, revealing muscular forearms. He then did the same thing to the sleeves on Jeff's little blue denim shirt. He made quite a production of it, as if they were about to make a seven-course gourmet meal instead of heat up chocolate milk. Vanessa couldn't decide whether the show was for her or for Jeff. Either way, she enjoyed every last second.

Nathan scrounged up a saucepan, set it on the range, then ordered, "Son, find a spoon. I'll need to stir this."

Jeff turned onto his belly on the counter, reached over the edge, and jerked open the drawer. The silverware in it jangled. "Dad, do you want a big spoon or a little spoon?"

"A little one," Nathan said as he wrestled with the milk carton. It didn't open neatly. Instead, the waxed cardboard wouldn't separate, so he scowled at the carton as if his dark look would make it cooperate.

Vanessa watched the whole process with nothing short of delight. *I would have gotten up at six for this show. This is a riot.*

Nathan gave up on the first side of the milk carton and attacked the other side. It yielded.

Probably out of fear.

He poured the chocolate milk into the saucepan and dumped the mangled carton into the trash with more emphasis than the poor thing deserved. When Nathan turned back around, he gave Jeff a blank stare. "What is that?"

"A little spoon."

Vanessa bit the inside of her lip to keep from laughing as Jeff held out the quarter teaspoon from a set of measuring spoons that had gotten separated.

"When we look in my toolbox, you know how I have the great big mallet, and I have the regular hammers, then I have that skinny, little finishing hammer?"

"Dad, you're not going to stir the hot chocolate with a hammer, are you?"

Vanessa started laughing.

Nathan shot her a disgruntled look, then suddenly perked up. "Yes, Sport, I am. See?" He took two strides, came close enough to Vanessa for her to inhale his expensive, spicy aftershave, and reached around her. He snagged her meat-tenderizing mallet and nodded. Holding it high, he declared,

"Always be sure to use the right tool for the job, Jeff."

Humor mingled with disbelief as Vanessa watched Nathan hold on to the business end of the mallet, dunk the handle into the saucepan, and proceed to stir. She had to give him credit. He'd managed to recover pretty smoothly.

"Dad, what am I s'posed to do with this little spoon?"

"Yeah, Nathan," she chimed in. "What's that bitsy spoon for?"

"That is. . ." He paused for a split second. "The tasting spoon. Yes, the tasting spoon. Whoever holds the tasting spoon has the important job of deciding when the hot chocolate is ready."

Vanessa dug out three mismatched party napkins from the pantry and put them on the table. Soon Nathan set the cups of steaming cocoa on the table. He dumped a telephone book onto a chair to act as a booster seat for Jeff, and they were ready. The rich scent of hot chocolate filled the air, and Vanessa curled her fingers around the mug. She stopped short when Jeff drummed his fingers on the table.

"Aren't we gonna say a prayer?"

❧

Nathan froze. He hadn't seen that coming, but he should have. Vanessa always took a moment to pray. For the past two Sundays, her father had prayed over the lunches. A man should be the spiritual head of the home. . .the adage went through his mind. *It's not my home,* he tried to reason, but that excuse sounded pathetic. There had once been a time when speaking to the Lord came so naturally, so freely. Now here he sat, mute.

"When I was a little girl," Vanessa said to Jeff, "I learned some prayers. Maybe you'd like to learn one of them. You can say the words after me."

"That's a good idea." Nathan breathed a silent sigh of relief. Listening to Jeff's pure voice repeat each phrase after Vanessa did something odd to Nathan. *Evie would have wanted this. She wanted our son to grow up in the Lord. She wanted me to fall in love again and live a full life. How many times did she tell me that? I didn't believe her. I refused to listen because I couldn't bear to think of going on without her—but I have. I've had to, mostly for Jeff. But now I want to for me. Thank you, Evie, for being so sweet to give me your blessing to move on. Had you known Vanessa, you would have been good friends.*

In those moments, Nathan sensed a momentous shift. He had a past, but he wanted a future. For five long years, he'd not looked ahead. Now he saw a bridge in the guise of a simple child's prayer.

Am I using God and religion as a way of making it acceptable to court and love Vanessa? I've done nothing but shake my fist in God's face for five years. Now, suddenly, I'm going to do this turnabout? How convenient is that? Is this a matter of my heart or of my soul?

"Da—ad. You're not listening."

"What?" Nathan snapped out of his contemplation.

"I asked you when you were going to tell Van about where we're going."

"If Van is willing to watch you, I'm going to Mexico."

"What about the arcade, Dad? I wanna play games!"

Nathan looked at Vanessa. "We'll play at the arcade today, but if that hammer in Vanessa's kitchen is anything like the ones going to Mexico, that team needs a lot of help to build that church."

"Why can't I go with you?"

"It's a school week." Nathan took a gulp of hot cocoa. He needed to get away to think. Vanessa needed time to be with Jeff to see if they could get along well for more than just a day at a time.

A short while later, while Jeff smacked buttons on a blaring machine at the arcade and Amber sat patiently at Vanessa's side, Nathan apologized. "I should have asked you privately about watching Jeff instead of blurting it out like that. If you'd rather not, I'll understand."

She hitched a shoulder and laughed self-consciously. "Oh—I'm happy to watch him. He's a lot of fun. I was trying to find a way of suggesting it might be easier if I stayed at your place with him than bringing Lick to mine."

"You wouldn't mind?"

"Why should I?"

"It's closer to the school, but it'll be farther for you to get to and from work."

She hitched the strap of her purse up onto her shoulder. "I'm glad you're going to go. The team needs guys like you who know what you're doing. You have a lot of talent. It's generous of you to want to use it for G—" She caught herself. "For others."

Nathan slid his hand over hers and laced their fingers. Her eyes widened. "I need a chance to do some soul-searching and thinking."

"I got hundreds of points and this many tickets on that game!" Jeff half shouted the words and intruded on the moment. He stood before them and held up a long trail of pale blue rafflelike tickets the arcade machine spit out. "I wanna get so many, I can get something really cool."

"Oh, is that so?" Vanessa broke away and rose. "I'm lethal on Uranium Thief."

"Can I play you? Can I?"

"You'd better. I'd be horribly disappointed to come all of the way here with you and not get a chance to razzle dazzle you with my ability."

"Oh, brother," Nathan scoffed. "Jeff, can you believe her?

She really thinks she knows what she's doing, but she doesn't know who she's playing against."

Vanessa's chin went up at a stubborn tilt. "I challenge you here and now—and if I get to the third level before you, you have to eat a fried pickle."

"A fried pickle?" Nathan and Jeff said together.

Vanessa dusted her hands together. "A fried pickle. Now prepare for doom. You're about to wish you'd never brought me along today."

"Even if I have to eat a fried pickle, I won't feel doomed." Nathan looked at her intently. "I'd never be glad that you hadn't come along."

eighteen

"Twenty-eight dollars?" Vanessa twisted in the seat and gave Nathan an appalled look. "We wasted twenty-eight dollars at the arcade?"

"It wasn't a waste, Vanessa. We had a good time, didn't we?"

"And look at all of the good stuff I earned!" Jeff sat in the middle of the backseat like Midas in the center of his golden treasures. He'd spent half of forever choosing bouncy balls, slink chains, squirt guns, a magnifying glass, crazy sunglasses, candy, and half a dozen other assorted "prizes" with the tickets he'd earned from the arcade machines. Had they gone to a five-and-dime, he could have bought all of it for five bucks, max. Nevertheless, they'd had fun, and his pride made it all worthwhile.

"Sport, here's that big, big bridge."

"Are we going on it? Really?"

"No kidding."

Jeff sat a little straighter and craned to look out over the very edge of the bridge.

The railing came up so high that Vanessa could barely see over it part of the time. The Coronado Bridge in San Diego swept in a huge, graceful, sideways arc. It boasted such height, military vessels passed under it with ease. This kind of height gave her a sense of freedom. She tried to concentrate on looking as far out at whatever horizon she could spot through the drizzle. Due to the weather, there wasn't the usual abundance of sailboats out.

Charming, little old houses covered the island. Well-manicured lawns and nicely sculpted shrubs reflected the orderly community of military officers and understated wealthy citizens. Vanessa watched a cat streak across a lawn and shoot up a tree.

"Oh! I was so busy gawking, I didn't notice we passed the restaurant. I'm sorry, Nathan. It was on the left back there."

He gave her a startled look. "You're serious."

"Of course I am. I blew it."

"No problem—that can happen to anyone. I meant, you're serious about that restaurant—that it has fried pickles!"

She bobbed her head. "And you two are going to eat them. I got to level three first."

Nathan pulled into a parking lot. Vanessa wrinkled her nose. "What are we doing here?"

"Getting antacids. If I have to eat a fried pickle, I want something to rescue my stomach afterward."

"Hey! Don't knock it until you've tried it!"

"Ever hear of 'an ounce of prevention'? Well, I'm subscribing to that theory." Nathan opened his door. "I'll be back in a sec."

Ten minutes later, he emerged from the drugstore. He carried a big paper sack and stuck it between the two front seats. Vanessa peeped inside and let out a disbelieving laugh.

At least a full-dozen bottles of pink liquid jumbled in the bag.

"If you don't want to eat the fried pickles, just say so. You didn't have to buy out the store."

He snapped his seat belt and hitched his shoulder. "I figured we'd need it for the Mexico trip. Two for one."

"You're a bargain shopper? Who woulda thunk it?"

"Bargain? Me? You've got to be kidding. I'm not talking about a sale. I'm saying I'm killing two birds with one stone—the pickles and the trip."

Ten minutes later, seated in the Red Oak Steakhouse, Jeff repeated the prayer after Vanessa said each line. Just before she said, "amen", he blurted out, "And God, please don't let Daddy kill those birds. Amen."

"What birds, Son?"

Jeff gave his father a sad look. "The ones on your trip that you wanna throw rocks at."

"It's just a saying, Sport. It means taking care of two things at the same time."

"Oh."

Vanessa gave Jeff's hand a reassuring squeeze. "But you were right. You can pray about anything that bothers you. I do, and it makes me feel better."

Vanessa saw emotion flare in Nathan's eyes, but she couldn't interpret it.

"Your mom did that too," he said quietly to Jeff. "She talked to God about all sorts of things."

The food came, and Jeff practically dove across the table. "I wanna try the pickle!"

Vanessa arranged the napkin in her lap and avoided looking at Nathan. Had she gone too far? Spoken when she should have held her tongue? Opened the door to his grief again? Being torn between living for Christ and being sensitive to Nathan's limits was like being stuck between third base and home—she was in a pickle, all right.

❧

Nathan didn't want the day to end. More to the point, he didn't want his time with Vanessa to be over. After lunch, he decided they ought to take in a movie. They'd just missed the beginning, so to burn up time until the next showing, he drove to the huge, red-roofed Hotel Del Coronado. "Why don't we wander and gawk? This old place is fascinating."

"I need to stop at the desk and make sure they're okay with Amber on the premises."

"I'll drive up to the front, then." He pulled up to the entrance of the white main building, and a bellhop immediately opened Vanessa's door.

"I'll only be a minute." She hopped out, and Amber started to follow. "Amber, stay."

When Vanessa slipped inside, Nathan reached down and petted the dog. "She'll be right back."

Indeed Vanessa came right back out. A gust of wind blew her hair into wild disarray, but Nathan could see her laugh in delight rather than become upset. She found so much joy in simple things. He loved that about her. She ducked her head into the car. "They're fine with Amber as long as I have the training jacket and gentle leader on her. How about if Jeff and Amber stay with me while you park? That way we won't have wet fur and a soggy boy?"

Nathan looked beyond the portico at the gloomy drizzle and shook his head. As he scooted out of the car, he said, "I'll just have them valet park. That way, we'll all stay dry, and we'll be able to get back to the theater on time."

They entered the lobby, and Vanessa started to get the giggles. Nathan gave her a questioning look. "What's come over you?"

"The valet is going to see all of those bottles you bought at the drugstore and think I'm the world's worst cook!"

"You're a good cook, Van," Jeff piped up. "I like the stuff you make, and you know how to make lotsa different junk. Dad's a pretty good cook too. He makes terrific hot chocolate!"

"Sport, you need to use your indoor voice." Nathan looked around. "So where do you want to go first?"

Vanessa looked around. "We can go downstairs and wander

through a few shops. If it's not raining, we can peek at the swimming pool."

Nathan nodded toward one of the antique elevators. The metal grillwork on it carried the grace of a bygone era. "They sure don't make beauties like that anymore. Should we give Amber a chance to ride?"

"Amber?" Jeff looked crestfallen. "What about me?"

Vanessa leaned down. "You get to be the tail guard. You come along and make sure her tail doesn't get caught in the door. That's an important job."

They spent a leisurely hour-and-a-half wandering around. Jeff kept twisting around to check on Amber's tail. "He's a responsible little guy," Vanessa praised.

When they got into the theater, Nathan used a small pen-light he'd brought in from his glove compartment to illuminate the floor. They found a spot that didn't have any spilled soda or popcorn, and Amber curled up. Vanessa took her seat, and to Nathan's dismay, Jeff hopped into the seat right next to her. He thought about picking the boy up and plopping him down in the next seat over. That way, Nathan could slip his hand over and hold Vanessa's hand during the movie. . .or he could put his arm around her shoulders.

"No, that's not a good idea."

Nathan turned his head sharply. One of the men from the ball team held a flimsy cardboard tray laden with popcorn and drinks. He was trying to get four kids settled in and keep them from grabbing a drink all at the same time.

Nathan extended his arm and shored up the bottom of the tray. "You're about to lose the battle."

Doug groaned. "Thanks. Janey's mom and sister are in town. I volunteered to take all of the kids for the day—but that was when we had a clear weather report." He spied

Vanessa and gave Nathan a keen look.

Nathan ignored it. "Hope you enjoy the movie." He sat down. Had he needed to give a review of the movie, he'd be sunk. The whole time it played, Nathan tried to sort out his thoughts. He liked her. . .as more than just a friend. Somewhere along the way, she'd burrowed into his heart and made him start to face life again. He wanted her to be an integral part of that life. As the movie flickered on the screen, Nathan didn't even follow the plot. He came to the rock-solid conclusion that he wanted to make their relationship a public thing. . . and hopefully a very private thing too.

But wanting wasn't enough. Vanessa deserved someone who shared the joy and innocence of her beliefs, and Nathan didn't know if he could ever again be the man of faith he'd once been. Amber had howled during that hymn "It Is Well with My Soul," but Nathan had to admit, *It still isn't well with my soul.*

❧

Two weeks later, Kip came into the pet shop. "Valene said you're going to watch Jeff so Nathan can go with the Mexico work-and-witness team. Knowing how clear he's been about not wanting to be involved with the church, I thought she got things mixed up. I couldn't imagine him hanging out with a bunch of us, building a sanctuary, of all things, but I just stopped by Seaside and got the paperwork. I'm sharing a tent with Nathan."

Vanessa stayed on her knees on the hard linoleum floor. She'd started cleaning the birdcages, and when she put the latest sheet of newspaper in the tray to line this one, she'd spotted the comic strips and had taken a moment to enjoy them.

Kip squatted down next to her. "Van, this isn't funny. I'm worried about you."

"You don't think I can handle Jeff and Lick for a week?"

"Stop it right there. You can play games and tease other people into changing a subject, but I know you too well to get sidetracked. You're losing your heart to Nathan." He held up a hand to keep Van from responding. "Don't bother to deny it or make excuses. It's a fact. The question is: What are you going to do about it?"

"Pray."

"That's a good first step. What about exercising some wisdom?"

Vanessa stared at Kip. He was known for being brutally honest at times. She had the sinking sensation she was about to get an earful. "I'm not going to pretend I'm at peace with everything, Kip. I'm being honest with God."

"But are you able to be honest with Him when you're not being honest with yourself?" He smacked his thigh in impatience. "I'm partially to blame. I told you to pursue the relationship because I hoped you might be the Lord's emissary to bring Nathan back into relationship with Him."

"You're not to blame, Kip. It's not that kind of situation at all. Since we're shooting straight from the hip, here's the truth: I really care for Nathan—as a friend and as a man. Until he can get over his grief and reestablish his relationship with the Lord, I know I can't let the relationship go any further."

"This whole thing bothers me a lot. Don't tell me you don't feel any hesitance, because you have to. Deep in your heart, you have to know God would want you to put a brake on this before it rolls out into dangerous territory."

Vanessa slid the tray back into the birdcage. "I was reading Philippians 4 today." She sat on the floor and quoted, " 'Let your gentle spirit be known to all men. The Lord is near. Be anxious for nothing, but in everything by prayer and supplication with thanksgiving let your requests be made known to God. And the peace of God, which surpasses all comprehension, will guard your hearts and your minds in Christ Jesus.' " She let out a prolonged sigh. "I have to trust the Lord with this. I need to be patient about His timing and believe that He'll guard my heart."

"Don't stop there. What about verses eight and nine?" He locked eyes with her and quoted, " 'Finally, brethren, whatever is true, whatever is honorable, whatever is right, whatever is pure, whatever is lovely, whatever is of good repute, if there is any excellence and if anything worthy of praise, dwell on these things. The things you have learned and received and heard and seen in me, practice these things, and the God of peace will be with you.' "

She waited. Tension sang between them.

"It's not right, and you know it isn't," Kip finally insisted. "Nathan hasn't renounced the Lord, but he's miles away from a strong walk. You're not feeling peace, and I think you need to reflect on it, because the Holy Spirit may be telling you to back off."

They both stood. Kip shook his head sadly. He reached over and cupped her cheek. "There was a time when I thought maybe you and I might make a go of things. I've always loved your sparkle and wit. I've accepted I won't ever be the man for you. You and Nathan have a special chemistry folks talk about that I've never really seen in action. I often struggle to tell you and Val apart when you're together; blindfolded, even as short a time as he's known you, he could figure out which one you are. I hoped maybe it was just infatuation and your family would step in and make you see the truth. I've probably put my foot in my mouth here, and you'll likely chalk all of this up to a wild, jealous rant. It's not, though. Van, as a brother in

Christ—and I know that's all I'll ever be—I felt compelled to speak the truth."

He patted her cheek, then pressed a chaste kiss on her forehead and walked out of the shop. The bell chimed over the door, and for once, its cheery noise seemed dreadfully out of place.

nineteen

Nathan stomped a few times and methodically dusted off his shirt front, sleeves, and the seat of his jeans before ducking into the tent. He was sore, dirty, and tired. He hadn't felt half as good in years.

"Place is really coming together," Kip said as he lounged on his sleeping bag. "We ought to be able to get the roof up tomorrow."

Nathan nodded. He rummaged through one of the athletic bags he'd brought, then pulled out a pair of granola bars. He tossed one at Kip. "I'm too hungry to wait for supper."

"I could eat the hind legs off a running buck." Kip chuckled as he peeled back the wrapper. "Who am I kidding? I'm getting so stiff, I couldn't catch a centipede."

"No more than anyone else."

Kip shook his head. "I was hoping playing ball would help get me back in shape. After all of that waiting at the hospital or sitting in a desk chair, I was pathetic."

"What were you at the hospital for?"

Kip set aside the Bible he'd been reading. "That was dumb of me. 'Course you wouldn't know. My sister had leukemia. She had a bone marrow transplant last year." He grinned. "She's doing great now."

"Wow. Bet your family feels pretty lucky."

"Blessed is a better word for it." He stretched and winced.

Nathan didn't say anything. For the past four nights, he'd stayed in the area after dinner for Bible study or fellowship. Around the fire they built in a big pit, they shared and spoke of life's disappointments and joys, of how God gave them strength in the hard times.

He'd learned Harriet, who was cooking all of their meals, normally took care of her mother with advanced Alzheimer's. Pete and Lily had a daughter who was away at cystic fibrosis camp. Hugo left Patsy at home, rejoicing in her pregnancy after they'd struggled in silence through several years of infertility. Ben's teenaged son was addicted to drugs.

Heartaches. Everyone has them. A little voice whispered, "But they turn to Me."

Kip grabbed a cell phone and toggled it in the air. "I'm due to check in with the folks back home."

"I just called home, myself. Everything is fine."

"That's always good news. See you at chow." Kip left the tent.

Nathan looked at the Bible Kip left behind. He'd brought his own. He hadn't read it in years. At first, it sat on the coffee table, but he'd moved it to the dresser, then finally tucked it in a drawer. Out of sight, out of mind. While packing for this trip, he'd tucked it in with his gear. He hadn't had the courage to open it. Steeling himself, he pulled it out of his bag.

The unusually thick latigo cover still felt supple in his hands. Sturdy. Enduring. *Unlike my faith.* He opened it up and braced himself for the pain. It didn't come. Instead, he traced the lettering inside with a wash of gentle feelings.

With all the love God has given me for you, Evie.

She'd given it to him the Christmas they were engaged. She'd fretted because the lettering went uphill slightly. He'd found it endearing. He'd told her it represented how they'd always look up.

But I didn't. To the end, Evie clung to her faith. Me? I railed at God, then hid away from Him.

He thumbed through the gilt-edged pages. . .many marked with sermon notes or comments. The faded purple ribbon placemarker lay with an odd twisted quirk at the center of Psalm 139.

Where can I go from Your Spirit? Or where can I flee from Your presence? If I ascend to heaven, You are there. If I make my bed in Sheol, behold, You are there. If I take the wings of the dawn, if I dwell in the remotest part of the sea, even there Your hand will lead me, and Your right hand will lay hold of me. If I say, "Surely the darkness will overwhelm me, and the light around me will be night," even the darkness is not dark to You, and the night is as bright as the day. Darkness and light are alike to You.

Nathan felt like he'd been punched in the gut. *I've been trying to hide, but it's impossible. In the darkness of my grief and anger, I was overwhelmed—but that was because I didn't look to the Light and hold fast to Him. People told me that, but I didn't listen.*

The memory of Lick's disobedience came back to him in a whole new light. He'd called, and Lick had ignored him; he'd commanded, and finally, when Lick did come, he'd petted and praised him—hoping it would make it easier for Lick to come back the next time. *And I've ignored God's voice. He's beckoned me, wooed me, called to me. . .yet He will still have a place for me like the father did for his prodigal son.*

"Nathan?" He hadn't heard Kip come back in the tent. Kip hunkered down beside him. "Do you need time alone, or do you need a brother right now?"

"I've been so bitter at God instead of holding fast to Him." His voice cracked. "I've been such a fool."

Kip sat down and gently pulled the Bible from him. He glanced down at the page, then looked up somberly. "David was a champion repenter. He messed up so many times. He went against God's will, but he knew the Lord's forgiveness was his if he confessed his sins and truly sought to restore his relationship. Is that how you're feeling?"

Tears burned Nathan's eyes. He barely choked out, "Yes."

Kip ran his stubby finger along the last verses of that chapter as he read aloud, "Search me, O God, and know my heart; Try me and know my anxious thoughts; And see if there be any hurtful way in me, And lead me in the everlasting way."

"That makes it all sound so simple."

"It is. You're complicating it. God knows you. He was waiting for you to turn to Him. His arms are wide open."

Someone slapped the side of the tent. "Supper's on!"

"Be there in a minute," Kip called.

Nathan grasped his hand. "Pray with me first."

❧

"Who was on the phone?" Vanessa came out of the bathroom with a towel wrapped around her head.

"Dad called." Jeff lay on his belly on the floor, his brow furrowed with concentration as he arranged several plastic figurines in specific places. "He said he'll call again tomorrow. I told him I'm fine."

"Good. I'm going to go start supper." Vanessa stood in the hallway for a second and sagged against the wall. *They're fine, but I'm not.*

Staying in Nathan's home was a huge mistake. She'd been sleeping in the guest bedroom next to Jeff's, but even it carried Evie's stamp. No matter where she turned, Vanessa felt the lingering ghost of Nathan's wife—in the silk pansy arrangement on the bedside table, the Battenburg lace comforter and curtains, the kitchen's pink flowered dishes, floor, and wallpaper. Nathan couldn't bear to change Jeff's room, even though it looked woefully infantile. The first thing Vanessa did was to shut the door to Nathan's bedroom. A pair of portraits hung in there—one of Evie in her wedding gown, and another of her and Nathan.

Father, I went into this with the right intentions. Where did I go wrong?

She rewrapped her turban and dragged herself downstairs. Consuelo normally came in to do the housekeeping and laundry, but she had the flu. Vanessa tried to keep the house picked up as she went along, but between Jeff and Licorice, it wasn't a successful operation. She tucked his book bag against the couch, out of the way of traffic, and made a mental note that he still had to take a ruler to class tomorrow.

With Consuelo sick, Jeff didn't have anyone to go pick him up after school or watch him until Vanessa got off work. She juggled her schedule so Jamie was at the shop for the twenty minutes each afternoon that it took for her to zip over to the school and back. Jeff would do his homework in the back room, show it to Vanessa, then help her out with filling water bowls or playing with the animals. The makeshift arrangement actually worked out fairly smoothly.

Vanessa headed into the kitchen. Somewhere along the line, she'd gathered that Nathan's culinary skills encompassed the vital ability to open cans and microwave frozen foods. All week long, Jeff sat wide-eyed at the table as she put home-cooked meals in front of him. Tonight, she didn't have the energy. She opened a can of chili.

As it heated on the stove, the phone rang.

"I've got it!" Jeff shouted from the stairs. He rocketed across the living room and snagged the receiver. In a breathless voice, he said, "Hellowhoisthis?"

Vanessa bit her lip. Maybe they should talk about phone manners tonight at dinner.

"Van, it's for you."

She took the phone. "Hello?"

"Vanessa, this is Dave."

Dave. Dave from Guide Dogs. . . She mentally placed him and said, "Yes?"

"I've got a tough one for you. They're starting a new training session up at the facility on Monday. One of the dogs they were going to use just got held back. He got into a tussle with an unleashed boxer."

"He didn't get injured, did he?"

For all of their work, the hardest thing the puppy raisers had to deal with was unleashed dogs. They disrupted all but the most polished, obedient, mature puppies, and even then, it could be dicey.

"No, but we think he needs another couple of months of citizen training before we put him through the program. You've done a marvelous job with Amber, and I'd like to go ahead and slip her ahead into that position."

Vanessa drew in a quick breath.

"I know we had her slated to go in six weeks, Van." He spoke quietly, his words measured with understanding of the sacrifice he asked. Vanessa knew he'd raised a puppy and relinquished it—he knew firsthand how much it hurt. "It's hard to let them go, even with a target date."

She let out a long, choppy breath. "Is there any other candidate you could have go?"

"That last trip we all made to Disneyland is what made me think of you. Amber performed like a pro. She got on and off the Haunted Mansion and Pirates of the Caribbean like she'd been on them a million times. When that little girl came up and yanked on her tail, she showed exceptional tolerance too."

Vanessa remembered that trip. The puppy training club went on monthly outings to socialize and to expose the dogs to challenging situations. She'd posed Amber with characters for photos, sat on Main Street and watched the parade, and had been proud that Amber didn't bat an eye at the huge draft horses pulling a trolley.

In a small voice, she said, "So Amber passed the final, and

I didn't even know it was an exam."

"It wasn't meant to be, Van."

"I know. You've always been right up front with me. It's heartache talking. You know me." She laughed sadly. "Always talking before I think."

"I'll make the flight arrangements and get back to you. You've done a fine job, and someone is going to be lucky to have Amber as their guide dog."

"Thanks, Dave." She tearfully whispered, "Bye," and quickly hung up the phone.

"Van?" Jeff tugged on the hem of her sleeve. "What's wrong?"

"Everything."

❧

Nathan scowled at his cell phone. He'd accidentally left it on, and the charge was almost shot. He dialed home. "Van? Listen, my battery's almost gone. I won't be able to call tomorrow. How are things going?"

"Jeff's over at the Wilsons's for Caleb's pizza party."

"I forgot about that! I didn't get a present."

"I called Caleb's mom to get approval. He's now the proud owner of a second hamster."

"I owe you, big time. How about you?" Just then, his cell phone let out a pitiful beep. "Van? Van?"

He kicked a small stone, sending it flying into a metal trash can. The *ping* wasn't loud enough to tattle on his frustration, but Nathan hated having to wait to tell Vanessa his good news. Then again, he smiled to himself, it's the kind of news best given in person.

The next day, hundreds of tools rattled in the back of the truck. At one of the preplanning meetings, he'd assessed what folks were taking and deduced their team was grossly under supplied. His construction company had donated materials, and he'd packed a generator and all sorts of power and hand tools in his truck. He hit a pothole, and everything made another loud *clunk*. Nathan didn't care. Normally, he took pains to treat his tools well, but it didn't matter this time. He was going home, and he wanted to get there as soon as possible.

Kip understood. He'd helped Nathan pitch the tools in and shoved him toward the cab. "I'll take down the tent. You go on ahead and get home. You have someone waiting for you. . .and I don't mean Jeff."

Nathan had paused for an instant and given Kip a searching look.

"Vanessa is yours, Buddy." Kip lifted his blistered hands in a gesture of surrender. "I gave it a try, but I know when to quit. You're the right man for her. Now that you squared things away with God, there's nothing standing in the way. Go home. Make her a happy woman."

Nathan remembered Kip's words as he pulled onto his housing tract. Everything had fallen into place. Life had a sense of rightness. A neighbor was mowing his lawn, and a few kids were tossing a Frisbee. His son and the woman he loved were just a street away.

Instead of the welcome he expected, his reception was anything but delirious. Vanessa sat on the steps with her arm around Amber. Jeff sat on the other side of the retriever. All three of them looked glum.

Nathan had barely jammed his truck into "Park" when he bolted over to them. "What's wrong?"

Jeff popped up and gave him a hug. "Van has to give Amber back."

Vanessa's pretty blue eyes were red rimmed and puffy. If ever she needed comfort, now was the time. Nathan plopped down beside her and slid his arm around her shoulders. "When?"

"Tomorrow."

Even choking out that one word stretched her. Nathan could scarcely stand seeing her hurt. He tilted her head onto his shoulder and whispered into her soft, golden hair, "You can keep her if you really want to, can't you?"

Vanessa shook her head. "I gave my word. From the day I got her, I knew I'd have to let go."

"She's being honor'ble, Dad."

"Yes, Sport, she is." He wondered aloud, "How are you going to do it?"

She lifted her head and looked at him. Tears glistened in her eyes. "God loved His Son supremely—but when it came time for mankind to stop walking in darkness, to shed spiritual blindness, God sent his beloved Son to lead us to eternal freedom. It was an unspeakable sacrifice—but I'm eternally grateful for it."

He let her talk, not knowing where she was going, but willing to let her talk if it gave her any comfort.

"Each time I've given up a guide puppy I've trained, I've remembered God's sacrifice for my soul. I've had to trust Him to give me consolation. He's been faithful, and that's why I've always taken on another puppy. By giving up Amber, someone who lives in darkness can find liberty. It's nowhere near the scope of the Lord's sacrifice, but drawing that parallel helps me let go because God proved that by giving, we're set free. I'm just following His example."

Tears ran down her pale cheeks. Nathan wrapped her in his arms and held her as she cried. He'd spent the last months thinking she was so innocent in her faith, yet she'd been far wiser than he'd been. She'd let God come alongside her in her times of loss. Oh, to be sure, the loss of a guide puppy didn't in any way equate with his losing Evie, but the God who cared about the lilies of the field and counted every hair on a man's head certainly covered every concern with His love.

Vanessa sniffled and pushed away.

"Van, we need to talk." He wanted to tell her his good news, to maybe shed some light in the midst of her sadness.

"No." She dipped her head. "I need time alone with Amber. I really need to go."

"Can't you stay just a little while? Maybe I could take a quick shower, and we could go out for supper."

"No."

"I'll drive you home. You shouldn't be driving right now."

"I need to drive. It'll help me clear my head." She flipped a swath of hair behind her shoulder and stood. Pasting on a smile that was anything but genuine, she said, "Jeff is a terrific kid. You can be proud of him."

"I'll help you put your stuff in the car."

She pulled her key ring from the pocket of her jeans. "Jeff already helped me. I need to go. G'bye."

He fought the urge to snatch her back, to hold her and let her pour out every last tear. She wanted to spend this last night alone with Amber, and she deserved that. Nathan stood on the porch and watched her drive off. If he had his way, she wouldn't be doing that again.

❧

Amber sensed something was wrong. She gently nosed Vanessa. That action opened the floodgates. Vanessa sat on the floor by her bed, wrapped her arms around her puppy, buried her face in her fur, and wept. Everything in her life felt like it was falling apart. She had no one to blame but herself.

She'd chosen to take on this puppy. All along, she'd known the time would come to give her up. What kind of fool was she to keep setting herself up for this kind of parting?

And then there was Nathan. The tears flowed even faster,

wetting Amber's soft coat. Mom and Dad and Val and even Kip had warned her. They'd each come to her and discussed their concerns. *Oh, but did I listen? No.*

In the week that she'd cared for Jeff, she'd come to realize how much she adored him. The feeling was obviously mutual. He was a great kid. Cute. Smart. Tenderhearted, grubby faced, and ultimately lovable.

The first few nights, she'd looked forward to a cell phone call from Nathan. Then she'd grown to dread them. As she stayed in his home, the truth became undeniable. What started out as an innocent business arrangement had ensnared her, and she couldn't let the relationship continue.

Vanessa had to face the heart-wrenching fact that she'd unwisely let her heart get ahead of her spiritual welfare. A huge ball formed in her throat.

God, I've been so foolish, so arrogant. All along, I thought I was in control of my feelings. Ever since I accepted You, I knew I was meant to fall in love with a man who wanted to serve You as much as I did. In my dreams, we were going to have a marriage based on You as our foundation.

I didn't listen. Mom and Dad came to me. Val tried to talk sense into me, and Kip even confronted me. Instead of listening to wise counsel, I charged ahead. I really thought I was doing the right thing. I wore my faith as a shield and thought it would serve as a barrier against any heartbreak. How wrong I've been!

I love him, God. I do. I hate to admit it to myself and to confess it to You. How did I come to this point? In the past, I'd been so positive about setting my affections on a man who was on fire for Your kingdom. Nathan is burned out, yet I want him.

I know I have to make a choice. Nothing can come between me and You. Abraham faced having to choose, and he was willing to sacrifice Isaac. You gave Your Son. Nathan professes to still be Your child, but he isn't walking with You. What kind of home would we have if the foundation isn't built on Your will and holy Word? If my husband isn't following You, how can he lead me? What about any children we'd have? I know it's wrong. Father, I know it's so very wrong.

But in my heart, I long for Nathan to be restored to You. His bitterness has faded into. . .emotionless acceptance. It's progress, but it isn't enough. I have faith You can reclaim him. Until he comes to that point, I see how I cannot let the love I feel flourish. I don't know how to stop it. I've never understood how Abraham could put his son on the altar. Can't you work a miracle for me, just as you did for him?

Give me strength to cling to You and let go of Nathan. Help me make the right choices. Give me the courage to let go.

No grand or glorious thing happened. She didn't feel a blanket of peace descend. If anything, her prayer only served to sharpen her awareness of just where she stood. Tears burned behind her eyelids, and a deep ache radiated behind her breastbone.

She'd hoped for a fleeting moment that Nathan would say something when she spoke about giving Amber away, but he'd been silent.

Even if he did reestablish a firm relationship with the Lord, Nathan still loved Evie. His heart belonged to the woman who had borne his child. So did his home—their home, the charming little saltbox Evie rescued on their honeymoon and Nathan lovingly reconstructed for her. Every single room still looked as she'd decorated it. Her pictures hung on walls and sat in frames on tables. All of the patience in the world wouldn't erase his memories, and Vanessa came to the conclusion she simply couldn't shadowbox the rest of her life with a memory.

Amber. Strike one. Nathan's soul. Strike two. Nathan's heart. Strike three.

Vanessa tipped her head back and stared at the ceiling. The light fixture wavered and formed a halo because of her tears. "God, I've struck out. I can't do this on my own. What more do You want from me?"

twenty

"Vanessa, let me drive you and Amber to the airport."

"Thanks, Nathan. It's nice of you to offer, but I have to do this myself."

"Honey—"

"I need to go. Bye." She hung up. Putting the bright green jacket on Amber was hard. It was yet another "last time" thing she was doing today. "You're a big girl now. You'll go to doggy college and wear a blue jacket."

Secretly, there was that selfish wish that Amber would go and "flunk out." Then, she could come back forever. . . . Vanessa clenched her eyes shut to keep from crying. *God, I really don't want to be that kind of person. Make me bigger than my selfish desires.*

Amber usually traveled in passenger compartments. She'd been on a plane twice and on a boat, busses, trains, even a hay wagon. Today was different. At the airport, Vanessa stayed with her until the very last moment, gave her a hug and kiss, and put her in a dog crate. She wept as they took Amber off to the plane, cried all of the way home, and flung herself across her bed. She lay at the very edge, her fingertips brushing the edge of Amber's bed. It was as empty as her aching heart.

❧

Nathan had tried to contact Vanessa a half-dozen times in the last twenty-four hours, and she'd given him every version of a polite brush-off he'd ever seen. He wasn't going to put up with it any longer.

Nathan chuckled under his breath. Vanessa, impulsive in so many ways, managed to model patience. Today, he was the impulsive one, and he had no patience left. He strode to her door with resolve, gave it three solid raps, and jangled the keys in his pocket as he waited for her to answer. She didn't come, so he banged on the door a few more times. Still no response.

Unwilling to give up, he hiked around the corner of her place and drummed his fingers on her bedroom window. When he'd helped move Val out, he'd had a conniption that they were on a ground floor with no security. He'd come back and put in a security window. Now, he wished he hadn't.

One side of the curtain inched back. "Whaddo you want?"

"Doing that well, huh?"

The curtains opened wider, revealing a very sleepy woman bundled in a robe the color of shamrocks. Nathan thought she looked as if someone tackled her and wrapped her up in AstroTurf. She'd never looked better to him. She scrubbed her face with her palm, then swept her wild hair back behind her left ear. "Do you have any idea what time it is?"

"Time to talk. Get dressed."

"Nathan, go home."

"No can do. Hurry up."

She turned to the side and wheeled back around. Her eyes were huge. "It's five-fifteen. Are you crazy? Who's watching Jeff?"

"Val is. I know what time it is, and we'll be late if you don't get a move on."

"The only place I'm going is back to bed." The curtains swished shut.

Nathan chuckled. He didn't doubt for a minute she'd be headed right back to bed, but he wasn't about to let her do it. He drummed his fingers on the window.

"Go away!" came the muffled shout.

A set of sprinklers started on the far side of the lawn. *I'm going to get soaked. May as well be a fool for love. . . .* He cleared his throat and began to sing. "It's rain-ing, it's pour-ing, the old man is—"

The curtains didn't open. Vanessa popped up from beneath them like a crazed jack-in-the-box and flipped the safety latch on the window. Her cheeks glowed scarlet. As she opened the double-thick, shatterproof pane, she hissed hotly, "If you had any sense at all, you'd just leave." She drew in a breath and added, "Can't you see the sprinklers are coming on?"

"Why do you think I'm singing this song?"

"I have no idea. I didn't recognize it as music. The first time you sang it with Jeff was cute, but this is irri—"

"Jeans and a sweatshirt, Van. Put 'em on and meet me at the front door." He glanced down at his wristwatch. "You have ten minutes."

"You have ten seconds to go away before I call the police. You're disturbing my peace!"

"Nine minutes."

She huffed and shut the window. He heard her mattress squeak.

Four minutes later, he used his cell phone and called her. "Five minutes, and I have chocolate."

❧

He'd given her five minutes. . .like he had any right to make any dictates to her. Still, he had her so tied in knots, she wasn't going to get back to sleep, anyway. Vanessa clambered out of bed and headed toward her closet. He'd specified jeans and a sweatshirt, but she wasn't going anywhere. Not at this hour. Not with him. She yanked on jeans, but her sweatshirts were in the bottom drawer over where Amber's empty bed lay. She couldn't go over there right now. Not a chance. She'd start crying all over again. Instead, Vanessa rummaged through her closet and pulled out a T-shirt that was as blue as she felt.

In her haste, she broke her shoelace. "Ohh!" She flung that shoe across the room and listened to the satisfying *thump* it made as it hit the floor right next to her shoe rack. Even in her frustration, at least she managed to keep her aim true. She scowled at her feet and hobbled over to that shoe rack. "Oh, forget it." She stopped looking and twist-stepped into big, rainbow-striped, fuzzy slippers.

Nathan Adams was about to get a piece of her mind. "Let's go." As soon as she said the command for Amber, she realized for the millionth time that Amber was gone. All of those things she said and did as a puppy trainer were empty gestures and phrases now—and painful reminders of the loss she'd sustained. A fresh wave of grief washed over her.

Nathan knocked at the front door.

Vanessa marched over, jerked open the front door, and gave him a belligerent look. How dare he show up at this ridiculous hour at all, let alone looking like that? Freshly shaven, lounging against her door frame, he could have just stepped from a magazine ad.

"Good morning, Sweetheart."

"Give me the chocolates, and you might not get hurt."

"They're in the car." He grabbed hold of her wrist and yanked.

Vanessa struggled to free herself. "What in the world are you doing?"

"Kidnapping you."

"You're nuts. I don't want to go anywhere or do anything. Just leave me alone."

He tilted his head to the side, and his dark brown eyes shone with compassion. "Hiding out won't take away the pain, Honey."

"Neither will running all over the place."

"True, but I have special plans. You'll have to trust me." He glanced down and shook his head. "I've got an extra sweatshirt in the car, but those slippers won't do."

"Just what is wrong with my slippers?" She folded her arms across her chest and tapped her toe.

"They'll get wet when you walk across the lawn."

"I'm not walking across the lawn!"

Nathan gave her a don't-be-difficult look. All of a sudden, he ducked, rammed his shoulder into her middle, and wrapped his arm around the backs of her legs. When he straightened up, she dangled over his shoulder like a rag doll. She turned her head to the side, saw him snatch her key ring from the hall table, then dizzily watched as he pulled the door shut and locked it.

She tried to stay calm. "What are you doing?"

"We've already discussed that. I'm kidnapping you and your goofy slippers. I'm even making sure they don't get wet."

A considerate kidnapper. She'd chalk this all up as another one of her wild nightmares, but blood rushed to her head. It pulsed and made her ears ring, proving she really was awake and Nathan truly had gone 'round the bend. "Let me get this straight. Valene is with Jeff and knows you're doing this?"

"Yup. So do your parents."

"Now I've heard everything."

"Almost. I've arranged for Jamie and your mom to mind the shop today."

"Great." She tried to catch her breath. It wasn't exactly an easy thing to do in this position. "I'm getting abducted by approval."

Nathan's shoulder shook as he chortled, and the action made her bounce. *It would serve him right if I threw up all over his legs. He's having far too much fun, and I don't want to play this game.*

"Really, Nathan, take me back. I'm lousy company right now."

"I'll take you however you come." He stopped, opened the car door, and lowered her inside with surprising care instead of dumping her like a sack of cement. He slammed her door shut, zipped around the car, and slid into the driver's seat.

Just then, Vanessa caught sight of herself in the visor's mirror and let out a breathless shriek. "Okay, the joke's over. I'm going back inside."

He started the car and put it into motion before she could open her door. "Buckle up, and the chocolate is in the glove compartment."

"I haven't brushed my hair. I don't have any makeup on, and I'm wearing slippers!"

"Yeah, so?" He shifted and pulled a black comb from his pocket. "Borrow this. Eat the chocolate."

She made a rude huff as she accepted the comb. The man needed to get his head examined if he thought this was going to mollify her.

"You're a natural beauty, Sweetheart. You don't need a bunch of stuff all over your pretty face, and as for your slippers. . ." He let go of the steering wheel momentarily and lifted his palms in an "oh well" gesture.

Vanessa pulled the comb through her tangles and gave him a disgruntled look. Leave it to him to give her a compliment on a morning like this. Clueless. The man was utterly clueless. Good thing too. It meant she could stay mad at him about this escapade and use it as an excuse to distance herself and cool the relationship.

"So ask me about what I found in Mexico."

"Obviously you lost your wits."

"This is important, Van."

"Sure it is," she said flippantly. She tossed his comb onto the dashboard and rooted around in the glove compartment for the chocolate. Nothing. She unbuckled her seat belt and twisted around.

"You're not listening to me."

Desperation had her rummaging through the stuff he had stored in the backseat. She didn't want to face him right now. "You promised me chocolate."

Nathan's baritone filled the car:

> " 'When peace like a river attendeth my way,
> When sorrows like sea billows roll,
> Whatever my lot, Thou hast taught me to say,
> It is well, it is well, with my soul.' "

Vanessa twisted around and stared at him. She clamped her hand around his arm and squeezed. "What?"

He gave her a soul-stirring smile. "I found my way back. My relationship with Christ is on track again."

"Oh, praise God!"

"The hurt and anger are gone, Van. I realized what a fool I was for blaming God for robbing me of my wife. Evie was His child, and He called her home. For a time, I was blessed to have her to love. I've mourned for her, and I'll always miss her, but now I can be at peace, knowing she's whole and healthy in heaven."

Vanessa took a deep breath. She didn't want to hear about Evie. Even the mere mention of her name was like a dagger through her heart, but how selfish was that? Nathan was freed of his shackles, and that was what was important. He'd begun to heal spiritually.

"Wow. Answered prayer."

"I know you were faithful to pray for me, Van." He gave her a piercing look, then trained his gaze back on the road. "I managed to push away everyone else, but you were different.

You didn't push back or walk away. You've stuck around and let God work in His own way."

"So tell me about how God finally got through to you!"

"It's been so subtle—gradual, you know? At first, I couldn't stand anything having to do with worshiping Him. All of the essentials for a strong walk stopped cold. But God's used you to patiently reintroduce them to me: associating with believers, prayer, attending church." He hitched his shoulder. "The final step was down in Mexico. Kip got me to start reading God's Word again."

"Kip's a great friend, Nathan."

"Yeah, he is—to me. What about you?"

Father, how do I respond to this? The biggest hurdle is behind us—Nathan is Yours. With time, can he let go of Evie and learn to love me? Do I play it safe and tell him Kip is just a friend, or do I focus on the relationship that may or may not ever blossom between me and this man?

Vanessa took a deep breath and looked Nathan in the eye. "I hope I'm a great friend to you too."

His rich, deep laughter filled the cab. Vanessa had the feeling she'd mistakenly answered Nathan's question the wrong way, but nothing mattered this morning.

"I finally realized the truth—I'd been longing for what was right in front of me all of those years. I was like a blind man, wandering around in darkness. I let anger and grief come between me and God instead of letting Him be my strength and solace at the darkest time in my life. Now I've come back to the Light. God's restored my spirit—just as he did for David in the Psalms."

"I'm so happy for you, Nathan."

"It's the craziest thing. I kept thinking the emptiness and loneliness were because I was a widower. I'm still a widower, but I can see that when grief should have started to wane, I stayed so empty because I'd shut down spiritually. You have no idea how free I feel."

His news started to fully sink in. He hadn't just made a decision with his mind—his heart and soul were behind it. The joy flowing from him touched her deeply.

"You once said God was bigger than my anger," Nathan continued. "I had plenty of people tell me I was a sinner for that; you were patient with me and let God chip away at my hardened heart. He is bigger than anything that I am or feel or do. But the other thing is, He doesn't expect me to pretend—He already knows how I feel, so I can live honestly before Him."

Vanessa nodded.

"I'm not trapped in the past anymore, Vanessa."

"The chains are broken. I'm glad for you."

He'd zipped down the freeway and turned onto a winding dirt road. Now he made a sharp hairpin and another wild jog to one side. A hot-air balloon came into sight.

"Oh, look!"

Nathan parked the truck and turned to her. "I wanted to celebrate with you in a special way. Let's go."

Still stunned by everything he'd said, Vanessa got out of the car when he opened her door. She watched him yank a paint-splattered, maroon sweatshirt from the back of his truck and gladly accepted it. Once she pulled it over her head, he slipped his strong hand along the back of her neck and freed her hair. The sudden warmth felt good in the nippy morning air, but she wasn't sure whether it was from the sweatshirt, his good news, or his touch.

"Come on." He took her hand and led her all of one step, then stopped. He looked down at her slippers and shook his head. "Upsy-daisy."

Vanessa let out a surprised squeal as he scooped her into his arms.

Nathan carried her toward the balloon and stopped briefly to speak with one of the men who seemed to be directing the busy ground crew. Seemingly satisfied, Nathan gave her a squeeze and carried her to the basket.

"Ready to go?" the operator inside the basket shouted above the din.

Nathan raised a brow as he looked at her. She nodded enthusiastically, so he lifted her into the basket, then climbed in beside her. He stood close in the tight quarters and bumped a picnic basket with his knee. He pointed down, then put his mouth by her ear and half-shouted, "Once we get underway, you can have some coffee. I ordered breakfast for us."

"Breakfast on thin air? How fun!"

The basket shifted a bit beneath their feet. Vanessa grabbed one of the lines. Nathan grabbed her. She didn't mind one bit.

Filled with hot air, the balloon barely started to rise. "Away we go!" someone said from behind her. The noise from the burners ripped through the air and made any conversation virtually impossible. The ground seemed to fall away and their balloon continued to rise. The movement felt smooth, but the height change seemed almost dizzying. Soon Nathan's car resembled one of Jeff's toys. A stand of trees looked like frilled toothpicks. As they reached cruising altitude, the noise from the burners diminished.

"Isn't this outta sight?" Nathan's arm around her waist tightened.

"Amazing! I've always wanted to ride in one of these!" She let go of one of the lines and reached out. "I almost feel like I can touch the clouds from here."

Nathan turned her and held her close. His warmth and strength felt marvelous. Slowly, one of his hands slid up her back to her nape. He spread his fingers out and speared them through her hair, forcing her to face him.

Vanessa didn't want to look at him. If she did, he'd be able to read her like a book and know exactly how she felt about him. She tried to turn her head to the side. "Look at the horizon. We're going right toward the sunrise!"

"I don't need to look out there to see today or tomorrow." He exerted gentle pressure and had her staring up at him.

Vanessa could scarcely catch her breath.

"I'm already walking on clouds, Van, and when I look at you, I see all of the bright days ahead."

He caught her gasp with a toe-curling kiss. When he lifted his head, he smiled. "I've been wanting to do that for awhile."

"Oh, my."

"I've already gone to your dad and mom. We have their blessing."

"Their blessing," she echoed, hoping she understood his meaning but afraid she was letting her wishes run wild.

"I know this is our first date, but I'm going to court you for a lifetime. I can't wait, though." Nathan's arm cinched tighter around her waist. He dipped his head and nuzzled her ear. "Marry me, Vanessa."

"Was that a request or a command?"

"It's a requirement." He pulled away a little and pressed his forehead to hers. "Live with me and love with me and laugh with me. God fills my soul, but you fill my heart."

There under a zigzag rainbow fabric canopy, soaring toward a sunny day, Vanessa didn't have to give more than a second's consideration to his proposal. "Yes, Nathan. I'd love to be your wife."

"Seal it with a kiss," he said in a husky tone.

After a kiss that promised happily-ever-afters, he cuddled closer. "Happy?"

She nodded, stood on the tiptoes of her slippers, and wrapped her arms around his neck. "I never want to touch down. I've been going crazy, loving a man who was so blind."

He looked deeply into her eyes. "Sweetheart, I can see forever from here."

epilogue

Vanessa sat in the bride's room, brushed on a touch of mascara, and winked at Della. "I have a feeling you like these clothes better than our baseball uniforms."

Della fluffed her hair. "Don't you just know it? You taught me how to bat and how to snag a ball. Think you can teach me how to catch a husband?"

"We'll have to see if Nathan invited any good prospects. I'll have him introduce you and Valene to them at the reception."

Valene groaned.

Vanessa gave her twin a saucy smile in the mirror. "Guess what I just figured out?"

"What?" Valene adjusted the skirt of her smoky blue maid-of-honor dress until it hung with sheer grace.

Her twin had been fussing all morning, and Vanessa suspected it was because she hated to be on stage at all. Even being a maid of honor was more spotlight than she'd prefer to handle, but she filled the role because sisterly love trumped shyness. Vanessa decided to tease her to help lighten her anxiety.

"When we walk down the aisle, it's the last time in my life I'm going to be the last one. Alphabetically, I've always been dead last."

Della snorted. "What did you expect? With a last name like Zobel, you were sunk."

"No kidding," Val agreed.

"Yeah, but you still came before me," Vanessa said to her sister. "Val, then Van. My married name will be Adams." She stood and twirled about in her rustling satin slips. "And the last shall come first. . . ."

Mom made a worried sound and started to take the bridal gown off of the hanger. "If you don't get into this gown, you're not going to be first or last. You'll be an old maid."

"Are you kidding? Nathan would marry me if I walked out there in my ugly orange baseball uniform. He proposed to me in my rainbow slippers."

Della gave her a silly look. "Let me get this straight. He was wearing your slippers?"

"And you all think I'm daffy? Of course he wasn't. Have you seen the size of his feet? I was wearing them when he kidnapped me. It was so romantic."

Val held part of the bridal gown, and Della took hold of another section. "Come on. Let's get this woman into her gown before she gets so besotted with those stupid slippers, she wants to get married in them." They lifted the gown so Vanessa could slip into it.

As Val started to do up the zipper of the dreams-come-true satin-and-lace bridal gown, Vanessa worried aloud, "You all have everything you need, right? Jeff will stay with Val for the next few days, then he'll go stay with Mom and Dad. Mom, you and Dad will stop by Nathan's and get Lick tonight? He'll tear up Val's condo. He needs your big back-yard to romp in."

"Stop worrying," Val chided. "You're chewing off your lip-stick."

"Girlfriend, you need to get your head examined." Della shook her finger at Van. "You're going off on a romantic honeymoon to Ireland and Scotland, and you're fretting about a dumb dog?"

"That dog and a silly goldfish are what brought them together," Valene said loyally.

"Yes." Vanessa dipped down so her mother could help her pin on an airy veil. She left the blusher veil back out of the way for the present. "And so did the grace and mercy of God."

Someone tapped on the door. Della opened it.

Dad stuck his head into the room. "We're ready."

Jeff nudged past him and stared up at Vanessa. His little mouth dropped open. He blinked, then said in an awed tone, "You look like a fairy princess."

"Yes, Kitten, you do." Her father's voice sounded choked.

Jeff walked all the way around her and asked, "Do I get to call you 'Mom' now?"

"That would make me so happy!"

"Okay, Mom. Daddy said he wanted you to hurry up. He said he's waited long enough for his sweetheart. Did you know that's what he called you?"

"Yes." She smiled at the way Jeff wrinkled his nose. At the rehearsal the day before, Nathan had been eager to sweep her into a theatrical dip and give her a heart-stopping kiss. Jeff ended it all with a loud, "Eww, yuck!" Nathan later borrowed her strawberry lip gloss and let Jeff take a whiff. After that, Jeff decided his dad hadn't gone crazy, after all. His favorite bubble gum smelled like that. Nathan then had extracted a pledge from his "honor'ble" son that he wouldn't make any noises during the real wedding ceremony.

They all went to the narthex. Mom gave Vanessa one last kiss and allowed Kip to seat her before he took his place as best man. The music started, and Jeff carried a satin pillow with the rings tied to it. He stopped partway down the aisle to scratch his knee, then continued on with all the decorum of an English butler.

Della stepped off, and Val turned to Vanessa. She didn't say a word. She didn't need to. They'd always been able to communicate at moments like this with just a look. She nodded, smiled, and headed down the aisle.

"Kitten, he's a good man, a godly man. I had some real doubts awhile back, but I know he's the man I prayed for God to bring to you."

"Thank you, Daddy." She gave him a kiss, accepted his fumbling help to pull down her blusher veil, and took his arm.

Vanessa walked down the aisle with every assurance that waiting for this moment was worth every prayer she'd ever whispered. When she could see Nathan at the front of the church, she knew she'd never known a more handsome man. Love and happiness shone in his eyes. Daddy gave her away, and she stood beside Nathan, then knelt at the altar.

They'd consulted and counseled with Pastor MacIntosh, and now he began to read the Scripture they'd requested for their wedding. It was from 1 Corinthians:

"Love is patient. . . ."

A Letter To Our Readers

Dear Reader:

In order that we might better contribute to your reading enjoyment, we would appreciate your taking a few minutes to respond to the following questions. We welcome your comments and read each form and letter we receive. When completed, please return to the following:

Fiction Editor
Heartsong Presents
PO Box 719
Uhrichsville, Ohio 44683

1. Did you enjoy reading *Love Is Patient* by Cathy Marie Hake?
❏ Very much! I would like to see more books by this author!
❏ Moderately. I would have enjoyed it more if

_____

_____

_____

2. Are you a member of **Heartsong Presents**? ❏ Yes ❏ No
If no, where did you purchase this book? _____

_____

3. How would you rate, on a scale from 1 (poor) to 5 (superior), the cover design? _____

4. On a scale from 1 (poor) to 10 (superior), please rate the following elements.

____ Heroine		____ Plot	
____ Hero		____ Inspirational theme	
____ Setting		____ Secondary characters	

5. These characters were special because?_____

_____

_____

6. How has this book inspired your life?_____

_____

_____

7. What settings would you like to see covered in future
   Heartsong Presents books? _____

_____

_____

8. What are some inspirational themes you would like to see
   treated in future books? _____

_____

_____

9. Would you be interested in reading other **Heartsong
   Presents** titles? ❑ Yes ❑ No

10. Please check your age range:
    ❑ Under 18   ❑ 18-24
    ❑ 25-34   ❑ 35-45
    ❑ 46-55   ❑ Over 55

Name_____

Occupation _____

Address _____

City_____ State_____ Zip_____

VANCOUVER

What's the best thing about living in a beautiful modern city— being surrounded by buildings, people, and activity? Or just getting away from it all? Meet four women who hold differing views of life in Canada's jeweled city.

Laugh and cry with these resourceful Canadian women and watch how faith and love uphold them on drifting currents of life.

Contemporary, paperback, 480 pages, 5 ³/₁₆" x 8"

CONTENTS

PART ONE
THE BASICS

PART TWO

RECIPES

Introduction

A few vegetables, some meat or seafood if desired, and water or stock: Soups are both as simple as that, and as complex as you choose to make them. Their deliciousness and variety are limited only by your imagination and the ingredients available, making them some of the most useful and versatile dishes in the cook's repertoire.

Soups have come a long way from their origins as humble staples, made from whatever meager ingredients were at hand. Now they range from quick snack to family meal to gourmet indulgence. Their versatility lends itself to myriad interpretations: a hearty and nutritionally balanced one-bowl meal, a chilled soup for a hot day, a delicate consommé to stimulate the palate, or a rich and creamy soup fit for an elegant dinner party.

These dishes are a boon to the busy cook, too, because although many soups require a long cooking time, they usually take little time to prepare. A bit of chopping, perhaps some sautéing, then it's time to sit back and relax while they cook,

filling the house with delicious aromas to whet the appetite for the meal ahead. Better still, most can be prepared ahead and then reheated with no deterioration in taste or texture. On the contrary, many soups improve in flavor when allowed to mature for a day or two before being served.

Another advantage of soups is that they are economical. They can be made with cheaper cuts of meat that benefit from long, slow simmering, becoming meltingly tender and imbued with the flavors of the vegetables with which they are cooked.

The book is divided into two parts. Part One covers the basics of making soups. It provides recipes for meat, chicken, fish, and vegetable stocks — the

flavorsome basis for all good soups. Also included are instructions on puréeing and storing stocks and soups.

Part Two presents over 120 recipes from around the world, from classics such as Wonton Soup and Lobster Bisque and contemporary recipes such as microwave Gingered Carrot Soup. Try Hanoi Beef and Noodle Soup from Vietnam, Italian-style Fish Soup, Seafood Gazpacho from Spain, or New England Clam Chowder. Also included are chilled soups and those cooked in the microwave oven.

With the Little Guide to *Soups*, you'll never be short of delicious mealtime inspiration.

U.S. cup measures are used throughout this book. Slight adjustments may need to be made to quantities if Imperial or Metric cups are used.

PART ONE

THE BASICS

This section tells you how to make full-flavored stocks to use as a basis for a variety of soups. Included are vegetable, chicken, beef, veal, and seafood stocks, as well as a quick microwave stock. There are also tips on equipment, and how to puree, strain, and store stock.

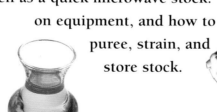

Different Types of Soups

Soups can be divided into several categories, according to their texture and ingredients. These are the main types:

Bisque Strictly speaking, the term bisque refers to a delicate soup made with seafood and cream. Shrimp and lobster are usually the stars of bisque. The stock on which bisque is based generally includes the shells of the seafood, which impart the essential color and flavor to the soup. In recent years, the term has broadened to include puréed vegetable soups as well.

Chowder This hearty soup typically contains seafood and/or vegetables. The base is a fish stock with tomato and/or cream.

Clear soups Many Chinese soups are of this type. They are much more substantial than consommé, and contain such ingredients as meat, seafood, vegetables, dumplings, and noodles in a rich-flavored broth.

Consommé (from the French, meaning to boil down or complete). This is soup at its most basic yet also its most refined. Consommé is a clear soup made from reduced stock. It is traditionally served as an appetizer, with or without additions, and may feature such items as a perfect ravioli, or delicate slices of vegetable.

Cream soups These are usually made with vegetables. Despite the name, they do not always contain cream. The common characteristic is that they have been puréed to a smooth, creamy consistency.

Gumbo A specialty of Louisiana, USA, this thick and hearty soup or stew is traditionally thickened either with okra or with filé powder (ground sassafras root). Its name is a corruption of *quin-gombo*, an African Congo word for okra. Gumbo is even better a day or two after it is made.

About Stocks and Broths

Stock, broth, and bouillon are all terms that describe an aromatic liquid produced by simmering vegetables and/or meat, plus herbs, in water for varying lengths of time. The resulting liquid is used as the basis for soups, sauces, gravies, and reductions. Because stock is the basis of other dishes, rather than a dish in its own right, it should be relatively bland, so as not to overwhelm other flavors, yet rich enough to add to the depth of flavor.

Onions, carrots, and celery are the traditional combination of aromatic vegetables used in stocks, but parsnip and swede are also good. The vegetables should be added sparingly about 30 minutes after the stock has begun to simmer and any scum that has risen to the surface has been skimmed off.

In some regional styles of cooking, the classic vegetable mixture varies. In parts of America, for example, the usual mix may include onions, bell peppers (capsicum), and celery. Mushrooms and leeks are also common. Fresh or dried herbs used include parsley, thyme, bay leaves, and peppercorns, in the form of a bouquet garni (see page 16). These flavor notes make an important contribution.

If you are in a hurry, there's no need to tie the seasonings in a bundle—simply toss them in with the vegetables.

Except when making vegetable stocks, it is best not to add salt during cooking. This makes it much easier to control the saltiness of the completed dish. The reduction process, during both the original simmering of the stock and any subsequent cooking of the soup, could concentrate the salt and spoil the dish. Vegetable stocks, however, being lighter in flavor, are rarely reduced, so you can add a small amount of salt during cooking to bring out the flavors:

Making Stocks and Broths

The quality of a stock is judged in terms of flavor and clarity. The best-flavored stocks are made with just enough water to cover the bones, shells, or vegetables. Additional water is needed only when it evaporates below the level of the ingredients before the stock is fully cooked. The following recipes give ideal ratios of liquid to solids, but the secret is simple: Keep the solids covered while cooking.

Cooking times for stock depend on how long it takes to extract all the good, rich flavor from the ingredients. Raw beef bones can be simmered for at least 8 hours to extract all their flavor, while chicken bones take much less time. Vegetable and fish stocks should be cooked much more quickly, because their delicate flavors deteriorate after about 30 or 40 minutes. Simmering the stock past the recommended cooking time can produce an unpleasant bitter taste, especially with fish stock.

When preparing vegetables and bones for making stock, it's a good idea to chop them to size according to the cooking time – large pieces for long cooking and small for quick cooking. This will allow the flavors to be fully extracted. To check if this has been accomplished, taste the meat from the stock. If it still has some flavor, allow the stock to simmer for longer. If the meat is tasteless and the bone joints are falling apart, it is time to strain the stock.

If a stock is lacking in flavor after straining, remove and discard the fat, then simmer the stock briskly to reduce the water content and concentrate the flavor. This technique, known as reduction, is used extensively in sauce making. It produces a stock with a deeper flavor. Reduction is not recommended for fish or vegetable stocks, because during the process

much of their aromatic, fresh taste is lost. Besides, not all dishes require a concentrated flavor. Sometimes a light stock is appropriate for its subtlety.

For dishes in which you want a hearty stock, first roast the bones and vegetables in a hot oven. Then transfer the bones and vegetables to the stockpot, pouring off the excess fat. Deglaze the roasting pan with wine or water by scraping up the browned, caramelized cooking juices—these have an intense flavor. Add the liquid to the stockpot. The resulting brown stock is darker and richer that a stock made by straight simmering, which is referred to as a white stock. This roasting technique is best used for meat and poultry stocks.

When choosing meat or bones for the stockpot, remember that meat adds flavor, while bones add body and give the stock a rich, smooth texture. This comes especially from the gelatinous joints (knuckles and shoulders) of young animals. Always use a combination of bones and meat, or look for very meaty bones. An economical way of making stock is to remove the meat or poultry from the pot before the stock is ready (while the meat still has some flavor) and serve it as a separate meal. The resulting stock will be lighter, but it can be used as is. Alternatively, return the bones to the pot after the meal and then cook the stock for a little longer.

Raw ingredients produce the best-flavored stock, but leftover meat or vegetables can be used. Leftover turkey carcasses, for example, make a fine stock.

The clarity of a stock is also important. A clear stock tastes clean and fresh, while a cloudy one may seem greasy and indistinct. The secret to a clear stock is to start with cold water, allow it to come slowly to the

boil, then immediately lower the temperature to barely simmering while you carefully skim off and discard any fat, or frothy scum containing impurities, that rises to the surface. This not only brings out the most flavor but also draws out impurities in the meat and bones that would otherwise cloud your stock. If the stock is allowed to boil, these impurities will, instead, be incorporated into the liquid. If time is short, a small batch of stock made quickly in the microwave may be a better option (see page 33), or consider using the quick beef stock recipe (page 27). Such recipes are great time savers.

Bouquet Garni

Small bunch of parsley or parsley stems

8 sprigs fresh thyme, or 1 teaspoon dried thyme

1 bay leaf

2 or 3 celery leaves (optional)

Herbs tend to float and get in the way as you skim the surface of your stock, so for greater convenience, tie them together in a little packet wrapped in a piece of cheesecloth (muslin). The contents of your bouquet garni can be varied to suit your dish, with additions such as whole cloves, dill, lemon zest, peppercorns, or garlic.

Tie the cheesecloth securely with a piece of kitchen string (this makes it easy to remove) or omit the cheesecloth and simply tie the herbs together by their stems.

Basic Tools and Utensils

Most kitchens have all the equipment needed to make stocks and soups, but you might like to invest in a specialized stockpot that is large enough to make batches of stock that you can freeze for later use. The best type of pot is tall and narrow, with a heavy base. Such pots allow the liquid to simmer away without too much evaporation, and are easier to skim. When making stock, just be sure the pot is large enough to hold the solids (bones, meat, shells, or vegetables) and enough water to cover them by 2 inches (5 cm). Avoid using an aluminum pot, which may react with some ingredients, spoiling the flavor.

Flameproof casseroles or wide soup pots also work well, as long as you add more water whenever the level drops below the solids. Using an 8–10 qt (8–10 l) stockpot, you can produce 2–4 qt (2–4 l) of stock at a time. A 4-qt (4-l) pot is about right for smaller batches.

A second large pot is handy for cooling strained stock; plastic containers will work, but as they insulate, the stock will not cool as quickly, which is important if you are planning to store it.

Little in the way of other special equipment is necessary. The basic tools called for are a ladle, a wooden spoon, and a sieve or colander large enough to catch the solids in the stock. Ideally, you should have two sieves, one coarse and one fine. The long-handled conical kind, called a chinois or China cap, is perfect, but a colander lined with a double layer of cheesecloth (muslin), or a layer of damp paper towels also works.

For brown stocks, you will need a large roasting pan, preferably with handles. Gravy separators, also called fat separators, are a convenient way to remove excess fat from stock when there is no time to chill the stock and let the fat solidify.

Vegetable Stock

2 tablespoons olive oil

1 cup (5 oz/155 g) diced carrot

¾ cup (4 oz/125 g) diced celery

¾ cup (2 oz/60 g) sliced leeks

1 small clove garlic

1 small red (Spanish) onion, cut in halves

12 oz (375 g) fresh white mushrooms, cut in halves

8 cups (64 fl oz/2 l) cold water

1 small plum (Roma) tomato, roughly chopped

½ teaspoon fresh thyme leaves or ¼ teaspoon dried thyme

½ teaspoon fresh marjoram leaves or ¼ teaspoon dried marjoram

4 sprigs fresh parsley

Salt and ground black pepper

Heat the oil in a saucepan over low heat. Add the carrot, celery, and leek and cook, stirring often, for 3–4 minutes, or until the vegetables are softened.

Add the garlic, onion, and mushrooms, and stir for 2 minutes, or until the onion has softened.

Add the water and bring to the boil. Using a large flat spoon, skim any scum from the surface. Add the tomato, thyme, marjoram, and parsley. Reduce the heat and simmer, uncovered, for 1 hour.

Strain the stock through a fine-mesh sieve lined with cheese-cloth (muslin) into an airtight container. Add salt and pepper to taste. Use immediately, or

cool, cover, and refrigerate for up to 3 days, or freeze in airtight containers for up to 3 months.

Makes 5 cups (40 fl oz/1.25 l)

Roasted Vegetable Stock

8 oz (250 g) fresh button mushrooms

1 onion, cut into fourths

2 carrots, peeled, and cut into chunks

8 cloves garlic, peeled, and crushed

1 small turnip, peeled, cut into chunks

7 cups (56 fl oz/1.75 l) water

1 bouquet garni, including sprigs of fresh herbs, such as parsley, thyme, oregano, and marjoram, plus a bay leaf and a pinch of crushed dried chili flakes (page 16)

Preheat the oven to 400°F (200°C/Gas Mark 5). Lightly grease a roasting pan, add the mushrooms, onion, carrot, garlic, and turnip, and toss well. Roast, turning occasionally, for about 1 hour, or until the vegetables are well browned.

Transfer the vegetables to a stockpot. Add 1 cup (8 fl oz/ 250 ml) of the water to the hot roasting pan and stir to deglaze the pan. Add this liquid to the stockpot along with the rest of the water and the bouquet garni. Simmer, uncovered, for 45–60 minutes, or until the vegetables are soft.

Strain the liquid through a fine-mesh sieve into an airtight container, pressing on the solids left in the sieve to extract as much liquid as possible. Allow to cool, then refrigerate until required (up to 3 days), or freeze in airtight containers for up to 3 months.

Makes 4 cups (32 fl oz/1 liter)

Chicken Stock

4–5½ lb (2–2.75 kg) chicken pieces (backs, necks, wings, legs, or thighs), or 1 whole roasting chicken, 4–5½ lb (2–2.75 kg), well rinsed

16 cups (4 qt/4 l) cold water, or just enough to cover

1 onion, coarsely chopped

1 carrot, peeled and coarsely chopped

1 stalk celery, coarsely chopped

1 bouquet garni (page 16)

Put the chicken pieces and water in a large stockpot. Bring to the boil over medium heat. Reduce the heat and simmer, skimming off any scum that rises to the surface, for about 30 minutes. Add the onion, carrot, celery, and bouquet garni. Simmer, uncovered, for 3 hours, adding water as needed to keep the ingredients covered. Strain into a clean pot or a heatproof plastic container. Cool quickly, uncovered, in a sink of ice water. Refrigerate until ready to use. Remove any fat that has solidified on top before using.

Makes about 12 cups (3 qt/3 l)

NOTE Using the lesser amount of chicken suggested here will result in a lighter stock, which will allow the flavor in many dishes to be more pronounced and less like chicken; the greater amount will yield a richer stock.

Lining the colander or sieve with cheesecloth (muslin) helps trap the fat, scum, and particles that make stock cloudy and impair its flavor.

STEP 1

Straining Stock

When the stock is cooked, remove from the heat and lift out the chicken pieces with tongs or a slotted spoon. Pour the stock through a large colander lined with 2 layers of cheesecloth (muslin) into a large bowl. Or, if you are making only a small amount of stock, you can strain it through a coffee filter. Cool the chicken pieces and remove the meat from the bones, if desired.

If you need to use the stock right away while it is still hot, blot up the liquid fat from its surface with a folded paper towel.

STEP 2

Removing Fat

Let the stock cool briefly, then refrigerate it for at least several hours, or overnight. With a large spoon or wire skimmer, skim off and discard the fat that has hardened into a layer on the surface of the stock.

Chicken stock
will keep, covered,
in the refrigerator
for up to 3 days.
Frozen stock can
be kept for up to
3 months.

STEP 3

Freezing Stock

After the fat has been removed, transfer 1-cup
(8-fl oz / 250-ml) portions of stock to freezer-safe,
heavy-duty plastic bags. Seal and date the bags, then
lay them on their sides on a tray; freeze, remove from
tray, and stack in the freezer until needed. Or, freeze
small portions of stock in ice-cube trays, release the
cubes, and store in labeled, dated, sealed plastic bags.

Roasted Chicken Stock

4–5½ lb (2–2.75 kg) chicken pieces (backs, necks, wings, legs, or thighs), or 1 whole roasting chicken, 4–5½ lb (2–2.75 kg), well rinsed

1 onion, coarsely chopped

1 carrot, peeled and coarsely chopped

1 stalk celery, coarsely chopped

16 cups (4 qt/4 l) cold water, or just enough to cover

1 bouquet garni (page 16)

Makes about 12 cups (3 qt/3 l)

Preheat the oven to 425°F (210°C/Gas Mark 7). Lightly grease a heavy roasting pan. Put the chicken parts and vegetables in the pan and roast, stirring occasionally, for about 1 hour, or until well browned.

Transfer the chicken and vegetables to a stockpot. Deglaze the roasting pan by adding 1 cup (8 fl oz/250 ml) of the water and scraping up any brown bits stuck to the pan. Add the liquid to the pot along with the remaining water and the bouquet garni.

Bring to a boil over medium heat, then reduce the heat and simmer for about 3 hours, skimming often during the first 30 minutes. Add more water as needed to keep the chicken and vegetables covered.

Strain into a clean pot or a heatproof plastic container. Cool quickly, uncovered, in a sink of ice water. Refrigerate until ready to use. Remove the fat that has solidified on top before using.

NOTE This chicken stock has a richer flavor than "white" chicken stock (which is made with uncooked chicken). It can be used for hearty chicken soups and stews or even as a substitute for beef stock.

Beef Stock

1 yellow onion, unpeeled

1 chicken (3 lb/1.5 kg), cut into 8 pieces, or 3 lb (1.5 kg) chicken pieces (thighs, drumsticks, wings, and/or necks)

1 lb (500 g) beef shin (shank), with the bone

8 oz (250 g) veal stewing meat, cut into large cubes

1 large carrot, peeled

1 stalk celery

1 tomato, cut in halves

16 cups (4 qt/4 l) cold water

Preheat a broiler (griller) and broil the whole onion until the edges are lightly browned.

Put the browned onion, the chicken, beef, veal, carrot, celery, and tomato in a deep stockpot. Add the water and bring to the boil over medium heat, skimming off any scum that rises to the surface. Reduce the heat to low and continue to simmer, partly covered, for 3 hours.

Remove from the heat. Strain into a clean pot or a heatproof plastic container. Cool quickly, uncovered, in a sink of ice water. Refrigerate until ready to use. Remove the fat that has solidified on top before using.

Makes about 12 cups (3 qt/3 l)

Quick Beef Stock

1 ½ lb (750 g) boneless beef chuck, cubed then pulsed in a food processor until coarsely chopped

5 cups (40 fl oz/1.25 l) water

1 onion, roughly chopped

1 small leek, white and tender green parts, washed thoroughly and chopped

1 carrot, peeled and sliced

1 tablespoon tomato purée

5 sprigs parsley

½ teaspoon dried thyme

3 black peppercorns, lightly crushed

1 whole clove

Put the beef and water into a stockpot and bring almost to the boil over medium heat. Reduce the heat and simmer, skimming off the scum that rises to the surface, for about 30 minutes.

Add the remaining ingredients and simmer, uncovered, for 1 hour. Strain into a clean pot or a heatproof plastic container. Cool quickly, uncovered, in a sink of ice water. Refrigerate until ready to use. Remove the fat that has solidified on top before using. The stock will separate, so whisk before using.

Makes about 4 cups (32 fl oz/1 liter)

NOTE If you do not have time to make even a quick stock, canned broths or consommés are an acceptable substitute, although often rather salty. Try to find a low-sodium brand, and do not add more salt without tasting the soup. If more salt is needed, add it at the end of the cooking time.

Any commercial stock can be made a little more flavorsome by adding a few finely chopped vegetables and herbs, and simmering for 15–30 minutes. Strain, then use as directed in the recipe.

White Veal Stock

1½ lb (750 g) veal breast

1½ lb (750 g) veal knucklebones, split

12 oz (375 g) chicken pieces (backs, necks, wings, legs, or thighs), well rinsed

12 cups (3 qt/3 l) cold water (or just enough to cover)

2 large onions, coarsely chopped

2 medium leeks, white and tender green parts, washed thoroughly and chopped

2 carrots, peeled and coarsely chopped

1 stalk celery, coarsely chopped

1 bouquet garni (page 16)

Put the veal breast and knuckle-bones in a large stockpot. Add cold water to cover and bring to a boil rapidly over high heat. Immediately drain and rinse the veal, the bones, and the pot.

Return the veal and bones to the pot and add the chicken pieces and water. Bring to a boil over medium heat, skimming off any scum that rises to the top. Reduce the heat and simmer for about 20 minutes. Add the onion, leek, carrot, celery, and bouquet garni. Simmer, uncovered, for 3–4 hours, adding water as needed to keep the ingredients covered.

Strain into a clean pot or a heatproof plastic container. Cool quickly, uncovered, in a sink of ice water. Refrigerate until ready to use. Remove the fat that has solidified on top before using.

Makes about 8 cups (64 fl oz/2 l)

Brown Veal Stock

1½ lb (750 g) veal breast

1½ lb (750 g) veal knucklebones, split

12 oz (375 g) chicken pieces (backs, necks, wings, legs, or thighs), well rinsed

2 large onions, coarsely chopped

2 medium leeks, white and tender green parts, washed thoroughly and chopped

2 carrots, peeled and chopped

1 rib (stick) celery, chopped

1 cup (8 fl oz/250 ml) red or white wine (optional)

12 cups (3 qt/3 l) cold water, or as needed

1 bouquet garni (page 16)

Preheat the oven to 425°F (210°C/Gas Mark 5). Lightly grease a roasting pan. Put the veal breast and bones into the prepared pan and roast for 15 minutes. Add chicken and vegetables and roast for about 1 hour, or until well browned.

Transfer the meat and vegetables to a large stockpot. Carefully pour off and discard any excess grease, while keeping the caramelized cooking juices. Add 1 cup (8 fl oz/250 ml) wine or cold water to deglaze the hot roasting pan. Scrape up all the browned bits and add the liquid to the stockpot with enough cold water to cover.

Bring to the boil. Reduce the heat and simmer, uncovered, skimming off any scum that rises to the top, for 30 minutes. Add bouquet garni and simmer, uncovered, for 3–4 hours, adding water as needed to keep the ingredients covered. Strain into a clean pot or heatproof plastic container. Cool quickly, uncovered, in a sink of ice water. Refrigerate until ready to use. Remove the fat that has solidified on top before using.

Makes about 8 cups (64 fl oz/2 l)

Fish Stock

2 lb (1 kg) fish heads and bones, or whole fish, scaled, gutted, gills and viscera removed, rinsed well and drained

1 small onion, sliced

1 large leek, white and tender green parts, cleaned thoroughly and sliced

½ fennel bulb, sliced (optional)

1–2 cloves garlic (optional)

1 cup (8 fl oz/250 ml) dry white wine (optional)

6 cups (48 fl oz/1.5 l) cold water (or just enough to cover)

1 bouquet garni (page 16)

Combine all the ingredients in a large stockpot. Bring to the boil over medium heat. Reduce the heat and simmer, uncovered, skimming off any scum that rises to the top, for about 30 minutes. (Do not cook for a longer period, or the stock may become bitter.) Strain into a clean pot or heat-proof plastic container. Cool quickly, uncovered, in a sink of ice water. Refrigerate until ready to use.

Makes about 6 cups (48 fl oz/1.5 l)

NOTE If fish bones are not available, use inexpensive whole fish. For a fresh-tasting, all-purpose fish stock, avoid using oily fish.

Shrimp Stock

2 tablespoons vegetable oil

5 oz (155 g) uncooked shrimp (prawn) shells, well rinsed and drained (shells from about 2 lb/1 kg shrimp)

2 small onions, chopped

2 small carrots, peeled and chopped

2 stalks celery, chopped

6 cups (48 fl oz/1.5 l) cold water

1 bay leaf

1 ½ teaspoons black peppercorns, lightly crushed

Splash Pernod or ¼ teaspoon fennel seeds (optional)

Heat the oil in a large stockpot over medium-high heat. Add the shrimp shells and cook, stirring occasionally, for about 15 minutes, or until they are bright pink and aromatic.

Stir in the onion, carrot, and celery, then add the water, bay leaf, peppercorns, and Pernod or fennel seeds, if using. Bring almost to the boil, then reduce the heat, and simmer, partly covered, for 20 minutes.

Strain into a clean pot or heat-proof plastic container, pressing down gently on the shrimp shells to extract all the liquid. Cool quickly, uncovered, in a sink of ice water, then refrigerate until ready to use, or freeze for longer storage.

Makes about 6 cups (48 fl oz/1.5 l)

Game Stock

1 rabbit or fowl, about 1.5 kg (3 lb), or 1.5 kg (3 lb) meaty game bones, rinsed and drained

16 cups (4 qt/4 l) cold water

1 medium onion, coarsely chopped

1 carrot, peeled and cut into pieces 1 inch (2.5 cm) long

1 stalk celery, cut into pieces 1 inch (2.5 cm) long

1 bouquet garni (page 16)

Put the rabbit, fowl, or game bones and water in a large stockpot. Bring to the boil over medium heat. Reduce the heat, and simmer, skimming off any scum that rises to the top, for about 30 minutes.

Add the onion, carrot, celery, and bouquet garni. Simmer, uncovered, for 2½ hours, adding water as needed to keep the ingredients covered. Strain into a clean pot or heatproof plastic container. Cool, uncovered, in a sink of ice water, then refrigerate. Remove the fat that has solidified on top before using.

Makes about 12 cups (3 qt/3 l)

NOTE This stock can be made with rabbit or with duck, guinea hen or other small game birds.

Quick Microwave Stock

To make a small amount of stock quickly, a microwave oven is a quick and easy option. Simply cook the meat or chicken scraps and bones with water and flavorings (such as chopped carrot, onion, celery, and turnip, and a bouquet garni, bay leaf, or other herbs of your choice). Remember to include a few celery leaves, which add greatly to the flavour.

Put the meat pieces or bones, chopped vegetables, and herbs in a microwave-safe bowl. Measure in enough cold water to cover. For each 2 cups (16 fl oz/ 500 ml) of liquid, microwave for 5 minutes on high (100%), then 10 minutes on medium (50%).

Set aside for 10 minutes, then strain. If using the stock immediately, skim off any fat by drawing a paper towel over the top of the hot stock to blot up the fat. Repeat until all fat is removed. Alternatively, chill the soup until the layer of fat rises to the surface and sets solid. It is then easy to lift off and discard.

The stock can be refrigerated, covered, for up to 3 days or frozen for up to 3 months.

Straining and Storing Stock

When the stock is cooked, strain it through a fine-mesh sieve into another pot. You can also use a colander lined with a double thickness of cheesecloth (muslin). With meat and seafood stocks, do not press heavily on the solids while straining, as that will cloud the stock. For vegetable stock, however, pressing on the solids in the strainer will release extra flavor from the cooked vegetables. Discard the solids.

Do not let the stock sit at room temperature for long, as it is a prime breeding ground for bacteria. Speed up the cooling process by placing the hot stock, uncovered, in a sink full of iced water. Stir the stock occasionally.

Once the stock is cool enough, cover it tightly and chill in the refrigerator. When the stock is chilled, any fat will rise in a solid mass, making it easy to remove before reheating. While cold, this fat layer actually protects the stock.

Storing Stock will keep for up to 5 days in the refrigerator. For longer storage, freeze stock in airtight containers or strong plastic bags in portion sizes that will be convenient for your needs. Store frozen stock for up to 3 months. Never thaw and refreeze frozen stock. Small amounts of stock, such as you might like to have on hand for gravies and sauces, can also be frozen in ice cube trays and then the ice blocks can be stored in sealed plastic bags. Always label the packages with the type of stock, the quantity, and the date.

Puréeing and Straining Soups

Thick soups can be puréed until smooth, or partly puréed to give them a creamier texture. Ingredients often used to make a soup that is suitable for puréeing are root vegetables, such as potatoes, pumpkin, or carrots. Grains such as rice and barley, and pulses such as beans and lentils are also useful.

The texture, or degree of smoothness, of a soup is largely a matter of personal taste. The following are some items of kitchen equipment commonly used in puréeing soup.

Food Processor This machine is especially good for thick soups.

When using a food processor, you may need to purée the soup in batches. Insert the metal blade. Ladle in a portion of the cooked solids and some of the liquid. Beware of overfilling the bowl or container, as liquids can leak out of the bottom or overflow. Put on the lid and pulse the machine several times, then process until the purée is the desired consistency. Or purée the solid ingredients with just enough liquid to keep the blade from clogging, then return the purée to the pot, and stir or whisk to blend through.

If there are fibers, skins, or seeds you wish to remove, pour the

purée through a sieve set over a large bowl. Using a wooden spoon, press the purée through the sieve, discarding any solids trapped in the mesh. Repeat with the remaining batches. Stir to give the soup an even consistency, and return it to the pan if necessary to gently reheat.

Food Mill Favored by professional chefs, this piece of equipment purées and strains simultaneously. A food mill will even strain out tomato seeds. Interchangeable discs help the cook to control the final texture of the soup. Cook the soup until the ingredients are quite soft. Assemble the food mill following

the manufacturer's instructions and set it securely over a large bowl. Ladle in some of the cooked soup.

Steady the mill with one hand, and turn the handle clockwise to force the ingredients through the disk. To dislodge any fibrous material from the surface of the disk, briefly turn the handle counterclockwise at intervals.

Continue ladling the soup and turning the mill handle until all the ingredients have been puréed. Remove the mill and stir or whisk the purée to give it an even consistency. Return it to the pan, and gently reheat.

Blender A blender works well for puréeing thinner soups. When blending hot soup, do not fill the blender more than one-third full. Wrap a kitchen towel around the lid (to absorb any liquid that may spray up and escape, spattering and perhaps burning anyone nearby). Start on a low speed, gradually increasing the speed until the soup is the desired consistency. Repeat, in batches, with the remaining soup. Return the soup to the pan, and gently reheat.

Wand Mixer or Hand-held Immersion Blender Portable and easy to clean, this tool is very convenient for the home cook, because the puréeing can be done without taking the soup off the heat. Just immerse the blade end in the soup and turn the wand mixer on, moving it around the soup until you achieve the desired texture.

The solid ingredients must be very soft for this type of blender to work properly, and it can never achieve a completely silken texture. But it is still an excellent tool for soups, especially those that are only partly puréed, such as some soups made with beans. For these, roughly purée just some of the soup and return it to the pan to thicken the soup.

Garnishing

A simple garnish added to a bowl of soup just before serving can add greatly to its appearance and flavor. All kinds of ingredients can be used: cheese, cream, croutons, fresh herbs, or even some decorative pieces of the main ingredient. Just remember not to overwhelm the soup with too many garnishes. Subtlety always gives the best results.

Cheese Scatter shredded Swiss, Cheddar, or another flavorful cheese over a thick, hearty soup.

Cream or sour cream To enrich a thick soup, spoon in a dollop of sour cream or heavy (double) cream, first whisking it slightly to liquefy it.

Croutons Cut slightly stale bread into thick slices and brush generously with olive oil, melted butter, or a mixture of the two. Cut into cubes and spread on a baking sheet in a single layer. Bake in a preheated oven at 350°F (180°C/Gas Mark 4), tossing occasionally, for about 30 minutes, or until crisp and golden. Alternatively, toss the prepared cubes, about a handful at a time, in a frying pan over medium heat until crisp and golden. Scatter over a thick or robust soup. Can be stored in an airtight container for 2 weeks.

Fresh Herbs Scatter fresh herbs, such as chopped or whole leaves of parsley, cilantro, or chives, over all kinds of soups.

Bell Pepper Roast, peel, and seed a bell pepper; purée in a food processor fitted with the metal blade, and spoon onto a rich, creamy soup. Alternatively, cut the peeled, roasted flesh into fine strips for a colorful garnish.

Vegetable pieces When making a puréed vegetable soup, cut up and reserve a few attractive pieces of the main ingredient. Parboil in lightly salted water until crisp-tender, and float them on the finished soup.

PART TWO

RECIPES

The following pages contain dozens of nutritious
and appetizing soups for all seasons and occasions.
Choose from delicate seafood consommés, robust
chowders, chilled soups suitable for summer menus,
hearty soups that are a meal in themselves,
and quick recipes for the microwave oven.

VEGETABLES
AND LEGUMES

Leek and Pumpkin Soup

2 teaspoons butter

3 lb (1.5 kg) pumpkin, peeled, seeded, and cubed

6 leeks, trimmed and sliced

8 cups (2 qt/2 l) milk

Salt

Melt the butter in a large saucepan, add the pumpkin and leeks, and cook over medium heat, stirring frequently, until lightly browned. Stir in two-thirds of the milk and add salt to taste.

Cook over very low heat for about 3 hours, or until the liquid is absorbed. Working in batches, transfer to a food processor or blender, add the remaining milk, and blend, retaining a slightly chunky texture. Return the soup to the pan and warm through over low heat. Serve immediately in warmed bowls.

Serves 4

Mushroom and Chili Soup

1 thick slice onion

1 clove garlic

1 lb (500 g) tomatoes

1½ lb (750 g) fresh white mushrooms, sliced

1½ teaspoons salt, plus extra to taste

2 cascabel chilis; 1 toasted and seeded, the other whole

1 tablespoon vegetable oil

1 tablespoon butter

4 cups (32 fl oz/1 liter) chicken stock (page 22) or vegetable stock (page 18)

Roast the onion and garlic on a cast-iron griddle or fry them in a frying pan until brown. Transfer to a bowl and set aside.

Using the same griddle or pan, roast or fry the tomatoes until they soften a little and the skins begin to split. Transfer, along with any juices, to the bowl holding the onion and garlic.

Place the mushrooms and salt in a saucepan with just enough boiling water to cover. Cook over high heat for 2–3 minutes, or until the mushrooms are tender. Drain.

Place the tomatoes, onion, and garlic in a blender. Add half of

the mushrooms and the toasted chili and blend until smooth.

Heat the oil and butter in a casserole. Strain tomato mixture into the casserole and simmer for 4 minutes. Stir in the stock, the remaining mushrooms, and the whole chili. Add salt to taste. Bring the mixture to a boil, then boil for 3 minutes to blend the flavors. Serve immediately.

Serves 6

French Onion Soup

½ cup (4 oz/125 g) unsalted butter

4 large yellow onions, thinly sliced

Salt and ground black pepper

5 cups (40 fl oz/1.25 l) beef stock (page 26) or veal stock (page 28)

2 bay leaves

½ lb (250 g) Gruyère or other Swiss cheese, shredded

4–6 slices French bread, ½ inch (1 cm) thick, toasted until golden brown

In a large saucepan, melt the butter over low heat. Add the onions and salt to taste. Stir to coat well with the butter, cover, and cook, stirring occasionally, until very tender, 20–30 minutes.

Uncover the pan, raise the heat slightly, and sauté, stirring frequently, until the onions turn a deep caramel brown, about 1 hour. Take care not to let them burn. Add the stock and bay leaves, bring to a boil, reduce the heat, cover, and simmer for about 30 minutes more. Toward the end of the cooking time, preheat a broiler (griller).

Discard the bay leaves. Add salt and pepper to taste. Ladle the soup into heavy flameproof serving crocks or bowls placed on a baking sheet or broiler tray.

Sprinkle a little of the cheese into each bowl, then place the toasted bread slices on top. Sprinkle evenly with the remaining cheese. Broil (grill) until the cheese is bubbly and golden, 2–3 minutes. Serve immediately.

Serves 4 to 6

47

Corn, Zucchini and Cilantro Soup

2 tablespoons vegetable oil

Kernels cut from 3 large ears of corn

1 tablespoon minced onion

6 cups (48 fl oz/1.5 l) chicken stock (page 22)

3 zucchini (courgettes), cut into small cubes or coarsely grated

½ cup (¾ oz/20 g) finely chopped cilantro (fresh coriander)

Salt and ground black pepper

4 oz (125 g) queso fresco, farmer's cheese, or mild feta, cut into small cubes

Heat the oil in a medium saucepan over medium heat. Add the corn and cook, stirring occasionally, for 6–8 minutes, or until softened.

Add the onion and cook, stirring, until it is translucent.

Stir in 2 cups (16 fl oz/500 ml) of the stock and cook until the corn is tender. Add the remaining stock, the zucchini, cilantro, and salt and pepper to taste. Bring to a boil, then reduce the heat and simmer until the zucchini is tender.

Serve immediately, topped with the cheese.

Serves 6

48

Summer Vegetable Soup with Pesto

1 tablespoon vegetable oil

2 onions, chopped

1 can (14 oz/440 g) tomatoes, chopped, juice reserved

8 cups (2 qt/2 l) chicken stock (page 22)

4 carrots, peeled and thinly sliced

2 potatoes, diced

4 leeks (white parts only), thinly sliced

2 large celery stalks with leaves, thinly sliced

2 cups (10 oz/315 g) sliced green beans

1 zucchini (courgette), sliced

3 oz (90 g) spaghetti, broken into 2½-inch (6-cm) lengths

1 cup (6 oz/185 g) dried great Northern (white haricot) beans, soaked, cooked until tender, and drained

PESTO

2 cloves garlic

¾ cup (¾ oz/20 g) fresh basil leaves

2 tablespoons olive oil

½ cup (2 oz/60 g) grated Parmesan cheese

Serves 8

Heat the oil in a frying pan over medium heat. Add the onion and cook, stirring, until tender. Add the tomatoes and their juice and cook, stirring, for 8 minutes. In a large saucepan, combine the stock, tomato mixture, carrots, potatoes, leeks, and celery. Bring to a boil, then reduce the heat and simmer gently for 15 minutes. Add the green beans, zucchini, spaghetti, and great Northern beans. Simmer until the vegetables are tender, about 10 minutes.

For the pesto, blend or process the garlic, basil, oil, cheese, and ¼ cup (2 fl oz/60 ml) of the soup liquid until smooth. Serve the soup topped with a dollop of pesto.

Summer Squash Soup

½ cup (4 oz/125 g) butter

2¼ lb (1.125 kg) small summer squash, such as yellow crookneck or zucchini (courgettes), sliced

1 clove garlic, finely chopped

2 large onions, chopped

10 oz (315 g) broccoli, chopped

⅓ cup (1½ oz/45 g) all-purpose (plain) flour

2 cups (16 fl oz/500 ml) milk

Pinch fresh thyme leaves

2 cups (16 fl oz/500 ml) chicken stock (page 22) or vegetable stock (page 18)

Melt the butter in a frying pan. Add the squash, garlic, and onions and cook, stirring, until softened. Add the broccoli and cook, stirring, until it softens.

Stir in the flour, being careful not to let the mixture burn. When well combined and slightly cooked, remove from the heat and gradually stir in the milk and thyme.

Return the pan to the heat and stir in the stock. Cook until thickened, then reduce heat to low and simmer for 5 minutes.

Serve immediately or freeze for up to 2 months.

Makes 12 cups (3 qt/3 l)

Provençal Garlic Soup

8 cups (2 qt/2 l) water

¾ cup (3 oz/90 g) cloves garlic, peeled

¼ cup (2 fl oz/60 ml) extra virgin olive oil

½ cup (2 oz/60 g) sliced white onion

⅓ cup (1⅓ oz/40 g) sliced celery

⅓ cup (1⅓ oz/40 g) sliced fennel bulb

½ cup (4 fl oz/125 ml) dry white wine

4 sprigs fresh thyme

½ teaspoon fresh rosemary leaves

1 bay leaf

5 cups (40 fl oz/1.25 l) chicken stock (page 22)

2¼ cups (18 fl oz/560 ml) heavy (double) cream

1 slice coarse country bread, preferably 1 day old, chopped

1 tablespoon salt

1 teaspoon ground white pepper

NOTE Despite the prodigious amount of garlic in this recipe, the resulting soup is surprisingly mellow. Trim any green tips from the garlic cloves, as they carry the sharpest flavor.

Place the water and garlic in a large saucepan and bring to a boil over high heat. Reduce the heat to medium and simmer, uncovered, until the garlic is translucent, about 5 minutes. Drain, reserving the garlic.

Return the saucepan to medium heat. Add the oil and heat for 30 seconds. Add the onion, celery, and fennel; cook, stirring, until just tender, 2–3 minutes. Add the garlic cloves, reduce the heat slightly, and cook, stirring often, for 2 minutes. Do not allow the garlic to brown. Stir in the wine and cook until the liquid has reduced by half.

Add the thyme, rosemary, bay leaf, stock, cream, bread, salt, and pepper. Stir well, reduce the heat to low, and simmer, uncovered, stirring occasionally, until the soup has reduced by one-fourth and is cream-colored, about 40 minutes. Set aside for 10 minutes to cool slightly.

Working in batches, blend or process the soup until smooth. Return the purée to the pan and reheat the soup over medium heat. Serve immediately.

Serves 4 to 6

Wild Mushroom Soup

⅓ cup (2 oz/60 g) pine nuts

½ cup (4 fl oz/125 ml) extra virgin olive oil

1 large yellow onion, finely chopped

3 cloves garlic, finely chopped

10 plum (Roma) tomatoes, fresh or canned, chopped

1 lb (500 g) shiitake mushrooms, stems discarded, caps sliced

8 oz (250 g) brown mushrooms (cremini) or white mushrooms, stems discarded, caps sliced

6 cups (48 fl oz/1.5 l) vegetable stock (page 18), meat stock (page 27), or water

1 tablespoon chopped fresh basil

1 tablespoon chopped fresh flat-leaf (Italian) parsley

1 tablespoon chopped fresh rosemary

1 tablespoon chopped fresh thyme

Salt and ground black pepper

Preheat an oven to 350°F (180°C/Gas Mark 4). Spread the pine nuts on a baking sheet and toast in the oven until golden and fragrant, about 5–8 minutes. Remove from the oven and set aside to cool.

Heat the olive oil in a large saucepan over medium heat. Add the onion and cook, stirring often, until soft and golden, about 5 minutes. Add the garlic, tomatoes, and mushrooms and increase the heat to high. Cook, stirring frequently, until the mushrooms begin to release their liquid, about 7 minutes.

Stir in the stock or water and all the herbs and bring to a boil. Reduce the heat to medium-low and simmer, uncovered, stirring occasionally, until the vegetables are tender, 25–30 minutes. Add salt and pepper to taste. Serve immediately, sprinkled with the pine nuts.

Serves 4 to 6

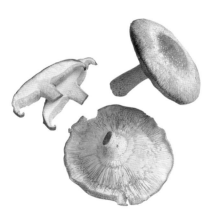

Pumpkin and Gruyère Soup

1 pumpkin, 5–6 lb (2.5–3 kg), or 5–6 lb (2.5–3 kg) acorn squash or other hard-shelled, orange-fleshed winter squash

¼ cup (2 oz/60 g) unsalted butter

1 large yellow onion, finely chopped

6 cups (48 fl oz/1.5 l) chicken stock (page 22) or vegetable stock (page18)

1½ cups (12 fl oz/375 ml) light (single) cream

2 tablespoons grated orange zest

2 tablespoons fresh orange juice

1 tablespoon fresh lemon juice

⅛ teaspoon ground nutmeg

⅛ teaspoon ground ginger

¾ lb (375 g) Gruyère or other Swiss cheese, shredded

Salt and ground white pepper

2 tablespoons chopped chives

Croutons, to serve (optional)

Cut the pumpkin or squash in half. Scoop out and discard any strings and seeds. With a sturdy knife, cut away the hard peel. Coarsely chop the flesh; you should have about 4 lb (2 kg).

In a large saucepan, melt the butter over medium heat. Add the onion and sauté until it begins to color, 4–5 minutes. Add the stock and chopped pumpkin or squash. Bring to a boil, reduce heat, cover, and simmer until squash is tender, 15–30 minutes.

In small batches, blend or process the soup until smooth. Return the purée to the pan and

stir in the cream, orange zest, orange and lemon juices, nutmeg, and ginger.

Reserve a handful of the cheese for garnish and sprinkle the rest into the soup. Stir over low heat until the cheese melts and blends in. Add salt and white pepper to taste.

Pour into a warmed tureen or individual bowls. Garnish with the reserved cheese, the chives, and croutons, if desired.

Serves 10 to 12

Cream of Broccoli Soup with Cheddar

1 ½ lb (750 g) broccoli, trimmed and tough stems peeled

2 tablespoons unsalted butter

1 yellow onion, finely chopped

¼ cup (1 oz/30 g) all-purpose (plain) flour

5 cups (40 fl oz/1.25 l) chicken stock (page 22) or vegetable stock (page 18), heated

½ teaspoon dried thyme

1 tablespoon lemon juice

2 cups (16 fl oz/500 ml) milk

½ lb (250 g) Cheddar cheese, shredded

Salt and ground white pepper

Reserve ½ cup (1 oz/30 g) small florets from the broccoli. Coarsely chop the remaining broccoli and set aside. In a large saucepan, melt the butter over medium heat. Add the onion and sauté until it begins to brown, 5–7 minutes.

Sprinkle in the flour and sauté, stirring, for about 1 minute more. Whisking continuously, slowly pour in the stock. Add the chopped broccoli, thyme, and lemon juice and bring to a boil. Reduce the heat to low, cover, and simmer until the broccoli is very tender, about 20 minutes.

About 5 minutes before the broccoli is done, bring a small saucepan of lightly salted water to a boil. Add the reserved florets and simmer until crisp-tender, 3–5 minutes. Drain and keep warm.

In small batches, blend or process the soup until smooth.

Return the purée to the pan, stir in the milk, and bring to a simmer over low heat.

Reserve a small handful of the cheese and sprinkle the rest into the soup. Stir over low heat until the cheese melts and blends in. Add salt and white pepper to taste.

Ladle into warmed bowls, garnish with the reserved broccoli florets and cheese, and serve immediately.

Serves 6 to 8

About Cheddar Cheese

Named for the English town in which it originated centuries ago, Cheddar is now the most copied cheese variety, made in factories all around the world. Almost 90 percent of all cheese sold in the United States is classified as a Cheddar-type cheese.

A firm, smooth-textured, cow's milk cheese, Cheddar ranges from mild, sweet, and smooth textured when fresh, to sharp, tangy, and slightly crumbly when aged. Normally, Cheddar varies in color from whitish to yellow. Orange-yellow Cheddar has had food coloring added.

Cheddar is generally matured for between 9 and 24 months. A good all-purpose cheese, it is suitable for eating out of hand, adding to soups or sandwiches, or melting atop grilled or baked foods. Store it in the refrigerator, wrapped in waxed or greaseproof paper rather than plastic wrap. It will keep for several weeks.

Fresh Tomato Soup

¼ cup (2 oz/60 g) butter

1 red (Spanish) onion, minced

1 small carrot, finely chopped

4 lb (2 kg) ripe tomatoes, peeled and coarsely chopped

4 cups (32 fl oz/1 liter) chicken stock (page 22) or vegetable stock (page 18)

1 sprig fresh basil

½ teaspoon dried thyme

1½ cups (3 oz/90 g) fresh white bread crumbs

1 cup (8 fl oz/250 ml) light (single) cream (optional)

Salt and ground white pepper

2 tablespoons shredded fresh basil

In a large saucepan, melt the butter over medium heat. Add the onion and carrot and sauté until the onion is translucent, 2–3 minutes. Add the tomatoes, 3 cups (24 fl oz/750 ml) of the stock, the basil sprig, and thyme.

Bring to a boil, reduce the heat, cover, and simmer for about 30 minutes. Stir in the bread crumbs. In small batches, blend or process the soup until smooth. Using a wooden spoon, force the purée through a fine-mesh sieve. Discard contents of sieve.

Return the purée to the pan and stir in the cream, if using, or the remaining 1 cup (8 fl oz/250 ml) of the stock. Warm the soup over low heat. Add salt and white pepper to taste.

Ladle into warmed bowls, garnish with the shredded basil, and serve immediately.

Serves 6 to 8

Tuscan Vegetable Soup

1 cup (7 oz/220 g) spelt, barley, or long-grain white rice

5 cups (40 fl oz/1.25 l) water

2 large broccoli florets

1 small leek, white part only

1 small celery stalk

1 large carrot, peeled

2 tablespoons extra virgin olive oil, plus extra to serve

1 cup (4 oz/125 g) chopped yellow onion

1½ cups (9 oz/280 g) peeled, seeded, and chopped plum (Roma) tomatoes, fresh or canned

½ cup (2½ oz/75 g) peeled and thinly sliced white turnip

5 cups (40 fl oz/1.25 l) vegetable stock (page 18) or meat stock (page 27)

¾ cup (3½ oz/105 g) diagonally sliced green beans

1 small zucchini (courgette), halved lengthwise, then thinly sliced crosswise

Salt and ground black pepper

Grated Parmesan cheese, to serve

TUSCAN VEGETABLE SOUP

In a bowl, combine spelt, barley, or rice and 3 cups (24 fl oz/ 750 ml) of the water. Set aside for 1 hour. Meanwhile, cut the broccoli, leek, celery, and carrot into ¼-inch (5-mm) thick slices.

Heat the oil in a large saucepan over low heat. Add the onion and cook, stirring often, until translucent, about 5 minutes. Add the tomatoes and cook, stirring often, for 2 minutes. Drain the spelt, barley, or rice and add to the pan, along with the broccoli, leek, celery, carrot, and turnip. Cook, stirring, for 3 minutes.

Add the stock and 1 cup (8 fl oz/ 250 ml) of the remaining water. Bring to a boil, then reduce the

heat to low, cover, and simmer for 15 minutes. Stir in the green beans and zucchini, cover, and simmer, stirring occasionally, until the vegetables are soft but still hold their shape and the grain is tender, 35–40 minutes. If the soup becomes too thick, add the remaining 1 cup (8 fl oz/250 ml) water. Add salt and pepper to taste.

Ladle into warmed serving bowls. Drizzle each serving with a little olive oil and sprinkle with the cheese. Serve immediately.

Serves 4

Spicy Seven-bean Soup

1/4 cup (2 fl oz/60 ml) olive oil

2 cloves garlic, finely chopped

1 green or red bell pepper (capsicum), seeded and diced

1 large fresh mild green chili pepper, finely chopped

1 yellow onion, finely chopped

1 carrot, finely chopped

1 celery stalk, finely chopped

1 teaspoon crushed dried chilis

1/4 cup (1 1/2 oz/45 g) of each of seven different types of dried beans (such as cannellini beans, chickpeas (garbanzo beans), black-eyed peas, red kidney beans, navy (Boston) beans, pinto beans, and borlotti (red) beans),

soaked in cold water to cover for 12 hours, then drained

4 cups (32 fl oz/1 l) chicken stock (page 22) or vegetable stock (page 18)

1 can (14 oz/440 g) crushed tomatoes

2 tablespoons tomato paste

1 tablespoon sugar

1 tablespoon dried basil

1 tablespoon dried oregano

1 tablespoon red wine vinegar

1 teaspoon dried thyme

2 bay leaves

Salt and ground black pepper

1/2 cup (2/3 oz/20 g) chopped fresh parsley

In a large saucepan, warm the oil over medium heat. Add the garlic, bell pepper, chili, onion, carrot, celery, and crushed dried chilis. Sauté until the onion is translucent, 2–3 minutes.

Add the drained beans, stock, tomatoes, tomato paste, sugar, basil, oregano, vinegar, thyme, and bay leaves. Bring to a boil, reduce the heat to low, cover partially, and simmer until the beans are tender, 2–2 1/2 hours.

Discard the bay leaves, add salt and pepper to taste, and stir in the parsley. Serve at once.

Serves 6 to 8

About Legumes

Peas, beans, and lentils (known collectively as legumes) are available dried and in cans. Most dried legumes (except for lentils and split peas) should be soaked before cooking. Canned legumes are precooked; they must be drained and rinsed before use. The following are some common types.

Black beans Small, flat, dried beans with a meaty flavor and mealy texture. Popular in Latin American cooking for soups, stews, dips, and in side dishes.

Cannellini beans A tender, meaty type of kidney bean. Prized in Italy for soups, casseroles, and salads.

Black-eyed beans Tiny dried beans with a black spot. They have an earthy taste and meaty texture.

Chickpeas (garbanzo beans) Earthy, round, dried beans, used in Middle Eastern, North African, and Indian cooking. Probably best known as the base for hummus, a seasoned spread and dip.

Great Northern (white haricot) beans Another type of kidney bean, these are large, white, plump, and mild flavored. Can be substituted for cannellini beans in soups, casseroles, and baked dishes.

Lentils Small, disk-shaped, dried seeds. High in protein, they have a mild, nutty taste and soft texture. There are red, yellow, pink, and greenish-brown varieties. Use in soups, salads, and side dishes.

Navy (Boston) beans These versatile beans can be used in any recipe that calls for dried white beans.

Pinto beans Brown-speckled beans with tannish-pink skins, a mealy texture and meaty flavor. Popular in the cuisines of Latin America, Mexico, and the American southwest.

Red kidney beans In Europe, India, Australia, and America, these large, meaty dried beans are familiar ingredients in salads, stews, and soups.

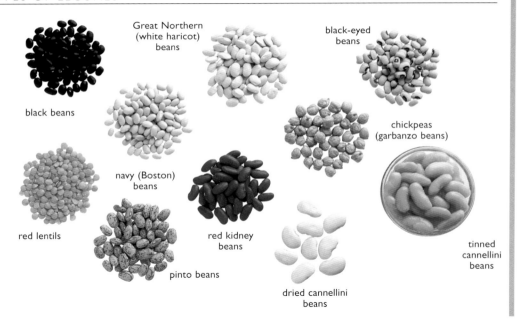

black beans

Great Northern
(white haricot)
beans

black-eyed
beans

navy (Boston)
beans

chickpeas
(garbanzo beans)

red lentils

red kidney
beans

pinto beans

dried cannellini
beans

tinned
cannellini
beans

Leek and Potato Soup

¼ cup (2 oz/60 g) unsalted butter

2 lb (1 kg) leeks, white part only, trimmed, carefully washed, and thinly sliced

6 cups (48 fl oz/1.5 l) chicken stock (page 22), vegetable stock (page 18) or water

2 lb (1 kg) baking potatoes, peeled, quartered lengthwise, and thinly sliced

Salt and ground white pepper

2 tablespoons chopped fresh chives

In a large saucepan, melt the butter over medium heat. Add the leeks and sauté until they begin to soften, 3–5 minutes.

Add the stock and potatoes, bring to a boil, reduce heat to low, cover, and simmer until the potatoes are very tender, about 20 minutes.

If desired, in small batches, blend or process some or all of the soup until smooth.

Add salt and white pepper to taste. Ladle into warmed bowls and garnish with the chives.

Serves 8 to 10

Hearty Peasant Soup

2 tablespoons extra virgin olive oil

1 onion, chopped

1 clove garlic, chopped

1 lb (500 g) ripe tomatoes, peeled, seeded, and chopped

8 cups (2 qt/2 l) beef stock

salt and ground black pepper

10 oz (315 g) ditalini (short pasta tubes), macaroni, or other small pasta shapes

6 slices coarse country bread

Heat the oil in a large saucepan over low heat, add the onion and garlic, and cook, stirring often, until translucent. Stir in the tomatoes, stock, and salt and pepper to taste. Simmer, uncovered, for 1 hour.

Stir in the pasta and cook until al dente, 10–12 minutes.

Toast the slices of bread. Place 3 slices in a soup tureen and pour over the boiling soup. Break the remaining slices of toast into pieces. Serve the soup immediately, garnished with the pieces of toast.

Serves 6

NOTE This soup lends itself well to improvisation; add a ham bone, diced root vegetables, a little chopped cabbage, or home-cooked or canned beans. For vegetarians, replace the beef stock with vegetable stock.

Tortilla Soup

2 tablespoons vegetable oil

1 yellow onion, diced

1 teaspoon salt

2 cloves garlic, minced

1 dried chipotle chili pepper, stemmed and seeded (optional)

1½ cups (12 fl oz/375 ml) purchased or homemade salsa

5 cups (40 fl oz/1.25 l) chicken stock (page 22), vegetable stock (page 18), or water

½ lb (250 g) corn tortilla chips

¼ cup (⅓ oz/10 g) chopped cilantro (fresh coriander)

½ small yellow onion, diced

1 lime, cut into 6 wedges

In a large saucepan over medium heat, warm the oil. Add the onion and salt and cook, stirring occasionally, until the onion is golden brown, about 15 minutes. Add the garlic and chipotle chili, if using, and cook for 1–2 minutes longer. Add the salsa and stock or water and bring to a boil. Reduce the heat to medium-low and simmer, uncovered, for about 20 minutes to blend the flavors. Stir in the tortilla chips and simmer until they soften and begin to break apart, 10–15 minutes more.

Remove and discard the chipotle chili, if used. Ladle the soup into warmed bowls and garnish each serving with cilantro and onion. Squeeze a wedge of lime over each bowl, then drop the wedge into the bowl. Serve at once.

Serves 6

Neapolitan Herb Soup

3 eggs

Pinch salt

3 tablespoons extra virgin olive oil

6 medium zucchini (courgettes), diced

8 cups (2 qt/2 l) chicken stock (page 22), boiling

1 tablespoon chopped fresh basil

1 tablespoon chopped fresh parsley

Ground black pepper

2 ripe medium tomatoes, peeled and diced

Place the eggs and salt in a bowl and lightly beat.

Heat the oil in a saucepan over medium heat. Add the zucchini and cook, stirring, for 2 minutes. Add the hot stock and bring to a boil. Boil for 2 minutes.

Remove from the heat and whisk in the egg mixture, basil, parsley, and pepper. Whisk constantly over very low heat for 1 minute, or until thickened. Stir in the tomatoes, add pepper to taste, and serve immediately.

Serves 6

Roasted Eggplant Soup with Mint

1½ lb (750 g) small to medium eggplants (aubergines)

2 tablespoons unsalted butter

1 small yellow onion, finely chopped

1 clove garlic, finely chopped

2½ cups (20 fl oz/625 ml) chicken stock (page 22) or vegetable stock (page 18)

½ tablespoon finely chopped fresh mint

1 cup (8 fl oz/250 ml) heavy (double) cream

Salt and ground white pepper

Fresh mint sprigs, to garnish (optional)

Preheat oven to 375°F (190°C/ Gas Mark 4). Place the eggplants in a baking dish and puncture their skins several times with a fork. Roast in the oven, turning occasionally, until the skins are evenly browned and deeply wrinkled, 1–1½ hours. Set aside at room temperature until cool enough to handle, then peel and roughly chop.

In a large saucepan, melt the butter over medium heat. Add the onion and garlic and cook, stirring occasionally, until golden, 3–5 minutes. Add the eggplant, cook for 2–3 minutes more, then add the stock and chopped mint. Bring to a boil,

then reduce the heat, cover, and simmer for about 20 minutes.

In small batches, blend or process the soup until smooth. Return the purée to the pan, stir in the cream, and gently heat through over low to medium heat. Add salt and white pepper to taste.

Ladle into warmed bowls and garnish with the mint sprigs, if desired

Serves 4 to 6

About Eggplants

Probably originating in India, eggplants (aubergines) have been cultivated for centuries in Southeast Asia, China, and Turkey. They are available in a variety of colors and sizes. Most common is the large, purplish-black type (also known as globe eggplant) that is popular in Mediterranean, Middle Eastern, and Indian cooking. If no particular type is specified, it is safe to assume that globe eggplant is intended. Other varieties range from pale green to yellow and white, and may be round, oval, long and slender, or little bigger than peas.

Choose firm eggplants with smooth, glossy, unblemished skin. They should be heavy for their size. Store uncut eggplants, unwrapped, for up to 2 weeks. They need refrigeration only in hot climates. Cut fruit discolors quickly, due to oxidization, so it is best to cook eggplant as soon as possible after preparation. Any unused cut fruit should be wrapped tightly in plastic wrap. The discoloration is of aesthetic concern only; the discolored part may be cut away and the rest of the eggplant eaten.

Fresh Tomato and Thyme Soup

1 tablespoon olive oil

2 onions, chopped

5 cloves garlic; 2 cloves crushed, others left whole

4 lb (2 kg) tomatoes, peeled, seeded, and chopped

1 tablespoon tomato paste

2 teaspoons sugar

1 bay leaf

4 large sprigs fresh thyme

½ teaspoon hot-pepper sauce, such as Tabasco

salt and ground black pepper

½ cup (4 fl oz/125 ml) vegetable stock (page 18) or chicken stock (page 22)

Corn bread, to serve (optional)

Heat the oil in a saucepan over medium heat. Add the onion and cook, stirring, until soft, about 5 minutes. Add the crushed garlic; stir for 1 minute.

Stir in the tomatoes, tomato paste, sugar, bay leaf, thyme sprigs, whole garlic cloves, hot-pepper sauce, salt and pepper to taste, and stock. Simmer, uncovered, for 20 minutes, or until the tomatoes are soft.

Discard the bay leaf, thyme, and garlic cloves. Blend or process the soup until smooth, then return it to the pan and reheat. Serve hot, with corn bread, if desired.

Serves 6

Two-mushroom Barley Soup

½ oz (15 g) dried porcini mushrooms

2 tablespoons vegetable oil

2 tablespoons unsalted butter

1 yellow onion, finely chopped

1 celery stalk, finely chopped

1 carrot, finely chopped

½ lb (250 g) fresh mushrooms, thinly sliced

10 cups (2½ qt/2.5 l) beef stock (page 26) or chicken stock (page 22)

2 cups (¾ lb/375 g) pearl barley

1 bay leaf

Salt and ground black pepper

¼ cup (⅓ oz/10 g) chopped fresh parsley

Place the porcini in a small bowl and add lukewarm water to cover. Soak until softened, about 30 minutes. Remove the porcini with a slotted spoon. Chop finely and set aside. Line a sieve with a double layer of cheesecloth (muslin) and set it inside a bowl. Pour the soaking liquid into the sieve and reserve.

In a large saucepan, warm the oil and butter over medium heat. Add the onion, celery, and carrot and sauté until the onion is translucent, 2–3 minutes. Add the sliced fresh mushrooms, raise the heat, and sauté until the mushrooms begin to soften, 2–3 minutes more.

Add the stock, barley, bay leaf, chopped porcini and reserved soaking liquid and bring to a boil. Reduce the heat to low, cover partially, and simmer, stirring occasionally, until the barley is tender and the soup is thick, 50–60 minutes.

Discard the bay leaf. Add salt and pepper to taste. Ladle into warmed bowls, sprinkle with parsley, and serve immediately.

Serves 8 to 10

About Mushrooms

For culinary purposes, mushrooms are classified as wild or cultivated, although this distinction is blurring as farmers succeed in cultivating more and more types. Of the almost 40,000 varieties that exist, the following are among the few to make it to the table.

White mushrooms These are the all-purpose type commonly found in supermarkets and grocery stores. Young white mushrooms with closed caps are known as button mushrooms.

Brown mushrooms Also known as cremini, these are closely related to, and interchangeable with, white mushrooms. They have a firmer texture and fuller flavor than white mushrooms.

Portobellos The name given to mature brown mushrooms. These have a rich flavor and meaty texture. The tough stems should be removed, but they may be reserved to add flavor to stocks or sauces.

Shiitake mushrooms A buff to dark brown Japanese variety, available dried or fresh. They are suitable for grilling, roasting, sautéing, and stir-frying. Remove their tough stems before using.

Oyster mushrooms Fan shaped and cream to pale grey. Choose small, young specimens; these mushrooms become tough and bitter as they age. Preserve their silken texture by cooking them only lightly, just until they are heated through.

Porcini Also known as cèpes or boletus, this uncultivated variety is difficult to find fresh outside of its native Europe. Reconstituted dried porcini may be substituted for fresh. These mushrooms are popular in soups, pasta sauces, and risottos, particularly in Italy.

Creamy Fresh Pea Soup

2 tablespoons butter

1 onion, chopped

1 lettuce heart (2 oz/60 g), finely shredded

4 cups (32 fl oz/1 liter) chicken stock (page 22) or vegetable stock (page 18)

2 lb (1 kg) fresh peas, shelled, or fava (broad) beans, shelled

Salt and ground black pepper

⅓ cup (2½ fl oz/80 ml) crème fraîche or sour cream

4 sprigs fresh chervil

Melt the butter in a large saucepan. Add the onion and stir over low heat for 2 minutes, or until softened. Add the lettuce and stir for 2 minutes more.

Stir in the stock and bring to a boil. Add the peas or beans, reduce the heat, and simmer for 20 minutes, or until tender. Add salt and pepper to taste.

Reserve ¼ cup of the cooked peas or beans. In small batches, blend or process the remaining peas or beans and the liquid until smooth. Strain through a fine-mesh sieve back into the pan, then bring just to a boil. Add the crème fraîche or sour cream, stir well, then remove from the heat.

Serve immediately, garnished with the reserved peas or beans and the chervil.

Serves 4

Corn Chowder

2 tablespoons unsalted butter

1 yellow onion, coarsely chopped

1 large golden (French) shallot, finely chopped

2 slices (rashers) bacon, chopped (optional)

6 cups (48 fl oz/1.5 l) light (single) cream

8 ears corn, husked, kernels removed with a sharp knife

Salt and ground white pepper

2 tablespoons chopped chives

1 red bell pepper (capsicum), roasted, peeled, seeded, and puréed in a food processor or blender (optional)

In a large saucepan, melt the butter over medium-low heat. Add the onion, shallot, and bacon, if using, and sauté until translucent, about 5 minutes. Add the cream and three-fourths of the corn kernels.

Bring to a boil, reduce the heat, and simmer, uncovered, until the corn is tender and the liquid has thickened slightly, about 10 minutes. In small batches, blend or process the soup until smooth, then force the purée through a fine-mesh sieve, pressing the solids with a wooden spoon to extract all the liquid. Discard the solids.

Return the purée to the pan over medium-low heat and add the remaining corn kernels. Simmer until the corn is tender-crisp, about 5 minutes. Add salt and white pepper to taste.

Ladle into warmed serving bowls and garnish with the chives. If desired, spoon a swirl of puréed bell pepper on top.

Serves 4 to 6

About Corn

Corn (more properly known as maize) is the only cereal known to have originated in the Americas. It has been cultivated in both North and South America for at least 3,000 years; no wild forms of maize now exist. The only cereal available to the Aztec, Maya, and Inca civilizations, it was taken to Europe by the Spanish in the late 15th century, and later to Asia by the Portuguese.

Corn comes in several varieties, and may be yellow, white, or blue. It is one of the world's most important crops. From it are made oil, corn starch (cornflour), corn syrup, breakfast cereal, cornmeal (polenta), bread, and tortillas. We eat some varieties as a vegetable; others are used as stock feed.

Corn is available fresh, canned, and frozen. Buy fresh corn still in its husk, as this retains its freshness for longer. Corn should be cooked as soon as possible after it is picked or purchased, as its sugar begins to turn to starch as soon as it is harvested. If you must store the cobs, leave them in their husks until the last moment before cooking so they don't dry out. Simmer for only about 5 minutes. If the corn is not quite so fresh, simmer for up to 15 minutes, or until the kernels feel tender when pierced with a sharp knife or skewer.

Pasta, Lentil and Pepperoni Soup

1 cup (6½ oz/200 g) red lentils

4 cups (32 fl oz/1 liter) chicken stock (page 22) or vegetable stock (page 18)

1 bay leaf

1 tablespoon olive oil

1 large onion, finely chopped

1 can (14 oz/440 g) tomatoes, roughly chopped, juice reserved

8 oz (250 g) ditalini (small pasta tubes) or similar short pasta

6½ oz (200 g) pepperoni, thinly sliced

Place the lentils, chicken stock, and bay leaf in a large saucepan. Bring to a boil, reduce heat, and simmer for 1–1¼ hours, until the lentils are very soft. In small batches, blend or process the soup until smooth. Return the purée to the pan.

Heat the oil in a frying pan and sauté the onion until soft. Add to the soup along with the tomatoes and simmer gently for 15 minutes.

Cook the pasta in boiling salted water until al dente. Drain and stir into the soup together with

the pepperoni. Heat until all ingredients are thoroughly warmed through, ladle into warmed soup bowls, and serve immediately.

Serves 6

Tomato and Bell Pepper Cream Soup

2 red bell peppers (capsicums)

2 tablespoons olive oil

1 large onion, chopped

2 cloves garlic, chopped

¾ cup (6 fl oz/185 ml) sherry

8 tomatoes, peeled and seeded

4 cups (32 fl oz/1 liter) chicken stock

1 bay leaf

3 sprigs fresh thyme

1 sprig fresh basil

1 large sprig fresh parsley

1 tablespoon black peppercorns

1 cup (8 fl oz/250 ml) heavy (double) cream

Juice ½ lemon

Salt and ground black pepper

CHILI CREAM

1 long fresh green chili

1 clove garlic

5 spinach leaves, blanched in hot water

⅓ cup (2½ fl oz/80 ml) heavy (double) cream, well chilled

1 tablespoon fresh lime juice

Salt and ground black pepper

Cook the bell peppers under a hot broiler (griller), turning occasionally, until the skin blisters and blackens. Place in a heatproof bowl, cover with plastic wrap, and set aside for 10 minutes. Peel, discard the skin, and roughly chop the flesh.

Heat the oil in a large pot. Add the onion and garlic and cook until softened. Add the sherry; cook until it evaporates. Stir in the tomatoes and stock. Tie the herbs and peppercorns in a square of cheesecloth (muslin) and add to the pan. Cook for 10 minutes, or until the mixture has reduced by a third. Stir in the cream and bell pepper.

Simmer for 15 minutes, or until liquid reduces slightly. Remove and discard the cheesecloth bag. In small batches, blend or process the soup until smooth. Return the purée to the pan. Add the lemon juice and salt and pepper to taste.

For the chili cream, place the chili, garlic, and spinach in a food processor and process until smooth. Add the cream and process until combined. Add the lime juice and salt and pepper to taste. Serve the soup topped with a dollop of chili cream.

Chili Corn Soup

6 long fresh green chilis

¼ cup (2 fl oz/60 ml) vegetable oil

2 onions, chopped

3 cloves garlic, crushed

4 tomatoes, peeled, seeded, and chopped

10 cups (2½ qt/2.5 l) chicken stock (page 22)

2 cups (10 oz/315 g) corn kernels, cut from 3–4 large cobs

8 oz (250 g) mild-flavored cheese, shredded

Under a hot broiler (griller), cook the chilis, turning occasionally, until the skin blisters and blackens. Place in a heatproof bowl, cover with plastic wrap, and set aside for 30 minutes. Peel, discard skin, and chop the flesh into strips.

Heat the oil in a large saucepan over low heat. Add the onions and cook, stirring frequently, for 5 minutes, or until softened. Add the garlic; stir for 1 minute.

Add the tomatoes and cook until the mixture forms a smooth paste. Stir in the stock and bring to a boil. Add the corn, reduce the heat, and simmer for 10 minutes, or until the corn is tender.

Serve at once, sprinkled with shredded cheese.

Serves 10

Sicilian Vegetable Soup

2 lb (1 kg) eggplants (aubergines)

Salt

⅓ cup (2½ fl oz/80 ml) olive oil

1 lb (500 g) onions, thinly sliced

1 lb (500 g) ripe tomatoes, seeded and cut into strips

2 tablespoons capers, rinsed

2–3 celery stalks, chopped

6 oz (185 g) black olives, pitted

2 cups (16 fl oz/500 ml) tomato juice

2 cups (16 fl oz/500 ml) vegetable stock (page 18) or chicken stock (page 22)

⅓ cup (2½ fl oz/80 ml) vinegar (use any kind)

1 teaspoon sugar

Wash the eggplants and cut into small pieces. Place in a large colander or sieve and sprinkle with salt. Set aside for at least 1 hour to drain.

Meanwhile, heat one third of the olive oil in a large frying pan. Add the onions and cook, stirring, until golden. Stir in the tomatoes, capers, celery, and olives and cook for 15 minutes. Set aside.

Rinse the eggplants and dry thoroughly on paper towels. Heat the remaining oil in a frying pan over high heat. When very hot, add the eggplant and fry until well browned. Drain on paper towels.

Stir the fried eggplant into the tomato mixture. Add the tomato juice, stock, vinegar, and sugar. Return to low heat and cook until all ingredients are heated through. Serve immediately.

Serves 4

Pasta and Bean Soup

2 lb (1 kg) fresh borlotti (red) beans or ¾ cup (5 oz/155 g) dried borlotti beans that have been soaked in water overnight

10 cups (2½ qt/2.5 l) water

4 ripe tomatoes, peeled and seeded

½ cup (4 fl oz/125 ml) olive oil, plus extra for drizzling (optional)

1 sprig rosemary

1 tablespoon garlic and parsley chopped together

5 oz (155 g) short pasta, such as penne, small rigatoni, or macaroni

Salt and ground black pepper

Combine the beans and water in a large pot. Salt lightly, bring to a boil, then lower the heat and simmer for 1 hour. Transfer a couple of ladlefuls of beans to a blender or food processor, add the tomatoes (work in batches if necessary,) and purée until smooth. Set the remaining beans aside in their cooking liquid.

Put the olive oil in a saucepan over low heat, add the rosemary, and cook gently for 5 minutes to flavor the oil. Discard the rosemary. Add the garlic and parsley and the tomato and bean purée. Stir to mix. Add the rest of the beans and their cooking liquid.

Stir in the pasta. Check for salt. Cook until the pasta is just slightly al dente and the soup has a creamy consistency.

Ladle into warmed serving bowls and drizzle with extra olive oil, if desired. Add pepper to taste and serve immediately.

Spicy Tomato Soup

1 tablespoon olive oil

1 yellow onion, finely diced

3 cloves garlic, crushed

½ teaspoon sweet paprika

2 cans (each 14 oz/440 g) whole peeled tomatoes, roughly chopped, juice reserved

1½ cups (12 fl oz/375ml) vegetable stock (page 18)

1 teaspoon sugar

Salt and ground black pepper

Crusty bread rolls, to serve

Heat the oil in a medium saucepan over medium heat. Add the onion and garlic, reduce the heat to low, and cook, stirring occasionally, for 10 minutes, or until the onion is soft.

Add the paprika and stir for 1 minute. Add the tomatoes, their juice, and the stock. Cover, increase heat to high, bring to a boil, then reduce heat to medium and simmer, uncovered, for 5 minutes.

Add the sugar, and salt and pepper to taste. Serve with crusty bread rolls.

Serves 4

Cream of Artichoke Soup

6 medium globe artichokes

⅓ cup (2½ fl oz/80 ml) olive oil

1 white onion, coarsely chopped

3 celery stalks, coarsely chopped

1 large russet potato, peeled and coarsely chopped

6 cups (48 fl oz/1.5 l) chicken stock (page 22)

⅓ cup (2 oz/60 g) hazelnuts

1 tablespoon salt

1 teaspoon ground white pepper

2 cups (16 fl oz/500 ml) heavy (double) cream

⅓ cup (2½ fl oz/80 ml) Armagnac, brandy, or dry sherry

Working with 1 artichoke at a time, cut off the top half. Trim the stem until it is even with the base of the artichoke. Snap or cut off the tough outer leaves until you reach the pale green, tender leaves. Carefully open the leaves and use a small spoon to remove the prickly choke, leaving the inner leaves intact. Cut each artichoke lengthwise into eighths and set aside.

Preheat an oven to 400°F (200°C/Gas Mark 5).

Heat the oil in a large saucepan over medium-high heat. Add the onion and celery and cook, stirring frequently, until golden, 8–10 minutes. Stir in the artichokes, potato, and stock; bring to a boil. Reduce the heat to medium, cover, and simmer until the mixture thickens slightly and the flavors have blended, about 45 minutes.

Meanwhile, spread the hazelnuts in a single layer on a baking sheet and toast in a moderate oven for 5 minutes. Place the warm nuts on a kitchen towel, gather up the corners to form a bundle, and rub the nuts gently against each other to remove as much of the skin as possible. Cool, then chop coarsely and set aside.

In small batches, blend or process the soup until smooth. Strain the soup through a fine-mesh sieve back into the pan. Stir in the salt, pepper, cream, and Armagnac, brandy, or sherry, then bring to a simmer over medium heat.

Serve immediately, sprinkled with the chopped hazelnuts.

Serves 6 to 8 as an appetizer

Mexican Garlic Soup

3 tablespoons olive oil

9 cloves garlic, halved

½ loaf crusty French bread, cut into 1-inch (2.5-cm) cubes

Salt and ground black pepper

8 cups (64 fl oz/2 l) chicken stock (page 22)

3 eggs, lightly beaten

2 tablespoons chopped fresh oregano

1 lime, cut into 6 wedges

Preheat an oven to 325°F (160°C/Gas Mark 3).

Heat the oil in a large pot over low heat. Add the garlic and cook, stirring occasionally, until the oil is well flavored and the garlic is soft but not browned, about 5 minutes. Remove from the heat and discard the garlic.

Place the bread cubes in a bowl and add about half the flavored oil (leave the remaining oil in the pan). Add salt and pepper to taste and toss well to coat. Spread over a baking sheet and bake until golden brown and crisp, 10–15 minutes. Remove from the oven and set aside.

Add the stock to the remaining oil in the saucepan and bring to a simmer over medium heat. Gradually add the beaten eggs to the simmering stock while stirring constantly in a circular motion. Add the oregano and continue to simmer until the eggs are set, about 3 minutes more. Remove from the heat.

Divide the croutons among warmed soup bowls and top with the stock mixture. Squeeze a wedge of lime over each bowl, then drop the wedge in the bowl. Serve immediately.

Serves 6

Vegetarian White Bean Soup

¼ cup (2 oz/60 g) vegetable oil

1 large yellow onion, chopped

1 clove garlic, finely chopped

1 large carrot, finely chopped

1 celery stalk, finely chopped

1 cup (7 oz/220 g) dried navy (Boston) beans, sorted, soaked in cold water to cover for 8 hours or overnight, then drained

5 cups (40 fl oz/1.25 l) vegetable stock (page 18)

1 can (14 oz/440 g) plum (Roma) tomatoes, roughly chopped, juice reserved

1 teaspoon dried summer savory

1 teaspoon dried thyme

1 teaspoon sugar

1 bay leaf

Salt and ground black pepper

2 tablespoons chopped fresh thyme

In a large saucepan, warm the oil over medium heat. Add the onion, garlic, carrot, and celery and cook until the onion is translucent, 2–3 minutes.

Add the drained beans, stock, tomatoes and their juice, savory, dried thyme, sugar, and bay leaf. Bring to a boil, reduce heat to low, cover, and simmer, stirring occasionally, until the beans are very tender, 2–2½ hours.

Discard the bay leaf. In small batches, blend or process the soup until smooth. Return the purée to pan and add salt and pepper to taste. Ladle into warmed bowls and garnish with the fresh thyme.

Serves 6 to 8

STEP 1

Rinsing and Sorting
As a first step, place the beans in a fine-mesh sieve. Rinse thoroughly under cold running water, tossing to wet all the beans. With your fingers, remove and discard any damaged or discolored beans or foreign matter.

STEP 2

Overnight Soaking
Put beans in a large pot. Fill pot with enough cold water to cover beans by about 2 inches (5 cm) or according to the recipe. Cover and set aside in a cool place for 8 hours or overnight. The beans will absorb almost all of the water and will expand and look plump. If the room is warm, let the beans soak in the refrigerator.

STEP 3

Checking Cooked Beans
After soaking, drain beans in a colander and rinse well. Cook beans until they are soft or as directed in the recipe. Taste a bean, or pick one up and squeeze it with your thumb and index finger to see if it is tender. If it is still firm in the center, cook a little longer. Add a little more more water if the beans are becoming dry before they are fully cooked.

Cream of Asparagus Soup

1½ lb (750 g) thin asparagus spears

9 sprigs fresh chervil

1½ tablespoons extra virgin olive oil

4 cups (32 fl oz/1 liter) water

1 tablespoon cornstarch (cornflour)

1 cup (8 fl oz/250 ml) milk

¼ teaspoon ground nutmeg

Salt and ground white pepper

3 tablespoons crème fraîche or sour cream

Cut 1¼ inches (3 cm) from the tips of the asparagus; reserve. Thinly slice the asparagus stems into rounds. Rinse the chervil and pat dry.

Heat the oil in a heavy-based saucepan. Add the sliced asparagus and cook, stirring, for 5 minutes, or until just browned. Add the chervil and water. Bring to a boil, reduce heat, and simmer for 15 minutes.

Blend or process the asparagus mixture until smooth. Strain the mixture through a fine-mesh sieve back into the pan. Discard the contents of the sieve.

Blend the cornstarch with the milk until smooth, then add to the pan. Add the nutmeg and salt and pepper to taste. Bring the mixture to a gentle boil over low heat. Add the reserved asparagus tips and cook, stirring, for 4 minutes, or until the tips are just cooked and the soup is thick.

Remove from the heat, add the crème fraîche or sour cream, and stir to combine. This soup may be serve hot or chilled.

Serves 4

Bean, Potato and Sauerkraut Soup

2½ cups (8 oz/250 g) fresh or 1¼ cups (9 oz/280 g) dried borlotti (red) beans

4–5 boiling potatoes, peeled

1 stalk celery

1 large onion

2 cloves garlic

2 bay leaves

3 oz (90 g) prosciutto

2 teaspoons olive oil

1 tablespoon all-purpose (plain) flour

8 oz (250 g) drained sauerkraut

Salt and ground black pepper

3 tablespoons olive oil

Pinch cumin

If using dried borlotti beans, soak in cold water to cover for 8 hours or overnight; drain.

In a large saucepan, place the beans, whole potatoes, celery, onion, 1 garlic clove, 1 bay leaf, and half the prosciutto. Add water to cover by about 2 inches (5 cm), bring to a boil over medium heat, reduce heat, and simmer for about 1½ hours, or until the beans are tender.

Meanwhile, warm the olive oil in a small frying pan, add the flour, and cook, stirring, until browned. Set aside.

Squeeze moisture from the sauerkraut and put it into another saucepan with salt and pepper to taste, the remaining garlic clove and bay leaf, the remaining prosciutto, the browned flour, and water to cover. Cook for 1 hour.

Take 2 or 3 ladlefuls of soup with the celery, some of the beans and 2 of the potatoes, and blend or process until smooth. Return the purée to the pan and add the sauerkraut mixture.

Cook for 30 minutes more and adjust the seasonings. Add the olive oil and cumin. Serve warm rather than hot.

Serves 4 to 6

Spinach and Fennel Soup

1 tablespoon olive oil

2 fennel bulbs, about 420g each, ends trimmed, outer layers removed, chopped

1 large brown onion, chopped

¼ cup (⅓ oz/10 g) chopped fresh oregano

2 cloves garlic, chopped

6 cups (48 fl oz/1.5 l) vegetable stock (page 18)

1 large potato, peeled, chopped

1 packet (8 oz/250 g) frozen chopped spinach, thawed, liquid reserved

Salt and ground black pepper

Ground nutmeg

Parmesan cheese shavings

Heat the oil in a large saucepan over medium-low heat. Add the fennel, onion, oregano, and garlic. Cook, stirring occasionally, for 10 minutes, or until the onion is soft.

Add the stock and potato to the pan. Increase the heat to high and bring to a boil. Reduce the heat to low and cook, covered, for 30 minutes, or until the fennel is very soft.

Add the spinach and its liquid to the pan, increase heat to high, and bring to a boil. Reduce heat to low and simmer, uncovered, for 10 minutes.

In small batches, blend or process the soup until smooth. Return the purée to the pan.

Reheat the soup over low heat. Taste and add salt, pepper, and nutmeg to taste. Ladle into warmed bowls and serve topped with the Parmesan shavings.

Serves 4 to 6

STEP 1

Trimming Fennel

Lay fennel on one flat side on a cutting board and anchor with your hand. With a sharp knife, trim the stalks and feathery leaves to within 1 inch (2.5 cm) of the bulb. Trim off any tough or damaged outer leaves.

STEP 2

Slicing Fennel

Using a sharp knife, slice each fennel bulb into quarters or sixths, or as called for in the recipe, from top to base. If the recipe calls for slices, take each of the fennel wedges and cut crosswise into slices about 1/4 inch (5 mm) thick.

Vegetables and Legumes

Pinto Bean Soup with Fresh Salsa

1 ½ cups (10½ oz/330 g) dried pinto beans

7 cups (56 fl oz/1.75 l) water

¼ cup (2 fl oz/60 ml) olive oil

2 yellow onions, diced

1 teaspoon salt

½ teaspoon ground black pepper

4 cloves garlic, minced

6 cups (48 fl oz/1.5 l) chicken stock (page 22), vegetable stock (page 18), or water

SALSA

3 ripe plum (Roma) tomatoes, seeded and diced

½ small red (Spanish) onion, finely diced

¼ cup (⅓ oz/10 g) chopped cilantro (fresh coriander)

Juice 1 lime

Salt and ground black pepper

Sour cream, to serve

Vegetables and Legumes

Sort through the beans and discard any misshapen beans or stones. Rinse well. Place the beans and water in a saucepan. Bring to a boil, reduce the heat to medium-low, cover, and simmer until all the beans are cooked through and creamy inside, about 1½ hours. Remove from the heat and set aside.

In a large pot over medium heat, warm the oil. Add the onions, salt, and pepper and sauté until the onions are lightly browned, about 10 minutes. Add the garlic and sauté for 1–2 minutes longer. Add the beans, their cooking liquid, and the stock or water.

Bring to a boil, reduce the heat to medium, and simmer, uncovered, stirring occasionally, until the beans start to break apart, 20–30 minutes. Remove the pan from the heat and let cool slightly.

Meanwhile, make the salsa: In a bowl, stir together the tomato, onion, cilantro, lime juice, and salt and pepper to taste. Cover and refrigerate until you are ready to serve.

In small batches, blend or process the bean mixture until smooth. Return the purée to the pan. Reheat over low heat, stirring often. (If not serving immediately, keep warm over very low heat, stirring often.)

Ladle the soup into warmed shallow bowls and top each serving with a spoonful of salsa and a dollop of sour cream.

Serves 6

NOTE If you prefer a spicier salsa, try this recipe using the Cherry Tomato Salsa (opposite). Alternatively, use a good commercial salsa.

Cherry Tomato Salsa

1 lb (500 g) cherry tomatoes

1 large golden (French) shallot, finely chopped

1 clove garlic, very finely chopped

2 tablespoons chopped cilantro (fresh coriander)

1 tablespoon white wine vinegar

Salt and ground black pepper

2 teaspoons fresh lime juice

2 jalapeño chilis, seeded and chopped

In a food processor, process the tomatoes until coarsely chopped. Transfer the tomatoes with their juice to a bowl. Mix in the remaining ingredients.

Cover the bowl, refrigerate, and let the flavors blend for at least 2 hours before serving.

The salsa may be refrigerated, covered, for 2–3 days.

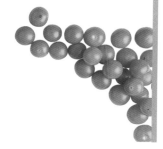

About Ginger

Native to the jungles of southern Asia, and now widely cultivated in warm climates around the world, ginger has been valued for centuries. It has been used in China as a flavoring and medicament for thousands of years, and was coming into Europe via the trade routes long before Roman times. A versatile ingredient with a warm, spicy flavor, it is used in ginger beer, sweet pastries and cakes, ice cream, and preserves, and is indispensable in many Asian cuisines.

Often erroneously called a root, ginger is in fact a rhizome, or underground stem. Fresh ginger may be grated, chopped, crushed, or sliced for use in savory dishes such as curries and stir-fries. As is the case with garlic, ginger will have a stronger flavor when grated or crushed than when simply chopped or sliced. Ginger is also available dried and powdered, crystallized, preserved in syrup, and pickled.

Young ginger, which is the cream- and pink-colored shoots of the rhizome, has the most delicate flavor and texture. As ginger ages, it darkens and develops in flavor but also becomes more fibrous. Choose ginger that is hard and heavy, with a smooth, pale, shiny, unbroken skin. Reject rhizomes that are wrinkled or that feel soft or rubbery. Store fresh ginger in a cool, dry place for up to 3 days or in the refrigerator for up to 3 weeks. If refrigerating, first wrap it in a paper towel then place in a plastic bag; this prevents the development of mold. Store dried, powdered ginger in an airtight container in a cool, dark place for up to 6 months.

Dhal with Indian Spices

1 cup (7 oz/210 g) red lentils

1 tablespoon vegetable oil

1 tablespoon yellow mustard seeds

1 tablespoon cumin seeds

1 large yellow onion, chopped

1 tablespoon grated fresh ginger

1 large clove garlic, finely chopped

½ teaspoon turmeric

4½ cups (36 fl oz/1.25 ml) chicken stock (page 22) or vegetable stock (page 18)

Salt and ground black pepper

1 fresh green chili, thinly sliced

Purchased naan bread, warmed, to serve

Lemon wedges, to serve

Place lentils in a sieve and rinse under cold running water until the water runs clear. Set aside.

Heat the oil in a medium saucepan over low heat. Add the mustard and cumin seeds and cook, stirring frequently, for 1 minute, or until aromatic and the mustard seeds begin to pop. Increase the heat to medium and add the onion, ginger, and garlic. Cook, stirring frequently, for 3 minutes, or until the onion softens slightly.

Stir in the lentils, turmeric, and stock. Cover and cook, stirring occasionally, for 25 minutes. Uncover and cook, stirring occasionally, for 15 minutes more, or until thick. Add a little more stock or water if the soup becomes too thick.

Add salt and pepper to taste. Set aside for 10 minutes before serving.

Ladle into warmed serving bowls, sprinkle with the chili, and serve with naan bread and lemon wedges.

Serves 4

Minestrone

¼ cup (2 fl oz/60 ml) extra virgin olive oil

1 small onion, finely chopped

1 clove garlic, finely chopped

1 stalk celery, finely chopped

10 oz (315 g) shelled fresh young peas

3 tablespoons yellow cornmeal (polenta)

8 cups (64 fl oz/2 l) beef stock (page 26) or meat stock (page 27)

10 oz (315 g) fresh or 5 oz (155 g) dried ribbon pasta, such as linguine or tagliatelle

Salt and ground black pepper

1 handful fresh basil leaves

Heat the oil in a frying pan over low heat. Add the onion, garlic, and celery and cook, stirring frequently, for 5 minutes. Add the peas, sprinkle with the cornmeal, and mix well. Stir in the stock and cook over low heat, covered, for 30 minutes.

Add the pasta, and salt and pepper to taste. Cook until the pasta is al dente.

Pour the soup into a warmed tureen or serving bowls, sprinkle with the basil, and serve at once.

Serves 6

Split Pea and Vegetable Soup

2 cups (12 oz/375 g) yellow or green split peas

1/4 cup (2 fl oz/60 ml) olive oil

2 yellow onions, finely chopped

2 carrots, finely chopped

2 stalks celery, finely chopped

2 cloves garlic, finely chopped

6–8 cups (48–64 fl oz/1.5–2 l) vegetable stock (page 18), chicken stock (page 22), or water

2 large sprigs fresh parsley

2 bay leaves

1 teaspoon dried thyme

Salt and ground black pepper

1/4 cup (1/3 oz/10 g) chopped fresh parsley

Lemon wedges, to serve

Sort through the peas; discard any impurities or discolored peas. Set aside.

In a large pot, warm the oil over medium heat. Add the onions, carrots, celery, and garlic and sauté until the onions are translucent, about 5 minutes.

Add 6 cups (1 1/2 qt/1.5 l) of the stock or water, the peas, parsley sprigs, bay leaves, and thyme. Bring to a boil, then reduce sheat, cover, and simmer gently, stirring occasionally, until the peas are reduced to a thick purée, about 1 1/2 hours. Add more water or stock from time to time, if necessary, to keep the peas moist.

Before serving, discard the bay leaves and parsley sprigs. Add salt and pepper to taste.

Ladle into warmed soup bowls, garnish with the chopped parsley, and serve with lemon wedges for diners to squeeze into their individual portions.

Serves 6 to 8

About Parmesan Cheese

Probably the most renowned of Italian cheeses, Parmesan takes its name from the town of Parma, in northern Italy, where it originated in about 1200. It is a hard, grainy, cooked cow's-milk cheese, straw yellow in color, with a distinctive sharp taste. Parmesan is a generic term for such cheeses, of which there are several varieties. The finest—the trademarked type known as Parmigiano-Reggiano—is produced only in certain parts of northern Italy under stringent standards that are protected by law.

Parmesan is valued both for its flavor and its ability to be used in cooking without forming strings, as many cheeses do. It is aged for 2–3 years and takes the form of huge wheels that commonly weigh 50–80 lb (25–40 kg). Best known as the world's favorite grating cheese, Parmesan can be also enjoyed as a table cheese, especially when young. It pairs well with such fruits as apples, pears, figs, and grapes, as well as with salad leaves, such as arugula (rocket). It is also added to risottos and soups.

Because it dries out and begins to lose its flavor soon after grating or shaving, Parmesan should be kept whole until just before serving. For this reason, packaged, pregrated Parmesan should be avoided. To grate small quantities, use a hand-held grater or a hand-turned winder-style grater. If grating large quantities, drop chunks into a running food processor fitted with a metal blade.

Store Parmesan wrapped tightly in plastic wrap or aluminum foil in the refrigerator for up to 2 weeks. For longer storage, wrap airtight and freeze for up to 2 months.

Stracciatella alla Fiorentina

6 cups (48 fl oz/1.5 l) chicken stock (page 22)

2 oz (60 g) stemmed fresh spinach leaves

4 eggs

¼ cup (1 oz/30 g) freshly grated Parmesan cheese, plus extra to serve

In a large saucepan, bring the stock to a boil, then reduce to a brisk simmer. Meanwhile, take half of the spinach leaves, stack them, roll tightly lengthwise into a cylinder, and slice crosswise into thin shreds. Repeat with the remaining leaves.

In a bowl, lightly beat the eggs, then stir in the cheese. While stirring the stock constantly, drizzle in the egg mixture, then add the spinach. Simmer for 2–3 minutes more.

Serve immediately. Pass extra Parmesan cheese for diners to add as they like.

NOTE Stracciatella is Italian for "little rags," and fancifully describes the shreds that form when egg and Parmesan cheese are stirred into the simmering stock. Alla Fiorentina, or Florentine, denotes a dish that contains spinach.

FISH
AND SEAFOOD

Rainbow Seafood Soup

2 teaspoons salt

2 teaspoons sugar

2 teaspoons cornstarch (cornflour)

1 teaspoon sesame oil

1 tablespoon water

6 conpoy (dried sea scallops)

4 oz (125 g) uncooked shrimp (prawns), peeled and deveined

4 oz (125 g) sea bass fillet, diced

4 cups (32 fl oz/1 liter) water

4 cups (32 fl oz/1 liter) fish stock (page 30) or prawn stock (page 30)

1 tablespoon shredded fresh ginger

2 oz (60 g) carrot, thinly sliced

1 tablespoon light soy sauce

1 teaspoon Chinese rice wine

2 tablespoons cornstarch (cornflour), dissolved in 2 tablespoons water

2 oz (60 g) cucumber, thinly sliced

1 tablespoon chopped cilantro (fresh coriander)

Serves 4 to 6

In a bowl, combine salt, sugar, cornstarch, oil, 1 tablespoon water, conpoy, shrimp, and fish. Allow to marinate for 15 minutes.

In a large saucepan, bring the 4 cups (32 fl oz/1 liter) water to a boil. Add the seafood mixture, return to a boil, then remove the seafood with a slotted spoon. Discard the cooking liquid.

Bring the stock to a boil in a separate large saucepan. Add the ginger and carrot and cook for 2 minutes. Add the seafood and return the broth to a boil. Add the soy sauce and rice wine. Stir in cornstarch solution. Serve at once, sprinkled with the cucumber and cilantro.

Italian-Style Fish Soup

3 lb (1.5 kg) assorted fish and seafood, such as octopus, cuttlefish, and squid, cleaned and cut into strips; red mullet, whiting, or other white fish, cleaned, washed, heads removed and reserved, flesh cut into chunks; mussels, scrubbed; lobster, flesh cut into chunks; and shrimp (prawns), peeled and deveined

2 onions

2 stalks celery

2 carrots

3 ripe tomatoes, coarsely chopped

Pinch of salt

1 cup (8 fl oz/250 ml) olive oil

1 sprig fresh parsley, chopped

1 small piece fresh chili, chopped

2 cloves garlic, finely chopped

1 cup (8 fl oz/250 ml) dry white wine

2 tablespoons tomato paste dissolved in ½ cup (4 fl oz/ 125 ml) hot water

4 slices coarse whole-grain (wholemeal) country bread, toasted

Coarsely chop 1 onion, 1 celery stalk, and 1 carrot. Place in a large saucepan with the reserved fish heads, the tomatoes, salt, and cold water to cover. Cook, uncovered, over medium-low heat for at least 30 minutes, until the liquid is fairly thick. Strain through a fine-mesh sieve into a clean pan and keep warm. Discard the solids.

Meanwhile, peel the remaining carrot. Thinly slice the carrot and remaining onion and celery stalk. Heat oil in a large heat-proof casserole. Add the sliced vegetables to the casserole and cook, stirring, until softened. Stir in parsley, chili, and garlic and let the flavors blend.

Add octopus, squid, and cuttle-fish (if using) to casserole. Cook until their liquid evaporates. Stir in wine; cook until evaporated. Add the tomato paste mixture, then the fish, then mussels, lobster, and shrimp (if using). Cover and cook over medium heat for 15 minutes.

Meanwhile, place a slice of toast in each serving dish, or place all of the bread in a soup tureen. Ladle the fish stock over the bread. Use a slotted spoon to lift the fish and seafood from the casserole and arrange on top of the bread. Drizzle with the cooking juices and serve hot.

Serves 4

Shrimp and Onion Soup

4 cups (32 fl oz/1 liter) water

1/4 onion

2 cloves garlic, unpeeled

1/2 bay leaf

1 sprig fresh thyme or 1 pinch dried thyme

1 teaspoon salt, or to taste

2 lb (1 kg) uncooked shrimp (prawns), unpeeled

3 tablespoons butter

3 onions, halved and thinly sliced

1 tablespoon all-purpose (plain) flour

2 cups (16 fl oz/500 ml) chicken stock (page 22)

1–2 canned chipotle chilis

Bring the water to a boil in a medium saucepan. Add the 1/4 onion, garlic, bay leaf, thyme, and salt. Simmer for 20 minutes. Add the shrimp and simmer for 3 minutes more. Pour the stock through a fine-mesh sieve into a bowl. Reserve the shrimp and discard the remaining solids. Peel the shrimp.

Melt the butter in a large saucepan over low heat and cook the sliced onions, stirring occasionally, for 25 minutes, or until tender. Add the flour and stir for 2–3 minutes. Add the reserved shrimp stock and the chicken stock. Stir to combine.

Add the shrimp and chilis to the pan and simmer for 3 minutes. Serve immediately.

Serves 6 to 8

NOTE This soup combines both French and Mexican elements. As in French onion soup, the onions are cooked gently in butter until tender, but here the shrimp (prawns) and chilis are the main flavorings, and chicken and shrimp stock are used instead of beef stock.

Crab Meat and Corn Soup

1 crab, about 12 oz (375 g), or 7 oz (220 g) drained canned crabmeat

1 tablespoon peanut oil

1 tablespoon shredded fresh ginger

3 cups (24 fl oz/750 ml) fish stock (page 30)

1 can (14 oz/440 g) creamed corn (sweetcorn)

1 tablespoon chopped cilantro (fresh coriander)

1 teaspoon Chinese rice wine

If using a fresh crab, place it, belly up, on a work surface and cut it in half. Clean thoroughly, then place in a saucepan and steam for 15 minutes. Remove the meat from the shell and set aside. Discard the shell.

Heat the oil in a large saucepan and add the ginger. When the ginger is fragrant, add the stock and corn, stirring to combine. Bring the mixture to a boil, add the crabmeat, and stir well. When the soup returns to a boil, stir in the cilantro and rice wine. Serve immediately.

Serves 4 to 6

Baja Seafood Chowder

2 tablespoons olive oil

2 cloves garlic, finely chopped

1 yellow onion, finely chopped

1 large green bell pepper (capsicum), seeded, deribbed, and coarsely chopped

1 fresh small hot green chili, seeded and finely chopped

1 cup (8 fl oz/250 ml) fish stock (page 30)

¼ cup (2 fl oz/60 ml) dry red wine or water

2 cans (each 14 oz/440 g) plum (Roma) tomatoes, coarsely chopped, with their juice

2 tablespoons tomato paste

1½ tablespoons sugar

1 teaspoon dried oregano

1 teaspoon dried basil

1 bay leaf

1 baking potato, peeled and diced

Salt and ground black pepper

12 small clams in the shell

½ lb (250 g) swordfish or sea bass fillets

½ lb (250 g) small uncooked shrimp (prawns)

½ cup (6 oz/20 g) finely chopped cilantro (fresh coriander)

Lime wedges, to serve

In a large pot, heat the oil over medium heat. Add the garlic, onion, bell pepper and chopped chili. Sauté until the onion is translucent, 2–3 minutes.

Add the stock, wine or water, tomatoes, tomato paste, sugar, oregano, basil, bay leaf, and potato. Bring to a boil, reduce the heat, cover, and simmer, stirring occasionally, until the soup is thick but still fairly liquid, about 30 minutes. Add salt and pepper to taste.

Meanwhile, discard any clams that are cracked or open. Scrub the rest well. Cut the fish into 1- to 2-inch (2.5- to 5-cm) pieces. Peel and devein the

shrimp. Add all the seafood to the pot. Raise the heat slightly, cover, and cook until the fish flakes, the shrimp turn pink, and the clams open, 7–10 minutes. Discard any clams that have not opened during cooking.

Ladle into warmed soup bowls and garnish with cilantro. Serve with lime wedges so that diners can squeeze lime juice as desired into their servings.

Serves 8 to 10

About Selecting and Storing Fish

Fresh fish should look moist and bright, and have clear eyes; bright, intact skin and scales; red, moist gills; and a clean, fresh scent. Avoid any fish that shows discoloration, dryness, or even a hint of a bad aroma. Whole fish, in general, should look almost alive.

Refrigerate fresh fish as soon as you get it home, and, ideally, cook it that day. To keep it until the next day, place the wrapped package in a container, cover with ice, and refrigerate. Always protect the flesh of filleted fish with plastic; direct contact with

ice will cause freezer burn and leach out flavor. Whole fish may sit directly in ice with no deterioration.

Frozen fish can also be very good. However, avoid any that looks dry, indicating freezer burn, or whose packaging contains liquid that has frozen, a sign of thawing and refreezing (a process that damages the fish's texture). Frozen fish will keep for 1–2 months in the freezer. To thaw, place on a plate, covered, in the refrigerator for 24 hours, then store in a pan or tray of ice until ready to cook.

Pasta and Seafood Bouillabaisse

2 tablespoons olive oil

1 large onion, chopped

2 cloves garlic, finely chopped

1 small fresh red chili, finely chopped

2 cups (16 fl oz/500 ml) fish stock (page 30)

1 large can (28 oz/880 g) plum (Roma) tomatoes, undrained

1 cup (8 fl oz/250 ml) dry white wine

4 oz (125 g) pasta shells or other small pasta shapes

2 tablespoons chopped fresh basil

Salt and ground black pepper

16 mussels, beards removed, scrubbed

1 lb (500 g) firm white boneless fish fillets, cut into 1-inch (2.5-cm) cubes

8 uncooked jumbo shrimp (king prawns), peeled, and deveined, tails left intact

Crusty bread, to serve

Serves 4

Heat oil in a large saucepan. Add onion, garlic, and chili and cook, stirring, for 4–5 minutes, or until onion is soft. Stir in the stock, tomatoes, and wine. Bring to a boil, then reduce heat and simmer for 25–30 minutes.

Meanwhile, cook the pasta in plenty of boiling salted water until al dente. Drain.

To the tomato mixture, add the basil, salt and pepper to taste, and the mussels. Cover and cook for 2–3 minutes. Add fish and shrimp; simmer for 2–3 minutes, or until just cooked. Discard any mussels that have not opened. Stir in cooked pasta and heat through. Serve with crusty bread.

Tomato Gumbo with Sea Bass

1 whole sea bass, about 3 lb (1.5 kg), cleaned, skinned, and filleted, head and bones reserved

⅓ cup (2½ fl oz/80 ml) olive oil or vegetable oil

½ cup (2 oz/60 g) diced yellow onion

¼ cup (1 oz/30 g) all-purpose (plain) flour

2 tablespoons diced spicy sausage

½ cup (2 oz/60 g) diced green bell pepper (capsicum)

1 celery stalk, diced

3 cloves garlic, sliced

1 teaspoon salt, plus extra to taste

½ teaspoon peppercorns

½ teaspoon dried thyme

1 bay leaf

4 cups (1½ lb/750 g) diced plum (Roma) tomatoes, fresh or canned

2 cups (16 fl oz/500 ml) water

2 tablespoons butter

¼ lemon, sliced

1 teaspoon chopped fresh flat-leaf (Italian) parsley, plus 4 sprigs extra, for garnish

¼ teaspoon filé powder

Cover and refrigerate the bass fillets. Wash the head and bones in cold water, then cut the bones into large pieces. Set aside.

Heat ¼ cup (2 fl oz/60 ml) of the oil in a large saucepan. Add the onion, flour, and sausage and stir until the flour browns, 6–8 minutes. Stir in the bell pepper, celery, garlic, 1 teaspoon salt, peppercorns, thyme, bay leaf, tomatoes, and water. Add the fish head and bones and bring to a boil. Reduce heat and simmer, uncovered, for 1 hour, occasionally skimming foam and impurities from surface.

During the final 10 minutes of cooking, prepare the bass. Cut

each fillet in halves and season with salt to taste. Heat the butter and remaining oil in a large frying pan. Add the fish and cook for 4 minutes. Turn and cook until fish is opaque, 4–5 minutes.

Remove the gumbo from the heat. Discard fish head and bones. Strain into a small pan, pressing on the solids to extract all their liquid. Add lemon and parsley, then stir in filé powder.

To serve, ladle gumbo into bowls, top with a piece of fish, and garnish with parsley sprigs.

Serves 4

Seafood Gazpacho

4 tomatoes, peeled and seeded

1 medium cucumber, peeled and seeded

1 small red bell pepper (capsicum)

1 yellow pimiento (sweet pepper)

1 medium red (Spanish) onion

2 cloves garlic, finely chopped

Dash of hot-pepper sauce, such as Tabasco

1 teaspoon ground cumin

Juice of 1 lime

4 cups (32 fl oz/1 liter) tomato juice

2 tablespoons balsamic vinegar

½ cup (4 fl oz/125 ml) olive oil

Salt and ground black pepper

¼ cup (⅓ oz/10 g) chopped cilantro (fresh coriander), plus extra leaves, for garnish

1 avocado, finely chopped

1 cup (8 oz/250 g) combined chopped cooked shrimp (prawns) and crab meat

Finely chop the tomatoes, cucumber, bell pepper, pimiento, and onion and place in a large bowl. Add the garlic, hot-pepper sauce, cumin, lime juice, tomato juice, and balsamic vinegar and stir to combine. Stir in the oil. Add salt and pepper to taste and the chopped cilantro. Refrigerate until the soup is well chilled.

Just before serving, stir in the avocado and combined shrimp and crab meat. Sprinkle with the extra cilantro and serve.

Serves 8

Mediterranean Fish Soup

2 lb (1 kg) mussels in the shells

4 lb (2 kg) assorted firm fish fillets (such as bass, flounder, halibut, haddock, snapper, cod, and grouper)

Salt

½ cup (4 fl oz/125 ml) olive oil

2 cups (7 oz/220 g) sliced yellow onions

1 cup (3 oz/90 g) sliced leeks, washed well

4 cloves garlic, finely chopped

2 celery stalks, chopped

1½ cups (9 oz/280 g) peeled, seeded, and chopped tomatoes (fresh or canned)

4 sprigs fresh thyme

1 bay leaf

½ cup (¾ oz/20 g) chopped fresh flat-leaf (Italian) parsley

1 cup (8 fl oz/250 ml) dry white wine

7 cups (56 fl oz/1.75 l) water

1 lb (500 g) uncooked shrimp (prawns), peeled and deveined

Fresh lemon juice

Ground black pepper

Discard any mussels that do not close to the touch. Scrub the mussels under cold running water and remove their beards. Place in a bowl and refrigerate until needed.

Cut the fish fillets into 2-inch (5-cm) pieces. Place on a plate, sprinkle with salt, and refrigerate until needed.

Heat the olive oil in a large saucepan over medium heat. Add the onions and leeks and cook, stirring often, until they are translucent, about 8 minutes. Stir in garlic, celery, tomatoes, thyme, bay leaf, and half of the parsley. Cook, stirring often, for 2 minutes.

Add the wine and water and bring mixture to a boil over high heat. Reduce heat to medium and simmer for 15 minutes. Stir in the salted fish pieces, cover, and simmer for 5 minutes. Stir in shrimp and mussels, cover, and simmer until the mussels open, 3–4 minutes. Discard any mussels that have not opened.

Season with lemon juice and salt and pepper to taste. Serve immediately, sprinkled with the remaining parsley.

Serves 6

Vietnamese Sour Fish Soup

1 whole catfish, striped bass, sea bass, or red snapper (about 2 lb/1 kg), cleaned, scaled, washed, and dried

1 tablespoon fish sauce

¼ teaspoon ground black pepper

1 green (spring) onion, thinly sliced

FISH SOUP

1 tablespoon vegetable oil

2 purple (Asian) shallots, thinly sliced

3 lemongrass stalks, cut into 2-inch (5-cm) lengths, crushed

6 cups (48 fl oz/1.5 l) water or chicken stock (page 22)

2 oz (60 g) tamarind pulp, chopped

1 cup (8 fl oz/250 ml) boiling water

1 cup (6 oz/185 g) diced pineapple

½ cup (2½ oz/75 g) drained, sliced, canned bamboo shoots

2 small fresh red chilis, seeded and thinly sliced

1 tablespoon sugar

2 tablespoons fish sauce, or to taste

2 small, firm tomatoes, cut into wedges

1 cup (2 oz/60 g) bean sprouts

Salt and ground black pepper

Cilantro (fresh coriander) sprigs or sliced fresh mint leaves, for garnish

1 lime, cut into wedges

Serves 6

NOTE Nearly every country in Southeast Asia has its own version of sour fish soup. This southern Vietnamese version has a wonderful combination of herbaceous, spicy, fruity, tangy, sweet, and savory flavors. Serve with steamed rice on the side.

VIETNAMESE SOUR FISH SOUP

Remove the fish head. Using a thin, flexible knife, carefully cut between the fillet and the backbone, working from the tail up. Remove the fillet, then turn the fish over and repeat to remove the remaining fillet. Reserve the fish head, bones, and any scraps. Cut fillets into 1-inch (2.5-cm) cubes and place in a bowl with the fish sauce, pepper, and green onion. Toss gently to combine. Set aside at room temperature to marinate.

For the fish soup, heat the oil in a large saucepan over medium heat. When hot, add the fish head, bones, and scraps and stir to combine. Add the shallots

and lemongrass and cook gently, stirring often, until fragrant, 3–5 minutes. Do not let the mixture brown. Add the water or stock and bring to a boil. Reduce heat to low and simmer, uncovered, for 20 minutes.

Meanwhile, in a small bowl, soak the tamarind pulp in the boiling water for 15 minutes. Mash the pulp using the back of a fork to help it dissolve. Pour the mixture through a fine-mesh sieve into another small bowl, pressing against the tamarind pulp to extract as much of the liquid as possible. Discard the pulp and set the liquid aside until needed.

Pour the fish soup through a fine-mesh sieve into a large saucepan. Discard the contents of the sieve.

Bring the soup to a boil. Stir in the tamarind liquid, pineapple, bamboo shoots, chilis, sugar, and fish sauce. Reduce the heat to medium and simmer for 1 minute. Add the tomatoes and marinated fish and continue to simmer until the fish is opaque and feels firm to the touch, 3–5 minutes. Add bean sprouts and salt and pepper to taste.

Serve immediately, garnished with cilantro or mint, and accompanied with lime wedges.

Steamed Clams in Garlic Broth

4 dozen clams in the shell, well scrubbed

1 tablespoon olive oil

4 cloves garlic, minced

4 cups (32 fl oz/1 liter) fish stock (page 30)

1 cup (8 fl oz/250 ml) dry white wine or ¾ cup (6 fl oz/180 ml) water and ¼ cup (2 fl oz/60 ml) fresh lemon juice

2 tablespoons unsalted butter

4 tablespoons coarsely chopped fresh parsley

2 large lemons, cut into wedges

Discard any cracked or open clams. In a large pot, warm the oil over low to medium heat. Add the garlic and sauté until translucent, 1–2 minutes. Then add the stock and wine or water and lemon juice, raise the heat, and bring to a boil. Reduce the heat slightly, add the clams, cover, and steam just until they open, 7–10 minutes.

Line a strainer with cheesecloth (muslin) and set inside a large bowl. Pour the contents of the pot into the bowl; discard any unopened clams.

Return the strained liquid to the pot over medium heat. Add the butter and parsley and stir until

the butter melts. Arrange the clams in warmed shallow soup plates and ladle the broth over them. Serve with lemon wedges.

Serves 6 to 8

NOTE Fresh mussels may replace the clams in this recipe. Serve the soup with plenty of crusty bread to sop up the broth.

New England Clam Chowder

3 dozen clams in the shell

2 tablespoons unsalted butter

1 clove garlic, minced

2 cups (16 fl oz/500 ml) water

1 cup (8 fl oz/250 ml) dry white wine or fish stock (page 30)

4 oz (125 g) lean bacon, chopped

1 leek, washed and thinly sliced

1 tablespoon all-purpose (plain) flour

2 cups (16 fl oz/500 ml) light (single) cream

1 lb (500 g) red potatoes, cubed

¾ teaspoon dried thyme

Ground black pepper

1 tablespoon snipped chives

1 tablespoon chopped parsley

Discard any cracked or open clams. Scrub well. In a large pot, melt 1 tablespoon butter over low heat. Add garlic and sauté until it softens, 1–2 minutes. Add the water and wine or stock, raise the heat, and bring to a boil. Reduce heat slightly and immediately add the clams. Cover and steam just until they open, 7–10 minutes.

Line a sieve with cheesecloth (muslin) and set inside a large bowl. Empty the pot into the sieve; discard any unopened clams. Set the clams and strained liquid aside separately.

Rinse out the pot, add the remaining butter, and place over medium heat. Add bacon and sauté until it just begins to brown. Add leek and sauté until it begins to soften, 2–3 minutes. Sprinkle in the flour and cook, stirring, 1 minute more. Stirring continuously, pour in reserved clam liquid and the cream. When the liquid reaches a boil, reduce the heat to a simmer. Add the potatoes and thyme.

Pull clams from shells. Cut any large clams into ½-inch (12-mm) pieces. When the potatoes are tender, after about 15 minutes, add the clams and simmer for 1–2 minutes more. Add pepper to taste. Ladle into bowls and garnish with chives and parsley.

Cadiz Fish Soup

1 whole white fish, about 2 lb (1 kg), cleaned, scaled, washed, and cut crosswise into steaks, head reserved

2 leeks, sliced lengthwise

2 carrots, sliced crosswise

3 cups (24 fl oz/750 ml) water

¼ cup (2 fl oz/60 ml) dry white wine

Salt

¼ cup (2 fl oz/60 ml) olive oil

1 onion, thinly sliced

Juice of 1 orange

1 loaf crusty French bread, sliced (4–6 thin slices per person)

Place the fish head, leeks, carrots, water, wine, and salt in a large saucepan. Bring to a boil, then reduce the heat and simmer for 30 minutes to make a broth. Strain through a fine-mesh sieve lined with cheese-cloth (muslin) and reserve about 2 cups (16 fl oz/500 ml) of the liquid. Keep warm. Discard the contents of the sieve.

Meanwhile, salt the fish slices on both sides and set aside.

Heat the oil in a heatproof casserole over low heat. Add the onion and cook, stirring often, until it begins to brown. Stir in half of the warm broth and cook for about 15 minutes,

or until the onion is very soft. Stir in the remaining broth and the fish. Cook over low heat for 10 minutes.

Stir in the orange juice and serve immediately accompanied with the bread.

Serves 4

About Mussels

Mussels are edible mollusks, closely related to the clam. Those used for culinary purposes are marine mussels of the genus *Mytilus*, which usually live in shallow waters along ocean coasts, and attach themselves to rocks or piers by producing strong, sticky threads made of protein. Fresh-water mussels, which are now scarce, are distant relations of marine mussels. They were once a major source of mother-of-pearl, a rainbow-colored material that lines their shells.

Commercially harvested mussels have usually spent some time in purifying tanks to cleanse them of pollutants and other impurities before they are sold. If you are not sure if the mussels you have bought have undergone this process, or if you have collected them yourself, put them in clean water in which a little salt has been dissolved and leave them for no more than two hours, or they will asphyxiate.

Before cooking, scrape mussels to remove barnacles and weed, then wash and scrub well. Pull off the coarse threads, known as the beard, attached to the shell. Use only fresh, live mussels, which have closed shells; discard any that do not pull their shells together quickly when disturbed, or that feel very heavy (a sign that they are full of mud). Cook mussels by placing them wet in a shallow layer in a pan. Add a small amount of water or white wine, if desired, and cook over high heat with the lid on just until all or most of the mussels have opened, about 2 minutes. Do not overcook, or the mussels will be tough. Discard any shells that have not opened naturally during cooking. Strain any cooking juices through cheesecloth (muslin) and use the liquid as a sauce.

Shellfish Soup

6 lb (3 kg) mixed shellfish (such as small clams, mussels, pipis, and scallops)

¼ cup (2 fl oz/60 ml) extra virgin olive oil

1 clove garlic, finely chopped

1 small onion, chopped

½ cup (4 fl oz/125 ml) dry white wine

1 lb (500 g) tomatoes, chopped

Salt and ground black pepper

1 fresh chili

1 handful chopped fresh parsley

6 slices bread, toasted

Wash and brush the shellfish thoroughly under running water. Transfer to a frying pan. Cover and cook over medium heat just until all or most of the shellfish have opened. Drain, reserving the cooking liquid. Discard any shellfish that have not opened. Also discard the empty half-shells, reserving the halves with the meat attached. Line a sieve with damp cheesecloth (muslin), place the sieve into a bowl, and strain the cooking liquid into the sieve. Set shellfish and cooking liquid aside.

Heat the oil in a frying pan. Add the garlic and onion and cook, stirring often, until browned.

Stir in the strained cooking liquid, wine, tomatoes, and salt and pepper to taste. Cook for 15 minutes, then stir in the chili. The soup should be fairly thin; add a little water if needed.

Add the reserved shellfish and cook for 1 minute. Stir in the parsley. Place a slice of toast in each serving dish. Pour over the soup and serve immediately.

Serves 6

Clear Broth with Grilled Seafood

6 cups (48 fl oz/1.5 l) fish stock
(page 30)

8 oz (250 g) sea scallops

8 oz (250 g) uncooked shrimp
(prawns), peeled and deveined

2 tablespoons unsalted butter,
melted

Salt and ground white pepper

Fresh chives, snipped into
1-inch (2.5-cm) lengths

Preheat a broiler (griller) or a gas or electric grill (barbecue) until very hot, or prepare a fire in a charcoal grill.

In a saucepan, bring the fish stock to a boil over medium heat. Reduce the heat to very low and cover the pan.

Meanwhile, brush the scallops and shrimp with the melted butter and season lightly with salt and pepper. Place the seafood on an unheated broiler rack or grill rack and cook close to the heat source until well seared and just cooked through, 1–2 minutes per side.

When the seafood is almost done, ladle the hot stock into warmed large, shallow soup plates, taking care not to fill them all the way. Neatly place the pieces of seafood in the stock; they should protrude slightly above the surface of the liquid. Float the chives in the stock and serve immediately.

Serves 4 to 6

Mussels in Saffron Broth

2 tablespoons olive oil

2 yellow onions, finely sliced

Salt and ground black pepper

4 cloves garlic, sliced

1½ cups (12 fl oz/375 ml) dry white wine

1 fresh thyme sprig

1 teaspoon saffron threads

2½ cups (20 fl oz/625 ml) bottled clam juice or fish stock

1 cup (8 fl oz/250 ml) tomato juice

3 lb (1.5 kg) small mussels in the shells

½ cup (¾ oz/20 g) chopped fresh flat-leaf (Italian) parsley

Heat 1 tablespoon of the olive oil in a large, heavy-based saucepan over medium heat. Add half of the onions, and salt and pepper to taste. Cook, stirring often, until the onions are light golden, 8–10 minutes. Add the garlic and stir for 1 minute. Stir in the wine and bring to a boil. Boil until the mixture has reduced by half, about 8 minutes. Stir in the thyme, saffron, clam juice or fish stock, and tomato juice and return to a boil. Reduce the heat to low and simmer for 10 minutes to blend the flavors. Strain the broth and discard the solids. Set aside.

Scrub the mussels under cold running water and remove their beards. Discard any mussels that do not close when touched.

Place 2 large frying pans over high heat (or cook in batches in 1 pan). Add 2 teaspoons of the remaining olive oil to each pan. When the oil is hot, add half of the remaining onions to each pan and cook, stirring occasionally, until they just begin to color, about 4 minutes. Add half of the mussels to each pan, spreading them out in a single layer, and cook, stirring occasionally, for 2 minutes.

Divide strained broth between the pans (or, if the mussels are being cooked in batches, add an equal amount to each batch) and bring to a boil. Reduce the heat to medium, cover, and cook just until all or most of the mussels open, about 2 minutes. Discard any mussels that have not opened.

Add half of the parsley to each pan or batch. Toss to combine and then spoon the mussels into warmed serving dishes. Divide the broth among the bowls and serve immediately.

Serves 4

Lobster Soup

Sea salt

2 medium spiny rock lobsters
(about 2 lb/1 kg each)

¾ cup (6 fl oz/180 ml) olive oil

2 medium onions, chopped

2 cloves garlic, finely chopped

2 medium tomatoes, peeled and
chopped

4 cups (24 fl oz/1 liter) fish stock

2 tablespoons finely chopped
fresh flat-leaf (Italian) parsley

2 bay leaves

Ground black pepper

Bring to the boil a large pot
of water to which sea salt has
been added. Add the lobsters
and cook for 8–10 minutes.
Remove, allow to cool a little,
then remove the meat from the
shells, chop up, and set aside.
Discard shells.

Heat the oil in a large heatproof
casserole and fry the onion
over low heat. When it starts
to brown, add the garlic and
tomatoes and allow to reduce
over low heat almost to the
consistency of a purée.

Add the lobster, fish stock,
parsley, and bay leaves. Cook
over high heat for 10 minutes.

Add salt and a little pepper to
taste. Lower the heat and cook
over medium heat for another
20 minutes. Remove bay leaves
and discard.

Serve in the casserole, or ladle
into warmed soup bowls.

Serves 4

Cream of Shrimp Soup

3 tablespoons unsalted butter

2 carrots, finely chopped

1 yellow onion, finely chopped

1 celery stalk, finely chopped

1 small baking potato, peeled and finely chopped

2 lb (1 kg) small shrimp (prawns), peeled, deveined, shells reserved

2 cups (16 fl oz/500 ml) fish stock (page 30)

2 cups (16 fl oz/500 ml) light (single) cream

½ tablespoon dried thyme

1 bay leaf, crumbled

Salt and white pepper

1 tablespoon fresh chervil or parsley leaves

In a large saucepan, melt the butter over medium heat. Add the carrot, onion, celery, potato, and shrimp shells and sauté until the onion is translucent and the shrimp shells turn pink, 2–3 minutes.

Add the stock, cream, thyme, bay leaf, and all but a handful of the peeled shrimp. Bring to a boil, reduce the heat, cover, and simmer gently for about 20 minutes.

In small batches, blend or process the soup until smooth. Force the purée through a fine-mesh sieve, pressing the solids with a wooden spoon to extract all the liquid. Return the soup to the pan and add salt and white pepper to taste.

Cut the remaining shrimp into small chunks and add to the soup. Simmer gently until cooked through, 2–3 minutes. Garnish with chervil or parsley.

Serves 4 to 6

Crab Bisque

1 large carrot, finely chopped

1 celery stalk, finely chopped

1 bay leaf, crumbled

1 teaspoon chopped fresh tarragon, plus extra for garnish (optional)

¾ cup (6 fl oz/180 ml) dry sherry (optional)

2 cups (16 fl oz/500 ml) dry white wine or fish stock (page 30)

2 cups (16 fl oz/500 ml) water

2 cups (16 fl oz/500 ml) heavy (double) cream

1½ cups (3 oz/90 g) fine fresh bread crumbs

Salt and white pepper

2 whole steamed crabs, cracked

¼ cup (2 oz/60 g) unsalted butter

2 golden (French) shallots, finely chopped

1 large yellow onion, finely chopped

Remove the crabmeat from the shells, reserving shells. Flake the meat and set aside.

In a large, heavy saucepan, melt the butter over low to medium heat. Add the shallots, onion, carrot, celery, bay leaf, and the 1 teaspoon tarragon. Sauté until the vegetables begin to soften, 5–7 minutes.

Add the crab shells and sauté, stirring constantly, for about 5 minutes more. Add the sherry, if using; raise the heat slightly, stir briefly, then add the white wine or stock, water, and half of the reserved crabmeat.

Bring to a boil, reduce the heat, and simmer briskly until the liquid reduces by about half, about 20 minutes. Remove the crab shell pieces and discard.

Empty the pan contents into a food mill set inside a bowl; purée. Or, pour the contents into a fine-mesh sieve set inside a bowl and press with a wooden spoon to extract all the liquid. Discard the contents of the sieve.

Rinse the saucepan, return the liquid to it, and bring to a boil. Reduce the heat to low and stir in the cream, then the bread crumbs. Simmer briskly until

thick, stirring occasionally, about 10 minutes more. Stir in the remaining reserved crabmeat and simmer for 5 minutes more.

Add salt and pepper to taste, ladle into warmed bowls, and garnish with tarragon, if desired.

Serves 4 to 6

NOTE The crab shells are essential to enhance the flavor and color of the soup.

Scallop Soup with Crostini

1½ lb (750 g) bay or sea scallops, with roe if desired

2 tablespoons extra virgin olive oil, plus extra for brushing

1⅓ cups (4 oz/125 g) sliced leeks (white parts only)

½ cup (2 oz/60 g) thinly sliced yellow onion

6 oz (185 g) pancetta, fat removed, cut into thin strips

4 cloves garlic, thinly sliced, plus 1 clove garlic, cut in half

2 cups (12 oz/375 g) peeled, seeded, and chopped plum (Roma) tomatoes (fresh or canned)

1½ cups (12 fl oz/375 ml) fruity Italian white wine

5 cups (40 fl oz/1.25 l) fish stock (page 30)

8 oz (250 g) fresh white mushrooms, stems discarded, sliced

4 tablespoons chopped fresh parsley

1 bay leaf

2 strips orange zest (rind), each 2 inches (5 cm) long and ½ inch (1 cm) wide

½ teaspoon fresh thyme leaves

¼ teaspoon fennel seeds

⅛ teaspoon powdered saffron

Salt and ground white pepper

4 slices coarse country bread

Small fresh basil leaves, for garnish

Grated Parmesan cheese, for garnish

If using sea scallops, cut crosswise into ½-inch (12-mm) thick slices. Set aside.

Heat the 2 tablespoons olive oil in a large saucepan or stockpot over medium heat. Add leek and onion and cook, stirring, until just translucent, about 3 minutes; do not allow to brown. Add the pancetta and cook, stirring, for 2 minutes. Stir in sliced garlic and tomatoes and cook for 1 minute.

Increase heat to high, add 1¼ cups (10 fl oz/315 ml) of the wine, and stir to dislodge any browned bits on the base of the pan. Bring to a boil, then stir in the stock, mushrooms, parsley, bay leaf, orange zest,

thyme, fennel seeds, and saffron. Return to a boil, then reduce heat to medium and simmer, uncovered, for 15–20 minutes, or until the mushrooms are cooked and the soup has reduced and thickened slightly.

Add the scallops and cook until almost opaque in the center, 2–3 minutes. Add the remaining wine and simmer until the scallops are just opaque, about 1 minute longer. Discard bay leaf and add salt and pepper to taste.

Meanwhile, toast the bread. Rub the cut sides of the halved garlic clove over 1 side of each piece of toast, then brush lightly with the extra olive oil.

To serve, place a piece of toast, garlic-rubbed side up, in each bowl. Ladle the soup over the toast and serve immediately, garnished with the basil leaves and Parmesan cheese to taste.

Serves 4

About Basil

Native to India, basil is one of the most popular herbs, and has been cultivated in the Mediterranean for thousands of years. Its name comes from the Greek *basilikon phyton*, meaning kingly herb, a title that attests to the high regard in which it is held. Of its many species, sweet basil is the most popular; other varieties include bush basil, lemon-scented basil, Thai purple basil, and the holy basil used in Hindu religious ceremonies. Like most herbs, basil has few calories (kilojoules), and reasonable quantities provide a good source of calcium and iron.

Basil is an annual plant that grows best in warm, humid conditions. Its curved, plump-looking, veined leaves vary greatly in size between species, but are always highly aromatic. The taste is reminiscent of of anise and cloves. Basil's culinary dominance is evidenced in its wide use in Italian cooking, bouquet garni, pesto, herbal oils and vinegars, salads, and for accenting any tomato dish. It is also used to flavor the liqueur chartreuse. Basil should be harvested in early autumn, before flowering. Dried basil has quite a different flavor from fresh basil, and is not an adequate substitute for it.

Seafood and Okra Gumbo

⅓ cup (3 fl oz/90 ml) vegetable oil

1 yellow onion, coarsely chopped

2 cloves garlic, finely chopped

3 tablespoons all-purpose (plain) flour

4 cups (32 fl oz/1 liter) fish stock, heated (page 30)

1 can (14 oz/440 g) plum (Roma) tomatoes, with their juice

1 lb (500 g) cooked lump crabmeat, coarsely flaked

½ lb (250 g) okra, trimmed and cut into ½-inch (12-mm) pieces

1 green bell pepper (capsicum), seeded, deribbed, and diced

2 bay leaves

1 teaspoon dried basil

1 teaspoon dried oregano

1 teaspoon dried thyme

1–2 teaspoons hot-pepper sauce, plus extra for serving

Salt and ground black pepper

1 lb (500 g) shrimp (prawns), peeled and deveined

2 cups (14 oz/440 g) steamed long-grain white rice

In a large, heavy pan, warm the oil over low to medium heat. Add onion and garlic and sauté until translucent, 2–3 minutes. Reduce heat to low, sprinkle in the flour, and continue sautéing, stirring occasionally, until the flour turns hazelnut brown, about 5 minutes more.

Whisking continuously with a wire whisk, slowly stir in the stock. Add the tomatoes, crushing them slightly with a wooden spoon. Then add the crabmeat, okra, bell pepper, bay leaves, basil, oregano, thyme, and hot-pepper sauce. Raise the heat and bring to a boil. Reduce the heat to low, cover partially, and simmer until thick but still fairly liquid, about 1 hour.

Add salt and pepper to taste and, if desired, more hot-pepper sauce. Stir in the shrimp and simmer until pink and cooked through, about 5 minutes.

Mound some of the rice in the center of individual soup bowls. Ladle the gumbo over it. Pass extra hot-pepper sauce.

Serves 8 to 10

NOTE This hearty soup from Louisiana, USA, is a meal in itself. If desired, add some chicken, diced ham, and/or andouille sausage when you add the crabmeat.

Leek and Salt Cod Soup

10 oz (315 g) dried salt cod, soaked in water for 12 hours

⅓ cup (2½ fl oz/80 ml) olive oil

4 cloves garlic, peeled

4 medium leeks, chopped

2 lb (1 kg) potatoes, cut into chunks

Salt and ground black pepper

Drain the cod. Remove the skin and bones, then break the flesh into small pieces.

Heat the olive oil in a heatproof casserole. Add the garlic and stir for 30 seconds. Add the leeks and cook, stirring often, for 3 minutes. Add the potatoes and cook, stirring often, until lightly browned.

Add enough water to cover the vegetables and bring to a boil. Stir in the cod. Reduce the heat to low, cover, and simmer for 45 minutes, stirring occasionally. Add salt and pepper to taste, ladle into warmed soup bowls, and serve immediately.

Serves 4

MEAT
AND POULTRY

Wonton Soup

8 oz (250 g) pork fillet, ground (minced)

2 teaspoons salt

1 teaspoon sesame oil

1 teaspoon cornstarch (cornflour)

4 oz (125 g) bamboo shoots, finely chopped

1 lb (500 g) Chinese cabbage, washed, dried, and finely chopped

48 wonton wrappers

6 cups (48 fl oz/1.5 l) boiling water

1 cup (8 fl oz/250 ml) cold water

4 cups (32 fl oz/1 liter) chicken stock (page 22)

1 teaspoon Chinese rice wine

1 tablespoon light soy sauce

½ teaspoon ground black pepper

Serves 4–6

Combine pork, salt, sesame oil, and cornstarch in a bowl. Mix well. Add bamboo shoots and cabbage and mix well. Spoon about 1½ teaspoons of pork mixture into the center of a wrapper. Wrap up and squeeze lightly. Repeat with remaining pork mixture and wrappers.

Drop wontons into a large pan containing the boiling water. Add the cold water. When water returns to a boil and wontons float to the surface, remove, drain, and place in soup bowls.

Bring the stock to a boil. Stir in the rice wine, soy sauce, and pepper. Pour over the wontons and serve at once.

Sour and Peppery Soup

2 teaspoons salt

1 teaspoon sugar

1 tablespoon cornstarch (cornflour)

2 tablespoons water

2 oz (60 g) pork fillet, shredded

2 oz (60 g) uncooked shrimp (prawns), peeled and deveined

2 cups (16 fl oz/500 ml) water, extra

4 cups (32 fl oz/1 liter) chicken stock (page 22)

12 pieces cloud ear fungus, soaked in cold water for 30 minutes, then drained

2 oz (60 g) bean curd, shredded

2 oz (60 g) bamboo shoots, sliced

1 tablespoon shredded fresh ginger

1 tablespoon chopped green (spring) onion

2 tablespoons aromatic or cider vinegar

1 teaspoon chili oil

½ teaspoon ground black pepper

1 teaspoon sugar

2 tablespoons cornstarch (cornflour), extra, dissolved in 2 tablespoons water

1 egg, lightly beaten

1 teaspoon Chinese rice wine

2 teaspoons dark soy sauce

Combine salt, sugar, cornstarch, and 2 tablespoons water in a bowl. Transfer half of the mixture to a separate bowl. Add the pork to one of the bowls and the shrimp to the other; toss well. Set aside to marinate for 15 minutes.

In a large saucepan, bring the 2 cups (16 fl oz/500 ml) water to a boil. Add the drained pork and cook for 1 minute. Add the drained shrimp and cook for 1 minute more. Discard the marinade. Drain the shrimp and pork and set aside. Wash and dry the pan.

Add the stock to the clean pan and bring to a boil. Stir in the cloud ear fungus, bean curd, bamboo shoots, ginger, green onion, vinegar, chili oil, pepper, and sugar.

When the mixture returns to a boil, add the pork and shrimp. Stir in the dissolved cornstarch mixture, then stir in the egg. Add the rice wine and soy sauce and heat through before serving.

Serves 4–6

Italian Mixed Vegetable Soup

2 tablespoons extra virgin olive oil

3 small white onions, thinly sliced

3 oz (90 g) pancetta, diced

5 oz (155 g) ground (minced) lean beef

3 tablespoons shelled green peas

6 artichoke hearts, cut into wedges

30 asparagus tips

3 tablespoons shelled fava (broad) beans

4 cups (32 fl oz/1 liter) beef stock, boiling

Coarse country bread, cubed and toasted

Heat the oil in a large saucepan over medium-high heat. Add the onion and cook, stirring often, until golden. Add the pancetta and beef and cook, stirring often, for 10 minutes, or until well browned.

Stir in the peas, artichokes, asparagus, fava beans, and boiling stock. Reduce heat and simmer for 15 minutes. Serve immediately, topped with the toasted cubes of bread.

Serves 4

Minestrone with Barley

1 cup (6 oz/185 g) pearl barley, soaked in cold water for 12 hours, then drained

3 oz (90 g) sausage meat, crumbled

1 oz (30 g) prosciutto, finely chopped

1 celery stalk, diced

1 onion, diced

2–3 potatoes, peeled and diced

Salt

14 cups (3½ qt/3.5 l) water

½ cup (2 oz/60 g) grated Parmesan cheese

Cook drained barley in boiling salted water for 45 minutes; drain and set aside.

Meanwhile, plunge the sausage meat into boiling water and then squeeze it to remove the fat.

In a large saucepan, combine the sausage meat, prosciutto, celery, onion, potatoes, salt, and water. Simmer for 30 minutes. Stir in barley and cook for 45 minutes more, or until barley is soft and creamy. Place 2 tablespoons of cheese in each bowl and ladle the hot soup over the top. Serve immediately.

Serves 4

Fava Bean Soup

⅓ cup (2½ fl oz/80 ml) extra virgin olive oil

3 oz (90 g) pancetta, chopped

1 onion, chopped

1 carrot, chopped

1 celery stalk, chopped

1¼ lb (625 g) plum (Roma) tomatoes, peeled and diced

3 oz (90 g) lean beef, cubed

1¼ lb (625 g) shelled fresh fava (broad) beans

8 cups (2 qt/2 l) clear chicken stock

Salt and ground pepper

Heat the oil in a frying pan over medium heat, add the pancetta, onion, carrot, and celery, and cook, stirring often, until onion is translucent, about 5 minutes.

Stir in the tomatoes, beef, and fava beans. Add the stock and cook over low heat, stirring occasionally, for 30 minutes. Add salt and pepper to taste and serve at once.

Serves 6

Green Soup with Kale and Potatoes

¼ cup (2 fl oz/60 ml) olive oil

1 large yellow onion, chopped

2 cloves garlic, finely chopped

3 baking potatoes, about
1 lb (500 g) total weight, peeled
and thinly sliced

6 cups (48 fl oz/1.5 l) water

Salt and ground black pepper

12 oz (375 g) kale, washed

4 oz (125 g) chouriço, linguiça, or
chorizo sausage

4 teaspoons olive oil, extra

Heat the oil in a large saucepan over medium heat. Add the onion and cook until tender, about 8 minutes. Add the garlic and potatoes and cook, stirring, for 3 minutes. Add the water and 1 teaspoon of salt. Cover and simmer until the potatoes are very soft, about 20 minutes.

Meanwhile, remove the tough stems from the kale. Stack the leaves, roll, and cut crosswise into fine strips.

Cook the sausage in a frying pan over medium heat until cooked through, about 10 minutes. Cool, then slice.

Use a potato masher to mash the potatoes in the liquid in the pan. Return to low heat, add the sausage, and cook, stirring, for 5 minutes. Add the kale, stir well, and simmer, uncovered, for 4 minutes. Add salt and pepper to taste. Drizzle each serving with 1 teaspoon olive oil, and serve at once.

Serves 4

Meatball Soup with Egg and Lemon

1 lb (500 g) ground (minced) lean beef and/or lamb

1 cup (5 oz/155 g) grated or finely chopped onion

⅓ cup (2½ oz/75 g) long-grain white rice or ½ cup (2 oz/60 g) fine dried bread crumbs

½ cup (⅔ oz/20 g) chopped fresh flat-leaf (Italian) parsley

2 tablespoons chopped fresh mint or dill

3 eggs

Salt and ground black pepper

6 cups (48 fl oz/1.5 l) chicken stock (page 22)

¼ cup (2 fl oz/60 ml) fresh lemon juice

Combine the meat, onion, rice or bread crumbs, half of the parsley, all the mint or dill, and 1 of the eggs in a bowl. Add salt and pepper to taste. Using your hands, knead the mixture until well combined. Shape into small balls, about ½ inch (12 mm) in diameter.

Bring the stock to a boil in a large pan over medium-high heat. Add the meatballs, reduce the heat to low, cover, and simmer gently until meatballs are cooked, 25–30 minutes.

Beat the remaining 2 eggs in a bowl until very frothy. Gradually beat in the lemon juice, then gradually beat in about 1½ cups

(12 fl oz/375 ml) of the hot stock, beating constantly to prevent curdling. (This tempers the eggs, so they won't scramble when added to the hot stock.) Continue to beat until the mixture thickens, then slowly stir the egg mixture into the hot stock. Heat through, but do not allow the soup to boil.

Serve immediately, sprinkled with the remaining parsley.

Serves 6

Pork and Hominy in Red Chili Broth

1 lb (500 g) stewing pork, cut into 1-inch (2.5-cm) cubes

½ teaspoon salt

4 cups (32 fl oz/1 liter) water

4 dried ancho chilis, stemmed, seeds removed

5 cloves garlic

1½ teaspoons dried oregano

2 tablespoons vegetable oil

1 large yellow onion, diced

2 cups (12 oz/375 g) well-drained canned hominy

3 cups (24 fl oz/750 ml) chicken stock (page 22), or as needed

sliced radishes, shredded lettuce, diced yellow onion, corn tortilla chips, diced avocado, and lime wedges, to serve

Combine pork, salt, and water in a saucepan over high heat. Bring to a boil, then reduce heat to medium and simmer gently, uncovered, until the pork is barely tender, about 20 minutes. Remove from heat and let the pork cool in the liquid. Drain pork, reserving the liquid in a bowl. Cover pork with a damp kitchen towel and set aside.

Soak chilis in the reserved warm cooking liquid for 20 minutes. Transfer the liquid and chilis to a blender. Add the garlic and oregano and blend until smooth. Set aside.

Heat the oil in a large saucepan over medium-high heat. Add

onion and cook, stirring, until light golden, about 10 minutes. Stir in chili mixture, hominy, chicken stock, and reserved pork. (Add more stock if needed to give a soupy consistency.) Bring to a boil, then reduce heat and simmer gently, uncovered, until pork is tender, about 30 minutes. Taste and adjust the seasonings, if necessary.

Place the radishes, lettuce, onion, tortilla chips, avocado, and lime wedges in separate small bowls. Ladle the soup into warmed serving bowls and serve accompanied by the garnishes.

Serves 4 to 6

Sausage and Black Bean Soup

1¼ lb (625 g) dried black beans

1¾ lb (875 g) spicy sausages

1 tablespoon olive oil

4 cloves garlic, finely chopped

2 yellow onions, finely chopped

2 celery stalks, finely chopped

2½ qt (2.5 l) meat stock (page 27)

4 tablespoons chopped parsley

1 teaspoon dried oregano

½ teaspoon ground cumin

2 bay leaves

½ tablespoon salt

½ cup (4 fl oz/125 ml) sour cream

2 tablespoons snipped chives

2 tablespoons chopped fresh cilantro (fresh coriander)

Sort through beans, discarding any foreign matter or discolored beans. Set aside.

Remove the casings from 1 lb (500 g) of the sausages. In a large saucepan, warm the oil over medium heat. Add the sausage meat and sauté, coarsely breaking up meat with a wooden spoon, until lightly browned, about 5 minutes. Pour off all but about 3 tablespoons of the fat. Return the pan to the heat, add the garlic, onions, and celery, and sauté, stirring, until onions are translucent, 2–3 minutes.

Add the beans, stock, parsley, oregano, cumin, and bay leaves; bring to a boil. Reduce heat, cover, and simmer gently until beans are tender, 2–2½ hours, adding half of the salt halfway through the cooking and adding a little water if necessary to keep the beans moist.

Discard the bay leaves. Blend or process a few ladlefuls of beans until puréed. Stir the purée back into pan with the remaining salt. Cut the remaining sausages into slices ½ inch (12 mm) thick. Sauté in a nonstick pan over medium heat until browned, about 3 minutes per side. Ladle the soup into warmed bowls; garnish with sour cream, sausage slices, chives, and cilantro.

Serves 6 to 8

Cabbage Soup with Flank Steak

¼ cup (2 fl oz/60 ml) vegetable oil

1 large yellow onion, chopped

2 cloves garlic, coarsely chopped

1 lb (500 g) flank steak, trimmed

Salt and freshly ground pepper

8 cups (64 fl oz/2 l) meat stock (page 27) or water

1 can (1 lb/500 g) plum (Roma) tomatoes with their juice

⅓ cup (3 fl oz/80 ml) fresh lemon juice

¼ cup (2 oz/60 g) sugar

¼ cup (1 oz/30 g) raisins

1 head Savoy cabbage, cored, cut into shreds ½ inch (12 mm) wide

2 bay leaves

In a large pot, warm the oil over low to medium heat. Add the onion and garlic and sauté until translucent, 2–3 minutes.

Lightly season the steak with salt and pepper, add to the pan, and sauté, turning once, until lightly browned, 2–3 minutes on each side.

Add the stock and deglaze the pan by stirring and scraping to dislodge any browned bits. Add the tomatoes, crushing them slightly with a wooden spoon. Add lemon juice, sugar, raisins, cabbage, and bay leaves. Raise the heat and bring to a boil. Reduce the heat to low, cover partially, and simmer gently

until the meat is tender, about 1 hour. Discard the bay leaves.

Remove the meat from the pot. Using a sharp knife and a fork, cut and tear it up into coarse, bite-sized shreds. Stir the shreds back into the pot. Taste the soup and adjust the seasoning. Ladle the soup into warmed bowls.

Serves 8 to 10

Wonton Noodle Soup

NOODLES

8 oz (250 g) fresh Chinese egg noodles

1 tablespoon peanut oil

WONTONS

8 oz (250 g) uncooked shrimp (prawns), peeled and deveined

1½ teaspoons coarse salt

¾ lb (375 g) medium-grind (minced) pork butt

1 tablespoon Chinese rice wine or dry sherry

2 teaspoons light soy sauce

1 green (spring) onion, finely chopped

2 tablespoons drained, finely chopped, canned bamboo shoots

¼ teaspoon sugar

Large pinch white pepper

1 teaspoon sesame oil

1 teaspoon cornstarch (cornflour)

60 wonton wrappers

1 egg white, lightly beaten

SOUP

6 cups (48 fl oz/1.5 l) chicken stock (page 22)

¼ teaspoon sugar

Light soy sauce, to taste

1 tablespoon sesame oil

Salt

1 lb (500 g) bok choy, cut into 2-inch (5-cm) lengths, or baby bok choy, cut in half

1 green (spring) onion, chopped

Gently pull strands of noodles apart. In a large saucepan of boiling salted water, cook the noodles, stirring to separate the strands, for 1 minute. Drain, rinse well, drain again, and place in a large bowl. Toss with oil to stop strands sticking together.

For wontons, rinse the shrimp, drain, and place in a bowl with 1 teaspoon of the salt. Toss well and set aside for 10 minutes. Rinse again, drain, pat dry, and chop coarsely. Combine shrimp, the remaining ½ teaspoon salt, the pork, wine or sherry, soy sauce, green onion, bamboo shoots, sugar, pepper, sesame oil, and cornstarch.

To wrap wontons, work with 1 wrapper at a time, keeping unused wrappers covered with a kitchen towel. Place 1 heaped teaspoon of filling in center of a wrapper. Moisten wrapper edges with water and fold in half to form a triangle. Bring the 2 long ends up and over to meet and slightly overlap. Brush the overlapping edges with egg white and press to seal. Place on a baking sheet and cover with a kitchen towel. Repeat with remaining filling and wrappers. You will need 36 wontons for this dish; wrap the remainder and any unused wrappers in plastic wrap and freeze for up to 2 months.

For the soup, heat the chicken stock in a saucepan. Season with sugar, soy sauce, and sesame oil. At the same time, boil the bok choy in lightly salted water for 1 minute. Use a slotted spoon to transfer to a bowl. When the stock is hot, add the noodles and heat through. Use the spoon to divide noodles among bowls; keep warm.

Drop 36 wontons into boiling water in batches. Cook until they float, about 3 minutes. Place wontons in bowls, add bok choy, and ladle over hot stock. Garnish with green onion. Serve at once.

Serves 6

About Noodles

Noodles are a staple throughout Asia, where they symbolize long life. Made of wheat, rice, or bean flour, they are eaten hot or cold at all times of day. Store fresh noodles, wrapped in plastic, in the refrigerator for up to 3 days. They also freeze well, but must be thawed fully before being cooked. Store dried noodles in a cool, dark place for up to 6 months. The following are a few common types.

Buckwheat noodles (soba) Grayish beige noodles, available fresh or dried, popular in Japan.
Mung bean noodles Also called cellophane noodles, glass noodles, or bean thread noodles, these dried noodles are made of mung bean flour and water. Soak in warm water for 20 minutes before cooking, or deep-fry without soaking to produce a bundle of fluffy white crisps.
Rice noodles are made of rice flour and water and vary in size from fine dried sticks to wide ribbons. Soak dried rice noodles in warm water for 20 minutes, boil for 2–3 minutes until al dente, then rinse in cold water. Cook fresh rice noodles in boiling water for 1–2 minutes, just until heated through and pliable. Take care not to overcook rice noodles; they turn to mush easily.
Wheat noodles are made from wheat flour, water, salt, and sometimes eggs, and are sold fresh or dried. Without eggs, they are generally paler than those with eggs, but both types come in a similar range of shapes and sizes. In Japan, thin wheat noodles are known as *somen* and thick ones as *udon*.
Wonton wrappers Also called dumpling wrappers, these are rolled into thin sheets from the same dough as wheat noodles, then cut into rounds or squares of varying size and thickness.

Spicy Lamb Soup

SPICE PASTE

1 piece fresh ginger, 1 inch (2.5 cm) long, peeled and coarsely chopped

6 cloves garlic

6 purple (Asian) shallots, about 8 oz (250 g), halved

1½ teaspoons ground fennel

1½ teaspoons ground cumin

1 tablespoon ground coriander

About 3 tablespoons water

SOUP

1½ lb (750 g) meaty lamb bones, for stock

12 cups (3 qt/3 l) water or meat stock (page 27)

2 tablespoons vegetable oil

2 leeks, including 1 inch (2.5 cm) of the tender green tops, washed and sliced

1 teaspoon curry powder

2 cardamom pods, bruised

2 star anise

1 cinnamon stick

4 cloves

1 large carrot, thickly sliced

2 teaspoons sugar

1 teaspoon salt, or to taste

1 large tomato, cut into large wedges

Fresh lime juice (optional)

For spice paste, place the ginger, garlic, shallots, fennel, cumin, and coriander in a blender. Blend to a smooth paste, adding a little water as needed to facilitate blending. Set aside.

For the soup, preheat an oven to 450°F (230°C/Gas Mark 6). Remove any meat from the lamb bones, cut into 1-inch (2.5-cm) cubes, and set aside. Place the bones in a roasting pan and roast, turning occasionally, until browned, about 20 minutes. Transfer the bones to a plate and set aside.

Drain off most of the fat from the roasting pan and place pan over medium heat. When the pan is hot, add 2 cups (16 fl oz/ 500 ml) of the water or stock and deglaze pan by stirring to dislodge any browned bits from base of pan. Set aside.

Heat the vegetable oil in a large stockpot over medium heat. Add leeks and cook, stirring often, until golden, about 2 minutes. Add the spice paste and curry powder and stir until fragrant, about 1 minute. Add the roasted bones, reserved meat, the liquid from the roasting pan, and the remaining water or stock. Wrap cardamom, star anise, cinnamon, and cloves in a piece of cheese-cloth (muslin), tie securely with kitchen string, and add to the pot. Bring to a boil, then reduce the heat to low and simmer, uncovered, for 30 minutes. Add carrot and simmer until meat is tender, about 30 minutes. Add sugar and salt to taste, and stir in the tomato.

Discard the cheesecloth bag and the bones and ladle the soup into warmed serving bowls. Add lime juice to taste, if desired, and serve hot.

Serves 8

Hanoi Beef and Noodle Soup

BEEF BROTH

3 lb (1.5 kg) oxtails, cut into sections

3 lb (1.5 kg) beef shins (shanks)

14 cups (3½ qt/3.5 l) water

3 pieces fresh ginger, each 1 inch (2.5 cm) long, unpeeled

1 large yellow onion, unpeeled, cut in halves

4 purple (Asian) shallots, unpeeled

1 lb (500 g) Chinese radishes, cut into 2-inch (5-cm) chunks

3 carrots, unpeeled, cut into chunks

4 star anise

6 cloves

2 cinnamon sticks

¼ cup (2 fl oz/60 ml) fish sauce

Salt

BEEF, NOODLES, AND ACCOMPANIMENTS

8 oz (250 g) beef round (1 piece, at least 2 inches/5 cm thick)

1 lb (500 g) dried flat rice stick noodles, ¼-inch (6-mm) wide

1 large yellow onion

2 green (spring) onions

2 small fresh red chilis

1 cup (1 oz/30 g) cilantro (fresh coriander) leaves

½ cup (½ oz/15 g) fresh mint leaves

1 lime, cut into 6 wedges

201

For the broth, place oxtails, beef shins, and water in a large pot and bring to a boil. Meanwhile, preheat a broiler (griller). Place the ginger, onion, and shallots on a baking sheet and broil, turning often, until browned on all sides, 1–2 minutes. Set aside.

When the water for the broth is boiling, use a large spoon or wire skimmer to skim the scum from the surface until it is clear of foam, about 10 minutes. Stir in the browned vegetables and the radishes, carrots, star anise, cloves, and cinnamon sticks. Reduce the heat to medium-low, partially cover, and simmer gently for 3½ hours.

Remove from heat and allow to cool. Strain the broth through a fine-mesh sieve into a bowl; discard the solids. Set aside until the fat rises to the surface. Use a large spoon to skim off the fat; discard. Stir in fish sauce and salt to taste. You should have about 8 cups (64 fl oz/2 l) of broth. (The broth can be made 1 day ahead and refrigerated, covered.)

For the beef, wrap in plastic wrap and freeze until partially frozen, about 1 hour.

Meanwhile, for the noodles, place in a large bowl, add enough warm water to cover, and set aside until the noodles are soft and pliable, about 20 minutes. Drain and set aside.

Cut beef across the grain into paper-thin slices about 3 inches (7.5 cm) long. Set aside.

Place the broth in a large saucepan and bring to a boil. Reduce the heat to keep the broth at a gentle simmer. Thinly slice the yellow onions, green onions, and chilis; set aside.

Bring a medium saucepan of water to a boil. Add noodles and boil until tender, about 1 minute. Drain well and then divide the noodles evenly among 6 deep soup bowls.

Divide the onions, beef slices, and chilis evenly among the bowls. Ladle the hot broth over the top (it will cook the beef). Garnish with the cilantro and mint. Serve with lime wedges.

NOTE This soup, known in Vietnam as *pho*, may also contain chicken or other ingredients. The best versions are available at street stalls or in coffee shops that specialize in *pho*. Light, hot, nourishing, and refreshing, it is eaten for breakfast and as a late-night snack.

Pork and Cellophane Noodle Soup

2 tablespoons peanut oil

2 slices fresh ginger (¼ inch/ 4 mm thick)

4 oz (125 g) pork fillet, shredded into 2-inch (5-cm) lengths

2 teaspoons Chinese rice wine or dry sherry

6 cups (48 fl oz/1.5 l) chicken stock (page 22)

6 dried shiitake mushrooms, soaked for 45 minutes, drained, stalks discarded, caps thinly sliced

2 oz (60 g) carrot, peeled, cut into thin strips

4 oz (125 g) zucchini (courgette), cut into thin strips

1½ tablespoons preserved mustard greens or Sichuan preserved vegetables (available at Chinese stores), shredded, optional

1 oz (30 g) cellophane noodles, soaked for 30 minutes in warm water, drained, and cut into 6-inch (15-cm) lengths

½ teaspoon salt

Pinch ground white pepper

¼ teaspoon sugar

½ teaspoon sesame oil

Heat the peanut oil in a stockpot over high heat until it is just beginning to smoke. Add the ginger and stir-fry until fragrant, 1–2 minutes. Add the pork and stir-fry until it changes color, about 3 minutes. Stir in the rice wine, stock, mushrooms, and carrot; simmer for 10 minutes.

Stir in the zucchini, preserved mustard greens or vegetables (if using), and noodles. Simmer for 2 minutes. Stir in the salt, pepper, sugar, and sesame oil; serve at once.

Serves 6 to 8

Chicken Soup

2 large yellow onions, finely chopped

2 cups (2 oz/60 g) loosely packed fresh flat-leaf (Italian) parsley leaves

4 cloves garlic, crushed

1/4 cup (2 fl oz/60 ml) fresh lemon juice

2 tablespoons soy sauce

1 whole chicken, about 2 1/2 lb (1.5 kg), rinsed; neck, tail and as much skin as possible discarded

5 stalks celery, cut into 1/2-inch (1-cm) slices

5 carrots, cut into 1/2-inch (1-cm) slices

2 medium tomatoes, halved

6 cups (48 fl oz/1.5 l) water

Salt and ground black pepper

Combine onions, parsley, garlic, lemon juice, and soy sauce in a large saucepan. Cook, stirring, over medium heat until onions are soft, 5–8 minutes. Add chicken, celery, carrot, tomatoes, and water and bring to a boil. Reduce heat to low and simmer, covered, for 1 hour, or until the chicken is tender and comes away easily from the bone.

Remove from heat, cool for 10 minutes, then place in the refrigerator to chill overnight.

The next day, remove the soup from the refrigerator. Using a slotted spoon, remove the layer of solidified fat from the surface of the stock.

Remove the chicken from the stock and place in a large bowl. Using your fingers, remove the meat from the bones and shred the meat. Discard bones and return chicken meat to the pot.

Bring the soup to a boil over medium heat until chicken and vegetables are heated through. Remove soup from the heat and skim a piece of paper towel over the surface to absorb any excess fat. Add salt and pepper to taste and ladle the soup into deep bowls. Sprinkle with a little extra pepper and serve at once.

Serves 6

Roasted Vegetable and Bacon Soup

6 slices (rashers) bacon, rind and excess fat removed, chopped

2 red bell peppers (capsicums), halved, seeds removed

2 leeks (white parts only), halved lengthwise, sliced

¾ lb (375 g) orange sweet potato (kumara), peeled, cut into ¾-inch (2-cm) pieces

3 cloves garlic, unpeeled

2 tablespoons olive oil

3 cups (24 fl oz/750 ml) chicken stock (page 22)

Salt and ground black pepper

Preheat oven to 350°F (180°C/ Gas Mark 4).

Place bacon, bell peppers, leek, sweet potato, garlic, and olive oil in a large nonaluminum roasting pan. Gently toss until coated with the oil.

Bake in preheated oven, stirring occasionally, for 1 hour, or until the sweet potato is golden and tender. Transfer the bell peppers to a large plate and cover with plastic wrap. Set the remaining vegetables aside for 10 minutes to cool slightly.

Peel bell peppers and place in the bowl of a food processor. Squeeze flesh from garlic cloves into food processor bowl. Add one fourth of the remaining vegetable mixture and ½ cup (4 fl oz/125 ml) of the stock and process until smooth.

Transfer the bell pepper mixture to a large saucepan. Add the remaining vegetable mixture and the stock. Bring to a boil over medium heat, stirring from time to time. Add salt and pepper to taste, ladle into warmed bowls, and serve at once.

Serves 4

Split Pea Soup with Bacon

2 tablespoons olive oil

1 yellow onion, finely chopped

1 celery stalk, thinly sliced

2 carrots, thinly sliced

1 clove garlic, finely chopped

1¼ cups (9 oz/280 g) green split peas, rinsed

6 slices thick-cut bacon

7 cups (56 fl oz/1.75 l) water

1 bay leaf

¾ teaspoon salt, or to taste

¼ teaspoon ground pepper, or to taste

1 tablespoon finely chopped fresh parsley

Heat the oil in a large, heavy-based saucepan over medium heat. Add the onion and cook, stirring, until it is softened, 3–5 minutes. Stir in the celery and carrots and cook until the carrots are tender, 2–3 minutes. Add the garlic and cook, stirring, for a further 1 minute.

Stir in the split peas, bacon, water, and bay leaf. Increase heat to high and bring to a simmer. Reduce heat to medium-low, partially cover, and cook until the peas are soft, about 1 hour, stirring often and occasionally skimming off the scum that rises to the surface.

Remove the bacon and bay leaf. Discard bay leaf. Cut the bacon into small pieces; set aside.

In a blender or food processor, purée the soup until smooth. Return the soup to the pan.

Reheat the soup over medium heat, stirring occasionally, until very hot. Add salt and pepper to taste, then stir in the reserved bacon. Serve immediately, sprinkled with parsley.

Serves 4 to 6

Lamb and Chickpea Soup

2 tablespoons olive oil

1½ lb (750 g) lamb shoulder

Salt and ground black pepper

1 yellow onion, finely chopped

1 carrot, finely chopped

1 clove garlic, finely chopped

¾ teaspoon ground coriander

¾ teaspoon ground cumin

¼ teaspoon cayenne pepper

5 cups (40 fl oz/1.25 l) beef stock (page 26) or chicken stock (page 22)

1¼ cups (8 oz/250 g) dried chickpeas (garbanzo beans), sorted and soaked in cold water to cover for about 12 hours, then drained

2 large plum (Roma) tomatoes, chopped

3 large lemons, cut into fourths

2 green (spring) onions, thinly sliced

4 tablespoons chopped fresh parsley

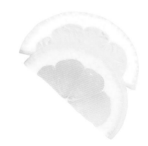

Heat the oil in a large pot over medium heat. Season lamb with salt and pepper and fry for 3–4 minutes on each side, or until evenly browned. Remove lamb and set aside. Pour off all but about 2 tablespoons of fat.

Add onion, carrot, and garlic to pan and cook over medium heat for 2–3 minutes, or until onion is translucent. Add coriander, cumin, and cayenne and cook for 1 minute more. Pour in the stock and deglaze the pot by stirring to dislodge any browned bits. Return the lamb to the pot.

Add the drained chickpeas, the tomatoes, and 4 of the lemon wedges. Bring to a boil, reduce

the heat to low, cover, and simmer, skimming regularly, for 2–2½ hours, or until the lamb and chickpeas are tender. Remove the lamb from the pot. Cut out and discard the bones and excess fat; cut the meat into small, coarse chunks and set aside. Discard lemon wedges.

Ladle about half of the chickpeas into a food processor or blender and purée until smooth. Stir the purée and lamb chunks back into the pot.

Gently reheat the soup. Ladle into warmed bowls and garnish with the green onions and parsley. Pass the remaining lemon wedges separately.

Serves 6 to 8

Pork and Green Chili Soup

1½ lb (750 g) fresh or drained, canned tomatillos

4 lb (2 kg) pork butt or shoulder, trimmed of fat and cut into 2-inch (5-cm) cubes

2 teaspoons salt

1 teaspoon ground pepper

All-purpose (plain) flour

¼ cup (2 fl oz/60 ml) vegetable oil

3 yellow onions, cut into 1-inch (2.5-cm) pieces

4 fresh green chilis, stemmed and seeded; 2 cut into 1-inch (2.5-cm) pieces, 2 finely chopped

2 green bell peppers (capsicums), seeded and cut into 1-inch (2.5-cm) pieces

3 cloves garlic, finely chopped

1 tablespoon dried oregano, crumbled

2 teaspoons ground cumin

2 tablespoons coriander seeds, crushed, soaked in water for 15 minutes, then drained

2 bay leaves

¼ cup (⅓ oz/10 g) coarsely chopped cilantro (fresh coriander)

4 cups (32 fl oz/1 liter) chicken stock

If using fresh tomatillos, preheat a broiler (griller). Husk the tomatillos, then place in a baking pan and broil, turning occasionally, until charred. Cool, then core and chop. If using canned tomatillos, core and chop them.

Season the pork with salt and pepper, then dust with flour. Heat the oil in a heavy-based frying pan over medium-high heat. Cook pork in batches until well browned, 5–8 minutes. Transfer to a large soup pot.

Discard fat in frying pan and return the pan to medium heat. Add onions and cook, stirring, until soft, about 5 minutes. Stir

in the chilis and bell peppers and cook, stirring, until fragrant, 3–4 minutes. Add garlic and cook for 1–2 minutes.

Add onion mixture, tomatillos, oregano, cumin, coriander seeds, bay leaves, cilantro, and chicken stock to the soup pot. Bring to a boil, reduce heat, and simmer, uncovered, until the pork is very tender, 2–3 hours. Ladle into warmed bowls and serve.

Serves 6 to 8

Meatball Soup with Cilantro Pesto

¾ cup (5½ oz/170 g) short-grain white rice

4 tablespoons (2 fl oz/60 ml) vegetable oil

2 white onions, diced

½ lb (250 g) ground (minced) pork

½ lb (250 g) ground (minced) beef

1 egg

1 teaspoon ground cumin

1 teaspoon dried oregano

1½ teaspoons salt

1 teaspoon ground pepper

1 clove garlic, minced

1 zucchini (courgette), diced

2 carrots, peeled and diced

2 ripe tomatoes, peeled, seeded, and diced

6 cups (48 fl oz/1.5 l) chicken stock (page 22)

CILANTRO PESTO

½ cup (¾ oz/20 g) chopped fresh cilantro (coriander)

1 sprig fresh mint, stemmed and chopped

Juice of 2 limes

2 tablespoons olive oil

2 tablespoons water

½ teaspoon salt

Serves 6 to 8

Place the rice in a heatproof bowl, pour over boiling water to cover, let soak for 40 minutes, then drain; set aside.

Meanwhile, in a frying pan over medium heat, warm 2 tablespoons of the oil. Add half of the onion and sauté until soft, about 5 minutes. Remove from the heat and let cool.

In a bowl, combine pork, beef, onion, soaked rice, egg, cumin, oregano, ¾ teaspoon of the salt and ½ teaspoon of the pepper. Using your hands, mix well and form into 1-inch (2.5-cm) balls.

In a large soup pot over medium heat, warm the remaining oil. Add the remaining onion and fry

until soft, about 5 minutes.
Add the garlic, zucchini, carrots,
and tomatoes and cook, stirring,
until fragrant, about 5 minutes.
Add the stock, stir well, bring
to a boil, and slip the meatballs
into the stock. Reduce heat
to low and simmer, uncovered,
until meatballs are fully cooked,
about 45 minutes. Add the
remaining salt and pepper.

Meanwhile, make the cilantro
pesto: In a mini food processor
or a blender, combine cilantro,
mint, lime juice, olive oil, water
and salt. Process to a paste.

Ladle the soup into warmed
bowls and top each serving with
cilantro pesto. Serve at once.

Lamb and Vegetable Soup

3½ lb (1.75 kg) lamb (a mix of shoulder, neck, and breast), cut into 2-inch (5-cm) cubes

Salt and ground pepper

1 tablespoon peanut oil

3 tablespoons butter

2 celery stalks, finely chopped

2 shallots, finely chopped

1 carrot, finely chopped

1 onion, finely chopped

1 teaspoon sugar

2 cloves garlic, halved

⅓ cup (2½ fl oz/80 ml) dry white wine

6½ oz (200 g) ripe tomatoes, peeled, seeded, and chopped

4 cups (48 fl oz/1 liter) chicken stock

1 can (14 oz/440 g) great Northern (white haricot) beans, rinsed and drained

chopped parsley (optional)

Season the lamb with salt and pepper to taste. Heat the oil and butter in a 6-qt (6-l) saucepan. Working in batches, add a few of the meat pieces and cook, stirring, until browned on all sides. Remove with a slotted spoon and set aside. Repeat with the remaining meat.

Add the celery, shallots, carrot, onion, sugar, and garlic and stir over low heat for 5 minutes. Add the wine and stir until it evaporates. Stir in the tomatoes and stock and cook, uncovered, for 1 hour; from time to time, skim off any scum that rises to the surface.

Add the beans to the pot. Cook
for 30 minutes, or until the
beans and vegetables are tender.
Ladle into warmed soup bowls
and serve at once, garnished
with parsley, if desired.

Serves 6

Thai Chicken and Coconut Soup

2 tablespoons vegetable oil

2 onions, chopped

3 cloves garlic, crushed

2 teaspoons ground cumin

1 teaspoon turmeric

1 teaspoon chopped fresh chili

1 tablespoon chopped fresh lemongrass, or 2 teaspoons grated lime zest

¼ cup (2 fl oz/60 ml) fresh lime juice

4 cups (32 fl oz/1 liter) chicken stock (page 22)

2 cups (16 fl oz/500 ml) unsweetened coconut milk (use light coconut milk if you prefer)

2 tablespoons Thai fish sauce

1 lb (500 g) boneless, skinless chicken breasts, thinly sliced

2 tablespoons chopped fresh coriander (cilantro)

Lime leaves, for garnish (optional)

Heat the oil in a frying pan, add the onion and garlic, and cook over low to medium heat, stirring, until the onion is soft, about 10 minutes. Add the cumin, turmeric, chili, and lemongrass and cook, stirring, until the lemongrass is tender, about 10 minutes.

Add the lime juice, stock, coconut milk, and fish sauce and bring to a boil. Stir in the chicken and simmer, uncovered, for about 3 minutes, or until the chicken is tender. Stir in the cilantro and lime leaves and warm through. Serve at once.

Serves 4

Turkey and Root Vegetable Soup

2 large carrots, cut into slices
½ inch (1 cm) thick

2 large parsnips, cut into slices
½ inch (1 cm) thick

2 large boiling potatoes, cut into
slices ½ inch (1 cm) thick

2 large yellow onions, thickly
sliced

2 bay leaves

½ cup (⅔ oz/20 g) coarsely
chopped fresh parsley

1 tablespoon dried thyme

1 roast turkey carcass, with any
meat attached, broken up, or 2 lb
(1 kg) fresh turkey pieces

10 cups (2½ qt/2.5 l) chicken
stock (page 22)

Salt and ground pepper

In a large pot, combine all the vegetables, the bay leaves, parsley, and thyme. Put the pieces of turkey carcass or fresh turkey on top and pour in the stock. Bring to a boil over medium heat, skimming away the froth from the surface.

Reduce the heat, cover, and simmer, skimming occasionally, until the vegetables are very tender, 45–60 minutes. Discard the bay leaves. Using a slotted spoon, remove the turkey pieces. Pick off the meat and return it to the pot. Discard the bones. Add salt and pepper to taste, ladle into warmed bowls, and serve.

Serves 10 to 12

Matzo Ball Soup

12 cups (3 qt/3 l) chicken stock (page 22), plus 1 cup (8 fl oz/ 250 ml) extra

2 large carrots, cut into chunks

2 large stalks celery, cut into chunks

1 large yellow onion, cut into 1-inch (2.5-cm) chunks

½ cup (¾ oz/20 g) coarsely chopped fresh parsley

2 cups (10 oz/315 g) matzo meal

8 eggs, separated

½ cup (4 fl oz/125 ml) rendered chicken fat or vegetable oil

1 teaspoon salt

½ teaspoon white pepper

Combine the 12 cups (3 qt/3 l) stock, the carrot, celery, onion, and parsley in a medium to large pot; you should have a depth of at least 4 inches (10 cm) of liquid for the matzo balls to float in. Bring to a boil over medium heat, then reduce the heat until the soup is barely simmering.

In a mixing bowl, combine the matzo meal, the remaining 1 cup (8 fl oz/250 ml) stock, the egg yolks, chicken fat or vegetable oil, and salt and pepper to taste. Mix well.

In a separate bowl, beat the egg whites with a whisk until very frothy but still liquid. Using a rubber spatula, fold the whites into the matzo-meal mixture until smoothly blended.

Moisten your hands with cold water, then gently and quickly shape the matzo mixture into smooth balls 2–3 inches (5–7.5 cm) in diameter. As the balls are formed, gently drop them into the simmering soup. Cover partially and cook for about 30 minutes.

Ladle the stock into warmed bowls, adding matzo balls and a few pieces of vegetable to each portion. Serve immediately.

Serves 8 to 10

Oriental Broth with Chicken Wings

6 dried Chinese mushrooms

3 lb (1.5 kg) chicken bones

16 cups (4 qt/4 l) water

Two 2-inch (5-cm) pieces fresh ginger; one sliced, the other finely shredded

6 green (spring) onions, chopped, plus 4 extra, sliced diagonally

1 teaspoon black peppercorns

4 chicken wings

1 leek, trimmed and thinly sliced

1 carrot, thinly sliced

¼ cup (2 fl oz/60 ml) reduced-sodium soy sauce

1 teaspoon sesame oil

1 teaspoon chopped fresh chili

Place the mushrooms in a heat-proof bowl, pour over boiling water to cover, and leave to stand for 20 minutes. Drain, then slice the mushrooms thinly.

For the broth, put the chicken bones, water, sliced ginger, chopped green onion, and peppercorns in a large saucepan and bring to a boil. Skim the surface, reduce heat, and simmer, uncovered, for 3 hours. Strain and let cool.

Refrigerate for several hours or overnight and then remove the fat from the surface. Return the broth to the pan and boil, uncovered, until it is reduced to 5 cups (40 fl oz/1.25 l).

Combine the broth and chicken wings in a large pan, bring to a boil, and simmer, covered, for 10 minutes. Add the shredded ginger, leek, carrot, and sliced green onion and simmer, covered, for a further 5 minutes, or until the chicken wings and vegetables are tender. Add the soy sauce, sesame oil, and chili and stir until hot. Place 1 wing in each serving bowl, then ladle in the broth and vegetables. Serve immediately.

Serves 4 as an appetizer

Chicken and Black Mushroom Soup

1 teaspoon salt

1 teaspoon sugar

1 teaspoon cornstarch (cornflour)

2 teaspoons Chinese rice wine

1 tablespoon water

4 oz (125 g) chicken breast, thinly sliced

2 cups (16 fl oz/500 ml) water

4 dried black mushrooms, soaked in warm water for 1 hour, drained, stems discarded, caps thinly sliced

4 cups (32 fl oz/1 liter) chicken stock (page 22)

1 tablespoon shredded ginger

1 tablespoon light soy sauce

1/4 teaspoon sesame oil

Combine 1/2 teaspoon of the salt, 1/2 teaspoon of the sugar, the cornstarch, 1 teaspoon of the rice wine, and the 1 tablespoon water in a small bowl. Add the chicken, toss to coat, and set aside to marinate for 15 minutes.

Bring the 2 cups (16 fl oz/500 ml) water to a boil in a saucepan and add the chicken. When it has turned white, remove, drain, and set aside.

Mix the sliced mushrooms with the remaining 1/2 teaspoon salt, 1/2 teaspoon sugar, and 1 teaspoon wine. Place on a steaming rack over a pan of boiling water and steam for 10 minutes. Remove from pan and set aside.

Bring the stock to a boil in a large pan and add the ginger, chicken, mushrooms, soy sauce, and sesame oil. Heat through and serve immediately.

Serves 4 to 6

Chinese Noodle Soup with Chicken

1 teaspoon salt

1 teaspoon sugar

2 teaspoons Chinese rice wine

2 teaspoons cornstarch (cornflour)

1 tablespoon water

4 oz (125 g) chicken breast fillet, thinly sliced

8 oz (250 g) egg noodles

1/3 cup (2½ fl oz/80 ml) water

2 tablespoons peanut oil

1 tablespoon shredded fresh ginger

4 oz (125 g) cabbage, shredded

2 dried shiitake mushrooms, soaked in warm water for 1 hour, drained, stems discarded, caps shredded

4 cups (32 fl oz/1 liter) chicken stock (page 22)

1 tablespoon light soy sauce

1 teaspoon dark soy sauce

½ teaspoon sesame oil

1 tablespoon finely chopped green (spring) onion

Combine the salt, sugar, 1 teaspoon of the rice wine, the cornstarch, and 1 tablespoon water in a bowl. Add the chicken, toss to coat, and set aside for 15 minutes to marinate.

Bring a pot of water to a boil and add the noodles. When the water returns to a boil, add the 1/3 cup (2½ fl oz/80 ml) cold water. Cook for 3–4 minutes, stirring to separate the noodles. Using tongs, transfer noodles to a colander. Reserve the cooking water. Rinse noodles under cold water. Return the cooking water to a boil. Return noodles to pan and cook for 1 minute more. Drain the noodles and divide among serving bowls; set aside.

Heat the oil in a wok or frying pan. Add the ginger, cabbage, and mushrooms and stir-fry for 30 seconds. Add 1 cup (8 fl oz/ 250 ml) of the stock and cook over medium-low heat for 3 minutes. Stir in the chicken, soy sauces, sesame oil, and remaining 1 teaspoon rice wine. Cook over medium heat for 1½ minutes. Spoon the chicken mixture over the noodles and sprinkle with the green onion.

Bring the remaining 3 cups (24 fl oz/750 ml) of stock to a boil. Ladle over the noodles and chicken mixture in each bowl, and serve immediately.

Serves 4

Chicken Broth with Rice and Shrimp

7 cups (56 fl oz/1.75 l) chicken stock (page 22)

½ cup (3 oz/90 g) white rice, rinsed well

1 teaspoon salt (optional)

½ cup (4 fl oz/125 ml) olive oil

4 tablespoons chopped cilantro (fresh coriander)

4 tablespoons finely chopped fresh chili

½ cup (4 oz/125 g) finely chopped tomatoes

8 medium shrimp (prawns), peeled, cooked, and finely chopped

1 lime or lemon, cut into 6 wedges

Bring the stock to a boil in a large saucepan. Add the rice and cook for 15–20 minutes, until it "flowers" (that is, until the grains open and break apart). Add salt, if desired.

To serve, place the olive oil in a small serving bowl on the table and place each of the remaining ingredients in separate small bowls. Ladle the rice soup into serving bowls and let each person add the other ingredients to taste, squeezing in a few drops of lime or lemon juice just before eating.

Serves 6

Chicken, Avocado, and Tortilla Soup

½ cup (4 fl oz/125 ml) vegetable oil

6 purchased tortillas, cut into thin strips

8 cups (64 fl oz/2 l) chicken stock (page 22)

1 skinless, boneless chicken breast fillet, cooked and shredded

1 fresh chili, seeded and chopped

Squeeze of fresh lime juice

1 teaspoon salt, or to taste

1 large avocado, peeled, stone removed, flesh sliced or cubed

2 tablespoons cilantro (fresh coriander), roughly chopped

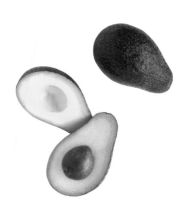

Heat the oil in a frying pan. Add the tortilla strips and cook until crisp. Drain on paper towels.

Put the stock, chicken, chili, lime juice, and salt in a large saucepan. Cook over medium heat until very hot.

Place the avocado and tortilla strips in separate bowls to pass around at the table. Serve the soup sprinkled with the cilantro.

Serves 8

Spicy Asian-style Chicken Soup

8 kaffir lime leaves or the zest (rind) of 1 lime

1 can (14 fl oz/440 ml) coconut milk

3 cups (24 fl oz/750 ml) chicken stock (page 22)

6 fresh or 4 dried galangal slices, each about 1 inch (2.5 cm) in diameter

4 stalks lemongrass, cut into 2-inch (5-cm) lengths, crushed

4 small fresh green chilis, halved

1 tablespoon Thai roasted chili paste (*nam prik pao*)

1 whole chicken breast, skin removed, cut into ½-inch (1-cm) cubes

½ cup (2½ oz/75 g) drained, canned whole straw mushrooms

½ cup (2½ oz/75 g) drained, canned bamboo shoots, sliced

¼ cup (2 fl oz/60 ml) Thai fish sauce

Juice of 2 limes (about ⅓ cup/ 2½ fl oz/80 ml)

¼ cup (¼ oz/7 g) cilantro (fresh coriander) leaves

In a large saucepan, place 4 lime leaves or half of the zest, the coconut milk, chicken stock, galangal, lemongrass, and chilis. Bring to a boil, then reduce the heat and simmer for 20 minutes. Strain through a fine-mesh sieve into a clean saucepan. Discard the contents of the sieve.

Bring the liquid to a boil, then reduce the heat until it is boiling gently. Add the remaining lime leaves or zest, the chili paste, chicken, mushrooms, bamboo shoots, and fish sauce. Boil gently until chicken is cooked through, about 3 minutes. Stir in the lime juice and cilantro and serve immediately.

Serves 6 to 8

Hearty Chicken Soup with Dumplings

½ cup (4 oz/125 g) pearl barley

8 oz (250 g) frozen fava (broad) beans

2 tablespoons oil

2 lb (1 kg) skinless, boneless chicken breast fillets, sliced

3 leeks, washed, trimmed, and sliced

2 cloves garlic, crushed

3 stalks celery, chopped

3 medium carrots, chopped

2 medium zucchini (courgettes), chopped

8 cups (64 fl oz/2 l) chicken stock (page 22)

½ cup (4 oz/125 g) tomato paste

DUMPLINGS

¼ cup (1½ oz/45 g) yellow cornmeal (polenta)

¾ cup (3 oz/90 g) all-purpose (plain) flour

1½ teaspoons baking powder

¼ teaspoon salt

½ cup (2 oz/60 g) grated Parmesan cheese

¼ cup (2 oz/60 g) butter, grated

½ cup (4 fl oz/125 ml) water, approximately

⅓ cup (½ oz/15 g) chopped fresh parsley

1 tablespoon chopped fresh thyme

Salt and ground pepper

Rinse the barley under cold water until the water runs clear, then drain. Pour boiling water over the fava beans, drain, and remove the skins.

Heat the oil in a large saucepan. Cook the chicken in batches until well browned all over. Set aside. Add the leek, garlic, celery, carrot, and zucchini to the saucepan and cook, stirring, until the leeks are soft, about 10 minutes.

Add the chicken stock and tomato paste and bring to a boil. Add the barley and simmer, covered, for 20 minutes. Return the chicken to the pan along with the fava beans.

Meanwhile, for the dumplings, combine the polenta, flour, baking powder, salt, cheese, and butter in a bowl. Mix well. Gradually add enough of the water to form a soft dough. Drop level tablespoonfuls of the dumpling mixture into the simmering soup. Cover and simmer for about 15 minutes, or until the dumplings are cooked through and the barley is tender. Stir in the parsley and thyme and add salt and pepper to taste. Serve immediately.

Serves 6

Chicken and Saffron Bouillabaisse

¼ cup (2 fl oz/60 ml) olive oil

2 leeks, washed, trimmed, and sliced

2 cloves garlic, crushed

4 chicken drumsticks, skin removed

6 large stalks celery, thickly sliced

1 can (14 oz/440 g) tomatoes, crushed, with juice

⅓ cup (2½ fl oz/80 ml) Pernod or Ricard

¼ teaspoon powdered saffron or saffron threads

1 tablespoon chopped fresh thyme

2 tablespoons chopped fresh dill

3 cups (24 fl oz/750 ml) chicken stock (page 22)

Hot-pepper sauce, such as Tabasco

Salt and ground pepper

Combine all ingredients except the stock, hot-pepper sauce, salt, and pepper in a large non-metallic dish. Stir well to coat. Cover and refrigerate overnight.

Transfer chicken and marinade to a large saucepan and bring to a boil. Reduce heat, cover, and simmer for 15 minutes. Stir in the stock and simmer, covered, for a further 15 minutes, or until the chicken is tender and cooked through. Add hot-pepper sauce, salt, and pepper to taste.

This recipe is best prepared a day ahead and then reheated gently just before serving.

Serves 4

Chicken Noodle Vegetable Soup

6 cups (48 fl oz/1.5 l) chicken stock (page 22)

1 yellow onion, finely chopped

2 carrots, halved lengthwise, thinly sliced

2 stalks celery, thinly sliced

2 zucchini (courgettes), thinly sliced

2 tablespoons finely chopped fresh parsley

2 oz (60 g) dried very thin egg noodles

½ cup (3 oz/90 g) shredded or cubed, skinless cooked chicken meat

Salt and ground pepper

In a large saucepan over low to medium heat, bring the chicken stock to a simmer. Add the onion, carrot, and celery and simmer until the vegetables are slightly soft, about 10 minutes. Add the zucchini and half of the parsley and cook until the zucchini is just tender, about 10 minutes.

Add the noodles and simmer until they are just tender, about 4 minutes, or according to the package directions.

Three minutes before the noodles are done, stir in the chicken. Just before serving, add salt and pepper to taste. Serve sprinkled with the remaining 1 tablespoon parsley.

Serves 4

Chicken Soup with Potato Patties

CHICKEN STOCK

1 chicken, 2½ lb (1.25 kg), cut up

3 leafy celery tops

1 yellow onion, cut into fourths

2 cinnamon sticks

2 cardamom pods

SPICE PASTE

3 lemongrass stalks, white part only, coarsely chopped

4 fresh or 2 dried galangal slices, about 1 inch (2.5 cm) in diameter, chopped (if using dried galangal, soak in hot water for 30 minutes, drain, then chop)

1 yellow onion, coarsely chopped

4 cloves garlic

6 candlenuts or blanched almonds

1 piece fresh ginger, 1½ inches (4 cm) long, peeled and coarsely chopped

2 tablespoons ground coriander

1 teaspoon ground pepper

1 teaspoon ground turmeric

2 teaspoons sugar

1 teaspoon salt

3 tablespoons water, approximately

2 tablespoons peanut oil or corn oil

POTATO PATTIES

1 lb (500 g) baking potatoes, peeled, boiled until tender

1 green (spring) onion, finely chopped

½ teaspoon salt

1 egg, lightly beaten

Vegetable oil, for frying

For the stock, place the chicken in a large stockpot and add enough water to cover. Bring to a boil over high heat, using a slotted spoon to skim off any froth that rises to the surface. Add the celery tops, onion, cinnamon, and cardamom. Reduce the heat to low, cover partially, and simmer until the chicken is white throughout, about 40 minutes.

Transfer the chicken to a plate and allow to cool. Simmer the stock for 20 minutes more, to reduce the volume and concentrate the flavor.

Allow the stock to cool, then strain through a fine-mesh sieve into a bowl. Refrigerate for several hours or overnight until the fat rises to the surface and solidifies. Use a large spoon to remove the fat. You should have about 8 cups (64 fl oz/2 l) stock.

Remove the skin and bones from the chicken breasts and shred the meat; set aside. Reserve the remaining chicken pieces for another use.

For the spice paste, place the lemongrass, galangal, onion, garlic, candlenuts or almonds, ginger, coriander, pepper, turmeric, sugar, and salt in a blender. Blend to a smooth paste, adding water as needed to facilitate blending.

Heat the oil in a large saucepan over medium heat. Add the spice paste and cook, stirring often, until well combined and fragrant, about 5 minutes. Stir in the chicken stock and simmer for 15 minutes. Taste and adjust the seasonings, if necessary. Keep warm over low heat.

For the potato patties, combine the potatoes, green onion, salt, and egg in a bowl. Use a potato masher or fork to mash the potato mixture. Shape the mixture into 1-inch (2.5-cm) balls (you should have 12) and flatten each into a patty about 1½ inches (4 cm) in diameter.

In a deep frying pan, add enough oil to to reach a depth of 1 inch (2.5 cm). Heat the oil to 375°F (190°C) on a deep-frying thermometer. Add the potato patties, a few at a time, and fry until golden brown underneath, about 3 minutes. Turn the patties and fry until golden brown on the other side, about 1 minute more. Transfer to paper towels to drain. Cover with aluminum foil and keep warm in a low oven while you fry the remaining patties.

Bring the stock to a simmer. Divide the shredded chicken meat evenly among serving bowls and ladle the hot stock over the top. Place 2 potato patties in each bowl and serve immediately.

Serves 6

NOTE This Indonesian soup is traditionally served with an array of garnishes—blanched bean sprouts, wedges of hard-cooked (hard-boiled) egg, noodles, sprigs of Chinese celery, and crisp-fried shallot flakes are some the customary additions. Prepare as many of the garnishes as you like.

243

Spicy Chicken and Corn Soup

1 tablespoon vegetable oil

4 skinless, boneless chicken breast halves, sliced

5 oz (155 g) chorizo, chopped

2 onions, chopped

2 cloves garlic, crushed

1 tablespoon ground cumin

¼ teaspoon chili powder

3 cups (24 fl oz/750 ml) chicken stock (page 22)

3 cups (24 fl oz/750 ml) tomato juice

2½ tablespoons tomato paste

2 teaspoons sugar

1 red bell pepper (capsicum), chopped

1 green bell pepper (capsicum), chopped

2 zucchini (courgettes), chopped

1 can (12 oz/375 g) red kidney beans, rinsed, drained

1 can (12 oz/375 g) corn kernels, drained

2½ tablespoons chopped cilantro (fresh coriander)

Salt and ground pepper

Serves 4

Heat the oil in a large pan over medium heat and cook the chicken and chorizo in batches, stirring, until lightly browned; remove and set aside. Add the onion and garlic to the pan and cook, stirring, until the onion softens. Add the cumin and chili powder and cook, stirring, until fragrant, about 1 minute.

Add the stock, tomato juice, tomato paste, and sugar and bring to a boil. Add bell pepper and zucchini and simmer, uncovered, about 5 minutes or until just tender. Stir in the reserved chicken and chorizo, the beans, corn, and cilantro. Heat through over low heat. Add salt and pepper to taste. This soup can be made a day ahead.

Beef Broth with Cilantro

8 cups (2 qt/2 l) clear chicken stock (page 22)

1 cup (8 fl oz/250 ml) sake (Japanese rice wine)

1 lb (500 g) prime-quality beef fillet (eye fillet), trimmed of excess fat and sinews

Salt and ground black pepper

½ bunch cilantro (fresh coriander), washed well, dried, and chopped into 1-inch (2.5-cm) lengths, including stems

In a stockpot, bring the chicken stock to a boil. Add the sake, reduce the heat, and simmer gently while you slice the beef.

Slice the beef fillet in half lengthwise and lay the open side down on the cutting board. Cut evenly on the diagonal into slices ¼ inch (5 mm) thick.

Add the beef to the broth and bring to a boil over medium heat. Reduce the heat to low and simmer for 1 minute. Taste the soup and add salt and pepper, if needed.

Add the cilantro, stir just until combined, and serve at once.

Serves 6

Miso Ramen

½ cup (4 fl oz/125 ml) Japanese mirin or rice vinegar

2 tablespoons soy sauce

1 lb (500 g) boneless pork loin

10 cups (40 fl oz/2.5 l) beef stock (page 26) or chicken stock (page 22)

1-inch (2.5-cm) piece ginger, sliced

1 lb (500 g) dried Japanese ramen noodles

¼ cup (3 oz/90 g) Japanese red or white miso paste

1½ cups (2½ oz/75 g) coarsely shredded spinach leaves

6 oz (185 g) bean sprouts

2 hard-cooked eggs, quartered

½ cup (1½ oz/45 g) thinly sliced green (spring) onions

In a mixing bowl, stir together the mirin or rice vinegar and soy sauce. Trim the pork of fat, add to the mirin mixture, and turn to coat well. Cover tightly and refrigerate for 1 hour, turning 2 or 3 more times.

Put the stock and ginger in a large saucepan and bring to a boil. Reduce the heat to low. Drain the pork and add it to the pot. Discard the pork marinade. Partially cover the saucepan and poach the pork in the barely simmering liquid until tender, about 1 hour, skimming the surface frequently.

About 10 minutes before the pork is done, bring a separate saucepan of water to a boil and cook the ramen until tender, 3–4 minutes. Drain well.

Remove the pork from the stock and discard the ginger. Using a sharp knife, cut the pork into slices ¼ inch (5 mm) thick. Stir the miso into the stock until it dissolves completely.

Divide the ramen among 4 large serving bowls. Ladle in the stock. Scatter the spinach along the edges of each bowl, immersing the shreds in the stock. Arrange the sliced pork, bean sprouts, and egg quarters in the center. Scatter the green onions on top.

Serves 4

CHILLED
SOUPS

Chilled Rich Tomato Soup

8 oz (250 g) dense-textured bread, crusts removed

2 cups (16 fl oz/500 ml) water

4–5 cloves garlic, peeled and chopped

Salt

1 lb (500 g) ripe tomatoes, peeled and chopped

1 cup (8 fl oz/250 ml) extra virgin olive oil

3 tablespoons (1½ fl oz/45 ml) white wine vinegar or lemon juice

3 eggs, hard cooked (hard boiled) and chopped (optional)

3½ oz (100 g) cured ham, diced, or 1 small can tuna in brine (optional)

Soak the bread in the water for a few minutes until soggy, then squeeze out as much excess liquid as possible.

The soup may be made with a mortar and pestle or a food processor. If using a mortar and pestle, crush the garlic with a little salt in the mortar, then add the tomatoes, followed by the bread. Blend with the pestle, trickling in the oil and then the vinegar to form a smooth paste. Do this carefully to prevent the mixture from separating. Add more salt to taste, if needed.

If using a food processor, purée the garlic, tomatoes, bread, and salt, then add the oil gradually, followed by the vinegar. Add salt to taste, if needed. Cover and refrigerate until well chilled.

Just before serving, garnish with the hard-cooked eggs and the ham or tuna, if desired.

Serves 4

Cucumber and Dill Soup

3 cucumbers, peeled, seeded, and chopped

1 onion, chopped

3 tablespoons chopped fresh dill

3 cups (24 fl oz/750 ml) chicken stock (page 22)

½ cup (4 fl oz/125 ml) heavy (double) cream

Combine the cucumber, onion, 2 tablespoons of the dill, and the stock in a saucepan and bring to a boil over medium heat. Reduce the heat and simmer until the onion is soft.

Allow the soup to cool a little, then purée in a food processor or blender. Return to the pan and gradually stir in the cream, reserving a little for decoration, if desired.

The soup may be served hot or chilled. To serve hot, reheat over low heat; do not allow the soup to boil. To serve chilled, refrigerate, covered, for several hours or until well chilled. Ladle into chilled bowls and garnish with the remaining dill and a swirl of cream, if desired.

Serves 6

253

Chilled Zucchini Soup

4 cloves garlic

12 large fresh basil leaves, plus
2 tablespoon finely chopped or
shredded fresh basil, extra

3 tablespoons extra virgin
olive oil

Salt

4 cups (32 fl oz/1 liter) water

13 oz (410 g) ripe tomatoes,
peeled, seeded, and coarsely
chopped

1 1/4 lb (625 g) zucchini
(courgettes), coarsely grated

Combine the garlic, whole basil
leaves, 1 tablespoon of the oil,
and salt to taste in a stockpot.
Add the water and tomatoes. Stir
well and bring to a boil.

Add the zucchini, cover the pot,
and cook over low heat for
40 minutes.

Allow the soup to cool a little,
then blend or process until
smooth. Set aside to cool
completely. Cover and refrigerate
until well chilled.

Serve the chilled soup drizzled
with the remaining olive oil and
sprinkled with the extra basil.

Serves 4

Gazpacho

6 vine-ripened tomatoes

1½ cups (7½ oz/235 g) finely diced cucumber

¾ cup (4 oz/125 g) finely diced celery

¾ cup (4 oz/125 g) finely diced green bell pepper (capsicum)

⅔ cup (3½ oz/105 g) peeled and finely diced carrot

½ cup (2½ oz/75 g) finely diced white onion

⅓ cup (½ oz/15 g) finely chopped fresh flat-leaf (Italian) parsley

1 tablespoon extra virgin olive oil

2 teaspoons sherry vinegar or wine vinegar

1 tablespoon salt

1 tablespoon chopped garlic

2 teaspoons dried oregano

1 teaspoon sugar

1 teaspoon ground black pepper

This recipe may be made with or without a food mill. If using a food mill, coarsely chop the tomatoes. Fit a food mill with the medium disk, position it over a large bowl, and pass the tomatoes through it. If you do not have a food mill, chop the tomatoes finely by hand. (Do not use a food processor, or the bright-red color necessary for the finished soup will be lost.)

Add the remaining ingredients and stir well. Transfer to a nonaluminum container, cover, and refrigerate overnight.

Pass the tomato mixture through a food mill fitted with the fine disk, or press the mixture

through a fine-mesh sieve using the back of a large spoon.

Add salt and pepper to taste, if needed. Return the tomato mixture to the container, cover, and refrigerate until well chilled. Ladle into chilled serving bowls and serve immediately.

Serves 6

Chilled Almond and Garlic Soup

1½ cups (8 oz/250 g) almonds

5 oz (155 g) bread, with crusts removed

2 cloves garlic, peeled

Salt

⅔ cup (5 fl oz/155 ml) olive oil

1 tablespoon sherry vinegar

4 cups (32 fl oz/1 liter) chilled water

1 lb (500 g) muscat grapes, peeled and seeded

Place the almonds in a heatproof bowl, pour over boiling water to cover, and leave for 2 minutes to loosen the skins. Drain, let cool for a few minutes, then slip off and discard the skins.

Soak the bread in a small amount of water. Crush the almonds, bread, garlic, and salt in a large mortar or bowl. Mix thoroughly with the pestle, gradually drizzling in the oil to form a spongy paste. Mix in the vinegar, then the cold water. Transfer to a bowl, cover, and refrigerate for several hours or until well chilled.

Just before serving, taste the soup, add more more salt or vinegar if needed, then add the grapes and serve well chilled.

Serves 4

Iced Melon Soup with Ginger

5 cups (2½ lb/1.25 kg) coarsely chopped fresh cantaloupe (rockmelon) or honeydew melon

1 tablespoon grated fresh ginger

1 tablespoon fresh lemon juice

3 cups (24 fl oz/750 ml) Champagne, sparkling wine, or sparkling apple or grape juice, well chilled

1–2 tablespoons confectioners' (icing) sugar

Fresh mint or chervil sprigs, for garnish (optional)

Fit a food mill with the medium disk, position it over a large bowl, and pass the melon and ginger through the food mill.

If you do not have a food mill, use a food processor fitted with the metal blade or a blender, taking care to avoid splattering. Then force the purée through a fine-mesh sieve set inside a bowl, pressing the solids with a wooden spoon.

Stir in the lemon juice. Cover tightly and refrigerate until well chilled, at least 2 hours or for up to 12 hours. Chill serving bowls.

Just before serving, stir the Champagne or sparkling wine

or juice into the melon purée. Then stir in just enough of the sugar to emphasize the melon's flavor without making the soup too sweet. Ladle into the chilled bowls and garnish with mint or chervil sprigs, if desired.

Serves 8 to 10

261

Iced Tomato Soup

2 lb (1 kg) ripe tomatoes, peeled, seeded, and coarsely chopped

1 cup (8 fl oz/250 ml) chicken stock (page 22)

¼ cup (2 fl oz/60 ml) extra virgin olive oil

⅓ cup (2½ fl oz/80 ml) aged wine vinegar

1 clove garlic, crushed

Salt and ground black pepper

4 teaspoons thick crème fraîche

12 small fresh basil leaves

Place the tomatoes, stock, oil, vinegar, garlic, and salt and pepper to taste in a food processor. Process on high for 2 minutes, or until the mixture is smooth. Refrigerate until ready to serve.

Serve topped with a teaspoon of crème fraîche and some basil leaves.

Serves 4

Chilled Cherry Soup

2 lb (1 kg) ripe red cherries, pitted, with pits reserved

1 cup (8 fl oz/250 ml) water and 1 cup (8 fl oz/250 ml) Riesling, Gewürztraminer, or other medium-dry white wine, or 2 cups (16 fl oz/500 ml) water

¼ cup (2 oz/60 g) sugar

¼ cup (2 fl oz/60 ml) fresh lemon juice

¼ cup (2 fl oz/60 ml) kirsch (optional)

1 tablespoon grated or shredded lemon zest, plus extra for garnish

2½ cups (20 fl oz/625 ml) sour cream

Fresh mint sprigs, for garnish

In a large saucepan, combine the cherry pits, water, wine, if using, sugar and lemon juice over medium heat. Bring to a boil, reduce the heat to low, and simmer, uncovered, for about 5 minutes. Remove from the heat, cover, and let steep for 5 minutes more.

Pour the liquid through a sieve set inside a bowl; discard the pits. Return the liquid to the pan. Add the cherries, reserving about ⅓ cup (½ oz/45 g) in a covered bowl in the refrigerator. Over medium heat, bring the liquid back to a boil; reduce the heat and simmer gently for 5 minutes more.

Blend or process the soup until smooth. Transfer to a mixing bowl and stir in the kirsch, if using, and lemon zest. Let the soup cool to room temperature, then cover tightly and refrigerate until well chilled, 2–3 hours. Chill the serving bowls.

Before serving, put 2 cups (16 fl oz/500 ml) of the sour cream in a tureen and whisk briskly to liquefy it slightly. Then gradually whisk in the soup. Ladle into the chilled bowls and garnish with dollops of the remaining sour cream, the reserved cherries, lemon zest, and mint sprigs.

Serves 6 to 8

Chilled Cream of Cucumber Soup

6 small cucumbers, each about 5 inches (13 cm) long, ends trimmed, unpeeled, cut into large chunks

3 or 4 sour dill pickles (pickled cucumbers)

2 cups (16 oz/500 g) low-fat or regular plain yogurt

2 cups (16 fl oz/500 ml) heavy (double) cream

2 tablespoons fresh lemon juice

2 tablespoons finely chopped fresh dill or 1 tablespoon dried dill, plus extra for garnish (optional)

Salt and ground white pepper

Working in batches, if necessary, put the cucumbers, pickles, yogurt, cream, lemon juice, and dill in a food processor fitted with the metal blade or in a blender. Blend or process until the vegetables are finely chopped. Add salt and pepper to taste.

Cover tightly and refrigerate until well chilled, 2–3 hours. Chill serving bowls.

Adjust the seasoning, if necessary, and ladle the soup into the chilled bowls. Garnish with dill sprigs or a sprinkle of dried dill, if desired.

Serves 6 to 8

NOTE This soup is also good with the addition of some finely shredded carrot or a little finely chopped red (Spanish) onion. Fresh mint may be substituted for the dill. Thinly sliced brown bread and butter is a good accompaniment for this soup.

Vichyssoise

¼ cup (2 oz/60 g) butter

3 leeks, washed and thinly sliced (white parts only)

1 onion, finely chopped

Salt and ground black pepper

5 cups (40 fl oz/1.25 l) chicken stock (page 22)

1 lb (500 g) all-purpose potatoes, peeled and thinly sliced

Crème fraîche, for garnish

4 sprigs fresh chervil, for garnish

Heat the butter in a large saucepan. Add the leek, onion, and salt and pepper to taste. Cover and cook over low heat until the vegetables are soft, but not browned. Add the stock and potatoes and bring to a boil. Reduce the heat and simmer until the potatoes are tender.

Remove from the heat and allow to cool, then blend or process until smooth.

Vichyssoise may be served hot or chilled. If serving the soup hot, return to the pan and reheat gently over low heat. Do not allow the soup to boil. If serving chilled, place in an airtight container in the refrigerator for several hours or overnight. Serve garnished with the crème fraîche and chervil sprigs.

Serves 6

Green Gazpacho

2 slices day-old white bread, crusts removed

1 stalk celery with leaves, chopped

6 tomatillos, husks removed, chopped

1 small green bell pepper (capsicum), seeded and chopped

2 large or 6 small cucumbers, peeled and chopped

1 fresh red or green chili, stemmed, seeded, and chopped

3 cloves garlic, chopped

1 teaspoon salt

Juice 1 lime

1/4 cup (1/3 oz/10 g) chopped cilantro (fresh coriander)

2 cups (16 fl oz/500 ml) vegetable stock (page 18) or water

MAYONNAISE

2 egg yolks

2 tablespoons tarragon vinegar

1 1/2 teaspoons salt

1/2 teaspoon ground black pepper

2/3 cup (5 fl oz/160 ml) olive oil

Chopped fresh chives

1/2 small avocado, stone removed, flesh peeled and sliced

Serves 4 to 6

Soak the bread slices in water to cover until soft, 3–5 minutes. Remove the bread and squeeze out the excess liquid.

Put the celery, tomatillos, bell pepper, cucumbers, chili, soaked bread, garlic, salt, lime juice, and cilantro in a food processor. Process until finely puréed. Working in batches, transfer to a blender with the vegetable stock or water and blend until smooth. Set aside.

For the mayonnaise, whisk together the egg yolks, vinegar, salt, and pepper in a large bowl. Gradually add the olive oil, drop by drop, whisking constantly until an emulsion forms. As the

mixture thickens, you can begin adding the oil more quickly. (If the mayonnaise becomes too thick or begins to separate, whisk in 1 tablespoon water and then continue.)

When all the oil has been added and the mayonnaise is thick, gradually add the vegetable mixture, ¼ cup (2 fl oz/60 ml) at a time, whisking until each addition is thoroughly blended before adding more. Taste and add more salt and pepper, if needed. Cover and refrigerate for 2–24 hours.

Ladle into chilled bowls, sprinkle with chives, and top each serving with a slice of avocado.

MICROWAVE

Cooking Microwave Soups

One of the joys of microwave cooking is that it enables you to have last-minute thoughts about your meal preparation. Soups that take hours to cook on the stovetop may take only half an hour or so when using a microwave oven. Another advantage of this method of cooking is that microwave energy does not affect the flavor of food. In fact, in many cases it enhances it, because the nature and speed of microwave cooking ensure that fewer nutrients and flavors are lost.

Cooking Times
It is difficult to be precise in giving cooking times for micro-

wave ovens, as individual ovens vary in power and thus in the time that they take to cook food. Read the manual that came with your oven, keep in mind the power level that your oven uses, and be prepared to check the soup frequently and make adjustments to the cooking time.

The following recipes have been written for a 650-watt oven. Ovens with less power will need a little more cooking time and those with more power will need less time. The table below will serve as a quick reference. If in doubt, always be guided by your oven's instruction manual or by how the food looks and tastes.

Power	Change of timing per minute (+ or −)
900 watts	− 40 seconds
850 watts	− 30 seconds
800 watts	− 20 seconds
750 watts	− 10 seconds
700 watts	− 5 seconds
650 watts	no change
600 watts	+ 5 seconds
550 watts	+ 10 seconds
500 watts	+ 20 seconds
450 watts	+ 30 seconds

The golden rule of microwave cooking is to undercook the food, then check to see if it is done and return it to the oven if necessary. If it is almost cooked, any further cooking should be done in bursts of only a few seconds to avoid overcooking. This is especially important when cooking seafood, which is easily overcooked.

Hints for Success

For best results, food that is to be cooked in a microwave should be as uniform in shape as possible. When preparing vegetables and meat for soup, dice or slice them to a similar size or thickness.

Microwave soup recipes usually call for the water or stock to be boiling when it is added to the vegetables and meat. This is contrary to the method used for cooking soups on the stovetop, but is done to quickly bring out flavors that would otherwise take much longer to extract.

When cooking soups in the microwave oven, remember to use a large cooking container, preferably one that is deep with straight sides. Stir well and frequently, to ensure that the ingredients cook evenly and that the soup doesn't boil over.

Adapting Recipes for the Microwave Oven

If converting conventional recipes for use in the microwave oven, remember that very little evaporation takes place, so cut down on any liquid by about one-third. Shorten the cooking time by always adding hot or boiling water or stock, and do not add salt until the cooking is complete.

When adding herbs and spices, keep in mind that their flavors are a little more concentrated when used in microwave recipes. Use less than you normally would, and taste to see if the amounts are correct.

Accompaniments

The microwave oven can also be used to cook accompaniments for soup. Try the following:

Croutons

The pleasant crunchiness of croutons is easy to achieve in the microwave oven. Use whole-grain (wholemeal) or multigrain bread, as white bread will not give as appetising a result.

Cut three thick slices of whole-grain (wholemeal) bread into cubes. Melt 2 tablespoons butter on high (100%) for 2 minutes. Stir in the diced bread. Cook on high for 4–5 minutes, tossing the bread occasionally during cooking, until crisp. Serves 4.

Puppadums

Cooking puppadums in the microwave is super-quick, and eliminates the mess of frying. It also gives a crisp, low-fat result.

Place purchased puppadums in a single layer on a piece of paper towel on the oven's turntable, or on a microwave-safe plate. Make sure they do not overlap. Cook on high (100%) for 45–60 seconds, or until crinkled and puffed. The puppadums will be slightly soft when removed from the oven, but will become crisp if left for a minute or two.

Cheesy Toast Fingers

For each person, spread 1 slice of hot buttered toast with 1 tablespoon purchased tomato-based pasta sauce. Spread with 1 tablespoon shredded tasty cheese, such as Cheddar. Place on a paper towel on a plate and cook on high (100%) for 1 minute, or until the cheese melts to your liking.

For variety, add some chopped green (spring) onions or chives before the cheese. Or cook a chopped slice (rasher) of bacon between 2 sheets of paper towel for about 2 minutes (depending on how crisp you like it) and sprinkle over before the cheese.

Basic Tools for Microwaving

Use microwave-safe dishes for microwave cooking. Choose a variety of dishes; some wide and shallow, others large and deep. Paper towel and microwave-safe plastic wrap are also essential.

microwave-safe dish

glass bowl

measuring spoons

spoon

wooden spoon

Oyster Soup

1 tablespoon butter

2 tablespoons all-purpose (plain) flour

2 cups (16 fl oz/500 ml) chicken stock (page 22), boiling

1 cup (8 fl oz/250 ml) fish stock (page 30) or water, boiling

½ cup (4 fl oz/125 ml) light (single) cream

24 bottled or freshly shucked oysters, well drained

Ground white pepper

Chopped fresh chives, for garnish

Put the butter and flour in an 8-cup (64-fl oz/2-l) microwave-safe dish or casserole. Cook on high (100%) for 1 minute, stirring after 30 seconds. Add the boiling stock and water, stir well, and cook on high for 5–6 minutes, stirring after every minute, until the liquid boils and thickens.

Add the cream, oysters, and pepper to taste. Stir well and cook on medium (50%) for 1–2 minutes, or until the ingredients are heated through.

Sprinkle with the chives and serve immediately.

Serves 4

Broad Bean Soup

3 oz (90 g) pancetta, chopped

1 onion, chopped

1 carrot, chopped

1 celery stalk, chopped

1/3 cup (3 fl oz/90 ml) extra virgin olive oil

1 1/4 lb (625 g) plum (Roma) tomatoes, peeled and diced

3 oz (90 g) lean beef, cubed

1 1/4 lb (600 g) shelled fresh broad beans

6 cups (48 fl oz/1.5 l) clear chicken stock (page 22), boiling

Salt and ground pepper

3 slices bread, cut into small dice

In a microwave-safe dish or casserole, combine the pancetta, onion, carrot, celery, and oil. Stir well and cook on high (100%) for 2 minutes, or until the onion is translucent, stirring after 1 minute.

Add the tomatoes, beef, and finally the beans. Add the stock and cook on medium (50%) for 10 minutes, or until beans are tender, stirring after 5 minutes. Add salt and pepper to taste.

Toast the diced bread in a preheated 350°F (180°C) oven until golden. Serve the soup accompanied by the croutons.

Serves 6 to 8

Green Vegetable Soup

½ onion, finely sliced

⅓ cup (2½ fl oz/80 ml) extra virgin olive oil

10 oz (315 g) cabbage, finely chopped

1 lettuce, finely chopped

10 oz (315 g) Swiss chard (silverbeet), finely chopped

10 oz (315 g) spinach, finely chopped

1 stalk celery, finely chopped

6 cups (48 fl oz/1.5 l) clear beef stock (page 26), boiling

Salt and ground black pepper

8 oz (250 g) shelled fresh peas

6 slices coarse country bread

2 cloves garlic

1 tablespoon chopped parsley

In a microwave-safe dish or casserole, combine the onion and half the oil and cook on high (100%) for 2–3 minutes, or until the onion is translucent, stirring after 1 minute.

Add the cabbage, lettuce, Swiss chard, spinach, and celery. Cover and cook on medium (50%) for 4 minutes, or until the leafy vegetables are wilted and the celery is tender, stirring once.

Add the stock and salt and pepper to taste, cover, and cook on high for 2 minutes. Stir, then cover and cook on medium for 10 minutes, stirring twice. Add the peas and cook on medium for 2 minutes, or until tender.

Toast the bread slices in a preheated 350°F (180°C) oven until golden. While still hot, rub each slice well with the cut side of a garlic clove to flavor it. Place the bread in a soup tureen. Pour the soup over the bread slices, sprinkle with the parsley and the remaining oil, and serve at once.

Serves 6 to 8

Shrimp Bisque

10 oz (315 g) peeled uncooked shrimp (prawns)

1 tablespoon butter

1 small onion, finely chopped

1 small carrot, peeled and grated

1 stalk celery, chopped

1 tablespoon tomato purée

½ cup (3 oz/90 g) long-grain white rice

1 bouquet garni (page 16)

¼ cup (2 fl oz/60 ml) white wine

2 tablespoons brandy

4 cups (32 fl oz/1 liter) fish stock (page 30), boiling

Salt and ground black pepper

2 tablespoons cream

Croutons, to serve (optional)

Devein the shrimp. Melt the butter in a 12-cup (3-qt/3-l) microwave-safe dish or casserole on high (100%) for 45 seconds. Add the prawns and toss well to coat. Cover and cook on high for 1 minute. Stir in the onion, carrot, and celery. Cover and cook on high for 2–3 minutes.

Stir in the tomato purée, rice, bouquet garni, white wine, brandy, and half of the boiling stock. Cover and cook on high for 10–12 minutes, or until the rice is tender, stirring every few minutes.

Remove 4 of the prawns; set aside. Discard the bouquet garni. Blend or process the soup until smooth, then return it to the casserole. Dilute the soup to the required consistency with the remaining stock. Add salt and pepper to taste.

Heat on high for 2–3 minutes. Stir in the cream. Ladle into warmed serving bowls, garnish each with a reserved prawn and some croutons, if desired, and serve immediately.

Serves 4 to 6

Mediterranean Seafood Soup

2 teaspoons butter

1 large onion, sliced

3 leeks, washed and thinly sliced

2 carrots, peeled and thinly sliced

1 celery stalk, thinly sliced

1 green bell pepper (capsicum), seeded and thinly sliced

4 cups (32 fl oz/1 liter) water, fish stock (page 30), or diluted chicken stock (page 22), boiling

1 bay leaf

1 teaspoon dried thyme

4 sprigs fresh parsley

Pinch powdered saffron

2 cloves garlic, crushed

6 fish steaks (such as gemfish or kingfish)

3½ oz (105 g) peeled uncooked shrimp (green prawns)

6 fresh oysters, shucked (or fresh bottled oysters, drained)

Salt and ground black pepper

Melt the butter in a 12-cup (3-qt/3-l) microwave-safe casserole on high (100%). Add the onion, leek, carrot, celery, and bell pepper. Stir well to coat with the butter. Cover and cook on high for 5 minutes.

Stir in the boiling water or stock. Stir in the bay leaf, thyme, parsley, saffron, and garlic, cover, and cook on high for 5 minutes.

Stir well, add the fish steaks, cover, and cook on high for 5 minutes. Stir in the shrimp and oysters and cook on high for 1 minute more. Add salt and pepper to taste, if needed. Serve immediately with crusty bread.

Serves 4 to 6

Curried Pumpkin Soup

1 kg (2 lb) pumpkin, peeled, seeded, and diced

2 cups (16 fl oz/500 ml) boiling water

1 chicken stock cube or 1 heaped teaspoon stock powder

1 clove garlic, crushed

1 teaspoon curry powder

Salt and ground black pepper

⅔ cup (5 fl oz/160 ml) heavy (double) cream

Croutons, to serve

Ground nutmeg

Sprig fresh tarragon, for garnish (optional)

Put the pumpkin in a 12-cup (3-qt/3-l) microwave-safe dish or casserole. Add the water, stock cube or stock powder, garlic, and curry powder. Cover and cook on high (100%) for 12–14 minutes, or until the pumpkin breaks down, stirring after 6 minutes.

Set aside for 3 minutes to cool slightly, then blend or process until smooth. Return the mixture to the casserole. Add salt and pepper to taste, if needed, and stir in the cream. Cook, uncovered, on medium-high (70%) for 4–5 minutes to heat through. Do not allow the soup to boil.

Sprinkle with croutons and nutmeg, garnish with tarragon, if liked, and serve immediately.

Serves 4

Beef and Vegetable Soup

1 cup (5 oz/155 g) macaroni

1 large potato, chopped

1 large carrot, peeled and chopped

2 stalks celery, chopped

1 tablespoon chopped fresh parsley

1 cup (3 oz/90 g) shredded cabbage

4 large cooking tomatoes, peeled and chopped

½ teaspoon dried oregano or marjoram

Salt and ground black pepper

½ cup (2½ oz/75 g) fresh or frozen peas (optional)

1 lb (500 g) ground (minced) beef steak

1 large onion, chopped

8 cups (64 fl oz/2 l) beef stock (page 26), boiling

Place the steak in a 16-cup (4-qt/4-l) microwave-safe casserole. Break up the meat with a fork and add the onion. Cover and cook on medium-high (70%) for 6 minutes. Stir well and cook on medium-high for 6 minutes more.

Add the remaining ingredients, except for the peas, and cook on medium-high for 25 minutes. (Stir in the peas, if using, after 15 minutes.) Set aside, covered, for 15 minutes to cool slightly.

Before serving, skim off any fat by drawing a paper towel over the surface of the soup. Repeat until all fat is removed.

Serves 8 to 10

Hearty Tomato and Zucchini Soup

1½ lb (750 g) tomatoes, peeled, seeded if desired, and chopped

4 medium zucchini (courgettes), thinly sliced

4 cups (32 fl oz/1 liter) chicken stock (page 22), boiling

1 tablespoon all-purpose (plain) flour

Ground black pepper

2 tablespoons butter

1 teaspoon ground nutmeg

1 tablespoon chopped fresh parsley

1 tablespoon chopped fresh dill

½ cup (4 fl oz/125 ml) sour cream

Put the tomato, zucchini, and half of the boiling stock in a 12-cup (3-qt/3-l) microwave-safe dish or casserole. Stir, then cook on high (100%) for 10 minutes, stirring occasionally, until the soup comes to a boil. Cook on medium (50%) for 10 minutes more, or until the vegetables soften. Set aside.

Put the flour, pepper, and butter in a small microwave-safe bowl. Cook on high for 1 minute, stirring after 30 seconds. Stir in the nutmeg, parsley, and dill. Pour a little of the soup into the bowl and stir to combine. Add to the dish or casserole with the remaining stock and stir well.

Cover and cook on high for 3–4 minutes, until the soup returns to a boil and thickens slightly, stirring after 2 minutes.

Garnish with sour cream and serve with crusty Italian bread.

Serves 6

Beetroot and Orange Soup

1 lb (500 g) fresh beetroot, peeled and diced

Finely grated zest (rind) and juice 1 orange

2 cups (16 fl oz/500 ml) chicken stock (page 22), boiling

1 cup (8 fl oz/250 ml) tomato juice

Ground black pepper

⅓ cup (2½ fl oz/80 ml) sour cream

Chopped fresh chives

Put the beetroot in a 12-cup (3-qt/3-l) microwave-safe casserole. Cover and cook on high (100%) for 6–8 minutes, or until tender. Set aside for 5 minutes to cool slightly.

Blend or process the beetroot and any cooking liquid until smooth. Return the purée to the casserole. Add the orange zest and juice, stock, tomato juice, and pepper and stir well. Cook on high for 5 minutes, stirring occasionally, until the mixture boils. Cook on medium (50%) for 5 minutes more, stirring occasionally, until the soup is thick and well combined.

This soup may be served hot or chilled. If serving chilled, set aside until cool, then refrigerate for several hours.

Serve topped with the sour cream and chives.

Serves 4

Gingered Carrot Soup

1 ¼ lb (625 g) carrots, peeled and sliced

2 cups (16 fl oz/500 ml) chicken stock (page 22), boiling

Finely grated zest (rind) and juice 2 oranges

1 cup (8 fl oz/250 ml) hot water

1 teaspoon ground ginger

½ teaspoon ground mace

⅔ cup (5 fl oz/160 ml) cream

Ground black pepper

Put the carrots in a 12-cup (3-qt/3-l) microwave-safe dish or casserole. Cover and cook on high (100%) for 5–6 minutes, or until soft. Stir in the hot stock, orange zest and juice, water, ginger, and mace. Cook on high for 6–8 minutes, stirring occasionally, until the liquid boils. Set aside for 5 minutes to cool slightly. Blend or process until smooth.

This soup may be served hot or chilled. If serving hot, remove from the heat and stir in half of the cream. Add salt and pepper to taste, if needed, and ladle into warmed serving bowls. If serving chilled, transfer the soup to an airtight container and stir in half

of the cream. Add salt and pepper to taste, if needed, and refrigerate until ready to serve.

Serve garnished with a spoonful of the remaining cream.

Serves 4 to 5

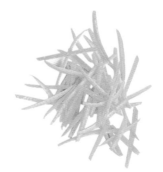

Minestrone

1 can (10 oz/315 g) four-bean mix, drained

2 tablespoons olive oil

1 large onion, finely chopped

2 cloves garlic, crushed

2 medium potatoes, peeled and diced

2 medium carrots, peeled and sliced

2 stalks celery, sliced

2 cups (6 oz/185 g) shredded cabbage

3 tomatoes, peeled and chopped

4 cups (32 fl oz/1 liter) chicken stock (page 22), boiling

1 bouquet garni (page 16)

1 cup (5 oz/155 g) small macaroni

3 oz (90 g) ham off the bone, diced

½ teaspoon paprika

Ground black pepper, to taste

1 medium zucchini (courgette), diced

½ cup (2 oz/60 g) grated Parmesan cheese

Sprigs fresh thyme, for garnish

Rinse the four-bean mix; drain. Heat the oil in a 16-cup (4-qt/ 4-l) microwave-safe casserole on high (100%) for 1–2 minutes, until hot. Stir in the onion and garlic, cover, and cook on high for 2 minutes. Add the potatoes, carrots, and celery, cover, and cook on high for 5 minutes.

Stir in the cabbage and tomato, then add the hot stock, bouquet garni, drained beans, macaroni, ham, paprika, and pepper. Stir well, cover, and cook on high for 20 minutes, stirring after every 5 minutes, until the vegetables and macaroni are tender.

Discard the bouquet garni and stir in the zucchini. Cook on

high for 5 minutes. Sprinkle
with the cheese and thyme and
serve immediately.

Serves 4 to 6

Split Pea and Bacon Soup

1½ cups (10 oz/315 g) green split peas

9 cups (2¼ qt/2.25 l) hot water

2 slices (rashers) bacon, chopped, plus once slice extra, cooked and crumbled, for garnish

1 large onion, chopped

1 large carrot, peeled and chopped

1 stalk celery, chopped

1 medium potato, chopped

2 bacon stock cubes

½ teaspoon dried thyme

½ teaspoon ground pepper

1 bay leaf

8 oz (250 g) bacon bones

Salt

Put the peas in a 16-cup (4-qt/ 4-l) microwave-safe casserole with 4 cups (32 fl oz/1 liter) of the water. Cook on high (100%) for 10 minutes, stirring halfway through cooking. Cover and set aside until needed.

Put the chopped bacon in a smaller casserole and cook on high for 1 minute. Stir in the onion, carrot, celery, and potato, cover, and cook on high for 5 minutes.

Crumble the stock cubes into the casserole containing the peas and add the remaining water, the vegetable mixture, thyme, pepper, bay leaf, bacon bones, and salt to taste, if needed. Stir well, then cook on high for 25 minutes, stirring after every 10 minutes.

Remove the bacon bones, pick off any meat, and return the meat to the soup. Discard the bones and bay leaf. Blend or process the soup until smooth, if desired. Serve garnished with the crumbled bacon.

Serves 6 to 8

Spicy Indian Cauliflower Soup

2 cups (4 oz/125 g) small cauliflower florets

2 tablespoons butter

½ red bell pepper (capsicum), seeded and cut into thin strips

1 large onion, finely chopped

2 teaspoons ground turmeric

Pinch chili powder, or to taste

2 cups (16 fl oz/500 ml) chicken stock (page 22), boiling

1 cup (8 fl oz/250 ml) milk

2 tablespoons besan (chickpea/garbanzo bean flour)

¾ cup (6 oz/185 g) natural yogurt

1 teaspoon garam masala

2 tablespoons chopped cilantro (fresh coriander) or fresh parsley

Make a small cut in each cauliflower floret stem. Melt the butter in a large microwave-safe dish or casserole on high (100%). Add the cauliflower, bell pepper, and onion. Cover and cook on high for 5 minutes, stirring after 3 minutes.

Stir in the turmeric, chili powder, and stock. Cover and cook on high for 8 minutes, stirring often.

Meanwhile, add a little of the milk to the besan to make a paste. Gradually stir in the remaining milk, then stir the besan mixture into the soup. Cover and cook on high until just boiling. Stir in the yogurt and garam masala. Heat on high until almost boiling. Stir in the cilantro or parsley, and serve immediately.

Serves 6

Mushroom Soup

2 tablespoons butter

½ cup (1½ oz/45 g) finely chopped green (spring) onion

2 cups (6 oz/185 g) fresh mushrooms, finely chopped

1½ cups (12 fl oz/375 ml) chicken stock (page 22), boiling

1½ cups (12 fl oz/375 ml) milk

1 tablespoon all-purpose (plain) flour

⅓ cup (2½ fl oz/85 ml) cream

1 egg yolk

Chopped fresh chives

Lemon slices, to garnish (optional)

Place the butter, onions, and mushrooms in a deep 12-cup (3-qt/3-l) microwave-safe dish or casserole. Cover and cook on high (100%) for 3 minutes. Stir in the stock and milk and cook on high for 3 minutes, or until the mixture is bubbling around the edges.

Combine the flour with a little water to make a smooth paste. Stir into the soup and cook on high for 2 minutes.

Whisk the cream and egg yolk together in a small jug. Stir in a little of the hot soup, then stir the cream mixture into the soup. Cook on high for 3 minutes or until the soup is bubbling around the edges. Stir well, ladle into warmed serving bowls, sprinkle with chives, and top with a slice of lemon, if desired.

Serves 4 to 6

French Onion Soup

2 tablespoons butter

2 large onions, sliced

1 tablespoon all-purpose (plain) flour

3 cups (24 fl oz/750 ml) beef stock (page 26), boiling

¼ cup (2 fl oz/60 ml) white wine

1 bay leaf

Salt and ground black pepper

4 thick slices French bread

2 oz (60 g) Gruyère or Cheddar cheese, grated

Melt the butter in an 8-cup (2-qt/2-l) microwave-safe dish or casserole on high (100%). Stir in the onion, cover, and cook on high for 5 minutes. Stir in the flour, cover, and cook on high for 1 minute. Gradually stir in the stock and wine, then add the bay leaf and pepper. Cook on high for 10 minutes. Add salt to taste, if needed. Discard bay leaf.

Meanwhile, sprinkle the slices of bread with the grated cheese. Place under a hot broiler (griller) until the cheese melts. Ladle the soup into serving bowls and place a slice of toast on top of each. Serve immediately.

Serves 4

Lentil, Carrot, and Pumpkin Soup

1 cup (7 oz/220 g) red lentils

2 tablespoons butter or olive oil

1 large onion, chopped

2 carrots, peeled and diced

1 clove garlic, finely chopped

1½ lb (750 g) peeled and roughly chopped pumpkin

6 cups (48 fl oz/1.5 l) chicken stock (page 22) or vegetable stock (page 18), boiling

1 bouquet garni (page 16)

Salt and ground black pepper

Rinse the lentils until the water runs clear. Drain and set aside.

Put the butter or oil in a 12-cup (3-qt/3-l) microwave-safe dish or casserole and heat on high (100%) for 45 seconds. Add the onion and carrot, cover, and cook on high for 3 minutes, or until the onion is translucent, stirring after each minute.

Stir in the garlic and cook on high for 1 minute. Stir in the lentils, pumpkin, stock, and bouquet garni. Cook, uncovered, on medium for 15–20 minutes, or until the lentils are soft, stirring every few minutes. Add salt and pepper to taste.

Allow to cool for a few minutes, then mash with a potato masher, or blend or process if a smoother consistency is desired. Reheat on high for 1–2 minutes, then ladle into warmed serving bowls.

Serves 6 to 8

NOTE If desired, some diced ham can be added to this soup at the same time as the stock. Or top each bowl with some crumbled, crisp-cooked bacon just before serving.

For a little extra heat, add 1 teaspoon grated ginger at the same time as the garlic.

Thick Lentil Soup

1 cup (6 oz/185 g) brown lentils, washed

1 tablespoon butter

1 large onion, finely chopped

1 clove garlic, crushed

1 large carrot, peeled and thinly sliced

4 cups (32 fl oz/1 liter) boiling water

1 tablespoon chicken stock powder

Ground black pepper

Pinch ground allspice

1 tablespoon chopped fresh parsley

Soak the lentils in enough water to cover while preparing the remaining ingredients.

Melt the butter in a 12-cup (3-qt/3-l) microwave-safe dish or casserole on high (100%). Stir in the onion, garlic, and carrot. Cover and cook on high for 2 minutes. Drain the lentils, add to the casserole, cover, and cook on high for 2 minutes. Stir in the boiling water, stock powder, pepper, allspice, and parsley. Cook, uncovered, on medium (50%) for 15–20 minutes, until the lentils are soft, stirring every five minutes.

Serve immediately. Or, if desired, blend or process the soup until smooth, then return to the casserole and heat through before serving.

Serves 4

Scallop Broth

2 cups (24 fl oz/750 ml) fish stock (page 30), boiling

1 cup (8 fl oz/250 ml) boiling water

1 cup (8 fl oz/250 ml) dry white wine

1 small onion, finely diced

1 small carrot, finely diced

1 small stalk celery, finely diced

Salt and ground white pepper

1 lb (500 g) bay scallops or small sea scallops, with roe, if desired

Chopped fresh parsley, to garnish (optional)

Put the stock, water, wine, leek, onion, carrot and celery in a large microwave-safe dish or casserole and heat on high (100%) until the mixture comes to a boil. Stir well, cover, and cook on medium-high (70%) for 5 minutes, or until vegetables are tender. Add salt and pepper to taste.

Add the scallops and cook on medium (50%) for 2 minutes, or until just cooked through, stirring after 1 minute. Ladle into warmed bowls and serve garnished with parsley, if liked.

Serves 4

NOTE Lobster, crayfish, shrimp (prawns), pieces of fish fillet, or a mixture of seafood can replace the scallops in this soup.

Tuscan Vegetable Soup

1 cup (7 oz/220 g) spelt, barley, or long-grain white rice

5 cups (40 fl oz/1.25 l) water

200 g broccoli florets and stalks

1 small leek, white part only

1 small stalk celery

1 large carrot, peeled

Extra virgin olive oil

1 cup (4 oz/125 g) chopped yellow onion

1½ cups (9 oz/280 g) peeled, seeded, and chopped plum (Roma) tomatoes (fresh or canned)

½ cup (2½ oz/75 g) white turnip, peeled and thinly sliced

6 cups (48 fl oz/1.5 l) vegetable stock (page 18), boiling

¾ cup (3½ oz/105 g) diagonally sliced green beans

1 small zucchini (courgette), chopped

Salt and ground black pepper

Grated Parmesan cheese

Soak the grain in water to cover for 1 hour. Cut the broccoli stalks, leek, celery, and carrot into ¼-inch (5 mm) thick slices; set aside.

Put 1 tablespoon of oil in a large microwave-safe dish and heat on high (100%) for 45 seconds. Add the onion and stir well. Cover and cook on medium-high (70%) for 5 minutes, or until the onion is translucent, stirring after every 2 minutes.

Add tomato, cover, and cook on medium-high for 2 minutes, stirring after 1 minute. Drain the grain and add to onion mixture along with the broccoli, leek, celery, carrot, and turnip. Cook

on medium-high for 3 minutes, stirring after each minute.

Add the stock, cover, and bring to a boil on high. Stir, then cover and cook on medium (50%) for 10 minutes, or until the grain is slightly tender, stirring after 5 minutes.

Add the beans and zucchini, cover, and cook on medium for 5 minutes, or until the grain is tender and the vegetables are soft, but still hold their shape. Add salt and pepper to taste. Ladle into warmed bowls, drizzle a little olive oil over the top of each, and sprinkle with cheese. Serve immediately.

Serves 4

Glossary

The following glossary provides advice on selecting, storing, and preparing some of the ingredients used in this book.

ARTICHOKES

Native to the Mediterranean, prickly artichokes look like tall thistles. The fleshy base of the inner leaves and the bottom of the bud are tender when cooked; the remainder, including the rest of the leaf and the fuzzy interior choke, are discarded. Fresh artichokes are sold all year in various sizes. Select compact, heavy globes with tightly closed leaves; store in a plastic bag, refrigerated, for up to 4 days.

ASPARAGUS

These tender stalks are prized for their delicate flavor and marvelous green hue, sometimes tinged with purple at the cap (white asparagus, a delicacy, is much less common). Crisp, straight, firm stalks with tight buds are best. Store wrapped in damp paper towels in a plastic bag, refrigerated, for up to 4 days.

AVOCADOS

Two main varieties of tropical avocado are common: buttery Hass, with a green-black, rough skin, and blander Fuerte, with a thin, smooth skin. Ripe avocados yield to gentle thumb pressure. Choose ripe but firm, unblemished avocados and store in the refrigerator for several days. Underripe avocados may be ripened at warm room temperature or, more quickly, in a paper bag, but they must not be refrigerated.

BEANS, FRESH

The familiar green beans and yellow wax beans are the edible immature pods of the bean plant, a legume. Another variety is the small delicate French bean, or haricot vert. Fresh beans are firm and smooth, without bruising or spotting; avoid those that are leathery or bulging with seeds. Refrigerate in a loosely closed plastic bag for up to 4 days. For information on dried legumes, see page 70.

BEETS

No part of a beet goes to waste; both the bulbous root and the leafy, deep-green tops are edible. The dense, deep-red flesh is enclosed by a dark, papery skin that is peeled away before eating; other varieties are golden yellow or creamy white. Store in a plastic bag, refrigerated (with root intact, but greens trimmed to 1 inch/2.5 cm), for up to 1 month; the greens will keep for up to 5 days.

BELL PEPPERS

Also known as capsicums, bell peppers are actually fruits, although they are eaten as vegetables. Crunchy and colorful, they are related to chilis, but are far milder in taste. They change color as they ripen, from green to orange, yellow, red, or purple. They can be eaten raw, added to salads, or cooked, when they become much sweeter and softer. Store uncut fruits in a plastic bag in the refrigerator for up to 1 week.

BROCCOLI

Both the rigid green stalks and the tightly packed dark green or purplish-green heads (also called florets) are edible. Choose firm stalks and closed heads with deep color and no yellow areas. Store, refrigerated, in a plastic bag for up to 4 days.

CABBAGE

A large and diverse family. Choose a cabbage with a firm, heavy head, unblemished leaves, and a moist core. Store in a plastic bag, refrigerated, for up to 2 weeks.

CARROTS

Choose firm, bright orange carrots; avoid those that are droopy, wrinkled, or have cracks or dry spots. Store in a plastic bag, tops removed, in the refrigerator for up to 2 weeks. Peel or scrub before using.

CHICKPEAS

Also known as garbanzo beans, chickpeas are medium-sized, light brown, wrinkled peas with a nutty flavor. Available dried or canned, they are used in Middle Eastern, Mediterranean, and Indian dishes. Chickpeas must be soaked for several hours or overnight before they are cooked.

CHIVES

The long, hollow green leaves of this herb add bright color and a mild onion flavor to many dishes. Fresh chives should not be wilted or damaged. Wrap in damp paper towels and store in a plastic bag in the refrigerator for up to 4 days. Chop chives finely and add them at the end of the cooking time so that their delicate flavor is not destroyed.

CILANTRO (FRESH CORIANDER)

This strongly flavored herb is very popular in Asian, Indian, Latin American, and Middle Eastern cooking. To store, rinse under cold running water, shake dry, then wrap in paper towels and refrigerate in a plastic bag for up to 1 week.

EGGPLANT (AUBERGINE)

Most forms have purple skins (although some have white). Cooked eggplant is mild flavored, with tender, creamy flesh. Look for plump, glossy eggplants that are heavy for their size and that have taut skin free of bruises or scratches. Store, refrigerated, in a plastic bag for up to 2 days.

FAVA BEANS

Also known as broad beans, these are large, slightly flattened, green or light brown beans. When they are very young, the whole pod can be eaten, but usually they are shelled like peas. Fava beans are available fresh, frozen, and dried.

FENNEL

Crisp, juicy fennel has a flavor reminiscent of licorice. Tubular stalks and feathery leaves attach to a bulbous base, which should be free of cracks or brown spots. Refrigerate in a plastic bag for up to 4 days.

GARLIC

A head, or bulb, of garlic is formed of numerous small cloves, all wrapped in a papery outer skin. Sharp when raw, the taste of garlic becomes delicate when cooked. Bulbs should be plump and firm; store in a cool, dark, dry spot and do not separate the cloves until you are ready to use them.

GINGER

Sometimes erroneously called ginger root, ginger is actually the rhizome, or underground stem, of a semitropical plant. This pungent seasoning has a lively, hot flavor and peppery aroma. Select stems that are firm and heavy, never shriveled, with taut, glossy skin. Wrap in a paper towel and store in the refrigerator for up to 2 days. For longer storage, unpeeled ginger may be wrapped airtight and frozen.

KALE

A member of the cabbage family, kale has ruffled dark green leaves and tastes similar to its cabbage relatives. It is eaten fresh or cooked, or can be used as a decorative garnish. Wash the leaves, dry well, and refrigerate in a plastic bag lined with paper towels for up to 3 days.

LEEKS

Although closely related to the onion, this long, white, tubular bulb with broad, flattish leaves has a much milder flavor. Buy small-to-medium, healthy-looking leeks with crisp green leaves; large ones more than 1 inch (2.5 cm) in diameter tend to be tough. Cut off the roots, trim the tops, and wash thoroughly before using. Bc sure to separate the leaves well, as dirt gets trapped between them Store in a plastic bag in the refrigerator for up to 1 week.

LENTILS

High-protein lentils come in several shapes and colors, but the most common are green (or brown) and yellow lentils. Red lentils are slightly smaller, and they fade to pinkish-yellow when cooked. Lentils are sold dried, either whole, split, or ground into flour. Before using lentils, pick them over to remove stones or foreign matter, then rinse well under cold running water.

MUSHROOMS

There are numerous varieties, colors, and sizes of edible fungi. Select firm, fresh, plump mushrooms that aren't bruised or slimy. Store in the refrigerator, lightly wrapped in paper towels or in a paper bag. Never store them in plastic, or they will sweat and perish. Use within 2 days. See page 85 for more information about different varieties of mushrooms.

OLIVE OIL

A staple of Mediterranean cooking, olive oil imparts a clean, fruity flavor and golden-to-green color to salad dressings, grilled bread, and pasta sauces. Use extra virgin oils, from the first pressing, for cold dishes and for drizzling over food just before serving. For sauces and pan-frying, use olive oil labeled "pure" or "light". Store in a dark spot away from heat for 6 months, or in the refrigerator for 1 year. (Chilled oil may become thick and cloudy; let it warm to room temperature before using.)

ONIONS

The onion is the most commonly used vegetable flavoring in the world, and has been cultivated for so long that its wild ancestors are unknown. Onions can be white, yellow, or reddish-purple. White and yellow onions generally have a sharper flavor than red varieties, although mild types are available. Green (spring) onions are immature, with more green stalk than white bulb. Papery-skinned shallots, members of the onion family, grow in clumps of small cloves like garlic. There are golden (French) and purple (Asian) varieties. Store onions and shallots in a cool, dark, dry place for up to 2 weeks. Refrigerate green onions in a plastic bag.

OREGANO

Aromatic and robustly flavored, oregano is a favorite herb of Italian and Greek cooks. Select bright green fresh oregano with firm stems. It is also available dried, both whole and ground, in the spice section of the supermarket. Refrigerate fresh oregano in a plastic bag for up to 3 days.

PARSLEY

Widely used for cooking and as a garnish, parsley has such a clean, refreshing flavor that it is sometimes enjoyed as an after-meal digestive. Curly-leaf parsley is mild, while flat-leaf (Italian) parsley is more pungent. Select healthy, lively looking bunches. To store, rinse under cold running water and shake dry, then wrap in paper towels and keep in a plastic bag in the refrigerator for up to 1 week.

PEAS

Only the seeds of the round, sweet English pea are eaten. Thin, crisp snow peas and plump sugar snap peas (mangetout) are eaten pod and all. All three varieties are available almost all year, both fresh and frozen. Choose crisp pods with bright green color and store, chilled, in a plastic bag for 2 to 3 days. Do not shell English peas until just before they are to be cooked, as the pod helps retain their freshness.

PUMPKINS

Also known as "winter squash," pumpkins have a very hard rind covering a firm, sweetish yellow or orange flesh. They range in size from very small to very large, depending on the variety. Pumpkins are usually peeled and cut up before cooking. Store whole pumpkins in a cool, dry place for 2–3 months. Once cut, remove the seeds, wrap well in plastic wrap, and store in the refrigerator for up to 3 days.

SUMMER SQUASH

Soft-skinned, slender green and yellow zucchini, yellow crookneck squashes, and pattypan squashes are classified as "summer" squash, although many are sold year round. They can all be used interchangeably. Choose well-shaped squash that are heavy for their size and that are free of cracks or bruises. They will keep for up to 4 days in the refrigerator.

SWEET POTATOES

The golden sweet potato and orange yam are neither potato nor yam but tuberous roots from the morning glory family (true yams are another vegetable entirely and very rare). Sweet potatoes are sweet and creamy when baked or boiled. Choose sweet potatoes with firm, smooth skins. Store in a cool, dark place and use within 1 week.

SWISS CHARD

This leafy relative of the beet has crinkly green leaves and either a white or scarlet stem (both types are interchangeable). Select chard with crisp, unblemished leaves. Wash in cold water, pat dry, and store in a plastic bag lined with a paper towel, refrigerated, for up to 3 days.

TOMATOES

Although they are botanically a fruit, tomatoes are eaten as a vegetable. Oval-shaped plum (Roma) tomatoes are thick and meaty, with less juice and smaller seeds than other varieties, making them ideal for soups and stews. Store fresh tomatoes at room temperature for several days; do not refrigerate them, or their flavor and texture will suffer. Underripe tomatoes will ripen in a few days if left on a sunny windowsill or countertop. For most soups, canned tomatoes are just as good as fresh ones.

WATER CHESTNUTS

These crisp, white tubers with dark brown skins stay crunchy and fresh tasting even when cooked. They are available fresh in specialty markets, or in cans from supermarkets and Asian markets.

Index

Entries in *italics* indicate illustrations and photos.

Acknowledgments

Weldon Owen would like to thank Tessy Grabo and Jennifer Losco, for editorial assistance, and Puddingburn Publishing Services, for compiling the index.

Photography Ad-Libitum/Stuart Bowey, John Callanan, Kevin Candland, Rowan Fotheringham, John Hollingshead, Peter Johnson, Joyce Oudkerk Pool, Penina, Alejandro Pradera, Chris Shorten.

Styling Janice Baker, Penny Farrell, Kay Francis, Stephanie Greenleigh, Jane Hann, Susan Massey, Pouké, Vicki Roberts-Russell. Cover styling by Sally Parker.

Published by Fog City Press
814 Montgomery Street
San Francisco, CA 94133 USA

Copyright © 2003 Weldon Owen Pty Ltd

Chief Executive Officer: John Owen
President: Terry Newell
Publisher: Lynn Humphries
Managing Editor: Janine Flew
Design Manager: Helen Perks
Editorial Coordinator: Kiren Thandi
Production Manager: Caroline Webber
Production Coordinator: James Blackman
Sales Manager: Emily Jahn
Vice President International Sales: Stuart Laurence

A catalog record for this book is available from
the Library of Congress, Washington, DC

ISBN 1 877019 63 1

Color reproduction by Colourscan Co Pte Ltd
Printed by LeeFung-Asco Printers
Printed in China

A Weldon Owen Production

THE LITTLE GUIDES

SOUPS

FOG CITY PRESS

SOUPS

John F. Kennedy habló de crear el Cuerpo de Paz antes de ser presidente.

5

Los gobiernos de otros países
le piden ayuda al Cuerpo de Paz.
El Cuerpo de Paz envía gente
a ayudar a los países necesitados.

¡Es un hecho!

¡Desde 1961,
el Cuerpo de Paz
ha ayudado
a 134 países!

Voluntarios

En el Cuerpo de Paz trabajan
voluntarios. Los voluntarios
no reciben dinero por su trabajo.

¡Es un hecho!

Más de
161,000 personas
han sido
voluntarios en el
Cuerpo de Paz.

Los voluntarios trabajan en
el Cuerpo de Paz por dos años.
Antes, les enseñan cómo ayudar.

¡Es un hecho!

Los voluntarios estudian tres meses antes de trabajar. Algunos tienen que aprender otro idioma.

Ayuda

Los voluntarios del Cuerpo de Paz
ayudan a cientos de miles de
personas cada año. El Cuerpo de Paz
les enseña a ayudarse por sí mismos.

Los voluntarios ayudan de muchas formas

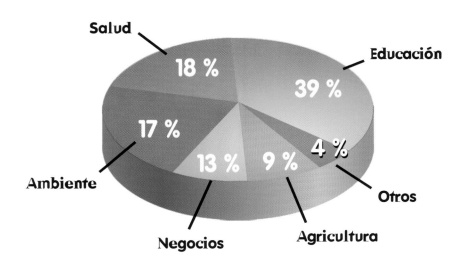

Salud **18 %**

Educación **39 %**

Ambiente **17 %**

Negocios **13 %**

Agricultura **9 %**

Otros **4 %**

 Un voluntario ayuda a sacar una colmena de unos arbustos en Ghana, África.

Los voluntarios enseñan nuevas destrezas en todo el mundo. Unos enseñan a los niños. Otros ayudan a construir escuelas y otros edificios.

Voluntarios del Cuerpo de Paz ayudan
a construir una escuela en Gabón, África.

Algunos países necesitan ayuda con la agricultura. Los voluntarios enseñan nuevas formas de cultivar alimentos. Otros países necesitan médicos o enfermeros. El Cuerpo de Paz ayuda donde se necesita.

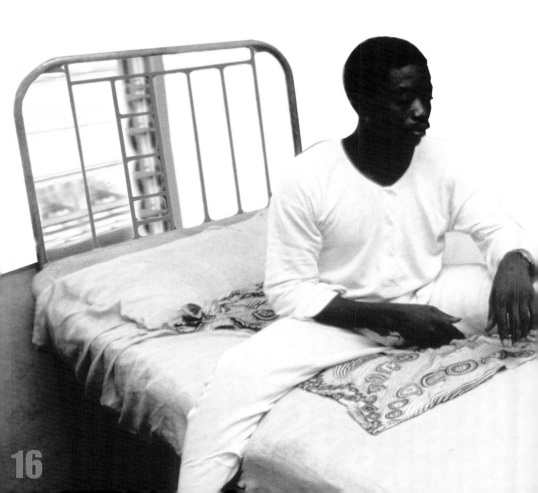

Los voluntarios del Cuerpo de Paz trabajan mucho pero también lo pasan bien. Conocen mucha gente y lugares diferentes.

Voluntarios del Cuerpo de Paz juegan
fútbol americano con los niños en un pueblo.

El Cuerpo de Paz ahora

Hoy, más de 7,000 voluntarios trabajan en 76 países de todo el mundo. Mucha gente tiene mejor salud y vive mejor gracias a la ayuda del Cuerpo de Paz.

Glosario

cuerpo (el) grupo de personas con conocimientos especializados

gobiernos (los) grupos de personas que manejan o administran países

idioma (el) lenguaje de un país u otro grupo de personas

paz (la) ausencia de guerra

voluntario (el) persona que se ofrece a hacer una cosa por voluntad sin recibir dinero a cambio

Recursos

Libros

So, You Want to Join the Peace Corps: What to Know Before You Go
Dillon Banerjee
Ten Speed Press (1999)

The Kid's Guide to Service Projects: Over 500 Service Ideas for Young People Who Want to Make a Difference
Barbara A. Lewis
Free Spirit Publishing, Inc. (1995)

Sitios web

Debido a las constantes modificaciones en los sitios de Internet, PowerKids Press ha desarrollado una guía on-line de sitios relacionados al tema de este libro. Nuestro sitio web se actualiza constantemente. Por favor utiliza la siguiente dirección para consultar la lista:

http://www.buenasletraslinks.com/ayuda/cuerpopazsp/

Índice

Número de palabras: 236

Nota para bibliotecarios, maestros y padres de familia

Si leer es un reto, ¡Reading Power en español es la solución! Reading Power es ideal para lectores hispanoparlantes que buscan un nivel de lectura accesible en su propio idioma. Ilustrados con fotografías, estos libros presentan la información de manera atractiva y utilizan un vocabulario sencillo que tiene en cuenta las diferencias lingüísticas entre los lectores hispanos. Relacionando claramente texto con imágenes, los libros de Reading Power dan al lector todo el control. Ahora los lectores cuentan con el poder para obtener la información y la experiencia que necesitan en un ameno formato completamente ¡en español!

Note to Librarians, Teachers, and Parents

If reading is a challenge, Reading Power is a solution! Reading Power is perfect for readers who want high-interest subject matter at an accessible reading level. These fact-filled, photo-illustrated books are designed for readers who want straightforward vocabulary, engaging topics, and a manageable reading experience. With clear picture/text correspondence, leveled Reading Power books put the reader in charge. Now readers have the power to get the information they want and the skills they need in a user-friendly format.